Association Brooklyn Ethical

Life and the conditions of survival, the physical basis of ethics,

sociology and religion

Association Brooklyn Ethical

Life and the conditions of survival, the physical basis of ethics, sociology and religion

ISBN/EAN: 9783337261368

Printed in Europe, USA, Canada, Australia, Japan

Cover: Foto ©Andreas Hilbeck / pixelio.de

More available books at **www.hansebooks.com**

LIFE AND THE CONDITIONS OF SURVIVAL

THE PHYSICAL BASIS OF ETHICS, SOCIOLOGY AND RELIGION

POPULAR LECTURES AND DISCUSSIONS
BEFORE THE
BROOKLYN ETHICAL ASSOCIATION

CHICAGO
CHARLES H. KERR & COMPANY
1895

PREFACE.

The lesson which this volume of lectures and discussions is intended to teach is one of great practical importance, both to the individual and to society at large. If heeded, it will correct, we believe, many of the false tendencies in modern life, the outcome of which is disastrous to social and personal well-being under the exigent conditions of our latter day civilization.

The Eighteenth Century closed with a pæan to Liberty which sounded the death-knell of chattel slavery and absolute monarchies, and fulfilled the promise of the Reformation by assuring to all men the right of free thought and private judgment. The Nineteenth Century, under the inspiration of the doctrine of evolution, warns men that this freedom is only the means to a higher end—a means which if rightly used will lead to that fullness of life, in the individual and in society, which is the ideal goal of the evolutionary process, but which if misused or abused will, with equal certainty, lead to degeneration and decay.

Ethics in practice is the supreme product of human evolution; and the moral life means not merely "necessitation to an end which is unwillingly adopted," but voluntary obedience to Cosmic as well as Sociological Law. Evolution sees an objective unity in the cosmic order of the starry heavens and those orderly activities which constitute morality in the soul of man. It points an objective as well as a subjective test of the rightness of our actions, and no longer delivers man over to the blind guidance of an exclusively subjective monitor—the "Mystic Ought"—which renders unattainable an intelligent consensus as to the true end of human endeavor.

Following the previous volumes on "Evolution," "Sociology," "Evolution in Science, Philosophy and

iii

Art," "Man and the State," and "Factors in American Civilization," this volume carries evolutionary principles into the field of individual life and character, and shows their application to the practical problems of hygiene, sociology, religion and applied ethics. The writers are for the most part masters of the topics assigned them for treatment, and we confidently commend their work to thoughtful and intelligent readers who would know the last word of the evolutionist upon the most vital of all the questions of the time.

CONTENTS.

Larger and narrower views of sanitation. The former seeks
to prevent disease and death—the latter to cure existing
evils by specific remedies. The former the evolutionary
view. Obedience to cosmic law the essential principle
of true sanitation. Ethical and religious aspects of the
problem.

By JAMES AVERY SKILTON.

The parallel lines of religious and governmental evolution.
From animism to cosmic theism. Religion as a cement
to society. Failure of cults based on efforts at dogmatic
unity. The church of the future—a federation, not a
negation of sects.

By REV. EDWARD P. POWELL.

COSMIC EVOLUTION, AS RELATED TO ETHICS

BY

DR. LEWIS G. JANES

COLLATERAL READINGS SUGGESTED.

Spencer's *First Principles, Principles of Psychology,* and *Principles of Ethics;* Fiske's *Cosmic Philosophy;* Powell's *Our Heredity from God;* Bain's *Mind and Body;* Picton's *The Mystery of Matter,* and *The Philosophy of Ignorance;* Clifford's *Body and Mind, Seeing and Thinking,* and *The Scientific Basis of Morals;* Wake's *Evolution of Morality;* Lankester's *Degeneration: A Chapter in Darwinism;* Hinton's *Life in Nature,* and *Mystery of Pain,* Arabella Buckley's *The Moral Teachings of Science;* Huxley's *Evolution and Ethics* (Oxford Address).

COSMIC EVOLUTION, AS RELATED TO ETHICS.*

BY LEWIS G. JANES.

Among the wonders of the beautiful White City by Lake Michigan, whither so many of us have made pilgrimages during these pleasant summer and autumn months, nothing is more instructive or suggestive to the thoughtful mind than the anthropological exhibit, so admirably and systematically arranged under the intelligent supervision of Professor Putnam. "Not things, but men," was the motto of the exhibition in its entirety, and of the Auxiliary Congresses, marshalled so successfully by President Bonney and his able corps of assistants; and here indeed, in the Anthropological Building, was a veritable history of man in the things which he had created. From the rude stone implements of a barbaric age, up to the time of polished stone and copper, and on again to the finest mechanisms of our own wonderful era, as we pass from the building especially dedicated to anthropological science to those larger evidences of human advancement in the vast temples of Agriculture, Machinery and the Liberal Arts, what a picture of evolution, what sublime testimony to man's achievements, what hope and promise for the future millennial expectations of mankind, did our marvelous Columbian Exposition—that great school of anthropology—afford! What wonder that this significant object-lesson embodied in the triumphs of science and art, so effectually demonstrating man's capacity for progress, so completely reversing the old theological dogma of the fall of man from an original state of human perfection, should take voice in the great Parliament of Religions in a pæan

---

* Copyright 1893, by the Brooklyn Ethical Association.

of sympathy and human brotherhood transcending the boundaries of sect, overleaping the walls of dogmatic belief, merging Christian and Buddhist and Hindoo, Confucianist and Shintoist, Catholic and Protestant, Orthodox and Liberal into one church universal, of which the Art Institute constituted the Sacred Synagogue, the Columbian Exposition the Holy Temple, and its manifold exhibits the appropriate symbols and sacramental altars.

It was my privilege to witness the impressive spectacle at the closing session of the Parliament of Religions, when the Buddhist monk, clothed in the yellow robe of his order, the white robed and turbaned Hindoo and Shinto priests, the intellectual looking and richly clad follower of Confucius, sat side by side on the platform, fraternizing with the Greek bishop, the Roman Catholic doctor of divinity, and the sombre-garbed Protestant divines; while earnest-faced Susan B. Anthony, intellectual and white-haired Julia Ward Howe, refined and elegant Mrs. Henrotin, representatives of America's noblest womanhood—and, *sui generis*, Joseph Cook, pompous of person and wrapped in a conceit of infallibility which overshadowed even that of the Roman Catholic potentates, completed the picturesque and cosmopolitan delegation. The enthusiasm of the vast audience when, one after another, the foreign delegates, whom we have been wont to define as "heathens," arose and in cultivated and scholarly phrase uttered their final words of appreciation, counsel and admonition, the interest culminating when the Shinto priest invoked the blessing of the thirty million gods of Japan upon the American people, presented a scene such as the world never beheld before, and into the perfect harmony of which even the "Boston Lectureship," for the nonce, contributed no discordant word. As I felt the thrill of the popular uplift and enthusiasm, it seemed to me that here, in the closing decade of the Nineteenth Century, the ethical and humanitarian sentiment had touched high-water mark; and that the conceit of an exclusive possession of saving truth by any sect, or even by Christianity itself, could never again obtain credence among the people who witnessed the inspiring scene. Sober second thought, however, suggested the reflection that mere emotional sentiment is always ephemeral in its effects, and must be impotent to furnish a permanent bond of unity for religious and philanthropic effort.

There must be some common ground of rational principle to substitute for the dogmatic foundations of sectarian segregation, which shall leave individuals free to formulate their own intellectual creeds while in a larger fellowship of the spirit they become helpers for the world's advancement. Can such a basis be found in ethics, as approached from the side of science and the doctrine of evolution? Can an ethical science be formulated in harmony with cosmic law, sufficiently rational and broad to command the allegiance of all liberal minded people? Can our little Association, with its cosmopolitan membership and free, scientific platform, offer a useful object-lesson in testimony to the utility and practicability of such a basis of spiritual fellowship?

Manifestly this problem, which involves the entire question of man's relation to the Universe, and those laws and processes by means of which worlds have grown out of chaos, life out of inanimate nature, consciousness out of life, self-consciousness and moral responsibility out of the lower forms of sentience and conscious apprehension, admits of two modes of superficial interpretation. Ignoring the earlier stages of the evolutionary process and judging exclusively by its final and most exalted manifestations, we may unhesitatingly pronounce all things "very good" and find a possible common basis for ethical sanctions and religious reverence in the Universe itself and the majesty of its eternal order. Or, on the other hand, viewing the "martyrdom of man" at shorter range, as he has mounted with bloody feet to the heights of a civilization yet all too sadly imperfect when judged by the loftiest moral tests, we may question the beneficence of life, condemn the cosmo-poietic energy manifested in the evolution of the Universe as unmoral and careless of human good or ill, and seek for some Nirvana wherein the extinction of desire shall remove all motive for continuing the struggle for existence.

If the doctrine of evolution be true, man is a product of the Universe, a child of the great World-Mother. This is true not merely of his physical organism, but of his higher nature as well. Mind and morals equally with muscles and sense-organs have been developed by the interaction of organism with environment throughout the entire period of his ancestral history. The consistent evolutionist can adopt no other view than this. Any deviation from it throws us back upon unscientific theories of special creation and the supernatural intrusion of extra-cosmic forces into Nature's eternal order. The doctrine of the soul as an eternally self-existent monad may seem to furnish the way out of the difficulty, but it is unscientific, unevolutionary, and has no basis save in metaphysical speculation. Such a doctrine may appear plausible to the mere literary student of philosophical systems, but it is totally lacking in scientific credentials, however imposing may be the names of speculative thinkers marshalled in its support.

There are certain logical implications in the evolutionary conception of cosmic and human origins that cannot possibly be evaded. The eternity and uncreatability of matter are now the conceded dicta of physical science; or, speaking more accurately and philosophically, it is conceded that to beings constituted as we are, the Universe would always have presented those properties and qualities which we designate as material. But the logic of evolution affirms no less emphatically, the eternity and uncreatability of mind; for if mind is an ephemeral time-product of material conditions, its primary appearance in a hitherto unconscious Universe of purely physical forces would be indicative of a new creation, which is an unscientific and anti-evolutionary conception. A truer psychology recognizes the phenomenal character of both mental and material processes as known to us, and their consequent dependence upon a common, unitary Reality which, in its essential constitution, is unknowable. That we do not recognize the presence of mind in connection with phenomena regarded as purely physical, is therefore no evidence that mind has no concomitant relation to such phenomena. The failure to recognize such a relation may be and doubtless is due to the limitations of our knowing faculties. As to the real nature of those energies which constitute essential elements in our conception of matter, we know absolutely nothing. For aught we can say to the contrary, that impulse which compels the coherence of atoms in a bar of iron, or which holds the whirling planets in their orbits, or which causes the union of chemical affinities, is as essentially psychical in its nature as the impulse which binds wife to husband, or mother to child, or holds together seventy millions of people in these United States.

Thus that "brave show of things," the visible Universe, as interpreted to us by modern science, seen as an ever shifting, never-resting panorama of atomic changes, blends ultimately with the inner world of thought, becoming not less real, but more real as we recognize its relationship to that which we know best and most intimately in experience, our psychic personality.

> 'Sweet the genesis of things,
> Of tendency through endless ages,
> Of star-dust, and star pilgrimages,
> Of rounded worlds, of space and time,
> Of the old flood's subsiding slime,
> Of chemic matter, force and form,
> Of poles and powers, cold, wet, and warm;
> The rushing metamorphosis
> Dissolving all that fixture is
> Melts things that be to things that seem,
> And solid Nature to a dream."

Diverse and antithetical, indeed, as are our conceptions of mind and matter, impossible as it is to interpret one in terms of the other, it is equally impossible to separate one from the other for independent investigation, analysis and study. Atoms and molecules are necessary hypothetical creations of our rational thought, and have never been revealed to our senses even by the most powerful microscope. They are known to us only as logical necessities for the interpretation of their known effects in combination.

The qualities of matter as we conceive them are thus conditioned upon and relative to the limited boundaries of our sense-perception. Light and color, hardness and weight, form and extension are mental concepts, showing us not what the external reality is in itself, but only what it is as related to our capacities of apprehension. But this is only one side of the shield—one aspect of the rounded globe of truth concerning the problem of existence. What we want is the whole truth—and nothing but the truth. On the other hand, we think no thought, we perceive no truth, we solve no problem of a mental character, save through the movement and tension, the wear and decay of physical atoms in the brain and nervous system; that which is a logical necessity of thought we are obliged to conceive as a reality transcending individual consciousness and inhering in the nature of the extra-sentient universe. No vision of beauty in landscape or human countenance gives rise in our souls to sentiments of joy and adoration, save through the pulsations of a physical æther. No musical harmony, however beatific, penetrates and enthralls the mind save as it is wafted on the physical waves of the atmosphere in accordant touch with the physical structure of the ear and brain. The new psychology finds its primary data in a scientific physiology. While it compels us to recognize the relative and symbolic character of our sense perception, its inevitable logic also forces us to recognize the reality behind the symbols—a reality constant and steadfast in its relations, independent of our volition, which compels our psychical nature to construct definite and unchangeable symbols for its interpretation. Materialist and idealist are thus alike baffled by the simplest facts of our every-day experiences, touching as they do at the ultimate depths of every problem, whether of physics, biology, psychology or ethics, a Reality external to the individual consciousness, well known or susceptible of scientific investigation in all its phenomenal relations thereto but unknown and unknowable to finite beings in its absolute and essential nature.

So intimate is the relation of concomitant mental and material phenomena, that it need not surprise us

when we discover certain obvious analogies between
their laws and operations which are useful, instructive
and infinitely suggestive to us in the higher regions
of thought and investigation. Surely the likeness
between those attractive forces of gravity and cohe-
sion which bind atoms and worlds into a cosmic unity,
and those sentiments of love and obligation which
constitute the psychical attractions of man to man in
the social organism, is so apparent that it compels
instant recognition. And that wonderful equilibration
of centrifugal and centripetal energies which holds
suns and planets in orderly relation and propulsion,
is paralleled by the sense of equity in the human mind
which balances the claims of egoistic and altruistic
obligation, demands rights for self, and recognizes corresponding duties toward others, and in its most perfect manifestation ultimates in the greatest possible
fulness of life, in the individual and in society at
large. May we not logically infer that these imperfectly understood but clearly evident analogies are indicative of a deeper unity than that which is directly
revealed to our finite faculties?

In the growth of worlds, the advent and development of life upon our planet, the progress from
moneron to vertebrate, from fish to saurian, from
lemur to ape, from ape to man; in the advancement
of man from the lowest savagery to the highest civilization; in the unfolding of mind from its simplest
manifestation in the unicellular organism up to the
triumphs of a Shakespeare, an Olmsted, a Beethoven
or a Spencer, we may trace the operation of one primary and consistent principle or law of evolution. In
the clash of atoms in the primeval nebulæ, the contests of life in the plant and animal world, the age-long
competitive strifes of man with man—at first on the
purely physical plane, then with the sharper weapons
of wit and cunning, finally in the loftier and yet keener
competition for moral supremacy—we see everywhere
the "struggle for existence," ultimating in the survival of that which is best adapted to existing physical,
social and intellectual conditions. We see through
all these developmental processes, the triumph of law,
every Present the child of the immediate and remoter

Past, effect always answering to cause; Nature everywhere efficient and sufficient to accomplish the observed
results; no evidence of supernatural intrusion anywhere; no "First Cause" in a series having a beginning in time, but a never-ending, never commencing
immanent and efficient Cause:—the sole miracle, the
always existent, ever-potent, self-revealing in its re--
lational aspects, but ultimately incomprehensible Reality.

We see the principle of order in the intercourse
of atoms and whirl of worlds rising to life in plant
and flower, to sentience in the brute creation, to self-
consciousness and moral supremacy in man. Everywhere disorder, dislocation from the inherent and eternal principles on which the process of evolution is
conducted, has meant disintegration, decay, dissolution. Everywhere unity with and obedience of these
principles has meant survival and advancement. The
impulse to self-preservation, relatively weak in the
lower organisms, becomes stronger in the higher, instinctive in most vertebrates, and of the greatest importance in the life of man, where for the first time
intelligent volition seeks to create ethical instincts
which shall aid in its triumph over the manifold difficulties of life. In gregarious creatures this primary
impulse impels a recognition of kinship in the herd or
flock or related colony, and the obligation to serve
one's self broadens into the obligation to serve the
local commonwealth. Here, indeed, is the germ of
conscience and ethical obligation, reaching its roots
down into the sub-stratum of order in the physical universe out of which it has sprung and to which it is
vitally and genetically related.

. With an excusable assumption based on an obvious
analogy, we may say that a colony of ants, a herd of
cattle, a flock of migratory birds, has developed a
morality of its own. In the evolution of language,
certain words have been exalted above their original
signification, while others have suffered degeneration,
decay, and degradation of meaning. The word "moral"
which at first meant merely that which is customary
or adapted to the existing social order, has come to
mean conformity to an ideal standard of right, often

far removed from the immediate conventions of society; thus adding the testimony of philology to the ethical advancement of the race. In its present use it implies a supreme act of volition in obligation to ideal ends. It is only by reverting to its primitive signification, however, that we can properly speak of a moral order among animals; since their action is instinctive rather than volitional, or volitional in the sense of striving for social ends only because they are seen to promote individual safety and happiness. With no necessity for assumption, however, seeing the relations of cause and effect which link the noblest human character to the principle of order in the inorganic universe, by insensible gradations, through animal instincts and egoistic efforts for self-preservation, we may say that this is in very truth a Moral Universe, quivering with ethical impulse and purposive moral life in every atom. The moral in man is a supreme *fact*, independent of all theories of free or determined choice, of intuitional or experiential origin. The final product of the long evolutionary travail, it is an ethical justification of the entire process which lies behind it. But in a stricter sense and in its purely human relations, we can only call that impulse moral which dissociates the sense of obligation from all conscious striving for egoistic happiness, and substitutes for this primary motive the secondary representative and altruistic motive of *obedience to a law of morals*, conditioned upon the nature of things, and conditioning the progressive stability of human societies; which has thus been found essential to the highest welfare and happiness of mankind. The discovery of such an abstract law appears to be the exclusive province of the developed human intellect, though the germs of abstraction may doubtless be found in memory and the association of ideas in the lower animals.

In a moral action, the conscious object of pursuit as indicated by an ethical science based on the doctrine of evolution can never be mere egoistic pleasure, but *fullness of life*, not only for self and family, but for society at large, including the life of posterity. To this end, if necessary, one must always be ready

to sacrifice individual happiness, immediate or remote. While it is true on the one hand, therefore,
that conventional and perfunctory actions, like those
regulating the social relations of brutes and savages,
however beneficent in their results, can not be regarded
as in the highest sense moral, it is also true that
the intuitive sense of obligation, however powerful, is
equally defective as an ultimate moral test.

The true tests of ethical action are both objective
and subjective; either one alone is illusory and unsat-
isfactory. Unless rightly guided by an adequate intellectual apprehension of the results of the volitional
activities, such an intuitive sense of obligation may
be a most serious obstruction to human welfare and
advancement—a fire-brand at the domestic altar, in-
quisition for the heretic, destruction to enemy or un-
believer. The consciences of the Joshuas, John Cal-
vins and Joseph Cooks of history, recent or remote,
like those of the domestic Bluebeards, and those ec-
centric minds which we term "cranks," warped and
distorted by false intellectual apprehensions of duty,
offer some of the most serious problems in rational
psychology and ethics. In such minds the sense of
duty may be absolutely supreme and unyielding; but
the hardest rock does not constitute the most useful
building material, nor does it become the most fruitful soil under the slow attrition of the elements. Its
unyielding nature dooms it to stand in lonely isolation, a monumental reminder of a primeval stage of
evolutionary progress which the living world has long
since left behind. An exalted sense of obligation must
be combined with a certain plasticity of the intellectual nature, freedom from dogmatism and willingness to
seek and learn, to constitute the highest ethical attainment.

Taking the process of evolution in its more general
aspects, it is perhaps not difficult to maintain an optimistic attitude toward the Power that has raised the
animate world out of the inanimate, and moral man
from the unmoral brute creation. But when we view
the process in detail, especially as it affects sentient
organisms, certain problems are presented which chal-
lenge our most thoughtful consideration. The evolu-

tion of life, from the lower to the higher organisms, is accompanied by an ever increasing differentiation of structure and function, finally culminating in highly developed brains and nervous systems of steadily augmenting refinement and complexity of organization. This physical advancement is accompanied by a corresponding differentiation and integration of sentient capacity, so that a much wider and more definite range of sense impressions is open to man and the higher animals than that of which the lower forms of sentient life are susceptible.

The struggle for existence which in inanimate nature and probably in vegetal organisms is unaccompanied by conscious apprehension, is reported to the unitary sensorium in the brain through the intricate network of nerve-fibres in man and the higher animals, and eventuates in conscious feelings of pleasure or of pain. The problem of pain and suffering in sentient creatures appears to some minds insoluble in accordance with the conception of beneficence at the heart of the cosmic process. In his recent Romanes address at Oxford, Professor Huxley, one of the most virile and versatile thinkers among the modern scientific apostles of evolution—an honored friend and Corresponding Member of this Association—takes the ground that all evolution is cyclical in its character—the alternation of growth and decay, of progress and degeneration, without any obvious intelligible or benenfient end or tendency. No moral character, therefore, he claims, is predicable of the cosmic process. On the contrary, all ethical progress has been achieved "not by imitating the cosmic process, still less by running away from it, but by combating it."

That I may do Professor Huxley no injustice, I will quote somewhat at length from his lecture. "From the very low forms up to the highest," he declares, "in the animal no less than the vegetable kingdom—the process of life presents the same appearance of cyclical evolution. Nay, we have but to cast our eye over the rest of the world and cyclical change presents itself on every side. It meets us in the water that flows to the sea and returns to the springs; in the heavenly bodies that wax and wane, go and return to their places; in the inexorable sequence of the ages of man's life; in the successive rise, apogee and fall of dynasties and of States which is the most prominent topic of civil history. But there is another aspect of the cosmic process, so perfect as a mechanism, so beautiful as a work of art. Where the cosmo-poietic energy works through sentient beings, there arises, among its other manifestations, that which we call pain or suffering. This baleful product of evolution increases in quantity and in intensity, with advancing grades of animal organization, until it attains its highest level in man. Further, the consummation is not reached in man, the mere animal; nor in man, the wholly or half savage; but only in man, the member of an organized polity; and it is a necessary accompaniment of his attempt to live in this way—that is, under these conditions, which are essential to the development of his noblest powers."

After a brief sketch of ethical theories as enunciated in Buddhism and the Greek philosophies, in the course of which he incidentally affirms that "Cosmic Nature is no school of virtue, but the headquarters of the enemy of the ethical nature," and that "the cosmos works, through the lower nature of man, not for rightcousness, but against it," he enters upon a criticism of modern theories, practically denying that any ethical system can logically be based upon the doctrine of evolution, and further emphasizing his position by the remarkable statement that "Cosmic evolution may teach us how the good and evil tendencies in man may have come about; but, in itself, it is incompetent to furnish any better reason why what we call good is preferable to what we call evil than we had before." He alludes to processes of degeneration as in conflict with the conception of an ethical aspect or tendency in cosmic Nature, and adds: "As I have already urged, the practice of that which is ethically best— what we call goodness or virtue—involves a course of conduct which, in all respects, is opposed to that which leads to success in the cosmic struggle for existence. Its influence is directed, not so much to the survival of the fittest, as to the fitting of as many as possible to survive."

Leaving out the remainder of his lecture, which is chiefly devoted to a much needed emphasizing of the importance of the human will in moral evolution, and with the general purport of which I heartily agree, let us consider whether Professor Huxley's indictment against the ethics of evolution must be permitted to stand unchallenged. And first, let us ask by what authority, as an evolutionist, does he tacitly and avowedly accept the old theological conception of an antithetical and antagonistic relationship between man and the Universe out of which he has sprung? If man's ethical nature is not a product of the cosmic process as certainly as his purely physical nature, whence does it come? By what means can man correct the methods by which the cosmic energy works in the lower plane of vital activities, without using the powers which he has inherited from these very struggles for existence? As an evolutionist, Professor Huxley can hardly fall back upon the scientifically obsolete doctrines of special creation and a supernaturally intruded grace, and herein would seem to be his only refuge from the conclusion which he so persistently ignores. If, as he affirms, "the cosmic process has no sort of relation to moral ends," how does it happen that the moral sense is itself the culminating product of all evolution, the fine Man-child of all the centuries, toward whose advent the long struggle for existence has constituted the natal throes?

Nor can we admit what seems to be implied in the whole tenor of Professor Huxley's address, that the physical nature of man is, *per se*, a lower or evil nature, or in necessary conflict with the moral ends of his being. Rightly used, every function of our complex human nature works for good and is the helper of moral ends. Abused, any, even the highest, may be productive of evil. The masterfulness of "the cosmic nature which is born in us," the inheritance from brute conditions, is the necessary and powerful instrument in ethical advancement as well as in the physical conflicts of life ; and that conventional morality which is the outcome of a mere deficiency of physical power and capacity is surely a condition not of positive, manly virtue, but of puerile and ascetic weakness, in-

dicative of mental as well as bodily defect. The
conflict with evil to which the Oxford address, as a
whole, is a trumpet call, can never be waged successfully without those very weapons which have been
forged in the fiery furnace of the age-long cosmic
struggle. He who does not conceive of the ethical
life as a conflict demanding every resource of manly
energy, must either live the life of an ascetic, withdrawn from the world and its temptations, or be lapped
in circumstances that favor his continuance in the
innocence of childhood—

> "A powerless, pulpy soul,
>   Showing a dimple at the touch of sin."

By what curious bias, moreover, has Professor Huxley been induced to debit Nature with all the pain and
suffering which enter into the experience of sentient
beings, and to fail to credit her with the manifold
pleasures and satisfactions which are equally the product of the cosmic process? It is man in his entirety
who is the child of the great World-Mother, and his
virtues as well as his weaknesses and vices, his enjoy-
ments as well his pains and sufferings, are a part of
his cosmic heritage. Nor can it be denied, I think,
that a progressively unfolding and enlarging life implies a constant surplus of satisfactions over the concomitant sufferings. To conceive otherwise, as Mr.
Spencer has ably shown, would bring the theory to a
reductio ad absurdum so complete as to be unanswer-
able. Pain and suffering are usually indicative of
some want of adaptation to the physical, social or
moral environment of the individual, and as such their
function may be and should be educational; if not always and effectively to the individual, at least to the
community and the race. And their educational effect-
iveness for the individual depends mainly upon that
very capacity for sympathy which can only grow out
of experience in and observation of their effects. It
does not appear to me to be either a manly, a rational
or a philosophical attitude to expect or desire a life of
enjoyment from which all suffering is eliminated. We
must take the shadows with the light. Were either
lacking, the picture of a progressive moral life would

be incomplete—nay, it would be an impossibility. As Professor Huxley well says, "We are grown men, and must play the man—

'Strong in will
To strive, to seek, to find and not to yield,'

cherishing the good that falls in our way, and bearing the evil, in and around us, with stout hearts set on diminishing it." But as we mount, step by step, up the "stairway of surprise" that leads to loftier heights of manly living, the relative good of the lower stage often becomes evil in the clearer air and wider view which opens before us, and the conflict must needs go on to yet higher ends. The clear perception of this fact must at once fashion our rational ideals of life, and urge us forward to their attainment. Those Oriental philosophies, which Professor Huxley seems to deem the highest products of human speculation, with their doctrines of cyclical change and of metempsychosis— of successive lives of desire and effort finally seen to be fruitless, ending in the search for Nirvana, the extinction of desire and endeavor—can offer no rational ideal to the modern scientific thinker. To him it is evident that something more than a mere cyclical alternation of growth and decay is indicated by the only processes of evolution which he is permitted clearly to study—those thus far exemplified on our planet and in our human lives. Differentiation, refinement, progress toward a higher individuality, has been so far, and in the long run, the actual result of the cosmic process. From a formless gas to a solid globe; from the theatre of fierce plutonic activities to a condition where such activities are rare and exceptional; from an inanimate mass to a home for manifold forms of life; from coarser to finer forms of vegetation; from moneron to ape and from ape to man; from savagery to barbarism and from barbarism to civilization: this has been the life history of our little world—the sole object-lesson from which we have the right to judge of the actual nature and tendency of cosmic evolution. Here is the large fact of progress, which is by no means reversed or seriously discounted by the incidental fact that this progress has not been serial, but rhythmical, that occasional and local degeneration has been an accompaniment of the general evolutionary process.

And now, at the culmination of the cosmic process, man stands forth—child of the great World-Mother—a being capable of reflection, investigation and rational volition as a guide to his own activities; a tremendous factor henceforward in the evolutionary process, who by thought, married to deeds, cannot only change his own stature—contrary to scriptural suggestion—but can form his own character, modify his environment, and vastly help or hinder the progress of the world. Nay, he *is* doing it, whether he will or not—for evil if not for good—wasting the riches which affluent Nature has placed in his hands by unwise prodigality, wasting his own life by heedlessly devoting it to selfish or unworthy ends, or wisely enlarging it and the world's prosperity by a well-considered balance of economy and expenditure of vital resource in the service of his fellows. A creature like man cannot be a mere make-weight in the economy of Nature: he must *tell*, either one way or the other—for good or for ill.

Nor has man been left without guidance as to the true method of combating the evils of life. The discovery of this method, indeed, is left to his own intelligent volition, but the rule by which his steps should be guided is planted deep in the very nature of things. The fact that cause and effect rule in his own mental activities as well as in the processes of external nature—that in all normally constituted minds action necessarily follows from adequate and equivalent motives—so far from banishing ethics from the world of human effort, constitutes the sole and essential condition of all moral action and ethical advancement. Nor does it even imply the negation of individual freedom in any rational, philosophical sense, since the motive which controls his action is not external to the man but the outcome of his own inherent nature in contact with the living world; and to say that the motive governs his action is therefore simply to affirm that his action is governed by his own volition, which is the clearest possible statement of his freedom. The conception of uncaused volition, or of action deter-

mined by a will acting independent of orderly and equivalent motive, on the contrary, is an affirmation of real
external constraint; for here the will is hypostasized
as an entity superior to and external to the other faculties of the mind, and constraining them to do its
bidding. The conception of the uncaused volition of
a self-determining will extrinsic to the natural order
of causation and equivalent motive, intrudes a supernatural element into human action of the character of
true external compulsion. This, however, is a purely
metaphysical and unscientific conception. It must be
evident, on reflection, that the only real constraint
which the moral nature of the individual can suffer,
is the constraint of external forces; while the only
rational conception of moral freedom consistent with
the possibility of ethical culture involves the recognition of an individual volition which is the resultant of
adequate and equivalent motives; such motives being
the outcome of the free activity of the psychical nature upon the circumstances submitted for its judgment.

Looking back, all along the line of social and moral
evolution, we see that progress has been made whenever man has acquired a true understanding of cosmic
laws, and has governed his life in accordance therewith. Recalling the anthropological collection at the
World's Fair, with which we started, and taking the
rudest stone implement to be found there as an example, we shall find that it was fashioned to human
uses by the discovery of and conformity, in some
small degree, to the laws of mechanics; and it is
merely by an amplification of this scientific knowledge and its uses that the powerful Allis engine, in
Machinery Hall, and the most intricate apparatus for
weaving or printing or fashioning articles for our
daily use has been constructed. If Nature has compelled man to fight his way up from barbarism to civilization, she has also furnished him with suitable
weapons all along the way; until the Krupp guns and
steel armor plates of our modern day promise by their
very perfection of mechanism to render brute conflicts
forever unprofitable as well as immoral. When a single shot costs a thousand dollars for powder and ball,

nations will think twice before they settle commercial quarrels or disputes about boundaries by appeals to arms. To this era of "peace and good will" the marvelous triumphs of the mechanic arts, in the field of manufactures and in the construction of the vehicles of commercial intercourse are also contributing factors more potent than pulpit sermons or the tracts of the Peace Society.

Whenever man has ceased to study Nature and endeavored to hew out a course of conduct for himself with the imperfect tools of his own unguided imaginings, hoping thus to blunder into some millennial condition of prosperity and happiness, he has always gone astray. That is the fault of metaphysical speculation everywhere, carried to excess, and divorced from experiential knowledge. It involves an immense waste of power, like the effort one makes to lift himself by his boot-straps. That is why India finds herself today a plaything in the hands of England, though intellectually her great thinkers are infinitely superior in culture and ability to the small-minded Occidental theologians who call them "heathens," and assume to dole out to them the conditions of salvation from eternal torment in a future life. Was it a gleam of real intellectual progress, or was it only reflected light from the Parliament of Religions, which induced the American Board of Commissioners for Foreign Missions, the other day, to send back Missionary Noyes with his gospel of a possible future probation for the "heathen," in spite of the awful warning and threatened secession of Joseph Cook?

Whatever religion we may profess, or if we think we have no religion, we are face to face, every day of our lives, with the actual facts of the Cosmos, and of our associated human life; with the problems of present duty—of salvation *here* and *now*. Underneath the facts are the eternal laws in accordance with which they have come into being. It is ours to study the facts, to learn the laws, and to conform our lives in harmony with them. Herein lie both our golden opportunity and our profound and unavoidable respon sibility. To obey is life—ever-enlarging life, reaching out to ever higher and more beneficent fruition.

To ignore or disobey is pain, degeneration and death. There is no royal road to that knowledge, either by "Mental Science"—which is nescience—or Theosophy, or any form, whether ancient or modern, of special illumination or supernatural grace. To hold up such hopes or expectations to men in the face of the impressive teaching of all history is to make one's self a blind leader of the blind—to cultivate an egoistic conceit of knowledge, which is no knowledge, and to place new stumbling blocks in the path of human progress instead of those which the travail of many generations has hardly yet, through weary labors and suffering and martyrdom, been able to remove.

Nature's mandate forever is, Here are my eternal laws, the conditions of all progress, the source of all true happiness, external to your own volition, which you cannot change by one jot or tittle, but by obedience to which you may transform yourself and the world into the likeness of the All-Perfect. If so you will, your own intelligent volition shall supplement the painful experience of the ages, and hasten the dawn of a higher and diviner civilization. Would you be helpers of the world? Study and obey these laws—be their prophet and evangelist, carrying their glad gospel of salvation by character, salvation by works, salvation by evolution, salvation by obedience, to all who are weary and heavy laden, whether with burdens of sin, or ignorance, or poverty or disease of mind or body. Serve the self which is higher than your individual self—the larger self of family, country and mankind, which is one in the last analysis with the very life and being of the Cosmos. Thus, by forming life and character, self and society, upon the divine order of Nature thou shalt become one with it, accomplishing at once the purest ethical and the loftiest religious ends of life.

It is the great virtue of the evolutionary ethic that it calls man from the cloud-land of metaphysical speculation, and seeks to enlighten his intellect and guide his steps by appeals to the scientifically ascertained facts of human experience, and the laws by which they are governed. Back to Nature—not in her statical aspects, as dreamed by Rousseau and the Eighteenth Century philosophers, but in her dynamical and evolutionary aspects—must we ever go for ethical guidance, encouragement and inspiration.

> "Man's thought is like Antæus, and must be
>   Touched to the ground of Nature to regain
>   Fresh force, new impulse, else it would remain
> Dead, in the grip of strong Authority.
> But once thereon reset, 'tis like a tree,
>   Sap-swollen in Spring-time, bonds may not restrain
> Nor weights repress; its rootlets rend in twain
> Dead stones, and walls, and rocks, resistlessly."

Calling men to obedience to the eternal laws of right which are a part of the Cosmic Order, not alien to it, the evolutionary ethic demands the most exigent service of all who clearly perceive the nature of its high behests. He who in this service would help to reform the world, has no idle or superficial task before him, nor can he hope for an immediate millennial future which shall establish a universal reign of righteousness in human societies. His philosophy of life, while the reverse of pessimistic, should perhaps rightly be styled melioristic rather than optimistic. Slowly, by the enlightenment and conversion of the individuals who make up the great social organism, must their wills be brought into unison for the accomplishment of beneficent social ends. Private emolument, pride of personal supremacy, and all unworthy seeking of individual advantage, must give place to a complete consecration of will and deed to wise efforts to know, to teach and to obey the great evolutionary laws which ultimate in the highest conduct of life.

> "Who dares to leave the life of private ends
>   And on himself the world's great burden take,
>   Who tramples selfishness, and turns to make
>   All men his friends,
>
> "In the large service of the common weal,
>   Virtues he needs of high and noble name;
>   He should possess such scorn of praise and fame
>   As martyrs feel.

"He should have faith too great for doubt to harm,
  Patience untouched through all the passing years,
  Wisdom, a jest to make of doubts and fears,
  Unmoved, calm.

"If he have these, and love, no fate can come
  To make his work as though it had not been;
  It serveth much, though Death should step between
  And strike him dumb.

"Or he be fallen, and none know where he fell,
  Crushed by the power that he would fain have served;
  E'en out of silence speaks who hath not swerved:
  His work is well."*

ABSTRACT OF THE DISCUSSION.

MR. JAMES A. SKILTON:

If it be a part of the opportunity and duty of discussing this paper to add something, that would seem
to be difficult, if not impossible; if to criticise and
condemn, that would seem ungracious, if possible. As
a paper devoted exclusively to ethics, I can give it
neither one of these methods of treatment, and only
highest praise and commendation. And yet, considering the implications that are found between its lines,
their proper discussion would seem to require as much
time, or space, as the paper itself, and the devotion
of an equivalent study, and an equal talent, if that
were possible.

In this paper the changes are constantly, and nobly,
rung on law, obedience, duty, obligation, good,
righteousness and words of related import, while emotion is put not simply under a ban, but flatly banished
as an unworthy and untrustworthy member of the select
brotherhood of virtues. (It may well be doubted if
such a thing as "mere emotional sentiment" even can
be properly condemned merely as such; for even that,
according to our fundamental thesis, is and must be

---

* The Reformer. By William Francis Barnard.

supported on a solid physical basis and have its proper place in an evolutionary system.) And this is, as I understand, no mere accident, no mere slip, no mere omission for want of time or space, but an exclusion intended and made necessary to round out an alleged all-sufficient system. So considered, the criticism could not well be too prompt or too vigorous. Treatment by process of exclusion, for clearness and definiteness, where the subject is large, difficult or obscure, is not only wise but safe; and is often necessary, where the purpose is to make a study or a speculative trial. But where the purpose is to frame a system for practical application, such a method is most dangerous, if not certainly misleading.

To be just, and truly ethical, perhaps my criticism should extend beyond the essayist and far enough to reach the board of trustees who selected and settled upon the topics of the season, myself included. Our general topic is: The Physical Basis of Ethics, Sociology and Religion. But devoting the opening essay to a general and preparatory treatment of ethics, we pass over or ignore such a treatment of Sociology and Religion and at once take up specific topics of physics. Ethics is, without religion, soulless, and without sociology homeless—a soulless, homeless wanderer. If all men were (like our genial friend) possessed of a clear and penetrating intellect transfused and all compact with beneficent emotion and righteousness, an ethical system might be framed for their use that would fairly engineer and guide the world and mankind on the hard and uphill road of progress; but, shall I say alas, they are not.

Mere law never developed or saved the family; nor can it develop or save the state, or society, which are only the larger family. It is interesting, however, as Arnold would have said, to note how the needed guest and Savior did creep in and find a snug corner for himself, "unbeknownst" like, just at the last. Faith, patience, wisdom—unmoved, calm, "If he have these, *and love*, no fate can come to make his work as though it had not been." Yes, Ethics shot through with love, we may all say, will answer. But while we may readily admit that—"The moral in man is a supreme fact," we cannot admit that it is the supremest fact or "The *final* product of the long evolutionary travail." The supremest fact we shall hardly find until we find that love which, while it has true abiding places in society and religion would in both fain extend into the domain of the limitless and the infinite.

The question has its practical bearings for us and our work. There are minds upon which lectures on mere ethics act as a sufficient stimulus, but they do not belong to the mass of mankind. Therefore, while we start from a foundation of physics we must rise thereform into the domain of the emotional, if we would have the aid of enthusiasm in giving motion, momentum and working energy to our *Propoganda Fide*.

Dr. ROBERT G. ECCLES:—

The aim of the present course that has been begun so admirably by Dr. Janes is to lay a physical foun·dation for moral law; or, as it were, "to lead from Nature up to Nature's God." The title of the course indicates its scope and shows the aim of those who mapped it out. Every lecture is to be upon some phase of life, and how it has survived and progressed among the ever-changing conditions of the physical world. It is to show that obedience to the laws of being leads toward the higher life while disobedience brings suffering and death. As in the nebulæ lay the potentialities in embryotic activity that have brought into being solar systems and worlds, and in an amœba those that have finally differentiated into man, so in the world of physical things lie the germs of the moral. Newton's first law of motion is potentially the first law of morality. Action and reaction are equal and opposite in moral things as well as in material, as every person learns sooner or later in life. The New Testament only states in other terms Newton's law when it says "as you sow so shall you also reap." Push a wall with a pressure of ten pounds and it pushes you back with the same pressure; crowd your fellow beings with a given amount of immoral conduct and your fellow beings will crowd you back with equal

force. If the wall gives way to your pressure it is
only to allow stones and bricks in unstable equilibrium above you to fall and injure you. If you injure
your fellows to the extent of forcing movement among
them it is only to bring down on your head greater
damage as a result. Nature by this law is incessantly
seeking for a balance. In physics we call it equilibrium, in morals equity. They are but different names
for what fundamentally is the same. Justice is well
typified by a pair of scales for this reason. Action
and reaction are equal and opposite in kind as well
as in amount. Every good deed gives a good reaction
to bless him who does it. In the proportion of one's
good deeds so is the rate of his happiness; and in the
proportion of his evil that of his misery. The very
plans pursued by animals in the past that enabled
them to survive amid the "rushing metamorphosis"
of things, are the plans that you and I must pursue
toward society if we would live. On the other hand
the plans pursued by iguanodons, megatheriums and
other such monsters, which have brought about their
extinction, are the plans for us to avoid in dealing
with our fellows. Lions, wolves, bears, condors and
eagles are fast disappearing. We should learn what
the nature of the reaction is that is extinguishing
them and avoid repeating their folly in dealing with
our fellows. Whenever a race is extinguished it is
because some act of its own toward Nature reacted to
its detriment. Whenever a race triumphs it is because some act reacts to its advantage. Our worst reaction toward our fellow creature is that of selfish hate.
Whenever you dislike a fellow creature it reacts to your
misery and the more you dislike that person the more
miserable you are. When you dislike two your misery is doubled, three trebled, four quadrupled, etc.
Here are action and reaction equal and opposite again.
Think of a man who hates everybody and everything
and you will have some conception of the immense
power of this law. Would it not be better for such
a man that he had never been born? Will he not
think so himself and be likely to try and extinguish
his own life? The opposite form of reaction is as
powerful for good and happiness as this for misery.

Jesus knew this when he taught that the whole gospel is summed up in the one word "Love." "Love is the fulfilling of the law." When young people love each other with their whole hearts, how intense the happiness. The more unselfishly devoted one creature is to another the more happy that creature becomes. In direct proportion to the number of people we like so is our happiness. In direct proportion, likewise to the intensity of our regard so too is our happiness. He who loves one is happy in that one's presence. To love two with unselfish love is to double our happiness. To love three is to treble it. To love the whole human family is to live within an atmosphere of beatitude and the more intense that love the greater the joy. The soul must make its own heaven and that too in obedience to this everlasting fundamental law of action and reaction as equal and opposite. The whole universe is seeking equilibrium and equilibrium is the other name for equity or justice.

Justice is the reaction of love on love as equilibrium is the reaction of attraction on attraction. The two phases are but aspects of the same thing. Physics is but the material way of viewing being. Psychics is the spiritual way of looking at the same thing. Turn attraction around, wherever you have the power to do so, and you discover in it love. Turn love around and it is only a form of attraction. Longing and desire are some of the simpler manifestations of love. Hunger is the chemical longing of our stomachs for food. Micro-organisms, so small that a wave of light can scarcely span them display hunger, love of light, love of certain chemicals, etc. They are too minute to have any structure like that of our nervous system. They are the uniting links between pure chemical activity and psychical activity. They show the two to be but aspects of one another. Love is attraction and all the evidence we are able to reach clearly implies that attraction is love. This last proposition, of course, awaits demonstration but we have this consolation that all the proof is in its favor. If the whole universe has a psychical aspect and every physical manifestation a corresponding psychical one, the conditions of survival of the remote past must be pregnant with meaning for the present and future when interpreted from the physical to the psychical signification. As the physiologist is constantly trying to find the material conditions giving rise to sensations of various kinds so the psychologist of the future will, perhaps, find work in interpreting the cosmos in a direction the reverse of this. To do so would lead toward a conception like that proclaimed as true by Paul on Mars' hill. It would show us God as over all, in all and through all. It is the only conception of Nature warranted by all the facts at present in our command. To study critically the conditions under which life has ever survived and to compare them with those that have brought about extinction, is to have our consciousness grow into the inevitable conclusion that the moral process of survival and the physical one are fundamentally the same.

Dr. Janes in reply:

The remarks of Dr. Eccles, sustaining and amplifying as they do my own positions, do not call for a reply. The criticism of my friend Mr. Skilton proceeds, it appears to me, from a rather surprising misapprehension or misinterpretation of the positions taken in my lecture. Had the topic assigned me called for a special discussion of the religious and sociological as well as the ethical bearings of the question before us, I should have had something further to say upon those aspects; but it certainly did not occur to me that a discussion of ethics could possibly be interpreted as an intentional exclusion of religion and sociology from consideration as factors in our main topic—"Life and the Conditions of Survival." The last lecture of the series, indeed, is expressly devoted to religion; while the sociological aspects of every specialized topic are brought out in the sub-titles as arranged in our programme. Indeed, since man's moral nature has to do chiefly, if not exclusively, with his social relations to his fellows, the separation of ethics from sociology is unthinkable, and is certainly nowhere implied in my lecture.

If my critic identifies religion with "mere emotional

sentiment," as I do not, it would be easy to show that this kind of religion has oftener led the world wrong than right. But if true religion include, as I think it must, the conception of morality as a part of the Cosmic order—a conception which I have every-where emphasized—then in one of its aspects it has rightly been defined by Matthew Arnold as "Morality touched by emotion," and it must logically recognize and enforce obedience to the moral as well as to the physical, and other sociological laws—if there be such —involved in the Cosmic process. If my friend can imagine "ethics without sociology" and "without love" —as I cannot—he might indeed find it a "soulless, homeless wanderer;" but that seems to me to be not only untrue but absolutely unthinkable.

In speaking of ethics as the "supreme fact," and "the final product of the long evolutionary travail" I merely alluded to the fact, so ably illustrated by Mr. Spencer and evidenced by all historical research, that religion, especially in its emotional aspects, antedates morality in the order of man's mental evolution, as these characteristics indeed, akin to the emotional instincts everywhere dominant in the brute creation, would necessarily imply, in a rational psychological system. In attacking this conception he is therefore attacking Mr. Spencer rather than myself. Surely, how-ever, I have not only impliedly but expressly recog-nized the value not only of the emotional but of the purely physical or animal nature of man as a neces-sary help to a true ethical and religious life. But if we *must* lack one or the other, the impressive warning of history is to give morality the infinite preference.

SOLAR ENERGY

A. EMERSON PALMER

COLLATERAL READINGS SUGGESTED.

Haeckel's *The History of Creation;* Spencer's *The Nebular Hypothesis;* Proctor's *Astronomy;* Carr's *The Sun: Its Constitution and Phenomena;* Tyndall's *Lectures on Light,* and *Heat as a Mode of Motion;* Molloy's *The Modern Theory of Heat,* and *The Sun as a Storehouse of Energy;* Flammarion's *The Wonders of the Heavens;* Gore's *The Visible Universe;* *Chapters on the Origin and Constitution of the Heavens;* Preston's *The Theory of Light;* Allen's *Solar Light and Heat;* Schellen's *Spectrum Analysis;* Croll's *Climate and Time;* Bell's *The Cause of the Ice Age;* Wright's *Man and the Ice Age.*

SOLAR ENERGY.

BY A. EMERSON PALMER.

From the astronomer's point of view, the sun is to be regarded in a two fold aspect. In the first place, it is the center and ruler of our planetary system. In the second place, it is a star, and therefore must be counted as a humble member of that vast company of "envoys of beauty" which come forth every night to "light the universe with their admonishing smile." In the present discussion we are to deal with the sun almost exclusively as the chief of what is termed the solar system. It will be necessary, of course, to make large use of facts and figures which are more or less familiar, and which are, as a matter of necessity, derived from standard works upon solar astronomy.

The sun has, very naturally and quite inevitably, been an object of profoundest interest to mankind from the earliest history of the race. It is as true now as it was when the book of Ecclesiastes was written that "the light is sweet, and a pleasant thing it is for the eyes to behold the sun;" and it was just as true a thousand and ten thousand years before. It is not in the least surprising that in a rude and primitive age men felt impelled to worship the sun. We know to-day better than they possibly could have known that it is far more worthy of adoration and worship than any other physical object within the range of human experience. That men should bow down before the sun, and offer sacrifices to it, and look upon it as a god, is as natural as anything in the world. To worship mere earthly fire, as some people have done, is to exalt to a lofty place something that is common and insignificant, compared with the majesty, glory, and life-giving power of the mighty—we may almost say the almighty—sun.

33

Of the sun it may truthfully be affirmed that, while unknown to us in many aspects, it is, nevertheless, well known. Nothing else in the range of astronomy, it is safe to say, arouses so much interest, piques so much speculation, or attracts so many telescopes and other instruments by means of which the astronomer is able to bridge the million-miled chasm dividing us from that which is the source of all that lives, and moves, and has its being on this little planet which we call the earth. This last is the literal fact. Nothing can be more certain that all life on the earth, that every object in the organic world, is absolutely dependent upon the sun. And, more than that, the maintenance of life depends upon the maintenance of the sun's temperature at a substantially uniform degree. If it should grow a little hotter, all living things would be scorched and shrivelled in its fiery breath. If it should grow a few degrees cooler, everything here would be quickly frozen, and the surface of the earth undoubtedly would, in a brief time, be encrusted with ice from pole to pole. We are pensioners upon the sun's bounty far more absolutely than most of us, I imagine, are in the habit of thinking.

THE SUN'S SIZE, DISTANCE, ETC.

Not only is all life on the earth due to the sun, but practically all forms of energy known to us are derived from this source. Before proceeding to that phase of the matter, however, let us consider a few of the leading facts that astronomy teaches in reference to the sun, for these are necessary to any clear understanding of the subject. We have to deal here with big figures—so big, in fact, that they can convey no very definite or adequate idea to the average mind.

The distance of the sun from the earth is about 93,-000,000 miles. The diameter of the sun is about 860,-000 miles. It is necessary to say "about," because, with all the accuracy of astronomical measurements, there is a considerable margin of error. How great it is, or, rather, how small it is, is shown by the remark of Sir John Herschel, that "the recent correction of the solar parallax corresponds to the apparent breadth of a human hair at a distance of 125 feet." The as-

tronomers tell us, further, that the quantity of matter
in the sun is 330,000 times as great as that in the
earth, and that its mean density is one fourth of that
of the earth, or one and one-fourth times the density
of water; that is to say, the mass of the sun is one
fourth greater than would be that of a globe of water
of the same size. Put into figures, the mass of the
sun is two octillions of tons—the figure 2, followed by
twenty-seven ciphers. The force of gravity at the
sun's surface is nearly twenty-eight times as great as
on the surface of the earth, so that a man weighing
150 pounds here would weigh in the neighborhood of
two tons there, and naturally would not cut much of a
figure on his feet.

As I said, these numbers are too vast for our minds
to grasp them. When I say that the sun is 93,000,000
miles away from us, I really convey no more definite
idea to you than if I said 193,000,000 miles—just as
if a hundred million miles were of no account whatever! For all practical purposes, either of these distances is infinite to us, although in reality the distance
of the sun is only a trifle in comparison with that of
the far-off fixed stars; so insignificant, in fact, that if
I represent the distance of the sun from the earth by
the distance from me of a man on whose shoulder I
can lay my hand, to indicate proportionately the stupendous distance of the nearest fixed stars, like Sirius
for instance, I should have to send the man away from
me more than one hundred miles!

SOME CONCRETE ILLUSTRATIONS.

Now let me endeavor to bring some of these figures
before your minds in a more concrete form. The diameter of the sun, as I said, is about 860,000 miles.
You all know that by traveling steadily one can make
the circuit of the earth pretty comfortably in eighty
days, or a little less. But going at that same rate it
would take not less than twenty-four years to put a
girdle around the sun. Still more impressive is another comparison. We know that the distance of the
moon from the earth is 240,000 miles. This is something that we can grasp more readily. Now, if the
whole interior of the sun were hollowed out and only

the shell remained, and if the earth were then placed at the center of this huge hollow sphere, with the moon still retaining its relative position to the earth —240,000 miles distant—the orbit of our satellite would extend only a little more than half way from the center of the sun to its enormous circumference.

Take, again, the distance of the sun, which, the astronomers tell us, is about 93,000,000 miles. If a man should walk four miles an hour for ten hours a day, and keep it up steadily, it would take him almost three-score years and ten to cover one million miles —sixty-eight and one half years, according to Professor Young; and walking at that speed it would take him more than 6,300 years to reach the sun. Benjamin Franklin was born in 1706. If when he was able to travel alone, say at the age of ten—that is, in the year 1716, the second year of the reign of George I.—he had set out for the sun on an express train running sixty miles an hour, and making no stops for fuel or water, he would be arriving at his destination somewhere in the present year of grace; and at the current rates he would have paid for railway fare something like $2,500,000.

One more illustration before leaving this part of the subject. So far as consciousness reveals it to us, the instant we prick a finger or burn it by bringing it into contact with something hot, that instant we are aware of what has occurred, the intelligence having been flashed along the nerves to the brain. Experiments have shown, however, that impressions travel along the nerves at a definite rate of speed—at the rate of about 100 feet per second. Some one has made the necessary calculation, and asserts that if a child should be born with an arm long enough to enable him to reach the sun, he would not live long enough to know that he had burned his fingers in it, since it would require nearly 150 years for the sensation, coming at the rate of 100 feet per second, to reach his brain.

So much for the mathematics of the case. Enough has been said to show that when dealing with the sun we are dealing with a very big thing, and that its distance from us is prodigious.

A MIGHTY STOREHOUSE OF RADIANT ENERGY.

The sun supplies us with light and with heat, and the sunbeams likewise have the capacity of producing chemical action. But these results are all diverse effects of the same thing. The last word of science on the subject, up to date, is that light, heat, and chemical action are all produced by an "uncompre-hended something radiated from the sun." This "un-comprehended something" is termed radiant energy. The sun is a mighty storehouse, an inexhaustible res-ervoir, of radiant energy, from which, as I said at the beginning, all organic life on the earth is derived.

It requires very little demonstration to prove that substantially all the energy involved in terrestrial phe-nomena is drawn from this source. The chief forms of energy known to us are water power, wind power, steam power, muscular power, electrical power, and the power of the ocean tides. Every one of these, except possibly the last, is plainly derived from this huge reservoir.

Water falls only because vast quantities of vapor are lifted into the air by the sun, to descend in rain or snow and feed the uncounted streams that flow cease-lessly into the ocean. "All the rivers run into the sea, yet the sea is not full,"* because the energy that comes pouring across 93,000,000 miles of space is con-stantly at work emptying it. We talk often of the power of gravitation that draws things down: think for a moment of the power of the sun's rays in pull-ing things up!

Wind, as everybody knows, is only air in motion. How is this motion produced? Here again we must look to the sun for the cause. Heated air expands and rises, and its place is taken by that which is cooler. So motion is established and currents are set up in the atmosphere; and so the wind which turns the arms of the wind-mill, or fills the bellying sails of the ship, or spreads the white wings of the peerless Vigilant—all this is seen to be directly due to solar energy.

The same is true of steam power, of muscular pow-

* Ecclesiastes, 1, 7.

er, of electrical power. Steam is produced by the combustion of coal or wood; and coal is the energy of the sun stored up in past ages, while wood and other forms of vegetable growth are produced by the direct action of the sun's rays. Muscular energy in man or other animals is derived, in the first instance, from the food eaten; and that food is either vegetable in itself or at one remove, having first passed into the flesh of some other animal. Electrical energy as produced in the dynamo is the energy of steam carried one step further on.

Only the energy of the tides remains. It is commonly supposed that this is the exception to the rule. But is it? It is true that the tides are caused mainly by the lifting power of the moon, although the sun plays some part even here, and that the sweep of the tides across the oceans is due to the rotation of the earth on its axis. But every one familiar with the nebular hypothesis knows that the motion which the earth has on its axis was derived in the last analysis from the sun; and, moreover, if the sun's radiant energy should be cut off, the tides would doubtless soon cease to ebb and flow in the tremendous cold that would ensue.

To the sun, therefore, we can trace all forms of energy upon the earth. Professor Tyndall's admirable words contain the poetry of science as well as the exactest scientific truth:—"Without solar fire we could have no atmospheric vapor, without vapor no clouds, without clouds no snow, without snow no glaciers. Curious then as the conclusion may be, the cold ice of the Alps has its origin in the heat of the sun."*

EVERYTHING DEPENDENT ON THE SUNBEAMS.

What Sir John Herschel wrote in 1833 needs little modification to bring it into harmony with the latest conclusions of science:—"The sun's rays are the ultimate source of almost every motion which takes place on the surface of the earth. By its heat are produced all winds, and those disturbances in the electric equilibrium of the atmosphere which give rise to the phenomena of lightning, and probably

---

* Forms of Water, p. 7.

also to terrestrial magnetism and the aurora. By their vivifying action vegetables are enabled to draw support from inorganic matter, and become in their turn the support of animals and man, and the source of those great deposits of dynamical efficiency which are laid up for human use in our coal strata. By them the waters of the sea are made to circulate in vapor through the air, and irrigate the land, producing springs and rivers. By them are produced all disturbances of the chemical equilibrium of the elements of nature, which by a series of compositions and decompositions give rise to new products and originate a transfer of materials. Even the slow degradation of the solid constituents of the surface, in which its chief geological change consists, is almost entirely due, on the one hand, to the abrasion of wind or rain and the alternation of heat and frost; on the other, to the continual beating of sea waves agitated by winds, the results of solar radiation. Tidal action (itself partly due to the sun's agency) exercises here a comparatively slight influence. The effect of oceanic currents (mainly originating in that influence), though slight in abrasion, is powerful in diffusing and transporting the matter abraded; and when we consider the immense transfer of matter so produced, the increase of pressure over large spaces in the bed of the ocean, and diminution over corresponding portions of the land, we are not at a loss to perceive how the elastic force of subterranean fires, thus repressed on the one hand and released on the other, may break forth in points where the resistance is barely adequate to their retention, and thus bring the phenomena of even volcanic activity under the general law of solar influence."

Regarding which Mr. Tyndall remarks: "This fine passage requires but the breath of recent investigation to convert it into an exposition of the law of the conservation of energy, as applied to both the organic and inorganic world."

In language that is even more striking, a recent writer has most graphically set forth the intimate relation which the energy of the sun bears to the earth and to all that exists and takes place on its surface.

"When one takes a country ramble on a pleasant
summer's day, one may fitly ponder upon the wondrous
significance of this law of the transformation of energy. It is wondrous to reflect that all the energy stored
up in the timbers of the fences and farm-houses which
we pass, as well as in the grindstone and the axe lying
beside it, and in the iron axles and heavy tires of the
cart which stands tipped up by the roadside; all the
energy from moment to moment given out by the roar-
ing cascade and the busy wheel that rumbles at its
foot, by the undulating stalks of corn in the field and
the swaying branches in the forest beyond, by the
birds that sing in the tree-tops and the butterflies to
which they anon give chase, by the cow standing in
the brook and the water which bathes her lazy feet,
by the sportsmen who pass shouting in the distance
as well as by their dogs and guns; that all this multi-
form energy is nothing but metamorphosed solar radiance, and that all these various objects, giving life
and cheerfulness to the landscape, have been built up
into their cognizable forms by the agency of sunbeams
such as those by which the scene is now rendered
visible."*

ONLY A SMALL FRACTION UTILIZED.

We may remark, in passing, how very small a part,
what an infinitesimal fraction, of the energy which
the sun provides for us is made use of by man. The
great majority of rivers and smaller streams flow unused, to find their level in the ocean. The winds blow
idly on sea and land. Vast quantities of coal and peat
lie untouched in Nature's storehouse. As for the immense power of the tides that beat on every shore,
practically all of it goes to waste, although the time
may come when men will learn to make use of what
is thus offered them with unfailing regularity twice in
every day, only to be indifferently rejected. All the
work done in the world is really insignificant, in comparison with the power which Nature furnishes in that
little part of the radiant energy of the sun which our
planet intercepts on its journey through space.

A little part, I say, for, of course, the sun's energy

is sent forth into space with equal force in every direction. The total would be sufficient to light and warm not less than 2,200,000,000 planets like ours. Think of it! There are 49,000,000 square miles in the cross-section of the earth exposed to the sun's rays; and yet the earth contrives to catch less than one-two-thousand-millionth part of the solar energy.

Insignificant as this may seem viewed on one side, viewed on the other it is enormous beyond our powers of conception. "The sun-heat falling on one square mile," says Professor Langley, "corresponds to over seven hundred and fifty tons of water raised *every minute* from the freezing point to boiling;" while the total amount of heat falling on the earth would in each minute boil 37,000,000,000 tons of ice-cold water. Still further, the sun's rays would in one year melt a coating of ice over the whole earth more than 160 feet in thickness; and if we could contrive to build a bridge of snow and ice, fifteen miles in diameter, from the earth to the moon, and could keep it intact until completed, and should then suddenly concentrate the sun's total radiation upon it, the entire mass would vanish into vapor in the space of a single second!

Truly, we are dealing with a "stupendous outflow of solar heat." And it is impossible not to speculate as to what becomes of by far the greater part of this prodigious total. The earth's share, as we have seen, is insignificant from one point of view, and all that is intercepted by the planets of our system and their satellites is but a minute fraction of the whole. What becomes of the vast remainder? Seemingly there is a most enormous waste; but it is impossible for us to think that it can be so. The law of the conservation of energy must apply there as well as here. Nature is said to abhor a vacuum. From what we know of her operations we may truthfully affirm that she abhors waste. There can be no room in the universe for waste. When considering the prodigious expenditure of solar energy, is it not entirely rational for us to affirm, with the poet, that—

> ' No ray is dimmed, no atom worn
> Its oldest force is good as new?"

How hot the sun is no one can tell, but it is a mat-

ter about which there has been considerable guess-
work. Professor Langley says on this point: "It is
probable, from all experiments made up to this date,
that the solar effective temperature is not less than
3,000 nor more than 30,000 degrees of the Centigrade
thermometer." This is a later statement than that of
Professor Young, which may also be quoted, that the
effective temperature of the sun is probably 10,000
degrees Centigrade, or 18,000 degrees Fahrenheit;
while Mr. Lockyer remarks that the temperature of the
sun is beyond all definition.

THE LIGHT OF THE SUN.

Thus far we have been viewing the sun as a gigantic
furnace at which we warm ourselves. But it is more
than that. It is also a tremendous reservoir of light.
On this head a word or two must suffice, although
the light is as obvious and in some respects as important as the heat. Measured in candle power—the ordinary method of estimating the illuminating intensity
of gas, or electricity, or any other light-giving substance—the light shed by the sun is represented, in
figures, by 63 followed by twenty-six ciphers—that
is, the sun has a candle power of six octillions, three
hundred septillions.*

Just here, and in connection with what was said a
moment ago concerning the seemingly unused heat of
the sun, a quotation from Stewart's Conservation of
Energy is pertinent. "It is a curious question," he
remarks, "to ask what becomes of the radiant light
from the sun that is not absorbed either by the planets
of our system or by any of the stars. We can only
reply to such a question, that *as far as we can judge
from our present knowledge*, the radiant energy that
is not absorbed must be conceived to be traversing
space at the rate of 188,000 miles a second." †

What a vision this conception opens up before the
imagination! We know that a large part of the light
received by the earth is reflected back from its surface.

---

* This is Professor Young's estimate, but it is considerably larger than that given
by Gore in The Visible Universe. He says: "Compared with a standard candle
placed at a distance of one metre from the eye, the Sun's light is equal in quantity to 1575 billions of billions of such candles (1575 followed by 24 cyphers.")

† P. 123.

Of this we have optical evidence in the earth-shine which is detectable on the moon in certain of its phases. Now all this reflected light that is not intercepted by the moon, the other planets, etc., must be regarded as flying through the regions of space at a speed so great that it leaps across the gulf separating us from the sun in eight minutes; and thus we may conceive of an eye behind a sufficiently powerful lens, placed at a sufficient distance, and traveling toward the earth with the velocity of light—we can conceive, I say, of such an eye beholding all that has taken place on our planet, not only since the beginning of history, but during that enormously long antecedent period, in comparison with which "the whole recorded duration of human history shrinks into nothingness."

Let us next ask how this solar energy in the form of heat and light reaches us. This is a question that cannot be answered with positiveness. "Physicists have to assume the existence of an all-pervading imponderable fluid inappreciable to any of our senses."* This fluid is commonly termed ether, and it is supposed to pervade all space. Through this ether the radiant energy is transmitted somewhat in the same way as sound is conveyed by vibrations of the air. The slower heat vibrations, says Professor Langley, are shown by experiments to "succeed each other nearly 100,000,000,000,000 times in a single second, while those which make us see"—that is, the light vibrations—"have long been known to be more rapid still." "All bodies, whether near or far," to quote Mr. Lockyer again, "are visible to us by means of their unrest. No motion of particles, no light. If all the bodies in space were absolutely tranquil we should never see them. But the normal condition of everything in nature is a state of most beautiful and exquisite unrest. Scientific men call this a state of vibration; but we need not quarrel about terms. Everything in Nature, far or near, is in this state of unrest, and if it were not so, there would be for us no External World."†

---

* Lockyer, Chemistry of the Sun, p. 2.

† The Chemistry of the Sun.

THE CAUSE OF THE SUN'S HEAT.

We now approach the most central and vital questions of all. What is the cause of the sun's heat? How long has this tremendous radiation of heat been going on? How long is it likely to last? Solar astronomy has answers for all three.

In the first place, it is the universal opinion of those who are wise on this matter that the solar heat is not maintained by combustion. The coal fields of Pennsylvania contain a sufficient quantity of that fuel to supply the whole country, at the present rate of consumption, for a thousand years. If the source of the sun's heat were to be cut off, and if all this coal could be transported thither and fed to the sun fast enough to maintain the present supply of heat, the entire amount would last less than one-thousandth part of a second. This is Professor Langley's calculation. If the sun were a solid sphere of anthracite coal, 860,000 miles in diameter, it would all have been burned out in less time than man is known to have been on the earth. The popular conception of the sun as a "ball of fire" is, therefore, erroneous.

It is believed that a considerable quantity of meteors fall into the sun each year, and from this source a small proportion of the solar energy is derived. At one time the theory that this was the principal source of solar heat gained considerable acceptance; but it has now been set aside in favor of the compression theory, which I cannot state better than in the words of Professor Langley:—"It is in the slow settlement of the sun's substance toward its center, as it contracts in cooling, that we find a sufficient cause for the heat developed."* The calculations of the astronomers show that a contraction of 300 feet per year would be enough to produce the stupendous results which we have been considering; and such a shrinkage during 10,000 years would scarcely be visible in the most powerful telescope.

The sun, then, is a mass of gases heated to an almost inconceivable hotness, and on account of the enormous heat prevented from liquefaction. In some

* The New Astronomy, p. 98.

way very imperfectly understood there is a tremendous
circulation going on among these gases, so that the
cooled products are carried within, heated, and forced
out again. Otherwise the outer surface, no matter
how hot, would gradually become cool, with disastrous effects to life in all its forms on the earth. We
may well believe, accordingly, that this solar circulation "is of nearly as much consequence to us as that
of our own bodies."

THE LIFE-TERM OF THE SOLAR SYSTEM.

But this process of contraction, which is deemed
sufficient to account for the vast outflow of radiant
energy from the sun, cannot go on indefinitely. There
must be an ultimate limit to the shrinkage. The
conclusion of astronomy on this point is that the
process has been going on for some 18,000,000 years,
and that in all probability it cannot continue as much
as 10,000,000 years longer. The whole extent of the
sun's existence in the state in which we know it is
placed at 30,000,000 years; and Professor Langley
says: "No reasonable allowance for the fall of meteors
or for all other known causes of supply could possibly at the present rate of radiation raise the whole
term of its existence to sixty million years."

"We are," says Professor Young, "inexorably shut
up to the conclusion that the total life of the solar
system, from its birth to its death, is included in some
such space of time as thirty million years." "At the
same time, it is of course impossible to assert that
there has been no catastrophe in the past . . .
producing a shock which might in a few hours, or
moments even, restore the wasted energy of ages.
Neither is it wholly safe to assume that there may
not be ways, of which we yet have no conception, by
which the energy apparently lost in space may be returned and burned-out suns and run-down systems restored; or, if not restored themselves, be made the germs
of new ones to replace the old. But the whole course
and tendency of Nature, so far as science now makes
out, points backward to a beginning and forward to an
end. The present order of things seem to be bounded,

both in the past and in the future, by terminal catas-
trophes, which are veiled in clouds as yet impenetrable."

Hence we see that Addison was in touch with the
latest word of science when he wrote, nearly two hundred years ago:

> "The stars shall fade away, the sun himself
> Grow dim with age."

But there is no warrant in modern science for the
notion that in the ultimate catastrophe the elements
are to "melt with fervent heat." We are far more
likely to be frozen than fried.

THE INFLUENCE OF OUR ATMOSPHERE.

In estimating the influence of sunbeams upon the
earth, we must not neglect to take into account the
very important part which our own atmosphere plays.
The old supposition was that the atmosphere extended
about forty-five miles above the earth's surface; but
it is now believed that that limit is far too small,
and that in reality the invisible cushion surrounding
the earth is hundreds of miles in thickness. Be that
as it may, we know that the sun's light and heat penetrate this cushion easily, but when they have once entered, the air has large capacity of retaining the heat
and preventing it from being radiated off into space.
It is this quality of the atmosphere which makes life
possible for air-breathing animals on the earth. The atmosphere at ordinary levels has the power of storing
up heat, whereas on the tops of high mountains, despite the immense amount of solar heat received, the
snow never melts, even in equatorial regions.

Incidentally, we may note the bearing of the facts
just stated upon the possibility that life like ours may
exist on other planets. The existence of such life, we
can readily see, may depend upon other things than
the distance of a planet from the sun and the amount
of solar radiation which it enjoys. Our moon gets
practically as much heat and light from the sun as the
earth does, in proportion to its size, but life for either
plants or animals is impossible there, because the moon
is without an atmosphere. But, with a suitable at-

mosphere, it is easily possible that organic life may exist on planets nearer to or farther from the sun than the earth, provided that the planets themselves have reached that stage in cosmic evolution at which living things, as we know them, can flourish.

CAUSE OF THE ICE AGE.

The amount of heat which the earth derives from the sun has, so far as we are able to ascertain, been from time immemorial substantially the same; but it cannot have been the same from the beginning. Without taking account of the heat sent forth from the earth itself during the ages when it was cooling down from a mass of fiery vapors, hardening its crust, and making ready for the work of the succeeding periods, the probabilities are that the solar radiation was for a long time greater in amount than it is now; and we are certain that the conditions of the atmosphere were such as to make possible those gigantic growths of which geology tells us, especially that vast growth of vegetable matter during the Carboniferous period, when the coal which is so indispensable to us was stored away.

How, then, is the age of ice, of the existence of which the evidence is indisputable in both America and Europe, to be accounted for? One theory is that the solar system on its journey through space has at times passed through regions of excessive cold, which greatly reduced the temperature of the earth. Other theories allege shifting of the earth's axis, and changes in the eccentricity of its orbit combined with the precession of the equinoxes, as the cause of the glacial epoch. Geologists, however, seem inclined to the opinion that the great cold which produced glaciation can be fully accounted for by changes in the level of land and sea, accompanied by corresponding changes in climate.

INDUSTRIAL USE OF THE SUN'S HEAT.

I have spoken of the astounding seeming waste of the radiant energy unstintedly and continuously emitted by the sun. There is one aspect of this matter which has a very practical interest for us. The in-

genuity of man has not yet devised a solar engine
which will do its work satisfactorily and economically;
but who can doubt that this will some time be accomplished? More than one promising experiment in this
direction has already been made, notably by the late
Mr. Ericsson. That there is a mighty power here
which is now totally lost is the most evident of facts.
It has been calculated that the noontide heat falling
each day upon Manhattan Island or the area of the city
of London is enough, if it could be harnessed and
utilized, to operate all the steam engines in the world.
The time will doubtless come when in a very literal
sense we shall hitch our engines to the sun, and make
it drive the world's machinery for us.

Although the deposits of coal in the earth are enormous, it is certain that they will one day be exhausted;
and it is equally certain that forests cannot be made
to grow fast enough to keep up the necessary supply
of fuel, even if, in a more densely populated world,
there should be room for them. Before that day ar-
rives I make no question that the problem of using
the solar energy at first hand will be solved. And
possibly also means will be devised of storing it up
during the summer, in order to heat the homes of that
coming generation during the winter's cold.

The utilization of this immense energy is not
unlikely to exert a vast influence upon the fortunes
and destiny of the human race. Professor Langley
has well said: "Future ages may see the seat of empire transferred to regions of the earth now barren and
desolated under intense solar heat—countries which,
for that very cause, will not improbably become the
seat of mechanical and thence of political power."
And he adds with great force: "Whoever finds the
way to make industrially useful the vast sun-power
now wasted on the deserts of North Africa or the
shores of the Red Sea, will effect a greater change in
men's affairs than any conqueror in history has done;
for he will once more people those waste places with
the life that swarmed there in the best days of Car-
thage and old Egypt, but under another civilization,
where man shall no longer worship the sun as a god,
but shall have learned to make it his servant."*

* The New Astronomy, pp. 115, 116.

As the servant of the planets of our system we have already learned to regard the sun. Indeed, "with our larger knowledge we see that these vast and fiery suns" which glitter nightly in the firmament "are after all but the Titan-like *servants* of the little planets which they bear with them in their flight through the abysses of space."* But only in a very limited way has man yet made a servant of the giant which rules our system. This task is reserved, mayhap, for that "crowning race of human-kind" which the poet in his glorious visions foresaw.

SOLAR ENERGY AND SURVIVAL.

The relation of solar energy to the question of survival is almost too obvious to need pointing out. The continuance of this energy as a condition precedent to the survival of life on the earth in any form is absolutely necessary. Not only is the sun's heat necessary for the maintenance of life, but the same is true of the sun's light. The plant kept in a dark place, if it grows at all, does so in a feeble and imperfect way; and if, for example, it is placed in a remote corner of a cellar into which some rays of light fall, it reaches out as best it can toward the light which is essential to its proper growth and development. So a human being becomes anæmic and abnormal if deprived of a due amount of sunlight, and all intelligent people recognize the importance, if not the necessity, of having their dwellings so arranged that the direct rays of the sun may penetrate into every room during some part of each day when the sun shines. The value placed on a "southern exposure" is a tribute of the most practical kind to the sun's life and health-giving power. In speaking of the sun, we may use with profoundest meaning, albeit with a variation, the words of the New Testament—"In him was light, and the light was the life of men."

EVOLUTION OF THE SOLAR SYSTEM.

The discussion of solar energy would not be complete without at least some brief account of the method by which the sun, with its attendant group of

---
* Fiske, The Destiny of Man, p. 16.

planets, came into existence, or, rather, took on the
form and characteristics with which we are familiar.

"This world was a fluid haze of light,
Till toward the center set the starry tides,
And eddied into suns, that wheeling cast
The planets."

So Tennyson, who did not neglect the world in its
scientific aspects in his devotion to its poetic side, has
sung. There has been no better succinct statement
of the theory of nebular genesis, which has gained
such wide acceptance among those who have studied
the subject most closely, and which, in spite of all
the objections that may be brought against it, and
all the difficulties which its adherents have to explain,
still affords the most satisfactory explanation of the
evolution of the planetary system with its central orb
and ruler.

All the researches of science go to prove that the
sun and the planets, together with their satellites, have
had a common origin.

In the first place, the spectroscope shows by in-
dubitable evidence that all the members of the solar
system are composed of the same substances, which
are merely very much hotter, or, on the other hand,
very much cooler, in some cases than in others. Then,
again, all the planets revolve around the sun in the
same direction, and this direction is the same as that
of the sun's own motion on its axis. Moreover, all
the planets revolve in planes which are but slightly
inclined to the plane of the sun's equator. As a rule,
the satellites conduct themselves in the same way
with reference to their primaries. With possibly one
or two exceptions, the planets, as well as the sun,
rotate upon their axes from west to east. Furthermore, all the planets and their moons move in ellip-
tical orbits of small or moderate eccentricity.

Even those who do not accept the nebular hypothesis as formulated by Laplace, concede that the evidence in favor of a common origin of the solar system
is overwhelming, and admit that the sun and the planets have been evolved from a primitive nebula, while
differing only as to the particular method in which the
evolution took place.

Briefly described, the nebular hypothesis assumes
the existence of a gigantic nebulous mass of gases,
presumably some six thousand million miles in diameter—that is, greater than the diameter of the orbit
of the planet Neptune, which is about 2,800 million
miles from the sun. By force of gravitation, this mass
began to contract, and thus to develop heat. Rotation
followed, resulting from time to time in the casting off
of concentric rings, which broke apart in their weakest places, the fragments finally coalescing and forming planet after planet, while in turn the satellites
were formed in the same way from rings cast off from
their revolving primaries.

Without stopping to consider the objections brought
against the nebular hypothesis, or the way in which
they are met by Faye and others, very strong evidence
in favor of the nebular genesis of our system is afforded by the fact of the existence in the universe of un-
doubted nebulæ, as the spectroscope discloses, which
very possibly are undergoing a process similar to that
by which our system came into its present shape. On
the whole, the nebular theory has been pronounced "a
conclusive and nearly satisfactory explanation of the
way in which those great demiurgic forces, heat and
gravitation, have wrought out the results we see."*

But when we have postulated the huge nebula from
which the sun and its attendant planets have been derived, we have taken only one step toward the solution
of the mystery which lies behind us. We have really
explained nothing. How came the nebula there? Some
recent astronomers have undertaken to account for its
existence by assuming that it was formed by the col-
lision of two dark bodies moving directly toward each
other in space with the enormous velocity of 476 miles
per second. This is the impact theory of the late Dr.
Croll. He objects to the nebular hypothesis, the general soundness of which he admits. on the ground that
it "begins in the middle of a process,"—which is undoubtedly true, but Dr. Croll's theory of dark bodies
is open to precisely the same objection. He not only
fails to account for their existence, but the origin of
their tremendous velocity he leaves equally unexplained.

* G. P. Serviss, Solar and Planetary Evolution.

THE MYSTERY OF THE UNIVERSE.

Thus, however far back we may go in time, however far off we may go in space, we come at last to a wall of mystery through which we cannot penetrate, beyond which it is impossible for us to advance a single step.

If we turn in the opposite direction, and seek to explain the universe by determining the nature of matter, our efforts are equally futile. According to the accepted theory among natural philosophers, matter is composed of ultimate atoms. But no eye ever beheld an atom; and it is hardly within the bounds of possibility that the microscope can ever reveal one. An atom is defined to be a hypothetical particle of matter'so small as to be indivisible,—"a thing," as Clerk Maxwell says, "which cannot be cut in two." It is estimated that "it would take 500 million atoms of ordinary matter placed in a line to measure an inch,"* and that if a drop of water were magnified up to the size of the earth, the atoms of which it is composed would, in that case, probably appear to the eye somewhat larger than shot and somewhat smaller than croquet-balls.

The telescope reveals a universe infinitely large. The microscope brings us into relations with a universe infinitesimally small. In this direction, as well as in that, we come at last face to face with an impenetrable barrier of mystery.

> "Shall any gazer see with mortal eyes
> Or any searcher know by mortal mind?
> Veil after veil will lift—but there must be
> Veil after veil behind."

In the attempt to solve the mystery of matter, its origin and its destiny, science breaks down. Even the things which are common, every-day matters to us, it cannot explain. How the sunbeams are metamorphosed into grass, how grass is transformed into flesh, and how this, again, is converted into human nerve and muscle and brain, and thence into thought, imagination, volition, aspiration, love,—it is a mystery of mysteries! What is more familiar to us than gravitation, and yet what an incomprehensible enigma it is!

* J. E. Gore, The Visible Universe, p. 65.

"I know the great worlds draw from far,
Through hollow systems, star to star:
But who has e'er upon a strand
Of those great cables laid his hand?
What reaches up from room to room
Of chambered earth, through glare or gloom,
Through molten flood and fiery blast,
And binds our hurrying feet so fast?
'T is the earth-mother's love, that well
Will hold the motes that round her dwell:
Through granite hills you feel it stir
As lightly as through gossamer:
Its grasp unseen by mortal eyes,
Its grain no lens can analyze."

Equally familiar, but even more elusive, is the lu-miniferous ether, by means of which the heat and light of the sun are brought to us and enabled to perform their gigantic work. Its very existence is a pure assumption; and so ethereal is it that some astronomers suppose it not to be matter at all! The theory has been proposed by a recent writer on these subjects that there may be a close connection between the mysteries of gravitation and ether; and he suggests that if the time shall ever come when we thoroughly understand the constitution of the now inconceivable ethereal fluid, such knowledge may not improbably lead us to a solution of the great mystery of gravitation.*

Truly, the awful mystery of the universe besets us behind and before, and we cannot lay our hand upon it!

BOUNDARIES THAT SCIENCE CANNOT PASS.

We have seen that astronomical science sets a definite limit to the power of the sun to radiate heat in sufficient quantity to maintain organic life on the earth, and tells us that the earth will ultimately be reduced to the condition of our moon, which is but "a burnt-out cinder of a planet." But, as we have also seen, it suggests that there may be ways, of which we know nothing, whereby the energy apparently lost in space may be returned, and burned-out suns and run-down systems restored; and that "when the sun is dead and the earth is in darkness, the wheels of life will still run in the light of other suns; and even our ashes

* Gore, The Visible Universe.

may thrill with a new life, on a new earth, in the beams of a new sun."*

But of this we can have no knowledge. A wise agnosticism is the becoming attitude of science here. Still we are justified in believing that no matter and no force are ever blotted out; and the law of conservation and persistence teaches, or at least suggests, that when existing systems have reached their term, the matter of which they are composed will take on new forms. At all events, we cannot think that any particle of this matter will ever be obliterated.

"An infinity and an eternity confront us, the secrets of which we may not hope to unravel. At the outermost verge to which scientific methods can guide us, we can only catch a vague glimpse of a stupendous rhythmical alternation between eras of Evolution and eras of Dissolution, succeeding each other 'without vestiges of a beginning and without prospect of an end.'"†

The imagination staggers at the tremendous possibilities here opened before it; at the mighty Power at the heart of things, which is adequate to the production of this marvelous series of never-beginning never-ending phenomena.

> "I saw the beauty of the world
> Before me, like a flag, unfurled,
> The splendor of the morning sky,
> And all the stars in company:
> I thought, How wonderful it is!
> My soul said, There is more than this!"

Aye, verily! All that we see, all star-eyed science reveals to us, only conducts us into the presence-chamber of that "invisible Power whereof the infinite web of phenomena is but the visible garment." We look for no great First Cause; but the universe is to us a meaningless riddle unless there is a mighty informing, immanent, all-pervasive cause—an infinite and eternal Energy behind, beneath, within all things, of which, indeed, all things that are, both physical and psychical, are but the manifestations. Emerson was never a truer *seer* than when he wrote:

---

* G. P. Serviss,

† Fiske, Cosmic Philosophy, Vol. I, p. 397.

"Ever fresh the broad creation,
A divine improvisation,
From the heart of God proceeds,
A single will, a million deeds."

The old "argument from design" is no longer in good and regular standing; but we are not thereby to assume that there is no design in Nature. If any are inclined to that belief, they will find the needful corrective in a few sentences of Professor Fiske's. "According to Darwinism, the creation of Man is still the goal toward which Nature tended from the beginning. Not the production of any higher creature, but the perfecting of Humanity, is to be the glorious consummation of Nature's long and tedious work." "He who has mastered the Darwinian theory, he who recognizes the slow and subtle process of evolution as the way in which God makes things come to pass, . . . sees that in the deadly struggle for existence which has raged through countless æons of time, the whole creation has been groaning and travailing together in order to bring forth that last consummate specimen of God's handiwork, the Human Soul."*

The circle is now complete. From the primitive fire-mist to the soul of man, what a chasm has been bridged! There is no break in the chain. There is no missing link. Rightly viewed, there is no such thing in Nature as chaos—there is no room for it. Everywhere we see cosmos instead—everywhere we find order, beauty, law.

THE SUN AS A STAR.

Coming back for a moment to the solar energy on which everything that is on earth is absolutely dependent, we have seen that this energy is practically infinite in amount, and the work it does is so enormous in extent that we can only begin to measure it. The sunbeams have so light a tread that the keenest ear cannot detect their footsteps; and the most delicate balance cannot register their weight. How they get here, we can only guess; how they perform their multifarious work, the wisest of us do not know.

Regarding the amount and the cause of the sun's

* The Destiny of Man, pp. 31, 32.

heat we have seen what astronomy has to teach; and we have gone a step further, and taken a glance at the way in which the sun and the planets were, most probably, evolved from the nebula which undoubtedly was their antecedent condition. Thus far we have been dealing with the sun as the center of the solar system; but we shall fail to comprehend him rightly unless we regard him for a moment in the second aspect to which reference was made at the beginning of the lecture. The sun is a star, though only a "private in the host of heaven." Seen from the distance of Sirius, he would probably present the appearance of a star of the sixth magnitude. But he is one of the members of the universe of stars which glitter in our firmament night after night, the number of which, counting all that can be detected by our most powerful telescopes, is estimated at not to exceed one hundred millions. Each of them, we may assume, though we may never know, is the center of a planetary system similar to our own, and each system, we may also assume, has had the same experience as ours; while in the hazy and irresolvable nebulæ we doubtless see systems undergoing the process of evolution which our sun and planets have gone through. Our sidereal universe, with its one hundred million stars, is by no means infinite; but to space itself we can set no bounds; and, for aught we know, beyond our furthest ken there may be universe upon universe of suns and planets, without end. Such knowledge is too wonderful for us; it is high, we cannot attain unto it!

THE GRANDEUR OF MODERN SCIENCE.

In bringing this imperfect consideration of so large and inspiring a subject to a close, I can find no more fitting words than those which Professor Tyndall wrote some thirty years ago, in the last chapter of his fascinating book on Heat as a Mode of Motion:—

"Presented rightly to the mind, the discoveries and generalisations of modern science constitute a poem more sublime than has ever yet been addressed to the imagination. The natural philosopher of to-day may dwell amid conceptions which beggar those of Milton. So great and grand are they, that in the contemplation of them a certain force of character is req-

uisite to preserve us from bewilderment. Look at
the integrated energies of our world,—the stored power of our coal-fields; our winds and rivers; our fleets,
armies and guns. What are they? They are all gen-
erated by a portion of the sun's energy, which does
not amount to one twenty-three-hundred-millionth of
the whole. This is the entire fraction of the sun's
force intercepted by the earth, and we convert but a
small fraction of this fraction into mechanical energy.
Multiplying all our powers by millions of millions,
we do not reach the sun's expenditure. And still, notwithstanding this enormous drain, in the lapse of human history we are unable to detect a diminution of
his store. Measured by our largest terrestrial standards, such a reservoir of power is infinite; but it is
our privilege to rise above these standards, and to regard the sun himself as a speck in infinite extension
—a mere drop in the universal sea. We analyze the
space in which he is immersed, and which is the vehicle of his power. We pass to other systems and
other suns, each pouring forth energy like our own,
but still without infringement of the law, which reveals immutability in the midst of change, which recognizes incessant transference or conversion, but neither
final loss nor gain. This law generalizes the aphorism
of Solomon, that there is nothing new under the sun,
by teaching us to detect everywhere, under its infinite
variety of appearances, the same primeval force. To
Nature nothing can be added; from Nature nothing
can be taken away; the sum of her energies is constant,
and the utmost man can do in the pursuit of physical
truth, or in the applications of physical knowledge,
is to shift the constituents of the never-varying total.
The law of conservation rigidly excludes both creation and annihilation. Waves may change to ripples, and ripples to waves—magnitude may be substituted for number, and number for magnitude—as-
teroids may aggregate to suns, suns may resolve themselves into floræ and faunæ, and floræ and faunæ melt
into air—the flux of power is eternally the same—it
rolls in music through the ages, and all terrestrial
energy—the manifestations of life as well as the display of phenomena—are but the modulations of its
rhythm."

ABSTRACT OF THE DISCUSSION.

PROF. PETER T. AUSTEN, PH. D.:—

In discussing the subject of energy the physicist must be especially careful to be exact in expression. There is a wide difference of opinion as to the essential natures of both matter and energy, the generally accepted view being that they are forms of vibration. The number of vibrations necessary to produce the sensations of heat, light and sound have been calculated. Particles of matter in vibration infringe upon a nerve-point, and the effect is transmitted to the brain, which has the power of transforming this molecular activity into sensations and images. It is important that we separate our ideas of energy from what it actually is in itself. Sound and heat do not exist in the different modes of vibration. The sensation as we experience it is due wholly to the brain and mental action, whereby motion is transformed into images and sensations into ideas. The brain correlates diverse material impacts into psychical coördination. Each mental sensation is caused by different modes of vibration. Sound vibrations do not produce the sensation of heat, or *vice versa.* Moreover, all these sensible vibrations take place within limited ranges. It is well known that there are both tone and light vibrations that we are unable to perceive, such as the noise of certain insects, and' the chemical or actinic rays of light. Must we not conceive that the possible range of vibrations is infinite? The senses are inexorably limited. No two individuals perceive exactly the same universe, and outside of all possible perception is a vast region to finite beings unknowable. There is no reason why beings may not exist capable of being affected by many of these vibrations which are to us imperceptible, and therefore constituted quite differently from ourselves.

The chemical elements have been demonstrated to stand in definite mathematical relations to each other, forming a spiral in which those elements that are in line with each other are found to constitute related families. The atom of the chemist is not necessarily an indivisible particle, but the smallest which can retain its elemental identity. Behind the atom the physicist cannot go. If the atom should prove to be further divisible, there would simply result another form of matter. Why may we not conceive it possible for the elements to stand to each other elsewhere in relations differing from those exhibited here? And if so, what limit could there be to the varying forms of different material universes, and to their chemical composition, inhabitants and products?

The physicist tells us that the slightest motion affects the entire universe. I wave my hand, and the motion is felt through all systems, and to the farthest heavens. We must do away with the former idea of a solid material mass: what we customarily so call is but the aggregation of minute particles in motion. The former conception of attraction as a force which pulls is giving place to that of pressure from without. Persistence of energy is the one great fact which renders science possible and stable and gives it unity. Persistence of force and the correlation of forces are the two great data on which all science rests.

The profound moral significance of these principles is the lesson we are to draw. If the slightest action and word not only, but our very thoughts are ineffaceably recorded in eternal material vibrations which persist and may be cognizable by us and others in their effects in the future, the most powerful incentive and stimulus to correct action is afforded by these ethico-physical sanctions. Some men's sins are evidently going before them into judgment, and some they follow after. The humblest worker in the line of his duty may not see its effect, but it may constitute an important thread of causation in relation to other threads. Thus the highest science is found to co-operate with the religious and moral impulses toward evolving the highest individual life.

DR. MARTIN L. HOLBROOK. : —

One of the important conditions of survival, it appears to me, is a larger use of sunlight for promoting health and vigor, especially by the inhabitants of cities. Light is one of the most powerful stimulants known to the nervous system, and it also promotes bodily growth. In former times, when children were permitted to work in mines in England, they never grew so large as those who were otherwise employed. Absence of sunlight was a chief reason. In Bavaria, half a century ago, in one deparmtent which had a population of about 3,000, half of whom worked in mines, and half in the fields, no men fit to become soldiers could be found in the mines, while among the field workers the usual quota could be selected. The miners were weak and deformed in body, had defective vision, and so escaped military duty. Children growing up in cities, unless special pains is taken to let them have plenty of light, also have bodily defects and weaknesses which prevent survival. All physicians have seen instances where families have become extinct by thoughtlessness in not supplying the growing children with sufficient light. Dr. Richardson has declared that the street children of London are healthier than the children of the better classes, who keep their little ones more indoors. The news boys of New York are more vigorous than many children of the well to do classes. They get more light as well as more air and exercise. I would advise the introduction of sun or solar baths as quite as important as water baths in every home. They are luxurious, and help to toughen the skin—a very debilitated organ in most well-clothed people. I am quite confident that the solar ray is directly appropriated by the body, and solar energy converted into bodily energy, if used rightly. Of course, too much sunshine, like too much food, may injure. Sun parlors at hotels and sanitariums at winter resorts are useful. The diffused rays act favorably on the body; but solar baths are still better. It is not always those who are morally best who survive, but the "fittest"—those best capable of resisting unfavorable conditions. If the best will see to it that their bodies are properly nourished and developed, they will stand a chance to become the "fittest;" and thus the intelligent will of every thoughtful individual may become a powerful factor in promoting the moral advancement and civilization of the world.

Mr. Palmer replied briefly, thanking the audience for their kind reception of his paper, and Professor Austin for his supplementary contribution to the scientific and philosophical aspects of the subject. He also appreciated the importance of its sanitary implications. The subject was so large that it was impossible to treat it exhaustively in an hour's discussion.

THE ATMOSPHERE AND LIFE

BY

ROBERT G. ECCLES, M. D.

COLLATERAL READINGS SUGGESTED.

Roscoe's *Chemistry*, Vol. I., pp. 434-457; Johnston's *The Chemistry of Common Life*; Angus Smith's *The Atmosphere*; Pettenkoffer's *The Air in its Relation to our Clothing, Dwellings and Soil*; Hartwig's *The Aerial World*; Parke's *Hygiene*; Fox's *Sanitary Examination of Water, Air and Food*; Kingzett's *Nature's Hygiene*; Becquerel's *Traité Elémentaire Privée et Publique*.

THE ATMOSPHERE AND LIFE.

BY ROBERT G. ECCLES, M. D.

We have all watched a fragment of ice melt and disappear in a glass of water. The earthy matter that
had been caught within its meshes during the process
of freezing, on being freed sinks to the bottom. No
longer ice, it has become indistinguishable from the
rest of the water present. Such a piece of ice is a
perfect illustration of our own origin and destiny.
We are enveloped in a vast fluid ocean that encom-
passes the earth. We live and move in it and are as
truly a part of it as the ice is of the water. Generation after generation of men and animals, trees and
herbs, crystallize out of it as the ice on freezing crys-
tallizes out of the water. Every succeeding generation
melts back into it again, as each winter's crop of ice
disappears before the heat of summer. All living
things, animals and plants alike, are neither more
nor less than masses of crystallized atmosphere in
the meshes of which a little mineral matter has become entangled. Out of the transparency of the atmosphere we grew, as ice crystals grow in water, and
into it again we are destined to sink, disappearing in
this common invisible ocean. An insignificant part of
our composition is from the earth. When a body is
burnt the handful of ashes that remains represents
all there was of it that mother earth can lay claim to.
These goings and comings of the matter that forms
organisms constitute the facts of the most remarkable

chapter in the genesis of things. They have made the atmosphere what it is and it, in turn, has both directly and indirectly conspired to mould living forms into the modern fauna and flora of the earth.

Calculations based on observations of luminous meteors lead us to believe that the atmosphere is not less than one hundred miles deep and may be two hundred. The laws governing the pressure of gases and the action of gravity tell us that it must in shape be an oblate spheroid with the poles markedly flattened, much more so indeed than is the case with the earth itself. Since it is able to support a column of mercury or water weighing about fourteen and three quarters pounds in a tube with a diameter representing one square inch, it must press upon the surface of the earth at every point with about this weight. When two very true and smooth surfaces are rubbed together, they adhere because of this pressure. When a boy presses a piece of wet leather on a stone and is able by an attached string to lift and carry that stone, it is due to this atmospheric pressure. The school experiment with the hollow hemispheres that after exhaustion by an air pump cannot be pulled asunder except with great effort, is another illustration of the same kind. An ordinary sized man bears constantly upon his body a pressure of about fourteen tons; but as this pressure is in all directions and from within outwards as well as from without inwards, the compensation is perfect and reduces the actual pressure to practically nothing. It takes 813½ cubic feet of air to weigh as much as one cubic foot of water. If 813½ cubic feet were compressed into the space of one cubic foot its weight would be about the same as an equal volume of water. Anything that volume for volume weighs less than air will be buoyed up and float in it. A balloon, to ascend, must have its total size represent less weight than the weight of air it displaces. Sir John Herschel calculated the total weight of the atmosphere at eleven and two-thirds trillions of pounds; and yet with this inconceivably vast weight it is only one one-million two hundred thousandth of the weight of the earth itself. The pressure of this vast mass of gaseous material varies quite considerably at different parts of the earth.

The higher one ascends, the less it becomes. It varies, too, at the same height at different times of day and night, and before and after storms. By keeping track of this pressure the mariner is often able to foresee and prepare for a storm, and the mountain climber can calculate his altitude at any moment. Wind is the flowing of air from regions of high to regions of low pressure. Where the difference in pressure is very marked the wind is fierce, and where but little, it is mild. Thus arise cyclones, blizzards, and hurricanes as well as the gentlest zephyrs. By a study and comparison of regions of high with regions of low pressure our weather officers are able to predict changes with a good deal of accuracy hours in advance of their occurrence. The time of year has a great influence on these variations of pressure. In April and October it is more even than at any other periods of the year. When water is evaporated and its volume thereby increased almost one thousand fold, it ascends just as a balloon would; but besides its light specific gravity when hot it is also subject to a law of diffusion that would carry it upward even though heavier than air. Since water is always evaporating and since diffusion is always at work, the air is constantly supplied with moisture, sometimes to the point of saturation. To this moisture in the air we are indebted for the maintenance of an even degree of temperature. But for it night would be colder than Greenland, even at the tropics. It is the water in the air that holds the sun's heat and keeps the earth warm where direct sunlight fails to fall upon bodies. The main constituents of air are the two gases, nitrogen and oxygen. In one hundred parts there are about 76 9 10 parts of nitrogen and 23 1 10 parts of oxygen. These gases are merely mechanically mixed together and not held by chemical bonds. Without the oxygen we could not live nor breathe, nor could any ordinary fire burn. The nitrogen seems to serve only as a diluent of the oxygen. In every ten thousand parts of pure air there are from four to six parts of carbon dioxide or carbonic acid gas. This is the same as the poisonous choke damp of the miner, and is the product of our breathing and of coal and gas fires. In still minuter amounts

the air contains ozone, ammonia, carburetted and sul-
phuretted hydrogen, carbon monoxide, sulphurous and
sulphuric acids, nitric acid, etc. The ozone and nitric
acid are the products of the action of electricity on the
contents of the air, especially during thunder storms.
The amount of ozone present is often chosen as a test of
the healthiness of a region, and that of the carbonic acid
of its unhealthiness. Many solid substances, in fine
division, float constantly in the air, and can be seen when
a beam of direct sunlight passes through a dark or
shaded room. In the struggle for existence among
both plants and animals, throughout all time, the atmosphere, through these and other qualities it possesses, has had an influence second, to nothing else, in
moulding their forms and directing their destinies.

The primitive atmosphere was a very markedly
different one from that described. When the fiery
mass of the earth began to crust itself over, the
weight, volume, composition and character of the air
were totally unlike that of to-day. Every particle of
oxygen must have been held in chemical union, since
the conditions for such union were present and more
than enough oxidizable material within reach The
only part of the atmosphere that would make a world
possible for us to inhabit was therefore totally absent.
All the water of the oceans was in the air. All the
carbonic acid in the mountain ranges and deep strata
of carbonates was likewise there. That which we now
know as coal must then have existed as carbonic acid.
Such an atmosphere, even had it been cool enough to
match our temperature, would have been absolutely
unfit to breathe, both because it did not contain the
element that makes life possible and because it did
contain in its stead more than an equal amount of deleterious gases.

The genesis of organic matter must have preceded
the production of organisms. Centuries before a
crust had formed upon the molten material of the
earth, the dance of the carbon atoms had begun and
the syntheses of the simpler forms progressed. Amid
the terrific tempests and almost ceaseless series of
deluges then going on the magic linkings of carbon, oxygen, hydrogen and nitrogen were steadily advancing in

complexity and reaching toward bioplasm. While the hot rock seethed and boiled like a cauldron over a furnace, in quieter and cooler spots additional new and more complex bodies were appearing. At last in the cradle of the deep appeared the infant protoplasmic germ in whose tiny form was locked the promise and potency of all that we can boast of. The earth was then an enormous piece of cooling slag and the atmosphere an equally forbidding mass of irrespirable poison. Every wind that then blew was a current of choke-damp and the rains as they fell becoming saturated with this gas, descended as deluges of soda water, identical with that drawn by druggists and confectioners from their fountains though perhaps scarcely as pure. No lamp, candle or fire could have burnt anywhere on our planet. Nothing that breathes could have survived such conditions for a moment. On the barren surface of the fire scarred earth there was no soil to harbor vegetation and no vegetation to be harbored. How life, in any form, however rudimentary, was able to develop or exist under conditions such as then obtained, it is difficult to understand. In an atmosphere that must have been almost or totally devoid of free oxygen how did protoplasm oxidise? Without oxidation of the substance constituting living things, life, as we know it, would be impossible. Late studies in bacteriology show us that many micro-organisms have the power of decomposing carbon dioxide and setting oxygen free independent of sunlight. The writer, in a paper read at the last New York meeting of the American Association for the Advancement of Science, showed that some of the higher fungi possessed this power and in such medicinal substances as dilute phosphoric acid were able to increase in weight without reducing the quantity of acid present in any perceptible degree. Prof. Farley of Harvard, our leading American mycologist, at that time doubted the accuracy of my results; but a number of German experimentors have since confirmed them on other species. It is now quite certain that many if not all fungi possess this power. At quite an early date in the study of micro-organisms Pasteur divided them into aerobic or air requiring microbes and anaerobic or such as could grow in the absence of free oxygen.

All the facts at our command concerning the early conditions of our planet force us to conclude that its first life was anærobic. The fogs, clouds and heavy atmosphere of those times forbade the struggling sunbeams admittance, so that "darkness was upon the face of the deep." Without free oxygen and in obscure gloom, living matter was forced to exist and begin the work of preparing this planet for us. Little by little oxygen was released from its bonds with other substances and as a free element kept increasing in amount and thereby making possible higher forms of life. At first the changes could not be other than slow. The life activities must have trod a pace so slow that our metaphor of "a snail's pace" would really over-estimate the same. The lower down we go in the biological scale the more sluggish is the metabolism of tissue found to be. Such sluggishness is incompatible with rapid adjustments to changing conditions. It was, however, the best that could then be found. The rapid, spontaneous and purposive release of energy from a body requires molecules of a certain definite structure, the most noticeable feature of which is the amount of nitrogen they contain. The peculiar characteristic of combined nitrogen is its instability. In all of its compounds it acts like a coiled spring that ever seeks to be released. In its free state, on the contrary, it is so stable that it is almost impossible to discover anything but negative properties with which to describe it. It is the very type of impassivity. Chemically, therefore, oxygen and nitrogen are almost opposites in characteristics. Nitrogen can only with difficulty be made to unite with anything, and once united it appears to be incessantly seeking release. Some of its well known compounds will rapidly become disrupted by a spark or blow. We all know how many accidents have occurred from the explosion of nitroglycerine or dynamite by merely a jar or blow. All of our dangerous explosives contain this element and owe their tremendous power to its desire for freedom from chemical bondage. The chloride, bromide and iodide of nitrogen are the most powerful explosives known, but their instability is so marked they are utterly useless. A mere jar will send off chloride of nitrogen with fearful and uncontrollable violence. Of course the power released is proportional to the amount going off. If we could separate the millions of molecules composing a few grains of it and have them explode one by one under the excitement of divers forms of stimulating jars, we should duplicate the conditions of life energy. When chloride of nitrogen suddenly explodes with merely a light jar, or even spontaneously without visible cause, it shows in a coarse or crude way what happens in a cell when a very slight stimulus makes it betray the fact that it is alive. In both cases molecules containing nitrogen are disrupted. Increase of nitrogen in living structures always signifies increased sensitiveness to external stimuli. This holds good throughout animated nature. The vegetable world displays less power of adjustment than the animal and shows a corresponding reduction in amount of nitrogenous material in its structure. The higher up the animal scale we travel the larger the amount of nitrogen that enters into the structure of the organism in proportion to weight or volume. In any given animal the higher the function of any tissue that enters into its structure, the larger the amount of nitrogen. The bones have the least and the nerve structure the most, while the brain has far more than any other part. As a mere rub or slight blow explodes chloride of nitrogen, so an image formed by light on the retina of the eye explodes our cerebral molecules and lets loose the energy we call will power. The break-up initiated among the nitrogenous molecules of the brain by causes so light, imparts energy to the coarser molecules containing more carbon and hydrogen. The breaking up of these requires oxygen, and this is supplied by the iron in the blood that holds this element in loose combination. In highly differentiated animals whose nervous structures contains a maximum of nitrogen, these decompositions are most numerous, and hence they require more oxygen. For this reason cold blooded animals can live where the warm blooded would perish. The combustion of their tissues is exceedingly sluggish. In plants the changes are still more slow. Plants likewise differ from animals in their

ability to produce; usually in the presence of direct
sunlight, more than sufficient oxygen, from the carbon
dioxide of the air, to supply their own requirements.

The breathing of plants and animals is the same. Not
long since it was believed that animals only required
oxygen, and that plants required carbon dioxide. This
was an error. Plants do not breathe carbon dioxide,
but, like ourselves, oxygen. They, however, find by
far the largest volume of their food in the carbon dioxide of the air. This they decompose by aid of direct sunlight, and by seizing upon the nascent carbon
convert it into plant tissue, while the oxygen escapes
into the atmosphere. Since they thus release far more
oxygen than they require for themselves, the air is
kept constantly pure by their good services. Because
they provide an oxygen balance of this kind and have
ever done so, to them we are indebted for the character of our present atmosphere and its most marked
difference from that of primitive times. They have,
during countless millenniums, been free oxygen man-
ufacturers. Beginning their work in an atmosphere
that was oxygenless, they have gone on with their good
services until it is now fit for the breathing of
healthy human beings. The change from the wholly
irrespirable air of early times to the perfectly respira-
ble air of to-day has come through slow, insensible
degrees. Step by step it has been transmuted into the
fitness that has made possible warm blooded, quick-
acting and quick witted creatures. Had the work of
plants not preceded us we could never have been;
and should they stop such work it would mean speedy
extinction for us. Our lives are bound up in theirs and
theirs in ours by a reciprocity so perfect that it is marvelous. Imagine two sets of machines so adjusted that
running down of one winds up the other, and that the
the stopping of either stops both, and you will have a
partial conception of the intimate relationship of the
two. Our breathing and the fires of our homes and
workshops supplies them with their daily food, and
they supply us not only with food and clothing, but
with pure air as well. Had the vegetable world succeeded in converting all the carbonic acid gas of the
primitive atmosphere into oxygen and carbon the pro-

portion of oxygen to nitrogen would have been much greater than it is. The weight, too, of the atmosphere would have been very materially increased and our coal beds would have proven far vaster than they are.

A very large part of the purification of the early atmosphere we must credit to the mineral world. It markedly diminished the atmospheric weight for us. In the burnt-up rocks of azoic times, calcium and other such elements were left as oxides and hydrates. Now we find them forming mountain chains and immensely deep strata as carbonates, the greatest proportion of their weight having been absorbed from the air. Every bed of limestone, chalk and marble illustrates this point. The quantity of carbonic acid gas these have absorbed from the air is so vast that if released again the world would be no longer fit for us to inhabit. One is almost constrained to believe that in this early absorption of the mineral world can be found a purposive act. It certainly looks as if æons of ages ago the way was being prepared for our advent. Every change led thitherward. Had the mineral world not absorbed the carbon dioxide, but left all the work to the plants, we might have had more oxygen than to-day, but we would likewise have had more pressure. This in turn would have required changes in the structure of our tissues that would have made such life as we now have impossible. At the proper point to save conditions favorable for us the bulk of the rapid absorption of oxygen by minerals was arrested. Had there been produced in the early world twice as much of these oxides and hydrates as there was, they would have stolen all the food from the plants and all the oxygen from us, thus leaving a barren earth. Had there been enough more than at present to have absorbed the gas which the plants used when forming our coal beds, what sort of civilization would have been possible to us? As it was, an evenly balanced strain was fixed upon minerals, plants and animals exactly at the point that made possible our present conditions. That matched strain is maintained in its perfection to this day. The number of plants which the earth is now capable of supporting is fixed by the amount of their food present in the air in the form of carbonic acid gas. The amount of this carbonic acid is kept up to their requirements principally by our fires and the breathing of animals. There are, however, a number of other sources. The fact that this is so shows us that the number of animals upon the earth and their character has a limiting power upon the number of plants, and the number of plants on the other hand limits the number of animals. Any great decrease in the number of plants would lower the oxygen supply that is now but little more than required. Any great decrease in the number of animals would lower the carbonic acid gas supply that is now little, if any, more than required. The quantity of each of these gases remains practically constant from year to year, showing that waste and supply do no more than balance. Such oscillations as may exist in favor of one side or the other cannot at present be detected with certainty. The plant world seems to utilize all the carbon dioxide as fast as it is produced, and the animal world all the oxygen; so that the bank account of each as found in the air is neither markedly increased nor diminished except in narrow limits for brief priods of time.

It is evident, from a survey of the facts already pointed out, that every breathing creature from the first dawn of time, has had to conform its structure to the conditions imposed by the nature of the air supply. The structure of our blood and its chemical composition is such that it can only perform its work properly where there is but little carbon dioxide and much oxygen. The structures of our lungs, hearts, livers and blood vessels are exactly adjusted to such a quality of blood and such air. Through all the countless years of the past every creature in the line of descent toward, ourselves has survived solely because these organs changed as the air changed, thus adapting themselves to the new environment. In every instance where such change did not occur, disease, followed by death, terminated their careers. Even in the slight changes of recent days, failure of adjustment must be leaving its mark. It is certain that slight deviations from the true physiological balance of structure cause certain families to be liable to certain diseases. We now know that the old notion that consumption is hereditary is wrong. But we also know that a very slight narrowing in the diameter of the pulmonary arteries and veins renders one more liable to consumption. Since some families have a structural deviation of this kind that is hereditary, all such people are more likely to have consumption of the lungs than others. The principal reason lies in the fact that they are unable to as fully aerate their blood and keep it in perfect vigor as their more fortunate fellow creatures. Where such people are constantly engaged in vigorous, healthy out-of-door work, they seldom catch the disease, even, though liable. Of course, if exposed to great changes of weather, out of door work may become the least favorable for them. When compelled to rapidly and completely inflate their lungs by reason of proper physiological exercise, they are safe under otherwise ordinary conditions of exposure to the disease. The causes that conspire to this and other serious forms of disease have been traced to the atmosphere. At one time miasmatic gases were blamed for some maladies, and to this day we hear of people suffering from malaria which when interpreted into plain English means "bad air." It is not the air itself, nor any gaseous constituent thereof, that is directly responsible for these troubles. The part performed by the air in the affair resides in its buoyant property by means of which light particles of solid matter are able to float in it. However pure the atmosphere may seem to be at any time, it is sure to be heavily laden with invisible dust particles. When a bright beam of light is projected into any dark or shady place you are always sure to see a mass of dust that looks as if it might smother us to breathe it. And yet such is the state of the air at all times under the ordinary conditions in which we live. This mass of floating dust we are constantly breathing and swallowing. There is not a spot in our homes or churches, streets or roads, that is not befouled by its presence. This dust is composed of the worn-out threads of our garments, the dried epithelium from our bodies, mineral particles from our walls, and the ground, decomposed material from our lungs and mouths, pollen from plants, spores from moulds, and worst of all, disease germs from infected soils and swamps, from dried-up sputa of consumptives and from the breath of people who walk our streets suffering from what to them with their resisting powers are merely slight ailments but to others is certain death. Go where we will we cannot escape. Air we must have, poisoned or pure, and it is always poisoned in some degree. That it has been ever so we have every reason for believing. Up to the present time, only creatures capable of resisting these invisible foes, that the air is the innocent means of carrying around, have survived. Whenever, in the past, a new germ appeared in a region and among people not able to resist it, they have perished by thousands, and history mentions the circumstance as a plague or pestilence. Subsequent attacks have usually been milder because the susceptible were nearly all killed before. When, however, physical filth or moral impurity has lowered the vital resistance of a people, even this rule of immunity does not hold good. We have also reasons for believing that such filth and such impurity render more vigorous the germs themselves, so that they can attack people who otherwise might, under ordinary circumstances, have escaped.

Nature thus holds us responsible not only for our own short-comings, but for those of our neighbors as well. As the best built fire-proof granite buildings melted before such a fire as Chicago witnessed, and more readily because many had been so imprudent as to put mansard roofs over their houses, so the strongest constitution is swept down by germs that are multiplied in numbers and virulence by the crimes of the filthy. Nature therefore declares that we are all our brothers' keepers, since their lives depend upon our deeds, and *vice versa*. These germs that under ordinary circumstances are unable to attack us, may by reason of our violating some law of nature and weakening our vitality, instantly find a home in our flesh, where they will live and multiply like weeds in a garden. If we get chilled beyond our margin of endurance they instantly begin to grow on our tongues, in our stomachs, in our intestines, in our lungs or in our blood. Then we have coryza, or dyspepsia, or rheumatism, or pneumonia, or pleurisy. But for that chilling they would have passed through us and been unable to get a foothold, since the strength of our cells would have been more than a match for them. If we get overheated, a similar train of maladies may arise. If we have overworked, that lowers the vital powers. Intoxication, loss of sleep, gluttony and excesses of every kind lay us liable to their attack by weakening the constitution and therefore its power of resistance. We are thus admonished of the fact that Nature is the relentless foe of every form of intemperance, and that the wages of all such sin is death. We see that not only our own sins but the sins of our fellows are charged up to us. In this we discover the duty that is imposed upon us to work for the elevation of the whole human family and its reclamation from filth, ignorance and crime. To live where wickedness rules is to suffer from it, although we may try ever so hard to escape its consequences. To tolerate ignorance of hygienic laws among our fellows is to endanger our own lives and the lives of our friends. An apt illustration of this is seen in the great prevalence of tuberculosis. This disease kills about one-ninth of our race, and its main source of propagation we make no effort to check. Consumptives are allowed to spit where and when they please, notwithstanding the fact that their spittle is death-laden for millions. It dries on the ground, floats in the air and is breathed in by others who die from such carelessness.

The diminished density of our present atmosphere as compared with that of primitive times gives it a very greatly reduced capacity for floating dust particles and germs. Its dangerous qualities then as compared with the present were therefore greater in this particular as well as in that of being laden with mephitic gas. During all the intervening years, the acquisition of immunity from certain kinds of disease-germs had been acquired. It is a remarkable fact that of the hundreds of known species of micro-organisms only a very few are pathogenetic. Whether this is due to an acquired immunity or not, of course no one can tell; but the existence of such a fact is significant. They are all capable of growing on dead animal—or

plant—matter under proper conditions of moisture and
temperature. In this we see that living matter somehow can resist most of them while dead matter cannot. Plants suffer from them as well as animals, and
by this means we have been able to isolate a number
of chemical products by which immunity is evidently
maintained. It is a quite remarkable fact that where
large numbers of related orders of plant life are highly
protected they are among the oldest and least specialized forms. Recently evolved, highly specialized forms,
when thus protected from pathogenetic organisms of
great virulence, usually stand alone among their kin-
dred, none of which are thus gifted. This would seem to
indicate that at an early period the danger of invasion
was greater, and that with the advance of time their
attacks were less marked over the world at large, but
equally well marked in special regions. This singular
condition is observed in the Gymnosperms, where
scarcely a species exists that is not charged with tur-
pentine and antiseptic resin. It could have been no
local necessity that evolved so general a characteristic.
Going higher up, we observe the willows and their
salicin. Here we see a less general endowment, and
note the fact that their swampy habitat may account
for their possessing this means of protection. With
the still more highly specialized Cinchonas we have
a very remarkable case. The environment, too, casts
a flood of light upon its significance, and the narrow
range of the protected species confirms the belief that
local and not general conditions evolved it. The
native home of these trees is on the Andean slopes in
South America, not far from the Equator. Their habitat is a region of perpetual fog and drizzle. For nine
months of the year scarcely a ray of direct sunlight
reaches them, and during the other three there is a
chasing of clouds and sunshine hour by hour during
the day, much like our April weather. It is an ideal
home of malaria, unfit for human habitation. In
those years when the fogs are densest and the sunshine
least, the yield of quinine from the bark is known to
be greatest. What other conceivable function can this
quinine serve the tree than as a destroyer of malaria
germs? It is only found in abundance in the parts of

the tree likely to be subject to their attacks. It multiplies under the very conditions that multiply the germs, and that would therefore make them more dangerous to the plant. The home of the tree is the natural home of such germs. In India, where Cinchona is now artificially cultivated they cover the bark of the growing trees with cotton and shield them from direct sunlight the year when they are going to strip them, having found experimentally that this treatment increases the quinine yield very markedly. Before they adopted this plan the yield was discouragingly small and becoming smaller. Now it compares favorably with that from wild trees in South America. By such treatment they imitate in a measure the conditions of their original homes, and the very conditions that indicate danger from germs to the tree. The tree has the power of anticipating such danger and guarding against it. The condition of the Cinchona belt on the Andean slope we have reason to think was the condition of most of the earth during that period of its history when Gymnosperms were the chief forms of plants. As a consequence, the protection instead of being confined to a single species, genera, or even order, covers a vast range of orders.

If the air by its buoyancy floats disease germs and enables them to kill off the weak and make room for the strong, it likewise floats the pollen of millions of plants and thereby aids healthy fertilization. Experiments made by Charles Darwin and others have shown that when plants fertilize themselves, or when fertilization is confined to close of kin, deterioration results. The intermarriage of plants of the same species raised at points remote from each other, and from seed without kinship, leads on the other hand to increase in vigor. Without cross-fertilization there is retrogression instead of progression, and therefore nature has adopted some of the most curious and remarkable methods of avoiding self-fertilization. The wind is, directly or indirectly, the marriage priest of nearly every plant on the earth. Sometimes it bears the pollen from enormous distances as in the case of the palms in Palermo, Italy, that were fertilized by others of their kind in Africa. Farmers who wish to grow sorghum when their neighbors are growing broom-corn, or vice versa, know well the power of the wind in spoiling their crops by this carrying of pollen. But while, in such an instance, cross-fertilization works mischief, the rule is the reverse. It has beautified the earth by leading to all the brilliancy of our finest floral displays.

The successive steps of change from wind-fertilization to insect-fertilization were all made possible by the air. Every insect and every little humming-bird that acts as a pollen-carrier to lilies and rhododen-drons, kalmias and sweet peas, roses and foxgloves can only fly by virtue of the air's support. The develop-ment of these lovely forms and brilliant colors could not have occurred but for this buoyant power of the air. It also carries the rich fragrance that at twilight hour guides and allures moths and butterflies to bright-colored and especially to white flowers. The recipro-cal action of flowers on insects is equally important in this connection. Only such insects as were able to fertilize the flowers by virtue of their forms and sizes could make a living and survive. Through countless generations each has fixed a line of conduct for the other, failure to pursue which meant death. Nature's changes are usually fair exchanges. She leaves no permanent place for dishonesty. When the wild bees of the Tyrolese Alps pierce the bases of the aconite flowers and steal the honey without ren-dering a return in service by carrying pollen to the stigmas, the penalty is paid in a succeeding year by starvation. Such inordinate haste to become rich on their part produces a dearth of aconite in succeeding years. No fertilization, no seeds; no seeds, no plants, no plants, no honey, and no honey, no bees. Here again we see that all suffer together, and that the moral lapses of others are charged to the account of the whole community. ❯We are our brothers' keepers. Nature does not consider individuals in her reckonings as much as she does whole races. Like the signers of the Declaration of Independence, "we must all hang together or we will hang separate."

The power that birds and insects possess of flying could not have become developed in a more appro-

priate time than when it did. The first efforts at flying among vertebrates were accomplished by bat-like
creatures with leather wings. The pterodactyls were
good illustrations of these primitive predecessors of
our birds. Feathers came as an after-growth. It is
probable that the first wings of insects were relatively
of equal coarseness and crudity. It is quite likely that
they appeared as an adjunct to an exaggerated jumping power. Their clumsy and awkward efforts were
fortunately favored by a very dense atmosphere. Had
they now to acquire such power the chances are that
natural selection would wipe them all out before a
favored pair appeared.

With the progressive rarification of the air, birds kept
pace by evolving hollow feathers and light down, while
insects' wings thinned themselves out to lightest gossamer. Of the unnumbered millions swept away because they did not or could not so change, we have no
record. We only keep account of Nature's successes.
We know, however, that every step of progress came
by selecting those with favorable qualities and discouraging or destroying those with unfavorable ones.
None ever came by trying to change lions into lambs,
or thistles into roses. Even the most insignificant
characteristics cannot be altered and maintained in
that way so far as science has yet demonstrated.

To the density of the atmosphere, human beings, and
the higher animals also, owe much of their progress.
But for it, our upright attitude could not have been
maintained by any such mechanism as the present ball
and socket arrangement of our thigh bones. These
bones are held in their places mainly by the pressure
of the atmosphere. The strength of our mucous membranes and possibly also of the outer cuticles is accurately adjusted to the terrestrial limits of this force.
Our eyes, too, are under control of its balances. To
rapidly remove the present atmospheric pressure from
any animal is to cause its death, not by absence of
oxygen, but from mechanical injuries to the tissues.
The slow removal of the pressure permits us within a
limited range to acquire new adjustments of the balance that save us from injury; but if we transcend
those limits the results are disastrous. Aeronauts,

in making high ascents in their balloons, find that on
passing a certain height their ears, noses, lips and
eyes begin to bleed spontaneously. With some, this
bleeding comes on at lower altitudes than others, and
there are people so susceptible to this trouble that
they cannot live in regions above the sea level. Such
people are known among medical men as bleeders.
Having been evolved in the midst of a definite range
of pressure we are only adapted to live within such
conditions, and must suffer when we undertake to
transcend them. As in the case of resisting certain
forms of bacterial attack, so also in resisting changes
in atmospheric pressure our powers vary with our
strength. The workings of our internal organs are adjusted to definite pressures and these in diseased conditions of the same are exceedingly sensitive to the
slightest changes in this particular. Minute barome-
tric alterations profoundly influence the very sick. The
rhythm of exacerbation and improvement often follows
the ups and downs of the mercury as the compass-
needle follows the direction of the pole. Then again
what we call good and bad weather have decidedly
marked effects on the sick, and changes in the weather
result from variations in the pressure of the atmosphere. Cold weather and hot weather, wet weather
and dry weather, foggy weather and clear weather,
calm weather and windy weather are all products of
variations in the pressure of the atmosphere. Every
one of these special kinds of weather brings upon the
community special types of disease and carries off the
sick where but for their advent the physician's skill
would have saved the patients. The Encyclopædia
Britannica sums this up as follows: "The curves show
that the maximum annual mortality from the different
diseases groups around certain specific conditions of
temperature and moisture combined. Thus, *cold and
moist weather* is accompanied by a high death rate from
heart disease, diphtheria and measles; *cold weather*, with
a high death rate from bronchitis, pneumonia, rheumatism, etc.; *cold and dry weather*, with a high death rate
from suicide and smallpox; *hot weather* with a high
death rate from bowel complaints; and *warm moist
weather*, with a high death rate from scarlet and typhoid fevers."

Almost every movement we make is influenced to some degree by changes in the weather. It would therefore, be a most interesting and instructive thing to know just how the great battles of the earth and the events that controlled the route and character of civilization were directed by the winds and the consequent weather. The winds that filled the sails of Columbus' ships and wafted them to America certainly brought to our modern world momentous results. The topography of the earth is what it is because of wind and weather. The courses of the winds are the routes of civilization. The directions in which they blow fix the characteristics of vast areas and determine whether they shall be rich prairies or barren deserts, deep forests or naked plains. In choosing the sites for cities we unconsciously are controlled by the way the winds blow. That we have built houses or cities at all has been due to the winds. That we are to-night clothed and comfortably housed instead of naked and roaming the forests as wild nomads, is all traceable with perfect certainty to the blowings of the wind. A warm, pleasant, stormless climate could never have produced our present civilization. The successive necessities that gave birth to all inventions were lodged in the winds. It was to overcome the exigencies of the weather that men struggled when laying the foundations of society. It was adversity and not prosperity that acted as a directing force to civilization. No prosperous savage ever voluntarily took a single step civilizationward. If we turn to the vegetable world we see the same lesson illustrated. Our finest and most enduring timber comes from trees usually weather exposed. The wind gave us the majestic oak because that stately tree knit its trunk into solid tissue that resisted the surly blast. Trees that naturally grow wind-exposed are most likely to be tough-grained; while those whose habitats are compact forests tend to become soft-wooded. The gnarled mahogany of the Rocky Mountains, exposed to every passing blast, has acquired a hardness that needs but slight exaggeration to be compared with steel; while the quaking aspens and cottonwoods of the secluded dells and weather-shielded declivities are quite soft

in comparison. In such illustrations we can find lessons of value. The fitness tnat proves best is the fitness born of adversity. What we are inclined to consider favorable conditions often in practice prove decidedly unfavorable. It is not the opportunity that
leads to true development, but the effort to make opportunity. The truly successful man is the one who
overcomes obstacles, just as the truly moral man is
the one who resists temptation, and the true hero is
he who, while conscious of danger, dares to brave it.
Without something.to resist we cannot progress. He
is not a moral man who has been in solitary confine-
ment for years though he has neither lied, stolen, killed
nor injured a single individual. He has kept the commandments unsullied, perhaps, because he had no op·
portunity to break them. He only is the truly moral
man who when tempted has the courage to resist. It
is only by being tempted that we can ever reach to
full manhood in morals. When resistance ceases,
progress ends. As long as the fight keeps up and
holds itself within the bounds of strained endurance
progress will be made.

It is impossible even to conceive of the profundity
and thoroughness of the interwoven relations that have
been kept up during past ages between the weather
and life of all kinds and to enumerate or estimate
them is simply out of the question. We can but
roughly scan them in a general way. The barren ig-
neous rocks that like immense lava beds originally
formed the crust of the earth have by the weather been
ground and worn into material to make the rich soil
in which vegetation develops. ´ If grass, grain, trees
and flowers grow it is because the weather made a soil
on which they could grow and brought in due season
refreshing showers to aid that growth. Every condition of life as well as the very materials of life, belongs
to the air. It tempers the solar heat to life's requirements. It floats the tiny particles of water raised by
the sunbeam from the sea, carries them into the high-
lands, deposits them as rain, hail or snow, where they
go to feed rivers, lakes and springs. It thus becomes
the universal purifier. Without such good services the
air would be death-laden, and stagnant ponds and lakes

would alone remain to supply for a brief spell the wants of plants and animals. The incessant distillations are ever-continuous purifications. The falling showers bring down to earth myriads of germs and tons of dust that would otherwise be deleterious to health. Each passing storm restores to normal conditions the distorted electric tension, and this in turn gives to the air vitalizing ozone. Nitric acid and ammonia are in the same manner supplied to plants for their maintenance. Nor has the atmosphere failed to contribute to our æsthetic development. God's bow of promise in the clouds is an arch of beauty no limner can match in brilliancy of colors. The rich blue dome of heaven in its cerulean grandeur surpasses every human art in decoration. The ruby glow of evening twilight and the bright crimson-to-gold Aurora brings at dawn, are master works of gorgeousness which the greatest genius can but faintly imitate. The magnificent landscapes and these enchanting settings are all gifts of the atmosphere. The crimson glow of health that mantles on the maiden's cheek and the rich-hued fragrant flower that nestles on her breast are each contributions from the same source. Beauty and utility, our lives, our all, develop from its mystic depths of invisible transparency only to return again in the circle of that season appointed for man.

ABSTRACT OF THE DISCUSSION.

Miss Ellen E. Kenyon, Ph. D. :—I believe the object of this entire course of lectures is to get the ethics out of physics. In this Dr. Eccles has succeeded so well that his lecture might be taken as a model. I agree with Dr. Janes that there has been no better sermon preached to-day. Of the many thoughts suggested, I shall be able to offer but a few.

We have been told this evening that animals produce carbon and consume oxygen and that plants produce oxygen and consume carbon, keeping up a constant balance in which each does little in excess of ministering to the other's needs. Now, let us suppose that forest destruction goes on indefinitely and that scientific farming and scientific feeding reduce the requisite area of cultivated land to a minimum, and that population increases beyond a certain point. This is to imagine a time when our race must learn to thrive on less oxygen or else suffer deterioration. It occurs to me in connection with this point that our friends who are so very anxious to have the world populated had better turn about and consider precautions against over population.

Our speaker grew eloquent and no wonder, in describing the vast preparation for our human advent that has occupied Mother Nature during such immeasurable periods of time. But the idea that all this was done for our little sakes, reminds me of the little girl who, in an astronomic ecstasy, murmured,

"Twinkle, twinkle, little star—
Don't you wonder what I are?"

Thus does humanity lose perspective in judging its own place in nature. We forget that we seem great to ourselves because we are near to ourselves. Coming, as we have done, and as of necessity we had to do out of the conditions that preceded us, for those conditions could not have resulted otherwise, we read in that chaotic past a plan of which we are the fulfillment!

True, there is much in the natural universe, there is much that has been pointed out to us to-night that seems to argue design in the cosmos; but when we consider that nature is everywhere ready to burst forth into life, but certain conditions and chains of conditions are necessary, we have only to apply the laws of evolution to explain more simply the concomitance of favoring conditions, and prospering forms of life. This question of design is a curious one in philosophy and an important one in Ethics. It is a question of where is the center of the universe?—where is ultimate responsibility? The center of the universe is the individual consciousness, and responsibility rests with intelligence. The more intelligent we are—the more we see in this great throbbing, breathing universe an infinite living organism—the less we are able to lay our individual responsibilities upon the shoulders of a Creator.

There are several questions I should like to ask the lecturer. I want to know why that great body of human benefactors, the scientists, who have ushered us into a new world during the comparatively short period of their activities, haven't done more while they were about it. For instance, this atmosphere which surrounds and sustains us is still burdened with three deleterious ingredients that frustrate the ethical plan of creation by causing rebellion in the soul of man and calling its sometimes emphatic expression from his lips. These are *noise, mosquitoes* and that *dust* which Dr. Eccles has so discouragingly analyzed for us tonight. Why are we still, in this age of pianos, subjected to several of them at once, if we happen to live opposite a row of genteel flats? Why have we as yet no means of annulling all sound waves but those we choose to listen to? Why have not the natural enemies of the mosquito been cultivated to the extermination of that destroyer of the summer moonlight? Why have we no way of killing the disease germs in that dust that trembles on every sunbeam?

Our speaker informs us that no prosperous savage ever made a single step toward civilization. I have a pessimistic question to ask right here. Dr. Eccles is always an optimist, and will doubtless answer it in his own cheerful way: Which is better—to be a prosperous savage, or an unhappy Londoner?

I am impelled to ask this question by the fact that we live in an atmosphere of opinion. The opinions of our neighbors are our constant scourge, and the more complex society and its conventions become the more points there are at which we must guard ourselves from the tongue thrusts and the eye-thrusts of our critics. But small peace is left us among them; but few interests are safe if we ignore them; but little liberty of thought, speech and behavior remains where formalism in schools, fashion and "good form" in society and orthodoxy in the churches reign. And they reign everywhere, in what we call the civilized world. They reign absolutely, too. There is not a man in this audience who would save himself from baldness at the

expense of wearing a form of headgear not approved
by Dame Fashion. There is not a woman present who
would dare run down a hill, in park or country, with
a soul in sight to comment upon her childishness, and
the woman who never wants to run down a hill is more
profoundly a victim of "good form" than she dreams.
Only yesterday a friend who takes cold easily and
whose life is in danger with every fresh one, complained to me, "It's these hats!" Yet she would not
dare wear one of those pretty worsted hoods that were
the privilege of a past generation, though duration
of life is the question at stake and that imminent! The
most harmless, the most wholesome, the most essential freedom is denied us by the spirit of criticism that
is abroad day and night.

The moral atmosphere we breathe not only forms
our manners and makes us wear what we wear, but it
builds up our characters into what they are, for better
or for worse. While the spoiled child of fashion is getting by heart all the superficialities of his narrow world,
the child of ignorance and poverty is feeding eye and
ear upon the sights and sounds of back streets and un-
cultured homes, learning vulgarity and uncouthness
with every breath he draws. What a heritage, the
surroundings of either! Teachers who have had experience with children of both these classes say that these
from the very haunts of vice have more in them that
responds to a humane culture's touch than the petted
ones from the lap of wealth. The kindergarten creates
an atmosphere that trains upward and outward and
cultivates all that is heavenly in infant character. Dr.
Rice in his "The Public School System of the United
States," published by the Century Company, tells of
the primary schools where this growth is continued
and of others where it is killed.

The anti-fatalistic element in the philosophy of
Evolution is the consideration that man makes his
own moral atmosphere. He has only to become intelligent, then, to make the right sort of an atmosphere
for every kind of innocent happiness and spiritual
growth to thrive in. One of our very best American
teachers never criticises his pupils. He *inspires* them!
This is what the human family must learn to do, mem-

ber for member. The greatest thing on earth is brotherly love. Universal love would make this earth a heaven, as Dr. Eccles so glowingly painted not long since. There is no need to search long for that "competent God" Mr. Skilton wants to find. The sweetest of history's voices has told us that God is Love. It is love that rules the universe, whether it manifests itself as gravitation, chemical affinity or human affection. Education must realize this and see to it that more love is poured into and out of the lives of succeeding generations. So shall be secured to some future race of human creatures the heaven that we have missed!

MR. JAMES A. SKILTON:—

Apparently Dr. Janes expects me to talk on the subject of ventilation, a subject to which I have given much attention; but I have a matter to present that in a certain aspect has here and now even stronger claims on our attention than the question as to how we shall get fresh air to breathe. It has been said that the topics of our season's course are too strictly scientific in character and that it will be difficult if not impossible to show their ethical, sociological and religious implications. Upon this question I have some evidence to produce, discovered or rediscovered on a recent re-reading of some of the writings of Ruskin. Despising science he still shows that the seers, prophets, poets and critics of the ages have derived their insight, influence and importance from their discoveries and presentation of the ethical, sociological and religious implications to be found, not only in nature, but in the material elements and laws of nature. This being true, we may not only bring men of this type of mind to our aid in the work of this season, but we may hope to reach, instruct and help many among our hearers and readers who are not themselves accomplished in science; for the seer, prophet, etc., speak to and for all mankind, out of hearts and minds common in varying degree and measure to all men.

He refers to the beauty to be everywhere seen in plant and animal life, and with it evidences of health, happiness and the enjoyment of life. He says: "We

are to take it for granted that every creature of God
is in some way good, and has a duty and specific operation providentially accessory to the well-being of all;
we are to look in this faith to that employment and
nature of each, and to derive pleasure from their entire
perfection and fitness for the duty they have to do,
and in their entire fulfillment of it."

But coming to the consideration of the human be·
ing, he draws a terrible but truthful picture of distortion, misery, unhappiness, and all downright ugliness,
due to his seeming inability to fit himself into nature
as do even plants and animals.

Later he calls attention to the powerful effects of
nature upon the Hebrew mind—the influence of both
the Egyptian lowlands, the mountains of Arabia, and
the fruitful valleys of Palestine, producing as he terms
it, "Sympathy with natural things themselves," which
gives grandeur to the imagery of the Hebrew literature.   Ruskin further asserts that education, until
lately, has been directed in every possible way to the
destruction of the love of nature; that children are
deprived of opportunities of free and full converse
with nature by a forced system of education, which
turns away from nature to books, and that such of
them as do secure for themselves the beneficent influence of the former, secure them under protest, even
at the risk of being classed with the idle and self-
willed.   Direct contact with nature is an incentive to
truthfulness and right feeling—it is the source of right
worship.   With merely mechanical and artificial contrivances, however happily adjusted, we can construct
no royal road to the attainment of the highest in character, art and life.

He further insists that the teachings of Christ himself, like those of the prophets and seers, derive their
power and obtain their influence over us from and
through nature, its implications and its sanctions.

If, then, these presentations of Mr. Ruskin are true,
in dealing properly with the topic of the evening and
with the other topics of this season, we are not only
working in harmony with nature and with a true and
broad science, but also with the seers, prophets, poets
of the ages, and with all the true ethical and religious
leaders and teachers of mankind.

Dr. Eccles in reply:

The awkward conclusion drawn by Miss Kenyon because of the present balanced condition of oxygen and carbon dioxide supply is hardly warranted from the facts. An increased supply of plants would make possible an increased supply of animals and vice versa. The large number of fires we now have, useless and useful, represent more consumption of oxygen than many times the number of human beings on the earth. The decomposition of organic matter by bacteria represents still more. All other animals not men, represent still more. When the number of human beings is great enough to take the places of all these oxygen consumers and carbonic acid makers, the population of the earth will be immensely greater than at present, and physical crowding will itself be likely to lead to decadence.

Noise, mosquitoes and dust may be reduced in future but science will not be apt to extinguish nore than the mosquitoes in ages and not then until stagnant pools are at an end. Disease germs are likely to get the best of any effort at their extinction owing to their minuteness and ability to grow wherever moisture and heat are supplied. There are uses for all these plagues or they would not long remain active. Even the fashions at which we rail have their true uses. Without "good form" society would be likely to disintegrate. Out of place they are evils.

WATER

BY

ROSSITER W. RAYMOND, Ph. D.

COLLATERAL READINGS SUGGESTED.

Huxley's *Physiography*, pp. 21-74, 100-184; Roscoe's *Chemistry*, pp. 202-287; Tyndall's *The Forms of Water in Clouds and Rivers, Ice and Glaciers;* Johnston's *The Chemistry of Common Life;* Fox's *Sanitary Examination of Water, Air and Food;* Parke's *Hygiene;* Wilson's *Hand-book of Hygienic and Sanitary Science;* Becquerel's *Traité Elémentaire;* Sir Henry Bell's *The Cause of the Ice Age;* Wright's *The Ice Age in North America;* Wallace's *Island Life,* and *The Geographical Distribution of Plants and Animals;* Heilprin's *Geographical and Geological Distribution of Plants and Animals.*

WATER.

BY ROSSITER W. RAYMOND, PH. D.

It is not expected, I trust, that I shall present to-night
either newly-discovered facts concerning water, or profoundly novel reasoning upon the facts already known.
My humbler purpose is to recall, in a very simple and
general way, some of the familiar characteristics of the
substance constituting my theme, and some of the relations which, in consequence of these characteristics, it
sustains to the world we inhabit, and to the processes of
evolution, inorganic, organic—even social and moral—
affecting the earth and man. Not impossibly, the mere
review of things so well known as to have been practically forgotten may serve to arouse a sense of their significance and importance "as good as new!"*

The first noteworthy fact concerning water is, that it
is almost the only liquid encountered in inorganic nature.
A little mercury is found now and then, trickling from
the ores of our quicksilver-mines; a comparatively small
amount of lava emerges here and there from the earth's
crust; and petroleum in greater abundance, yet, after
all, in insignificant amount compared with the earth's
supply of water, is furnished by springs or reached by
deep borings. Apart from such small exceptions, we
may fairly say that water is our only liquid.

This being the case, it is noteworthy that there is so
much water. The ocean alone contains some three million billion cubic yards of it; and if we take into account
the quantity that is constantly suspended in the atmosphere, or circulating in springs and rivers, or in the
earth's crust, or in the substance and veins of plants and

---

* This lecture, an informal talk without manuscript, was not intended for publication, and does not deserve to be printed as a contribution of any original value
to the literature of its subject. In hastily writing it out, with the aid of the sten-
ographer's notes, I am keenly conscious that all of it has been said, and better
said, before, and (what is still more mortifying to me) I cannot now precisely
specify where, or by whom. The current text-books on physics and mechanics,
and such works as Elisee Reclus' *Ocean*, and Geikie's *Geology*, will doubtless be
found to be the sources of much that I said. But I think a larger debt is due to a
lecture by Prof. Cooke, contained in his volume, "Religion and Chemistry," in
which the teleological argument from the peculiar properties of water is stated in
the good old-fashioned way, with great clearness and force. R. W. R.

animals, we must admit that the total is indeed vast. To this we might add again the amount that has been withdrawn from circulation, being fixed in the hydrated minerals of the rocks. But it is not probable that this quantity is as large as either of the other two.

Looking further, we are impressed with the fact that the abundant supply of water is due to its retention mainly on or near the surface of the earth. The contents of the ocean amount to only 1-500th part of the mass of the globe, and if they were distributed equally through that mass, would not perceptibly dampen it. If the sea-basins were leaky, and their water had escaped into the earth's interior, we should have a condition like that of the barren moon, which, indeed, is supposed by some selenologists to have lost its water in that way. The fortunate preservation of the water of our globe in the region where it is needed for a thousand functions, is the effect of many combined causes, which I will not pause to discuss.

Among them is the specific gravity of water, which is such that most solids sink, while many natural objects float, in it. What a different world we should have (supposing we had any world at all, in such a case), if our ships would not float, or the piers of our bridges would not stay where we put them. In an ocean of quicksilver, the bottom would be continually coming up!

As to the need of this one liquid, so abundantly supplied and so widely distributed, we shall have more to say. Meanwhile, let it be remembered that it is not only in the sea or in the air or in the aqueous circulation between earth and sky, that water is demanded. It is the principal element in all organic substances. We learn in school that potatoes contain 25 per cent, water-melons 93 per cent, and cucumbers 97 per cent, of water. Professor Agassiz found certain sun-fishes that contain 99.9 per cent. And even a man, as some one has said, consists of six pailfuls of water, with a few pounds of solid matter in it.

But this liquid is practically unique, not only in its quantity and distribution, but also in the remarkable qualities with which it is endowed. Let us briefly mention some of these.

In the first place, we possess water in three forms as

solid, liquid, and gas or vapor; and there is no other substance which passes so often and so easily, within the
range of ordinary temperatures, from one of these states
to another. All the known gases can be artificially
changed by cold and pressure to liquids or solids. Nearly
all usually solid elements have been artificially fused
or vaporized by heat. But the series of changes in water
goes on without our intervention, under the ordinary
conditions which surround us.

Here we encounter a remarkable fact, that while these
changes in the aggregate molecular condition of water
are so frequent and familiar, they are exceptionally slow,
and they consume or liberate, as the case may be, more
heat than the similar changes of any other substance.
In other words, water becomes solid or gaseous within a
comparatively small range of temperature; but its specific heat, i. e., the amount of heat absorbed when water
rises, or liberated when it falls, one degree in temperature, is the greatest known to us (one or two comparatively rare substances being disregarded). The amount
of heat that will raise one pound of water a given number
of degrees would raise a pound of iron about ten times,
and a pound of silver about sixteen times, as many degrees in temperature. Hence, while water is heating or
cooling, it changes temperature more slowly (under the
same conditions) and absorbs or gives out more heat in
doing so, than almost anything else in the world.

But this is not all. At the moment of condensing from
steam to water at the same temperature (say 212° Fahrenheit) water gives out suddenly an enormous quantity
of heat, called the latent heat of steam, and vice versa,
the same amount of heat is absorbed when water is
evaporated into steam. This quantity is more than
1,000 heat-units, that is, an amount of heat is required
to turn a pound of water at 212° into a pound of steam
at 212°, which would raise the temperature of the water
to more than 1200°, but for this change of condition.
In a similar way, the latent heat of ice is about 143 heat-
units.

Illustrations of these properties of water are familiar
to us all. We know how much quicker the poker gets
hot in the fire than the water in the tea-kettle over the
fire. The reason is the great specific heat of water.

We know how long it takes the ice in the pitcher to melt, or ice or snow to be reduced to water by building a fire upon it. This is an illustration of the heat absorbed and made latent in thawing ice. And we know that when the contents of a kettle are at boiling heat throughout (say 212° F.) a great deal of heat is still necessary to maintain the boiling; for the water will not all fly into steam just because it has reached the temperature of steam. Every pound of it wants 1,000 heat-units more. And, if the fire which is supplying this extra heat should be suddenly removed, the boiling would stop at once. These are illustrations of the latent heat of steam.

This property is utilized in our steam-heating apparatus, in which the steam, as it condenses into water, gives out its 1,000 heat-units of latent heat, and thus becomes, for the space it occupies, the most effective vehicle for the transfer of heat (or its equivalent energy).

But what we do in our steam-radiators and steam-boilers, Nature does on a vast scale universally. For these three qualities of water, unique in measure, if not in character, namely, its change of molecular condition within a comparatively short range of temperature; its high specific heat, and its high latent heat of solidification or evaporation, combined with its exceptional abundance and distribution, make it a wonderful storage-reservoir for heat, and an equally wonderful carrier and supplier of heat. These qualities are necessary to the aqueous circulation which perpetually goes on between the sea and the land and the sky, equalizing or modifying everywhere the extremes of temperature; both by the direct effect of the ocean and its currents, and by the indirect effect of evaporation and condensation. It is never as cold where ice is forming as it would be under the same conditions if there were no forming ice present to give out the latent heat of the water; and it is never as hot when snow is thawing as it would be if there were no snow to absorb heat in melting. The air will carry at 90° Fahr. twenty times as much aqueous vapor as at 32°; and yet the tremendous precipitation of rain which might follow, under other circumstances, every cooling of the atmosphere is checked and regulated by the specific and latent heat of the aqueous vapor. Moreover, this vapor is a screen to prevent the too rapid heating of the earth's surface by the sun and the too rapid cooling of that surface by radiation into cold space. It has been called "a trap to catch a sunbeam," and conversely, it is a blanket, especially in the form of clouds, shielding us against extremes of cold. But for the presence of a sufficient quantity, in adequately active circulation, of a substance having (as no other known substance has) the peculiar properties of water, the earth would have been, would now be, and would forever remain, uninhabitable for any form of plant or animal life.

But we have to note in addition what is perhaps the most peculiar property of all. Namely, water is the only liquid known to us which has a maximum density at a given temperature, as a liquid. At about 39.2° Fahr. or 7° above the freezing-point, water is denser under atmospheric pressure than at any other temperature. Below and above that temperature it expands. It is this peculiarity that prevents our rivers and lakes from freezing solid to the bottom, and becoming like glaciers, which only great continental and climatic changes can completely remove. So long as the surface-water of a lake is being cooled in winter down to 39.2 , it is becoming heavier as it cools, and sinking to the bottom, while warmer water takes its place, to be chilled in turn. By this circulation, the whole body of water grows cooler. By mere conduction through still water, this would not take place, because water is a bad conductor of heat. Now when the whole of a body of water has thus become nearly as cold as 39.2 Fahr., and the surface-water has actually reached that temperature, the circulation stops; and when the surface finally freezes, it forms a lid over a mass of water which is rarely colder, in depth, than 40°. This protects organic life in the water, and also permits the gradual unlocking of the stream or lake in the spring. The same process is equally effective as regards the moisture in the soil. The maximum density of water checks the descent of frost to kill the roots of plants; and the snow itself gives out heat in forming, and lies as a bad conductor over the ground, to shield it from the piercing cold in winter, while, reversing the process, it prevents too early starting of organic life in the first heat of spring.

But again, water is the universal solvent. The "alka-

hest" of which the old alchemists talked so much (and
which some of them thought they had found, but lost
again, because it dissolved every vessel in which they
tried to keep it), remains to this day a dream. But the
true alkahest is water, which will dissolve to greater or
less extent every known element, solid or gaseous—not
always in simple form, indeed, but at least in combination, for which it supplies the agency. In falling through
the atmosphere, it takes up carbonic acid, nitrogen and
oxygen—and, curiously enough, a larger proportion of
oxygen than of nitrogen, so that the air thus delivered
to the sea and river is richer in oxygen than that of the
atmosphere. If it were not so, those air-breathing animals, the fishes, could not survive. They take their air
with water, but they want it strong!

Moreover, the dissolved gases and salts in water make
it a tremendous agent of change underground, where it is
continually dissolving, transporting and redepositing in
new forms the constituents of the rocks. To this process we owe nearly all our economical mineral deposits.
They are local concentrations by means of aqueous
solutions (i. e., mineral springs) of materials originally
disseminated in the rocks in such minute proportions
that they could never be mined with profit.

Again, the solvent power of water makes it the great
scavenger and purifier of the world. It washes the sky;
it washes the land. Partly by solvent and chemical
action, partly by mechanical energy, of which it is so admirable a vehicle, it planes down the rising continents,
disintegrates, distributes and continually renews the soil,
and thus prepares the way for that organic life of which
it is itself the principal basis and the essential condition.

The most famous instance of the manufacturing of
soil, for the support of life, by a river, is the Nile. As
Herodotus says, "Egypt is the gift of the Nile." There
is no soil in Egypt from which human life could be sustained, except that which the Nile has left there. The
Nile valley from the Mediterranean up to the Lower Cat-
aract is an old estuary of the sea; and if you go down
twenty to fifty feet, almost anywhere, you will come to
sea-sand; but upon that has been deposited year after
year this fertilizing layer of mud from Abyssinia, through

the rains and freshets that join where the White Nile comes into the Blue Nile. These freshets raise the quantity of water up to about forty-fold, and flow over the whole land of Egypt, and by the scientific use of that water, after the system in use in the days of the Pharaohs, and another system now, it is made to irrigate all Egypt. Under the present system of the English engineers in Egypt there is practically, at low water, not a drop of that great river which flows into the Mediterranean to be wasted; it is all utilized, and it suffices to irrigate nearly all the land of Egypt that is fit to irrigate.

Another important property of water is its incompressibility. While it will of itself assume at a particular temperature a maximum density, mere pressure will not force it to do so. Remember that, if this were otherwise, the water at the bottom of the sea would be so heavy through the weight upon it that it would never come up, or take part in the all-important aqueous circulation.

This incompressibility of water is highly valuable to us when we utilize it for power. Sailors know how solid a blow a wave can strike, shattering sometimes the heaviest pier or lighthouse, and breaking up the stoutest ship. Hence when, with our hydraulic engines or Pelton percussion-wheels, we utilize the weight and momentum of falling water, we know it is not wasting itself in self-compression. A dramatic illustration of this property is furnished by the nozzles of the hydraulic miners, from which issue, under great "head," streams that seem as solid as round bars of steel, and irresistibly tear away the bluffs of earth and gravel at which they are directed.

The use of water-power has been somewhat cast in the shade, of late, by the great extension of steam-power. One drawback has been that it was necessary to put manufacturing centers and establish railroad connections close by the site of the water-power. As a result, those water-powers which were not commercially accessible had to be in the main neglected, while, on the other hand, those which became the centers of great industries, were gradually impaired by the effect of deforestation and agriculture, incidental to the large population they had collected.

But with the general introduction of the electric current as the conveyor of energy, our natural water-powers will receive fresh attention. The inaccessible cascades of the mountains, which will never be exhausted, can be harnessed to move the wheels of industry many miles away. I recall a place in Colorado where a small mountain stream, falling 600 feet, has been utilized so as to give 1,000 horse-power, about 75 per cent of which is actually realized at several distant points. Power is carried fourteen miles in one direction to run a stamp-mill of one hundred and twenty stamps; four miles in another direction to a mill of forty stamps, and to the pumps and hoisting engines of a mine; and in another direction to light a whole city with arc-lights.

I have scarcely passed the threshold of my subject. The relations of water to light and color, to electricity, and to chemical change, are as wonderful as those which I have thus imperfectly sketched. Of the two great classes into which the material world is divided—fuel and ash—water belongs to the category of ash. It is the ash of hydrogen. It has been already oxidized. It should have no potential chemical energy left. The ashes of the world are expected to be quiet. But this bland and indifferent substance proves to be one of the mightiest agents of chemical change, furnishing by its own decomposition fresh fuel, and burning other fuels continually. And not only is it concerned in perpetual oxidation. In some mysterious way it takes part in those strange processes of reduction by which plants live.

Equally remarkable and by no means yet completely understood, are the optical and electrical features at which I have only hinted above, and the sanitary and therapeutic relations which I must leave for my friend Dr. Shepard to discuss.

In view of the foregoing hasty and imperfect outline of some of the familiar, yet unique and wonderful properties of water, what shall we say of its relation to the universe of matter and of life, and to that process which we call in modern times evolution? As you know, this process consists in the reaction of every individual with its environment. And we are forced to recognize in water an element of the *universal environment* without which our earth could not have become what it is in shape or substance, and the very first steps of organic evolution could not have taken place. Such evolution without water is unthinkable.

Consider that this one liquid, armed with these unique properties, was preserved to our earth in sufficient quantity to perform all the vast and innumerable functions which are required of it; that it was prevented from disappearing permanently either into the depths or into the sky; that it was set in perpetual motion as a vehicle of energy, as an agent of progressive change, as a protector of every step in the advancing development of crystals and cells, plants and animals, men and societies, yes, social and moral and physical life. Consider how failure in any one of its qualities would have rendered our world and ourselves impossible. Think what would have been the result if quicksilver, instead of water, had been the surviving liquid when the earth-crust had solidified, or what, if the supply of water had been small and quickly absorbed or consumed. Then remember that this marvelous substance was provided, and these essential properties were stamped upon it, ages before organic evolution began upon the earth; and tell me whether you can see in all this no evidence of "design!"

My friends, there is no question concerning the exhibition of intelligent design in the universe. The fundamental postulate of science, as of faith, is this, that only a rational universe can be rationally interpreted. Our fathers may have made innumerable mistakes in trying to state what are the details and methods of the design they thought they perceived; and our mistakes will seem as ludicrous to future generations as those of our ancestors to us. But the vision is there, because the reality is there; and every age receives it in new glory and with new reverence!

I am not one of those who think it either practicable or profitable to frame schemes of reconciliation between the first chapter of Genesis and the ever-advancing discoveries and hypotheses of physical science. I do not believe the Mosaic account to be an infallible statement of scientific truth. Its significance and its inspiration mean something very different to me. But I find in it a far more scientific view than in any other account of equal antiquity which has come down to us; for it is pervaded with the conception of the unity of the creative power, which means the universality of natural law; it is free from the errors inevitably involved in the deification of natural forces, or the recognition of the warring wills of wanton gods; and it exhibits an insight, which I for one am quite willing to call inspired, into the order of the universe. I find it therefore noteworthy that in this primitive story, the all-importance of water is so impressively conceived. Even before the first "Let there be light!" the Spirit "moved upon the face of the waters"; and after that great command, the next act in the creative drama is the separation of the waters above and below the firmament—the hanging of a part in the sky, the collection of a part in seas and rivers—the institution, in other words, of that aqueous circulation which is forever the mechanism of the world. If this is poetry, it is poetry of a high order. Even as science, whatever its vagueness or error of detail, it strikes the keynote which has sounded ever since. We cannot wonder that water, thus recognized as the source, the vehicle, the agent, and almost the very substance of life, should be taken throughout the Bible as the symbol also of healing, cleansing and spiritual power; and that the climax of the splendid vision of the Seer of Patmos should be the River of the Water of Life, flowing from the Throne of Central Goodness and Power, in the City Celestial. The Bible begins and ends with water; and the wisest of us, when we contemplate the nature and the work of water, are not too wise to accept it in the spirit of the Bible, and to thank for it, neither happy accident, nor blind unconscious fate, but the loving foresight of our God.

ABSTRACT OF THE DISCUSSION.

Charles H. Shepard, M. D.

The large proportion of water that is required in the structure of our bodies, as well as that of both plant and animal life, shows at once the importance of this subject when viewed from a vital standpoint. When it is understood that a vigorous condition of the body and its best work is secured only by cleanliness, the conviction is quickly reached that too much attention can scarcely be given to this question, and it might be readily inferred that man would search diligently for the most effective means to attain so desirable a result. But such has not been the fact. His education has not been in that direction. It seems necessary that man should suffer in order to bring him to a consciousness of his needs.

Man is the microcosm of the universe, his condition the correlation of the forces of his nature, and his diseases the result of the transgressions of the laws of his being. The man who lives in the contravention of these laws, even through ignorance, as surely commits suicide as he who ends his life with a pistol. The law makes no excuse for ignorance, therefore there is no mitigation of the penalty. As eternal vigilance is the price of liberty, so is unceasing obedience the price of health. Without this, man's survival is but a dream, but with it all things are possible. The more readily he adapts himself to his environment, the pleasanter become his paths. By unwholesome food, unsanitary surroundings, and neglect of the body, he invites diseased conditions which shorten life. Furthermore, these conditions produce discouragement, cynicism, ill-temper, despair, and not infrequently lead to suicide. A man in an unwholesome condition has an unwholesome influence upon every one about him. The normal, healthy man, on the contrary, is strong, alert, ambitious, happy and hopeful, and his influence is like that of sunshine, brightening every thing in his vicinity. Thus we perceive that health, in itself, has an ethical value to the community that can be appreciated but not measured.

The conditions of man's survival may well occupy the earnest attention of all evolutionists. Why should the mass of mankind be obliged to leave the field of active work before arriving at fifty years of age? When occasionally a man lives one hundred years, it is regarded as exceptional, but may not the exceptional become the rule? Why put the limit at three score and ten?

The first condition of survival is health, which may be defined as the harmonious action of every function of the body. When it is understood that disease and dirt are almost synonymous terms, the importance of cleanliness is quickly recognized. Two-thirds of man's body is water, some authorities estimate it at five-sixths, and this is constantly undergoing the change of waste and repair. We are continually taking into the stomach water in different forms, and a full-grown man is supposed to discharge from his lungs and skin into the air, about two pounds daily.

The first thing a child needs on arriving in the world is a bath. Mr. Dick, when asked what should be done with dirty David Copperfield, meditated profoundly, and said, "Wash him!" Purification of the body is the only way in which we can escape the suffering of sin and disease.

Inasmuch as the skin is the most important organ of the body, enveloping all others, and constantly in contact with the outside world, its healthy condition and action takes precedence in the care of the body, and this cannot be fully secured without a free use of water. There is a natural limitation to the functions of the kidneys, the bowels, and the lungs, but there seems to be no limitation to the functions of the skin.

The action of heat upon the fluids of the body is one of the most valuable agencies that protects and conserves every function of the human organism, because it tends to human survival. It is easily demonstrated that dirt, debility, disease, despair, and death, are always dependent upon a deficient or obstructed action of the fluids of the body. The law of expansion by heat obtains with the fluids and tissues of the body as with all else in nature. By expansion and relaxation induced by perspiration, the circulation of the blood is perfected throughout the body, and thus the tissues are quickly renewed and obstructions overcome. Man's purification can thus be attained, and his life prolonged.

A most important law of nature is that the temperature of the blood, about 98 degrees, remains the same, wherever man is placed, whether in arctic regions or under the equator. The beauty of this law, and its practical application, is everywhere apparent. When man is in a cold atmosphere, the action of the skin is limited, and heat is conserved, but as soon as he enters a warm region the skin relaxes, and with an increase of heat, active perspiration is induced, by means of which all superabundant heat is thrown off. The same law is true in regard to water, which cannot be heated above 212 degrees, so long as the steam is allowed to escape. We cannot boil the water in a man, but it is possibly by a high degree of heat, to make his perspiration so active as to remove all the impurities from the blood, and thus rapidly renovate his whole system. The remarkable ease and comfort with which mankind can endure high temperatures is shown by the large population of warm countries.

Medical men and sanitarians are awakening to the serious and growing evils of the prevailing and utterly reckless use of the so called "mineral-waters," and "soda-waters," that have no soda in them. A medical writer has stated that the capital invested in the "mineral-waters," and carbonated beverage traffic, would erect and equip more school-houses and churches than now stand on the face of the earth, while the horses employed in preparing and distributing these countless products would form a tandem team long enough to girdle the earth. This estimate does not include the immense consumption of fermented and distilled liquors.

With us in America, drinking is a natural craze, and the market is supplied with concoctions and waters of every conceivable variety, good, bad, and indifferent. None are so obnoxious but that eager patrons can be found to praise them for their mysterious power to cure, and many intelligent people cling to the plausible delusion that every natural solution of alkaline, saline, sulphurous, or other nauseous earths and minerals was beneficently designated as a legitimate and "natural" medicine. Theirs is but an expression of a dearth of water in the tissues, and to allay it nothing is so grateful as pure water.

The character of the public water supply is the first and chief concern of every intelligent sanitarian, for in that lurks the means of transmission of all the most virulent and fatal of the infectuous diseases. Many of the epidemics that have desolated different countries have been caused by the use of impure water. Cholera, typhoid fever, and dysentery, are fostered and disseminated almost exclusively through the medium of drinking water.

These diseases have come through the milk-supply, though not from the milk itself, but from the processes concerned in its manipulation and distribution, and they have been known to come from the use of impure water for cleansing milk vessels, as well as the milk-man's use of it to increase his supply. It is scarcely possible to be too careful in the use of pure water for either drinking or cooking purposes, or cleansing of vessels to contain milk. Where impure water abounds, an important safeguard is that of boiling the water as well as the milk, by which both are sterilized.

In a late number of an English magazine, it is stated that in England alone, more deaths are attributable to impure water than to pure, impure, and adulterated spirits and alcoholic drinks altogether, and the diseases from which the miserable victims die are hideous and repulsive as those caused by drink.

Great scourges, formerly known as dispensations of Divine wrath, are now known to be the results of sanitary pollution. The fact that large classes of diseases which assume an epidemic form, and carry off large numbers of victims, are essentially filth diseases, may well emphasize the subject under discussion to all who have any regard for the welfare of their fellow men. With a proper attention to cleanliness, public as well as personal, we should have none of those epidemics.

The reason why cholera, a water-borne disease, is so continually prevalent in India, is because of the abominable water used. There is no public water supply, and the natives use water that has been contaminated by their own secretions. The effect of this is shown in a marked degree at the time of their religious pilgrimages, when thousands are literally swept out of existence by the use of this impure water.

It was the impurities contained in the waters of the river Elbe, that caused the great calamity to the city of Hamburg last year. The expense of that, to the city alone, has been estimated at £25,000,000!

A recent report from the Health Commissioner of Chicago states that during the year ending September 30th, 1892, when the water supply of that city was taken from points along the lake front liable to pollution from sewage, the number of deaths from typhoid fever alone was

1790. As a contrast, he states that during the year ending September 30th, 1893, when the water supply was
brought through tunnels from a point four miles from
the lake shore, the number of deaths from typhoid fever
was reduced to 712, or less than one half.

From youth up to old age, nothing so develops man,
physically, mentally, and morally, as an intimate acquaint-
ance with soap and water. The sacred rite of Baptism
is simply symbolic of the Bath, the two words having
the same derivation. The baptistry, originally was a
building, often of great architectural beauty, separate
from the church, and only after many years absorbed
into it. Even to-day in some churches, washing of the
feet is made a sacred rite, and the use of water for the
prevention and cure of disease has the sanction of experience from the remotest ages. The ancients had water-
gods, water-nymphs, and water-spirits, to preside over
different bodies of water. There are numerous cases of
river worship in Africa. Among other rivers in India,
the Ganges is considered sacred, and the natives believe
that to bathe in its waters, particularly at great stated
religious festivals, will wash away the stain of sin. In
our own country the Dakotas are said to worship a god
of the waters.

Sir Lyon Playfair, in an address before the British
Association, of which he was President, said, that the
whole of Sanitary Science could be comprised in two
words, "Be Clean!" Most fortunately this condition is
placed within man's reach. The clean man, other
things being equal, will be the healthy man, and the
moral man. To attain this condition he must secure
pure air, pure water, cleanliness in and around the house,
cleanliness of person, dress and food, cleanliness in life
and conversation, in other words, purity of life, and temperance in all things, to the end that his days may be
long, and that these days may be productive of good to
his fellow men.

Dr. Lewis G. Janes:—It is of interest to us as Americans to note the effect which water has had in forwarding
our own national development, and favoring our survival
as an integral political organization. It is the surrounding
oceans which make America a continent—or twin conti-

nents, if you please—and which thereby give to our
national ambition, continental scope and opportunity.
The natural protection which the seas afford us is of far
greater import and value than the artificial protection of
forts or tariffs.   Upon the perception of this fact was
based that great principle of public policy, recognized
by our government from its earliest days, the Monroe
doctrine.   Tersely stated, this doctrine affirms that no
foreign nation shall hereafter be permitted to colonize
any part of these two continents, or to interfere with the
autonomy of American nationalities; and on the other
hand, it gives assurance that we will not interfere with the
affairs of other nations beyond our own continental limits, and within these limits only for their own or our just
protection. We do not claim the right to appropriate territory even in this continent without the full consent of its
inhabitants and owners; but within the bounds of equity
and justice, our legitimate ambition may well find a continental scope. Without annexing other American territory than that which we now possess, we may cultivate reciprocal relationships of friendship and commercial intercourse with the nations of these two continents to our
mutual advantage. Though not a special admirer of the
political methods of the late Mr. Blaine, as some of you
are aware, his plan for friendly reciprocity between the nations of America had in it some elements of a true states-
manship.   Thomas Jefferson defined the proper limitations for territorial expansion to be where no navy would
be required for the protection of our possessions. If we
adhere to this wise and established policy of our government, resisting all temptations to territorial acquisition
beyond our continental limits, recognizing the natural
barrier and protection of the seas, not stretching out a
mercenary hand to those beautiful islands 2,000 miles
from our Pacific coast, but encouraging their people to
work out their own political salvation in their own way,
while we vigorously repel encroachments on American
domain and conserve that wise principle of local autonomy and federal union which constitutes the very
essence of our national life, we may find in this all-embracing element which at once integrates us as a people
and differentiates us from alien communities, not only the
universally recognized symbolism of purity, but the

promise and potency for us of more perfect internal unity and a continuance of international amity and peace.

After some remarks by MR. JAMES A. SKILTON upon the general topic of the lecture course, DR. RAYMOND replied briefly to Mr. Skilton's criticism.

FOOD AS RELATED TO LIFE AND SURVIVAL

BY

PROF. W. O. ATWATER

Miller's *Chemistry*, Vol. III., pp. 899-916; Johnston's *The Chemistry of Common Life*; Edward Smith's *Foods* (International Scientific Series); Fox's *Sanitary Examination of Water, Air and Food*; Bennett's *Nutrition and Health*; Pavey's *Food*; Fothergill's *Manual of Dietetics*; Holbrook's *Food and Work*; Goodfellow's *Dietetic Value of Bread*; Bellows's *Philosophy of Eating*; *Ethics of Diet*.

FOOD AS RELATED TO LIFE AND SURVIVAL.

BY W. O. ATWATER,

Professor of Chemistry in Wesleyan University.

Mr. President, Ladies and Gentlemen:—The subject assigned for our consideration this evening is Food Supply as related to the present condition and the future welfare of society. Will you allow me to present a few facts and figures as they appear from my point of view, which is that of chemist rather than physician, economist or moralist? Or rather, will you let me tell you some things which studies in the chemical laboratory have brought to my attention and which may perhaps be suggestive to you who are interested in hygiene, in sociology and in ethics?

In so doing I wish to speak of:—

First, the nutritive ingredients of food and the ways they nourish our bodies.

Second, the fitting of our food to our actual needs for nourishment, in other words, food and health.

Third, saving and waste of food; that is the pecuniary side of the subject.

Fourth, the food supply of the future.

Finally we may draw a few inferences regarding some of the sociological and ethical problems in which we are all so deeply interested.

In order that we may get through before you are too much wearied, I will pass as lightly as may be over the first three topics. It is not easy to dismiss them with a word, however, for they are interesting and weighty, and people in general know all too little about them.

Food constitutes the chief item of the living expenses of the people of this country and of Europe. The health and strength of all are intimately dependent upon their diet. Yet the most of us understand very little about what our food contains, how it nourishes us, whether we are economical or wasteful in buying and preparing it for use, and whether or not the food we eat is rightly fitted to the demands of our bodies.

The result of our ignorance is great waste in the purchase and use of food, loss of money, and injury to health. The reason for this ignorance is simple enough. Fifty years ago no man knew what our bodies and our foods were composed of; how the different nutritive ingredients of the food served their purposes in nutrition; how much of each of the ingredients was needed to supply the demands of people of different age, sex and occupation; and how best to adjust the diet to the wants of the user. We do not to-day know as much about these things as we ought. For that matter, we never shall be able to lay down hard and fast rules to apply to all cases, because of the differences between individuals in respect to their demands for nutriment and the ways in which their bodies can make use of different kinds of foods. But the research of the past twenty-five years has brought a great deal of definite information. Nearly all of the exact inquiry in this direction has been done in Europe, and the greater part of it in Germany. We are only beginning in the United States.

The statistics which I shall use here are based mainly upon the results of European inquiry and on some studies of food and dietaries carried out under my direction in the chemical laboratory of Wesleyan University. In the course of the latter studies, which have been made in connection with the Storrs Experiment Station, the Massachusetts Bureau of Labor, the United States Department of Labor, the United States Fish Commission, the Smithsonian Institution, and the World's Fair Commission, nearly a thousand specimens of food materials have been analyzed, and estimates have been made of the amount and composition of the food used by somewhat over one thousand persons, mostly wage workers, with a few college students and men in professional life, in some fifty families and boarding-houses, chiefly in Massachusetts and Connecticut. Of course the American data are extremely meager, and while the European are very extensive, even they are much less complete than is to be desired.

Let us, then, give our attention to our first topic. For this we must take a different view of food from that to which we are accustomed. We must consider, not the food as a whole, but the nutriment it actually contains, which is a very different thing. We must take account of its chemical composition, its nutritive ingredients, their actual cost in food as we buy it, and the ways in which they are used to nourish our bodies. We must talk, not of beef and bread and potatoes, but of nutritive ingredients and their potential energy.

A pound of lean beef and a quart of whole milk contain about the same amounts of actually nutritive material. But the pound of beef costs more than the quart of milk, and its nutrients not only differ in number and kind, but are, for ordinary use, more valuable than those of the milk. This illustrates a fundamental fact in the economy of foods, namely, that the differences in the values of different foods depend upon both the kinds and the amounts of the nutritive materials which they contain. Add to this that it is essential for health that the food shall supply the nutrients in the kinds and the proportions required by the body and that it is likewise important, from a pecuniary standpoint, that the materials be obtained at the minimum cost, and we have the fundamental principles of food economy.

Those who are interested in this special subject may find explanations of the chemical terms, and accounts of analyses of food materials, and studies of dietaries and food consumption, in the Reports of the Storrs Experiment Station for 1891 and 1892, which are published in the Reports of the Connecticut Board of Agriculture* for those years. It will suffice to say here that we estimate the nutritive values of foods from their proportions of protein, fats, carbohydrates and their potential energy or fuel value.

The terms protein, proteids, and albuminoids are used somewhat indiscriminately for the nitrogenous compounds in plants and in the animal body. The myosin which forms the basis of lean meat and of the flesh of fish, the ossein of bone, albumen of egg, casein of milk, gluten of wheat, and the like, are protein compounds. Of the fats we have examples in butter, olive

---

* To be obtained of Hon. T. S. Gold, Secretary Conn. Board of Agriculture, West Cornwall, Conn.

oil, and the oils of corn and other vegetable foods. Sugar and starch are carbohydrates. Carbohydrates do not occur to any extent in meats and fish, but are found in milk as milk sugar, and are the chief nutritive ingredients of vegetable foods. The mineral matters, and water also, are necessary for nourishment; but we do not generally take them into account in studies of dietaries.

In general the animal substances contain the most water, and the vegetable foods the most nutrients, though potatoes and turnips and allied green vegetables are exceptions. Meats have more water in proportion as they have less fats. Thus, very lean beef is nearly three fourths water, while other and fatter cuts are less than one half water. The flesh of fish is in general more watery than that of ordinary meats. Flour and meal have very little water, and sugar almost none. In examining the proportions of individual nutrients, the most striking fact is the difference between the meats and the fish, on one hand, and the vegetable foods on the other hand. The vegetable foods are rich in carbohydrates, and the meats abound in protein and fats, of which the vegetable foods usually have but little. Beans and oatmeal, however, are rich in protein, while fat pork has very little.

The following figures will serve to illustrate the quantities of the different ingredients and estimated fuel values of common food materials.

Composition of Ordinary Food Materials.

Food Materials.	Refuse: bones, skins, skulls, etc.	Edible portion.						
		Water.	Total.	Nutrients.				Potential energy in r pound.
				Protein.	Fats.	Carbo-hydrates.	Mineral matters.	
	per cent	per cent	per cent	per cent	per cent	per cent	per cent	Calories
Beef, side, well fattened	19.2	44.3	36.5	13.9	21.8		0.8	1180
Beef, round, rather lean	10.0	60.0	30.0	20.4	8.1		1.2	725
Beef, sirloin, rather fat	25.0	45.0	30.0	15.0	14.3		0.7	880
Beef, flank	12.1	43.7	44.2	12.4	29.2		2.6	1460
Mutton, side, well fattened	17.3	44.2	38.5	14.0	23.7		0.8	1260
Smoked ham	11.4	36.8	51.8	14.8	34.6		2.4	1735
Pork, very fat, salted		12.1	87.9	0.9	82.8		4.2	3510
Codfish, fresh, dressed	29.9	58.5	11.0	10.6	0.2		0.8	205
Mackerel	44.8	40.4	15.0	10.0	4.3		0.7	365
Salmon, whole	35.3	40.6	24.1	14.3	8.8		1.0	635
Salt codfish	42.1	40.3	17.6	16.0	0.4		1.2	315
Hens' eggs	13.7	63.1	23.2	12.1	10.2		0.9	655
Oysters, average		87.1	12.9	6.0	1.2	3.7	2.0	230
Cows' milk		87.0	13.0	3.6	4.0	4.7	0.7	325
Cheese, whole milk		30.2	69.8	28.3	35.5	1.8	4.2	2090
Butter		10.5	89.0	1.0	85.0	0.5	3.0	3615
Wheat flour		12.5	87.5	11.0	1.1	74.9	0.5	1644
Beans		12.6	87.4	23.1	2.0	59.2	3.1	1615
Corn (maize) meal		15.0	85.0	9.2	3.5	70.6	1.4	1645
Potatoes	10.0	71.0	19.0	2.0	0.1	16.0	0.9	340
Sugar, granulated		2.0	98.0	2.0	0.1	97.8	0.2	1820

Food nourishes our bodies in two ways: it builds and repairs our tissues and it serves for fuel to yield heat to keep the body warm and to give it force and strength to do its work. The protein compounds are the building material. They are sometimes called "flesh-formers," because the flesh, i. e., muscle and sinew, is formed from them, though they make blood and bone as well and can also be transformed into fat. The fats and carbohydrates are the fuel ingredients. Both of them are transformed into the fat of the body, which is its reserve of fuel. The protein can serve as fuel also, but the fats and carbohydrates cannot build nitrogenous tissue, for protein contains nitrogen and they do not. Chemists have devised ways for estimating the fuel value, or, to use a more correct term, the potential energy of the nutrients of food. This is expressed in heat units, called Calories, the Calorie being the amount of heat that would raise a kilogram of water one degree centigrade or one pound of water about four degrees Fahrenheit. One Calorie corresponds to 1.52 foot-tons. A gram (453.6 grams make a pound avoirdupois) of protein or a gram of carbohydrates is estimated to yield, on the average, 4.1 Calories, and a gram of fats 9.3 Calories, of energy. A pound of rather fat sirloin of beef would contain about 900, a pound of butter 3,00, a pound of wheat flour about 1,650, and a pound of potatoes 340 Calories. The potatoes yield so little because they are three-quarters water, the butter so much because it is mostly fat. In the adjusting of diet to the demands of the body the important matter is to provide enough protein for the building and repair of tissue and enough energy to keep it warm and do its work. Considering the body as a machine, there must be material to make it and keep it in repair, and fuel to supply heat and power. If there is not food enough or the nutrients are not in the right proportions, the body will be weak in its structure and inefficient in its work. If there is too much, damage to health will result.

This brings us to our second topic: the fitting of our food to our actual needs for nourishment.

Scientific research, interpreting the observations of practical life, indicates that we make a four-fold mis-

take in our food economy. First, we purchase needlessly expensive kinds of food. We do this under the
false impression that there is some peculiar virtue in
the costlier food material, and that economy in our
diet is somehow detrimental to our dignity or our welfare. Secondly, the food which we eat does not always contain the proper proportions of the different
kinds of nutritive ingredients. We consume relatively
too much of the fuel ingredients of food, such as the
fats of meat and butter, the starch which makes up
the larger part of the nutritive material of flour and
potatoes, and sugar and sweetmeats. Conversely, we
have relatively too little of the protein or flesh-forming
substances, like the lean of meat and fish and the
gluten of wheat, which make muscle and sinew and
which are the basis of blood, bone, and brain. Thirdly,
many people, not only the well to do, but those in
moderate circumstances, use needless quantities of
food. Part of the excess, however, is simply thrown
away with the wastes of the table and kitchen; so
that the injury to health, great as it may be, is doubtless much less than if all were eaten. Probably the
worst sufferers from the evil are well-to-do people of
sedentary occupations—brain workers as distinguished
from hand-workers. Finally, we are guilty of serious
errors in our cooking. We waste a great deal of fuel
in the preparation of our food, and even then a great
deal of the food is very badly cooked. A reform in
these methods of cooking is one of the economic demands of our time.

Some of these statements cannot be made as confidently as if we had more exact information, but
they express the facts as far as they are known to-
day.

Take, for instance, the quantities of food consumed
by people in New England Here are some figures
selected from the studies of dietaries of people in Massachusetts, Connecticut and Canada, and of people in
corresponding walks in life in Europe. With them are
dietary standards as proposed by leading European
authorities and also by myself. The table is from
the Report of the Storrs Experiment Station for 1892,
above cited.

I have said that our diet is one-sided—that the food which we actually eat, leaving out of account that which we throw away, has relatively too little protein and too much fat, starch, and sugar. This is due

DIETARIES.	Protein.	Fats.	Carbohydrates.	Potential Energy	Nutritive Ratio.
American (Massachusetts and Connecticut).	gm	gm	gm.	Cal.	1:
Family of glass blowers in East Cambridge, Mass.........	95	132	481	3,590	6.2
Boarding house, Lowell, Mass.; boarders, operatives in cotton mills, ...	132	200	549	4,650	7.6
Boarding house, Middletown, Conn.; { Food purchased	126	188	426	4,010	6.8
well-paid machinists, etc., at moderate work,............. { Food eaten......	103	152	402	3,490	7.3
Blacksmiths, Lowell, at hard work........................	200	304	795	6,905	7.4
Brickmakers, Mass.; 237 persons at very severe work....	180	365	1150	8,850	11.0
Mechanics, etc., in Massachusetts and Connecticut; average of 4 dietaries of mechanics at severe work (not including No. 5)..........................	215	296	749	6,705	6.6
Average of 20 dietaries of wage-workers in Massachusetts and Connecticut.......................	152	225	625	5,275	7.5
Average of 5 dietaries of professional { Food purchased	133	163	508	4,140	6.6
men and college students in Middletown, Conn.,............... { Food eaten	126	152	489	3,925	6.6
European (English, German, Danish and Swedish)					
Well-fed tailors, England, Playfair........	131	39	525	3,055	4.7
Hard-worked weavers, England, Playfair,...........	151	44	622	3,570	4.8
Blacksmiths at active labor, England, Playfair..	176	71	667	4,115	4.7
Well-paid mechanics, Munich, Voit................ .	151	54	479	3,085	4.0
Carpenters, coopers, locksmiths, Bavaria; average of 11 dietaries................	122	33	570	3,150	5.3
Miners at severe work, Prussia, Steinheil.	133	113	634	4,195	6.7
German army ration, peace footing...................	111	39	480	2,800	5.0
German army ordinary ration, war footing	134	58	489	3,095	4.6
German army extraordinary ration, in war	192	45	678	3,985	4.1
University professor, Munich; very little exercise,.......	100	100	240	2,325	4.7
Lawyer, Munich, Forster, ...	80	125	222	2,100	6.3
Physician, Munich, Forster,............................	127	89	362	2,830	4.1
Physician, Copenhagen, Jürgenson,...................	135	110	239	2,835	4.1
Average of 7 dietaries of professional men and students	114	111	285	2,670	4.7
Dietary Standards.					
Adult in full health, Playfair (English)	119	51	531	3,140	5.5
Active laborers, Playfair (English)...................	156	71	568	3,630	4.7
Man at moderate work, Voit (German)........	118	56	500	3,055	5.3
Man at hard work, Voit (German)	145	100	450	3,370	4.7
Man with moderate muscular work, writer..............	125	135	450	3,520	5.9
Man with active muscular work, writer..............	150	150	500	4,060	5.6
Man at severe muscular work, writer.................	175	250	650	5,705	6.9
Man at very severe muscular work, writer........	200	350	800	7,355	7.9

partly to our large consumption of sugar and partly to our use of such large quantities of fat meats. In the statistics above referred to, the quantities of fat in the European dietaries range from one to five ounces per day, while in the American the range is from four to sixteen ounces. In the daily food of well-to-do professional men in Germany, who were amply nourished, the quantity of fat is from three to four and one-half ounces per day; while in the dietaries of Americans in similar conditions of life it ranges from five to seven and one-half ounces in the food purchased. The quantities of carbohydrates in the European dietaries range from nine to twenty-four ounces, while in the corresponding American dietaries the carbohydrates were from twenty-four to sixty ounces.

Chemists estimate the proportion of fuel ingredients to protein in what is called the "nutritive ratio." In this estimate one part by weight of fats is counted as equivalent to two and one quarter of carbohydrates. Adding the two together gives the amount of the fuel ingredients. In the American dietaries the proportion of fuel ingredients to one part of protein ranges from six and six-tenths to eight and two-tenths, and even higher. In the European dietaries of well nourished people and in the dietary standards which express the average needs according to the teachings of the best physiological observations, it is from four and one-tenth to six or thereabouts. The rejection of so much of the fat of meat at the market and on our plates at the table is not mere willful wastefulness. It is in obedience to nature's protest against a one sided and excessive diet.

Our chief excesses are in our consumption of meats and sweetmeats. Our agricultural conditions have caused the excessive fatness of our meats. A taste, perhaps not vitiated but certainly not correct from the hygienic standpoint, has given preference to the very fat meats. though fortunately a reaction is beginning to make itself manifest. We are fond of sugar and of the delicacies of which it forms a part. But the most remarkable thing about our food consumption is the quantity. The American dietaries examined in the inquiry mentioned above were of people living at the time in Massachusetts and Connecticut, though many came from other parts of the country. It would be wrong to take their eating habits as an exact meas- ure of those of people throughout the United States.

For that matter, a great deal of careful observation will be needed to show precisely what and how much is used by persons of different classes in different regions. But such facts as I have been able to gather seem to imply that the figures obtained indicate in a general way the character of our food consumption. Of the nearly fifty dietaries examined, the smallest was that of the family of a chemist who had been studying the subject and had learned something of the excessive amounts of food which many people with light muscular labor consume. This dietary supplied 3,200 Calories of energy per man a day. The largest was that of brickmakers at very severe work in Massachusetts. They lived in a boarding-house managed by their employers, who had evidently found that men at hard muscular work out of doors needed ample nourishment to do the largest amount of work. The food supplied 8,850 Calories per day!

Voit's standard for a laboring man at moderate work, which is based upon the observation of the food of wage workers who are counted in Germany as well paid and fell fed, allows 118 grams of protein and 3,055 Calories of energy. The dietaries of Massachusetts and Connecticut factory operatives, day laborers, and mechanics at moderate work averaged about 125 grams of protein and 4,500 Calories of energy. For a man at "severe" work, Voit's standard calls for 145 grams of protein and 3,370 Calories of energy. The Massachusetts and Connecticut mechanics at "hard" and "severe" work had from 180 to 520 grams of protein and from 500 to 7,800 Calories of potential energy, and in one case it rose to the 8,850 just quoted. In the dietary standards proposed by myself, in which the studies of American dietaries have been taken into account, it did not seem to me permissible to assign less than 4,000 Calories to that for a workingman at 'hard" and 5,700 for a man at "severe" work. Just what compounds in food are required for the nutriment of the brain, physiological chemistry has not yet told us; but it is certain that people with little muscular exercise require less food than those at hard muscular labor. Many men whose work and strain are mental rather than physical suffer from over-eating.   In a number of dietaries of professional men in Germany, Denmark, and Sweden, including a university professor, a lawyer, physicians and students, all of whom were in comfortable circumstances, in good health, and amply nourished, the energy varied from 2,325 to 2,835 Calories; the average of all was 2,670 Calories.   The average of five dietaries of professional men and students from the Northern and Eastern States, residing in Middletown, Conn , was 4,140 Calories; the range was from 3,205 in the family of the chemist to whom I have referred to 5.345 in a students' boarding club.   These figures, like the others of the American dietaries cited, refer to the food purchased.   In the students' dietary the food eaten supplied 4,825 Calories.

Now, it is not easy to see why these men required so much more than was sufficient to nourish abundantly men of like occupation, but unlike temptation to over eating, in Europe. Difference in climate cannot account for it.   We are a little more given to muscular exercise here, which is very well for us, but it cannot justify our eating so much.   In the German army, where especial attention is given to diet and it is an axiom that soldiers to march well and fight well must be well fed, a ration for time of peace has been computed at 2,800 Calories, for time of war at 3,095; and an extraordinary war ration for service in the field, in which the soldiers are most severely tried supplies 3,985 Calories.   If a man with a tremendous physical and nervous tension required in such terrible service as the German soldier was a few years ago called upon to render in his victorious contests with the Frenchman, is well supplied by a ration of less than 4,000 Calories of energy, and German professional men in their quiet but active and successful intellectual work at home are amply nourished with 2,700 Calories and less, how happens it that men of like occupation here consume food with 4,000 Calories and more?

I think the answer to this question is found in the conditions in which we live.   Food is plenty.   Holding to a tradition which had its origin where food was less abundant, that the natural instinct is the measure of what we should eat, we follow the dictates of the palate. Living in the midst of abundance, our diet has not been regulated by the restraints which obtain with the great majority of the people of the old world, where food is dear and incomes are small. How much harm is done to health by our one-sided and excessive diet, no one can say. Physicians tell us that it is very great. Of the vice of over-eating, Sir Henry Thompson, a noted English physician and authority on this subject, says:

"I have come to the conclusion that more than half the disease which embitters the middle and latter part of life is due to avoidable errors in diet, . . . and that more mischief in the form of actual disease, of impaired vigor, and of shortened life accrues to civilized man . . . in England and throughout Central Europe from erroneous habits of eating than from the habitual use of alcoholic drink, considerable as I know that evil to be."

We now come to our third topic, which has to do more particularly with the economic and pecuniary phases of the subject.

Roughly speaking, half the total earnings of wage-workers in this country and in Europe is spent for the food of themselves and families. In the report of the Massachusetts Bureau of Labor for 1894, Hon. Carroll D. Wright, now Chief of the United States Department of Labor, has summarized the result of investigations into the cost of living of people with different incomes, especially workingmen's families, in Massachusetts and in Great Britain, and has quoted similar results obtained by Dr. Engel in Germany. Dividing expenses into those for subsistence (food), clothing, rent, fuel, and sundries, the percentage of the whole income expended for subsistence varies with the amount of income. The smaller the total earnings, the larger is the proportion spent for food.

The averages in Massachusetts were, for incomes of $750 to $1,200, fifty-six per cent expended for food, and for incomes of from $350 to $400, sixty four per cent. In other words, according to these figures, the

workingman in Massachusetts who earned $1,000 in a
year expended, on the average, $560 for the food of
himself and family, the man with $700 spent $300,
and the man with $400, $250 a year. In Great Britain
and Germany incomes are much smaller, but the proportions expended for food are about the same. Later
investigations, by the United States Department of
Labor, of the costs of living of families in the central,
southern and western States, where food is cheaper than
in New England and the eastern States, make the relative expense for food somewhat less. But it is safe
to say that, in general, wage-workers use half their
money to buy their food. This means simply what
they pay the butcher and the grocer and the milkman
and does not cover the cost of cooking except where
food is purchased ready cooked, as in the buying of
bread.

It seems a little strange that when food costs so
much more than clothing, rent, and other necessaries
of life, indeed as much as all the rest together, people should know so little about its real value for
nourishment. When an intelligent man buys a coat
he has a pretty fair idea as to whether it fits him or
not, how much wear there is in it, and whether he
can get as good a fit and as much wear in another
kind of coat at less cost. But when he buys his meat
and flour and potatoes, he has really very little definite information as to how much nutriment they contain, whether the nutritive materials are of the kinds
and in the proportions that are best adapted to the
bodily wants of himself and his wife for their work
and of his growing children for the healthy building
up of their bodies, nor does he know exactly whether
or not he might obtain what is needed in equally useful forms and at much less cost. He is very apt to
have the idea that what his family wants and must
have is "good, nourishing food and enough of it." This
is a most excellent principle, but in its practical application it is apt to mean, "Get the kind of food
you like; do not mind the cost, for the best is the
cheapest, and be sure that you get enough." The
result is bad economy—vicious wastefulness indeed.

One of the ways in which a great deal of bad econ-

omy is practiced is in the buying of high-priced foods.
The cheapest food is that which supplies the most
nutriment for the least money.   The most economical
food is that which is the cheapest and at the same
time the best adapted to the wants of the user.   The
maxim that "the best is the cheapest" does not apply
to food.   The best food, in the sense of that which
is sold at the highest price, is not generally the
cheapest, nor is it always the most healthful or economical.   Salmon and tenderloin of beef at seventy-five
cents a pound are no more nutritious than halibut or
shoulder steak at ten or fifteen cents a pound.   There
is as much of the actual nutrients, and these are just
as valuable for supplying the wants of the body, in
the cheaper as in the dearer material.   A large part
of the price we pay for the costlier food materials
goes for the flavor.   A cook who understands how can
make a toothsome dish from a cheap cut of beef; one
who does not can spoil a tenderloin.

The relative expensiveness of actual nutriment is
illustrated by the figures in the table herewith, which
shows the quantities of the different nutrients which
one would buy for twenty-five cents in the materials
at the price stated.*

If I buy a pound of sirloin steak for twenty-five
cents, I get about three tenths of a pound of actually
nutritive material, with fifteen-hundredths of a pound
of protein and enough fat in addition to yield some
870 Calories of energy.   If I am content with a cheaper
cut of beef, say from the fore-quarter at twelve and
a half cents a pound and of like composition, of course
I get twice as much nutritive material for the same
money.   The same twenty-five cents invested in a pint
of oysters, weighing a pound, would bring only six-
hundredths of a pound of protein and 230 Calories of
energy; but if it be invested in flour at three cents a
pound, it will buy seven and one-quarter pounds of
actually nutritive material, with nearly a fuel value of

---

*   Other statistics bearing upon this point may be found in the
Reports of the Storrs Experiment Station for the years 1891, 1892 and
1893. which are published with the Reports of the Connecticut
Board of Agriculture for those years.   An interesting lecture upon
the same subject by Mr. C. D. Woods is to appear, I understand,
in the Report of the New Jersey Board of Agriculture for 1893.

Nutrients and Potential Energy obtained for Twenty-five cents in Food Materials, purchased at ordinary prices.

FOOD MATERIALS AS FOUND IN THE MARKETS.	Price per lb.	Total Food Materials.	Nutrients.			Calories of Pot'n'l En'gy
			Protein.	Fat.	Carbohydrates.	
ANIMAL FOODS. *Beef.*	Cts.	Lbs.	Lbs.	Lbs.	Lbs.	Cal.
Rib..........................	20	1.25	.16	.34	—	1755
	16	1.56	.20	.43	—	2190
Sirloin.....	22	1.14	.18	.20	—	1105
	18	1.39	.22	.21	—	1350
Round	16	1.56	.28	.23	—	1335
	12	2.08	.37	.30	—	1780
Cooked and canned...........	18	1.39	.37	.24	—	1700
	14	1.79	.48	.31	—	2200
Mutton.						
Shoulder.....................	.20	1.25	.19	.24	—	1345
	15	1.67	.25	.31	—	1795
Leg	22	1.14	.17	.18	—	1065
	18	1.39	.21	.22	—	1300
Loin..........................	22	1.14	.14	.34	—	1690
	18	1.39	.18	.41	—	2055
Pork.						
Smoked ham..................	16	1.56	.25	.58	—	2915
	12	2.08	.31	.72	—	3615
Fat salt pork..................	16	1.56	.01	1.29	—	5475
	12	2.08	.02	1.72	—	7295
Fish, etc.						
Mackerel.....................	18	1.39	.14	.06	—	515
	10	2.50	.25	.11	—	930
Cod, dressed.................	10	2.50	.20	.00	—	390
	8	3.13	.25	.01	—	485
Dry salt cod..................	5	5.00	.53	.01	—	725
Salt mackerel	12	2.08	.31	.32	—	1925
Canned salmon...............	20	1.25	.26	.18	—	1220
Oysters, solids, 50c. qt. / 35c. qt.	25	1.00	.06	.01	.04	236
	18	1.43	.09	.02	.05	345
Eggs and Dairy Products.						
Eggs, 25c. per doz...........	18	1.37	.20	.14	—	985
Milk, 6c. per quart.	3	8.33	.30	.33	.39	2675
Butter........................	35	.71	.01	.60	—.	2550
Cheese, full cream...........	20	1.25	.35	.44	.02	2590
	16	1.56	.44	.55	.02	3230
VEGETABLE FOODS.						
Potatoes, 75c. per bu.........	1.25	20.00	.36	.02	3.04	6400
Granulated sugar	5.5	4.54	—	—	4.52	8375
Dried beans..................	5	5.00	1.15	.10	2.96	8075
Corn meal (maize)	3	8.33	.77	.32	5.88	13700
	1	25.00	2.30	.95	17.65	41100
Oat meal.....................	5	5.00	.74	.36	3.42	9225
Wheat flour	2.5	10.00	1.11	.11	7.49	16450
Wheat bread..................	8	3.13	.28	.05	1.76	4005

12,000 Calories of energy. It is a noteworthy and lamentable fact that a very large body of people of moderate incomes insist upon purchasing the dearest kinds of food. Well-to do people are apt to be con·tent to economize, but many with small incomes insist on having "the best" regardless of cost. The wage-workers of the United States waste enough in this way to make a very great difference in the comfort and satisfaction of their living if the money were saved and used in wiser ways.

It would be an interesting study of our social economy to find how much of our food we literally throw away. In the dietary investigations above cited, numerous cases were observed in which from an eighth to a tenth of the actual nutrients of the food were rejected in the wastes of the table and kitchen. People in this country eat whatsoever is set before them, asking no questions for economy's sake, provided it suits their taste. The saddest part of the story is that it is the poor man's money that is worst spent in the market and the poor man's food that is worst cooked and served at home.

But there is another side to this picture. It is brought out by the comparison of the food of the wage-workers here and in Europe. The smallest among the American dietaries of this class examined furnished 3,500 Calories of energy per man per day. The average of seven dietaries of 421 persons in Massachusetts, of factory operatives, mechanics, etc., at moderate work, was 4,415 Calories; and that of four dietaries of mechanics and laborers in Connecticut at severe work, 6.705. In this latter the dietary of the Massachusetts brickmakers with their 8,850 Calories was not included. The average of twenty dietaries of wage-workers in the two States named was 5,275 Calories. In a large number of European dietaries of which I have obtained statistics there are many which range from only 1,700 to 1,900 Calories. Of course these are of relatively poor people. The average of eleven dietaries of poorly fed wage-workers in Saxony and Prussia was 2,290. The average of the same number of dietaries of well paid mechanics in Bavaria was 3,150. The largest European dietary I have found

on record for men in ordinary conditions, even with
the severest labor, gives in the neighborhood of 4,500.
The American workingmen whose dietaries were examined were better nourished by half than their trans-
atlantic brethren. These comparisons have, I believe,
a profound significance.

The dietary statistics above cited, taken with the
collateral facts, lead to the inference that ordinary
people have with us what only the exceptionally well-
fed have on the other side of the Atlantic—the food
they need to make the most of themselves and their
work. Indeed, is it not safe to say that so far as the
facts at hand go, they imply very distinctly that to the
American workingman is vouchsafed the priceless gift
which is denied to most people of the world, namely,
the physical conditions, including especially the liberal nourishment, which are essential to large production, high wages, and the highest physical existence, and that as a corollary he has a like peculiar
opportunity for intellectual and moral development
and progress? To my own mind, the saddest part of
the picture that one sees among the industrious and
worthy members of the poorly paid and poorly fed
classes in Europe is not the physical want, but the
spiritual poverty, the lack of buoyancy, the mute,
hopeless endurance of their lives. And, by contrast,
the happiest feature in the condition of wage-workers
with us is not simply that they have better food, better
clothing, better houses, and a better material existence in general, but that they have what these things
bring—the vigor, the ambition, the hope for higher
things—and that their effort leads them to the realization of their hope.

The general principle here urged is that liberal food,
large production, and higher wages go together. If
this be true, the connection between the American's
generous diet and his high wages is very clear. The
question naturally follows: What is to be done for the
future maintenance of the position of our laboring people at home and in their competition with others in the
markets of the world? Part of the answers, at any
rate, must be sought in a reform in the purchase and
use of food. Instead of our present wastefulness,

there must be future saving. With increase of population and closer competition with the rest of the world, the abundance which tempts us to our lavishness must grow gradually less, and closer economy will be needed for living on our present plane of nutrition.

How will the coming man be nourished? If he follows the teaching which the science of nutrition will supply and the teachings of economy will enforce, his diet will be better fitted to his wants. If his work be intellectual, he will avoid excess. If it be physical, he will have enough to make the most of himself and his work. He will learn to economize in the purchase and use of his food, and devote that part of his income which he saves thereby to meeting his higher needs. These considerations suggest another question: Has man yet reached his highest development? The poorer classes of people—and few of us realize how numerous they are—the world over are scantily nourished. The majority of mankind live on a nutritive plane far below that with which we are familiar. We may hope for the best culture, not only of the intellectual powers, but of the higher Christian graces also in the minds and hearts of men, in proportion as the care of their bodies is provided for. Happily, with advance of knowledge comes the improvement of material conditions. May we not hope that the future development of our race will bring that provision for physical wants which is requisite for the best welfare of mind and soul?

Biologists tell us of the improvement in structure and qualities of plants and animals during long periods of development. Notice the sugar beet with its increase from four to sixteen per cent of sugar by proper culture, the development of many flowering plants by the art of the horticulturist, and what is much more to the point, the remarkable improvement in our breeds of domestic animals. Compare the Jersey cow and Shorthorn steer with the best breeds in this country or Europe two centuries ago, or the speed of the race horse with that attained in the last century. If these things are possible with other living things are they not so with man?

THE POSSIBILITIES OF A FUTURE FOOD SUPPLY.

But what of the promise of food for the future? Will the earth produce enough for the use of man? Before coming to the direct answer to this question let us note two or three ways in which the food supply may be increased.

One of these is in the better use of the sea as a source of food for man.

After we have used our food, the refuse, which contains material that should serve to nourish plants to be used as food again, is to a greater or less extent wasted. In various ways an immense amount of plant-food ultimately finds its way through soils, sewers and streams into the sea. What makes the matter worse is that the costliest and most precious of all of the elements of plant-food, nitrogen, is the one which is most carried from the land into this great receptacle. The plant-food thus conveyed to the ocean is commonly looked upon as lost for future use. But we recover it to some extent and may recover far more. Late research has shown that part of the nitrogen is transformed within the waters of the ocean to ammonia, which is continually evaporated from the ocean's surface and carried by winds to the land again, there to be brought to the soil by rain and serve as food for growing plants. The nitrogen is thus passing through a ceaseless round, from air to soil, from soil to plants, from plants to animals and men who use them as food, and then to the sea, from which more or less returns to the air again. But this is not all the saving of nitrogen from the sea. There is vegetation in the sea as well as on the land. That on the land yields us bread and meat. That in the sea yields fish. Here is the source of an almost inexhaustible supply of nourishment for man. Such reliable authorities as the late Professor Baird, of the United States Fish Commission, and Professor Huxley, serving in a similar capacity in England, have made calculations of the quantities of fish in the rivers, the lakes and the sea, and of the possibility of increasing this supply by fish culture. The conclusion as to the amounts of fish which may be made available for food for man seem, almost incredible, until we look into the facts and find how well they are founded.

Few who have not studied the subject realize the possibilities of crop-growing by irrigation. The lands of Egypt, that would otherwise be a desert, have been kept in fertility for centuries by the overflow of the Nile; the irrigated plains of Lombardy can yield nine crops of grass in a single year; the sewage farms of England over which is spread the sewage of cities that usually flows direct into the streams, yield almost fabulous produce. In the geographies that were used in our schools a generation or two ago, a large portion of the territory between the Mississippi and the Pacific was designated as the "Great American Desert." The largest yield of corn in the United States now and for years past has come from the midst of this region and without increase of water supply except that which comes with tillage, and by irrigation portions of it are made to rival the plains of Lombardy and Egypt.

Already our government is preparing the way for a vast system of irrigation. It is proposed to build dams and make reservoirs in the mountains of the west to hold the waters of winter until the time for them to bring their store of food for the nourishment of plants and to enable them to withstand the summer drought In the belief of those who have studied the matter most thoroughly, such an enterprise put into effect will make the region, which covers two-fifths of the whole United States, the garden of the continent, and capable of sustaining a population as dense as that of Italy or Spain.

There are those who prophesy that the agriculture of the future will be carried on largely by irrigation, and the more one looks into the matter the more plausible the idea appears. But tillage and manuring without irrigation work wonders in farming. The produce which the Prussian farmer gets from his sandy plains excels that of our virgin prairies. Countless illustrations of this could be cited.

Prince Kropotkin describes a case in point:
' If we want . . . . to know what agriculture
can be, and what can be grown on a given amount of
soil, we must apply for information to the market-
gardening culture in this country, in the neighbor-
hoods of Paris, Amiens, and other large cities, in
France and in Holland. There we shall learn that
each hundred acres, under proper culture, yield food,
not for forty human beings as they do on our best
farms, but for 200 and 300 persons; not for 60 milch
cows as they do yield in the island of Jersey, but for
200 cows and more if necessary. . . . . The gardeners there have created a totally new agriculture.
They smile when we boast about the rotation system
having permitted us to take from the field one crop
every year, or four crops every three years, because
their ambition is to have six, nine, and twelve crops
from the very same plot of land during the twelve
months. They do not understand our talk about good
and bad soils, because they make the soils themselves,
and make it in such quantities as to be compelled
yearly to sell some of it; otherwise it would raise up
the level of their gardens by half an inch every year.
They aim at cropping, not five or six tons of grass on
the acre, as we do, but from fifty to one hundred
tons of various vegetables on the same space; not 5£
worth of hay, but 100£ worth of vegetables, of the
plainest description, cabbage and carrots. That is
where agriculture is going now."

Of this *culture maraichère*, the distinctive feature
of which is replanting, Prince Kropotkin says:

"In such a culture the primitive condition of the soil
is of little account, because loam is made out of the
old forcing beds. . . . . No less than 2,125 acres
are cultivated about Paris in that way by 5,000 persons and thus not only the 2,000,000 Parisians are
supplied with vegetables but the surplus is also sent
to London.

"The above results are obtained with the help of
warm frames, thousands of glass bells, and so on. But
even without such costly things, with only thirty-six
yards of frames for seedlings, vegetables are grown
in the open air to the value of 200£ per acre, and even,

with some most successful gardeners, 200 £ on the half-acre. . . . . In fact, we are totally unable to realize what the soil will give, unless we have seen its liberality with our own eyes. Let me add also that all this wonderful culture is a yesterday's growth. Thirty years ago the *culture maraichère* was quite primitive. But now the Paris gardener not only defies the soil— he would grow the same crops on an asphalt pavement—he defies climate. His walls, built to reflect light and to protect the wall-trees from the northern winds, his wall-tree shades and glass protectors, his frames and pépinières have made a real garden, a rich Southern garden, out of the suburbs of Paris. He has given to Paris the 'two degrees less of latitude' after which a French scientist was longing; he supplies his city with mountains of grapes and fruit at any season; and in the early spring he inundates and perfumes it with flowers. But he does not only grow articles of luxury. The culture of plain vegetables on a larger scale is spreading every year; and the results are so good that there are now practical maraichères who venture to maintain that if all the food, animal and vegetable, necessary for the 3,500,000 inhabitants of the departments of Seine and Seine-et-Oise had to be grown on their own territory (3,250 square miles), it could be grown without resorting to any other methods of culture than those already in use, methods already tested on a larger scale and proved to be successful."

The essential features of this system are the selecting of vigorous plants, providing them with proper warmth and moisture, especially in their earlier growth, transplanting them so as to give them the best opportunity for development, and supplying them with abundant food. All this is simply the practical application of the principles which modern science is coming to explain. It is the improvement of varieties of plants and the economizing of plant food and energy.

Prince Kropotkin adds, "that in the hands of men there are no unfertile soils; that the most fertile soils are not in the prairies of America, nor in the Russian steppes; that they are in the peat bogs of Ireland, on the sand-downs of the Northern sea cost, on the craggy mountains of the Rhine, where they have been made by men's hands." The experience of tillers of the soil past and present, explained by modern science, upholds his statement. More than this; there is valid ground to expect that the food-production of the future may far exceed anything that these state· ments can even suggest.

Toward the realization of all these things that agency which is the fruit of rationally interpreted experience, and to which we give the name of science, is an indispensable and most efficient aid.

"About the middle of the last century a lighthouse, known as the Dunston Pillar, was built on Lincoln Heath, in Lincolnshire. England. It was erected to guide travelers over a trackless, barren waste, a very desert, almost in the heart of England; and long it served its useful purpose. The pillar, no longer a lighthouse, now stands in the midst of a rich and fertile farming region, where all the land is in high cultivation. For many years no barren heath has been visible, even from its top. Superphosphates of lime, a chemical invention, first applied to land by the British chemist Murray, and brought to the notice of reading farmers by Baron Liebig, has been the chief means through which this great change was effected. Superphosphates over great stretches of English soil makes, or once made, the turnip crop. Turnips there support sheep, and with sheep the English farmer has been · able to get rich on the poorest light lands."

Had no chemists busied themselves to find out what makes plants grow, and had practical farmers not been ready to use their discoveries. Lincoln Heath would perhaps still remain a waste. What is true of this bit of English soil is true in greater or less degree of wide areas of our own and other lands. Whether poor by nature or exhausted by cropping without return of the plant food taken away, soils can be made fruitful by proper treatment How to do this science helps us to find out. The veteran agricultural chemist, Professor Johnson of Yale University, Director of the Connecticut Agricultural Experiment Station, who cites the above instance, tells the exact truth in saying further:

"Agriculture, as well as other industries, has received large benefits from the systematic investigations of science. Chemistry, for example, has taught agriculture how to utilize the refuse of slaughter horses and fisheries—the bones, the flesh, the blood, which but a few years ago were waste, a nuisance and a peril to the public health. It has found vast mines of fossil phosphates in England, Norway, Spain, France, Germany, Russia, in Austria, Canada, and many parts of the United States; and has shown how they may be quickly and profitably converted into a precious fertilizer.

"Chemistry, by discovering and actually defining the food elements of vegetable growth, and by revealing their sources and realizing the means of making them cheaply available to the farmers, has triumphantly overcome one of the previously insuperable obstacles to the development of national wealth.

"Italy, Germany, France, Britain, and the United States have seen or are seeing the productiveness of thousands of their fields decline to a profitless minimum, until lands once beautiful with harvests are desolate and abandoned. But the artificial barrenness and exhaustion, like the natural barrenness of the heath, or sand-down, yields to the touch of science; and in all the older countries I have named, the work of reclamation is in full progress, and barring some great calamity of politics or nature, we are confident that the producing power of their soil will never again be less than now, but will increase many fold in the future, until they become gardens in all their breadth and to the very hill-tops."

THE DOCTRINE OF MALTHUS AND THE FOOD SUPPLY OF THE FUTURE.

This last statement promises wonderful things   It also brings us to the gist of the whole matter.

The doctrine of Malthus regarding the future food supply of the world and the ultimate starvation of a portion of the race, has been greatly misrepresented, but even the most favorable interpretation is a gloomy one. Briefly stated, the theory is that population increases

in a geometrical, and food supply in an arithmetical ratio and hence the time must come when there will
not be food enough. Perhaps the simplest and most
correct reply to it is that the assumption that the
race increases and will continue to increase in a geometrical ratio is not borne out by observed facts. The
theory that the food-supply increases in only arithmetical ratio and must ultimately reach its limit is doubtless nearer the truth. But while there is a limit to
the possible production of food, it transcends all the
ideas that ever occurred to Malthus or to the people
of his time. It has always been assumed that the capacity of the soil to produce plants is measured by
what is popularly called its fertility; that is to say,
the amount of production possible under ordinary conditions of culture. The science of to-day, however,
shows this measure to be incorrect, and the practice
of agriculture is already beginning to add its testimony
to the same effect. And remarkable as is the story
told of fertility in market gardens, the reclaiming of
the desert and in irrigation, it is only the first chapter
of a tale whose already attested wonders almost rival
those of the Arabian Nights.

The fundamental mistake out of which grew the
gloomy doctrines of the older theorists was in meas-
uring the possibilities of production by what they knew
of soil culture. Science had not revealed to them that,
aside from proper temperature and moisture, the
essential factor in vegetable production is plant food;
that this may be given to the plant without the aid
of the soil; that what they understood by soil fertility
is a comparatively unessential factor of agricultural
production; that in short, the possibilities of the food
supply in the future are measureless. Since some
of these facts are of comparatively late discovery and
not very generally understood and their bearing upon
the present question is not always appreciated, they
demand, perhaps, a few words of explanation here.

Modern research, in discovering the laws of nutrition
and growth of plants, has shown that they can flourish on the most barren soil or even without any soil
at all. Of the materials that make up the plant, only
a very small proportion, say two per cent or there-

abouts of the weight of grass when ready to be made into hay and a still smaller proportion of the ripened grain of wheat or corn, for instance, has come from the soil, the rest has been supplied by the air from its stores, which are inexhaustible. If we heat a wisp of hay, a grain of wheat or a piece of potato, in an oven long enough, it will be dried. The water thus driven out came from the air, though the plant obtained most, if not all, of it from the soil through its roots.

If we put the dried material into the fire, the bulk of it will burn away and only ashes will remain. The combustible portion consists mainly of four chemical elements, carbon, oxygen, hydrogen, and nitrogen. The carbon was obtained by the plant from the air, mainly through its leaves. Oxygen and hydrogen are the constituents of the water, which the air also furnished, and the nitrogen likewise came from the air, though a large part of it (until lately it has been claimed that practically all), was first accumulated in the soil and taken up by the plant roots.

The only food which the soil supplies to plants from its original sources is the small quantity of mineral matter which we call ashes when the plant is burned. Of every hundred pounds of the flour we use for bread or the pasture grass from which cattle feed and our meat is made, only a little over a pound in the case of the flour and about two pounds in the case of the grass was furnished by the soil on which the wheat and grass were grown. And that small quantity which the soil contributes from its own original stores is made up of a certain list of chemical elements the majority of which are contained in ordinary soils in such abundance that the cropping of ages would not begin to exhaust them.

It is hard to think of anything more barren, more destitute of fertility, than sea-sand. In connection with some studies of the chemistry of vegetable production in the laboratory of Wesleyan University, we have been growing plants in just such sand, brought from the shore of Long Island Sound. To divest it of every possible trace of material which the plants might use for food except, the sand itself, it was carefully washed with water and then heated. The young man who prepared the sand for use, in his zeal to burn out the last vestiges of extraneous matter, heated the iron pots in which it was calcined so hot that they almost melted. The sand was put in glass jars, water was added, and minute quantities of chemical salts, which plants take from the soil, were dissolved in it. In the sand thus watered and fertilized, dwarf peas were grown. Peas of the same kind were culti vated by a skillful gardener in the rich soil of a gar-den close by and grew to a height of about four feet, while those in the sand with the water and the mi-nute quantities of chemical salts reached a height of eight feet.

This is an old story. For that matter, plants will thrive without even the sand. Experimenters have devised the method of water-culture, by which plants are grown, not in soil at all, but with their roots immersed in water in which are dissolved the ingredients of their food which the roots ordinarily gather from the soil. The stems and branches are upheld by ap-propriate supports. Thus cultivated, they are in every way healthy and attain a more than tropical luxuri-ance, a development rarely equaled in field culture. This method of growing plants by water culture, as it is called, has been developed in Germany more than anywhere else. Professor Wolff, of the Agricultural Ex-periment Station in Hohenheim, raised four oat plants in this way with 46 stems and 1,335 well-developed seeds. Professor Nobbe, of the Experiment Station in Tharand, thus grew in jars of water a Japanese buckwheat plant, nine feet high, weighing, when air-dry, 4,786 fold as much as the seed from which it was produced and bearing 796 ripe and 108 imperfect seeds. Wheat, maize and other plants, and even trees, are grown in this way. Professor Nobbe now has some trees produced by water culture from seeds of others which also had never been in soil at all, but had grown with their roots immersed in water. The requisites for such plant growth are proper temperature, water, and certain elements of plant-food, of which very minute quantities suffice. Given these and the air will supply the rest, and if other conditions are right, abundant yield will be sure.

The experimenters have found just what are the chemical elements that plants take up by their roots. The list includes phosphoric acid, sulphuric acid, chlorine, iron, lime, magnesia, potash, and, for many plants, at any rate, some compounds of nitrogen. It transpires that the most of these substances exist in abundance in even the most barren soils. Iron and chlorine never, magnesia rarely, and the sulphuric acid and lime seldom fail to be supplied in abundance. The elements most frequently lacking in our ordinary soils are phosphorus which is contained in phosphoric acid; potassium, the basis of potash; and nitrogen. These soil elements are quickest exhausted in our ordinary way of farming; it is they more than any other that are wanting in worn out land, and they are the most precious constituents of manure. With plenty of them and proper water supply, we need have no fear for the agriculture or the world's food-supply of the future.

Although it has been reserved for the science of the present to show that warmth, water and plant food are the prime factors of successful crop-growing, the principle has been acted upon from time immemorial. It is at the basis of the irrigation that has been practiced since the most ancient times. It is actually applied in market gardens about Paris, where such surprising results are obtained; on the sands of Belgium and Holland, that yield food for a dense population, and on the soils of North Germany, which, though they are naturally poor, and have been in cultivation for many centuries, excel to-day the rich soils of our new West in their produce. Not the natural fertility of the soil, but its rational culture, is what brings the largest, the surest, the most enduring harvests.

THE FUTURE SUPPLY OF PLANT FOOD.

But can we obtain the phosphoric acid, the potash and the nitrogen? It seems to be a law of human progress that when a great want is defined, the discovery of its supply soon follows. When advancing science had revealed the need of phosphoric acid in poor and exhausted soils, mines of phosphate were

found in England, France. Germany, Spain, the islands of Caribbean Sea, Canada, different parts of the
United States, and elsewhere, and the already visible
supply, that which has been discovered in the present
century, is sufficient for the agriculture of untold thousands of years to come.

For the potash there was for a time no adequate
promise. The soapmaker long ago outbid the farmer
for the potash of wood ashes; that of saltpeter is very
limited in quantity, and wanted for making gunpowder,
salting meat, and other purposes. A process was invented for obtaining potash from sea water, which
contains a very minute percentage, but the cost of ex-
traction was too great to make it feasible. But some
years ago it was discovered that this costly process of
evaporation had been carried out on an immense
scale, in past geologic time, over an area of some
sixty square miles, in the region of Staasfurth, in Germany, and that in this almost inexhaustible bed of sea
salt, the potash compounds were on the top. The
use of the German potash salts speedily became common in European agriculture and has extended to the
United States and to the coffee fields of Brazil and
Ceylon. The results have been remarkable. Muriate
of potash, mined and refined in Germany, brought to
this country, and applied at the rate of one hundred
and fifty pounds, costing $3.50, per acre, on the worn-
out soil of a farm within a mile and a half from where
I am now writing, has made the difference between
corn so poor as to be hardly worth the husking and
a crop of sixty bushels per acre of the finest shelled
corn and a most excellent growth of stalks. Even if
in the far distant future the Staasfurth potash mines
should be exhausted, it is by no means improbable
that others may be found. It is evident, then, that we
need not be troubled about the phosphoric acid or the
potash.

With the nitrogen the case has, until lately, been
somewhat different. Although four-fifths of the air
are made up of this element, and over every acre of
land there are hundreds of tons of it, crops often fail
for lack of it. The prevailing doctrine has been that
plants do not avail themselves of the nitrogen of the

air to any extent, but are dependent solely on that which has been accumulated in the soil in past time or is supplied as manure. The scientific interest of the subject and its incalculable importance have made the question of the acquisition of atmospheric nitrogen by plants one of the hardest fought in the annals of biological and agricultural chemistry.

That plants should be without this power appears strange, and many observed facts in agricultural practice imply, very decidedly, that leguminous plants, such as clover, vetch, beans, and peas, somehow succeed in getting hold of the free nitrogen of the air and using it for their growth. But the experiments of the most noted investigators have seemed to bring positive evidence to the contrary, and the prevalent doctrine has been that atmospheric nitrogen is not available to vegetation.

In discussing "The Economy of Nitrogen" from the standpoint of the then prevalent view, a writer in the Quarterly Journal of Science, some fifteen years ago, said,—"To economize nitrogen, phosphorus, and potash, to recover these bodies from waste, and to find substitutes for their present 'profligate' applications is the most sacred task which the chemist can take in hand. The reforms which may shield us from occasional pestilence sink into insignificance compared with those required to guard posterity, in a not very remote future, from chronic scarcity, from recurrent famine, and from a wolfish struggle for food, in which man must relapse into a worse savagery than that from which he has emerged."

The evidence against the assimilation of atmospheric nitrogen by plants came from experiments in which the conditions differed considerably from those of ordinary plant growth. In a series of experiments by the writer, the results of which were published in 1883, plants (peas) were grown in sand to which water with plant-food in solution was applied, but under conditions otherwise normal. They were found to contain, when ripe, much more nitrogen than was supplied in the nutritive solution and seed. The only possible source of this extra nitrogen was the air. A conclusion, so opposed to the commonly accepted belief, was received with hesitation, and very naturally so. But in the years following, a number of other experimenters obtained similar results Several, among whom Professor Berthelot of Paris is chief, have found evidence that soils acquire nitrogen from the air to a much greater extent than was formerly supposed, and it is now probable that they get this nitrogen by the aid of micro-organisms. And what is still more to the point, Professor Hellriegel, of Germany, has, during the past ten years, made several hundred experiments and not only found that the leguminous plants, pea, lupine and serradella, which he has grown, acquire large amounts of the free nitrogen from the air, but has brought very strong proof that microbes are the agents by which it is done. These results have been most abundantly confirmed by those of a number of other investigators.

How many species of plants have this power of getting nitrogen for themselves from the air, and the details of their ways of doing it, are matters still to be found out. But it is certain that clover, and probable that the legumes in general, have this power. That this is all true is being admitted to-day even by those who have formerly been the strongest upholders of the opposing doctrine.

The practical bearing of all this is evident. Nitrogen is the costliest of the elements of plant-food used in fertilizers. Farmers throughout the older portions of our country and in Europe pay from 10 to 25 cents per pound and more for it in guano, nitrate of soda, sulphate of ammonia, dried blood, meat scrap, and other commercial fertilizers. For these materials the farmers of the United States expend millions of dollars, and the supply of some of them is being gradually used up. By raising leguminous crops which are in many ways the most valuable for fodder, this nitrogen can be had from the air without money and without price.

ENERGY AND FOOD-PRODUCTION.

The supply of plant food thus seems to be assured. But the population of the earth may become so dense that very general irrigation will be necessary. The rivers, the lakes and the sea will furnish water, if it can only be transported. This requires power, energy. Will the energy be forthcoming? Is it at hand?

We are accustomed to think of burning wood and coal as the chief sources of power. But their energy is nothing in comparison with that of moving wind, rivers and tide, and even that fades into insignificance in comparison with the energy of the sun's heat, a source of power so great that we can scarcely conceive of its vastness. When we reflect that, remarkable as are the uses we already make of the different forms of energy, our knowledge of them is still in its infancy, that we are apparently much nearer the storage and transport of the energy of stream and wind and sun than our grandfathers were to what we realize to-day in the use of steam and electricity, it takes no great faith to believe that science and invention will, in due time, supply the need. And with this use of mind to make the forces of nature do what has before been either done by the labor of our hands or left undone, the natural order of events will continue to bring what the progress of the past has brought, more product and larger profit with less manual toil.

Instead of the yield of a dozen bushels of wheat from the poor or exhausted soil of an acre, which was, a comparatively few years ago, a common average in England and is to-day in a large portion of the United States, thirty bushels of wheat per acre has come to be an average with better culture in England and will come with us when the demand calls for it. It is not to such increase as this, however, that we must look for the food supply of the future, but to such yields as come with sand and water culture. We are not restricted to the thirty or sixty or one hundred fold of the New Testament parable, but may look for the thousand-fold that is realized with abundant supply of plant food and water without any regard to soil.

Nor is there anything abnormal in such vegetable production. That a single plant should produce eight hundred seeds, as Professor Noble's buckwheat plant did, when fifty would be a large yield in ordinary practice; that the produce of a given area should

be scores or even hundreds of times what we ordinarily
see; that half a dozen crops should be grown on the
same area every year instead of one, is not what we are
accustomed to, but is not at all unnatural. What we
call luxuriant growth is really stunted growth. Our
plants are subject to fluctuation of temperature; they
have too much or too little moisture; their food-supply
is scant or one-sided, and the very hindrances to their
growth have had the further effect of preventing the development of varieties capable of producing the largest
amount of the most valuable material. Let plants be
trained by selection and cultivation to do their best;
let them have the opportunity which comes with proper
regulation of temperature and moisture and food;
then perhaps we shall see what nature can and will
do for us. As well say that the philanthropist is the
abnormal, and the untutored child of nature the normal man, as that there is anything abnormal in such
large vegetable production.

ARTIFICIAL PRODUCTION OF FOOD.   CHEMICAL SYNTHESIS.

But even if there were no such probability of almost
unlimited vegetable production, there is still a possibility for food-supply in artificial manufacture by
chemical process. Plants take the elements, carbon,
oxygen, hydrogen and nitrogen, and combine them,
in the forms of starch, sugar, oils, gluten and other
compounds which serve to nourish animals and man.
Within the memory of many chemists now living, it
was believed to be impossible to build up such compounds from their elements by artificial means. But
chemistry has found means to imitate these processes
of combination. Within the past few years many such
compounds have been produced in the laboratory by
synthesis. The advance of science in this direction
is not enough to warrant any prophecy of the synthesis of food-material—indeed, such a feat seems almost
visionary—but it is hardly safe to say that it is impossible, and there are those who are confident that
it will be done.

Farming by water culture or the artificial manufacture of food-compounds would not be feasible or
profitable to-day. The growing of a buckwheat plant

with a thousand seeds and the synthesis of sugar and protein are now only curious and costly experiments, but will they always be so?

A few years ago an interesting but troublesome lecture experiment consisted in providing a large galvanic battery and causing the current to pass from one piece of carbon to another. A bright light was produced and there were persons with faith enough to predict that electric lighting would at some time in the distant future be made a practical success. The light of the electric lamp at every street corner suggests most forcibly that we may be nearer the realization of other triumphs than we think. What we know of these things to-day more than the Romans knew sixteen centuries ago has nearly all been discovered within the last sixty years. The rate of discovery far exceeds the rate of increase of population. Long before population becomes dense enough to demand such production as I have been suggesting, we may hope that the details will have been worked out to make it easily feasible.

A German chemist, Professor Knop, wrote a book on agricultural chemistry. When it was done he gave it the title *Der Kreislauf des Stoffs;* the Circulation of Matter. He realized that he had been simply describing the way in which the elements pass through a ceaseless round of changes by which they are made parts of air and earth, then of plants and animals and man, then of air and earth again. In this round our food is made, our bodies are built up, and then both are resolved into their elements again. Chemical elements are combined by natural forces into starch and protein; into bread and meat, into muscle and brain. The supply of the elements is limitless, for the simple reason that none is ever lost. Like the water which, after moistening the soil and nourishing the plant passes away to sea or sky only to come again as rain, the elements of food are resolved into their simpler forms only to be formed into food again. How much food mankind may have is not a question of area, of arable land, or of soil fertility at all, but of man's control of the forces of nature. That control increases with the increase of human knowledge.

In the past man has had the strength of his hands and that of the beast which he has subjected to his will to do his work. In the present he uses the power that came from the sun and is stored in the coal. This makes possible the industrial advancement, the lessening of the hours of labor, the rise of the scale of living, and the spread of knowledge. The material and intellectual progress of the nineteenth century is the using of potential energy.

With a supply of material exhaustless and enduring as air and water, with power to utilize it unbounded as the supply of the sun, with prospect of new discovery unlimited as the sphere of human knowledge, what bound dare we set, what fear need we entertain, for man's future sustenance?

The role of the political economist is hardly fitting for the chemist. But one inference continually occurs to me. To make manufactured products abundant and cheap, large demand has been necessary. With the hand-loom of the past, a given number of people, living in a given area, could weave a small amount of cloth. In the factory of the present, each operative produces many times more than the weaver of the olden time, many more work in a given territory, and cloth is produced at a much lower price. The agriculture of the future will perhaps be a manufacturing process with correspondingly increased product. It may seem paradoxical to say that the dense population, which the older economy told us is to be the precursor of starvation, will be actually the antecedent condition of a cheap and abundant food supply; but is this anything more really than the re-assertion of a principle which has proven itself true in the manufacture of cloth in the factory, of machinery in the machine shop, and in countless other ways?

To resume briefly. In the light of our present knowledge, the problem of the world's future food supply is conditioned upon two things. One is plant food, the other is energy, power to manufacture and transport plant food and to transport water. The visible supply of plant food is such that the only element about which there has for some time been any question is nitrogen. Late research implies that this can be

easily derived from the atmosphere in unlimited quantity. With the unmeasured energy of the wind, flowing water and tide, to say nothing of the immensely
greater energy of the sun's heat, and the possibility
of storage, transfer and use of energy by electricity
and other agencies, we may hope that the science of
the future will provide the power. The amount of
vegetable growth that is possible within a given area
is entirely outside our ordinary calculations. The old
way of estimating possible food-production by land
area and soil fertility is wrong. We have only to
assume that as the population of the earth increases,
there will be a corresponding improvement in the use
of plant-food and energy, cf which the supply is
practically inexhaustible, and the problem is solved.

So strangely yet simply it comes about, that in the
providing of what is essential for the best welfare and
highest happiness of mankind in the future, the things
which have seemed farthest from our reach, nitrogen
and energy, are the very ones which Providence places
about us at all times and in utterly inexhaustible
amounts. To make them available requires only the
pushing of discovery a little farther along the lines
in which it is now moving rapidly and surely. To
make a practical use of them requires only the demand
for the product. If it is conceivable that population
should become so dense as to demand far more food
than can be thus produced by natural growth of plants,
there still remain the sources of artificial production.
And if it be allowable to reason from analogy, what
is needed to make food more abundant and more
cheap is enough population to make sufficient demand.

The capacity of men to consume food is limited.
The possibility of its production is almost limitless.
The very increase of population which the Malthusian
doctrine makes the cause of starvation will thus become the condition of cheap and abundant sustenance.
So the use of man's brain transforms the prospect of
dire calamity, of misery ineffable, into the promise of inexpressible blessing.

The doctrine of Malthus is the product of a time
when men's thoughts ran in gloomy channels, when
a current theology taught that millions of God's crea-

tures were foreordained to eternal torment, when a
stern logic, arguing ruthlessly from premises which
to-day we cannot accept, led to conclusions at utter
variance with the kinder teachings of nature and revelation, and the gentler aspirations of the human soul.

From the primeval curse, "In the sweat of thy face
shalt thou eat bread," human progress is bringing
knowledge, which is power, as a belief. This replacing of labor of the hand by the labor of the brain,
this enlarging of means to support men's bodies and
to improve their minds, this saving from want, increase of profits, and elevation of physical and intellectual living, all this is the fruit of experiment and
experience, of that definitely acquired and classified
knowledge to which we give the name of science and
which is advancing so rapidly in our time. If so much
has already been discovered, and so much has been
reaped, what may we not hope for in the future?

War, pestilence and famine will not be needed to
remove part of the people of the earth in order that
the rest may be kept from starving. Instead of using
the sword to kill, it may be turned into the plow-
share to help abundant harvests. Pestilence, once
thought to be the visitation of Divine wrath, we
know to be the work of the microbes of disease. Not
only are we finding how to prevent the ravages of
these creatures, but we are learning that they are the
upholders as well as the destroyers of life, and may
be the agents to protect our children from the very
starvation our fathers so much dreaded. In place of
the rule of famine, which has been prophesied, we
have the promise of a reign of plenty.

The doctrine here maintained is optimistic, decidedly so. But what was the earth made for? Is it
governed by a beneficent power or is it not? Are
mankind the creatures of Almighty malevolence or are
we the children of a loving, as well as omnipotent
Father? Are we placed here in a world which is bad
and growing ever worse, or is there a continual evolution toward higher and better and happier things?
Faith has always had its reply to Malthusian pessimism,
though that reply has been vague. The science of
to-day makes it clear. So faith and science, rightly
joined, ever lead us to the light.

ABSTRACT OF THE DISCUSSION.

Mr. John C. Welch:—

Professor Atwater has given us an eloquent and instructive discourse, which cannot fail to add to the potential energy of our minds.

It was my lot to conduct experiments in the use of food, that were not laboratory experiments, like many interesting ones to which Professor Atwater has referred, and they were involuntary.

When a man goes to war, and takes upon himself the vicissitudes of actual campaigning in the field, the process by which his body receives its nourishment is apt to undergo very much of a revolution; he finds that many forms of taking food are purely conventional; that regularity is not the thing that he had deemed it to be; that choice of viands is largely a matter of indifference in maintaining health and strength; and he is able to emancipate himself in great degree from what we now call a slavery in the use of food, to which many are subject.

To illustrate our indifference to the forms of taking food, and to what we take, I will refer to some of my war experiences.

Aside from participating in campaigns in the field, it was my lot to be a prisoner of war, and also to be an escaping prisoner of war; of the two latter experiences the first lasted between six and seven months, and the second for over a month. Concerning these two I will speak briefly.

The food given us first (there were 1,800 of us captured at Plymouth, North Carolina, in April) was almost exclusively corn bread, about two inches thick, that probably had no constituents but cornmeal, salt and water. Only the absolute necessity of taking food enabled us to eat it at all. We were taken by cars to Georgia, after a march of about fifty miles, the entire trip requiring a number of days. At Savannah there were distributed to us sea-biscuit and bacon, so much to each carload of us, which we were to divide among ourselves. There was no opportunity to cook the bacon, and, in fact, it was not necessary. In comparison with what we had had the bacon and sea-biscuit seemed delicious. We had been comfortably situated at Plymouth for over a year, with abundant and well-prepared food, yet I do not know that we suffered any impairment of health from this sudden change in diet.

I was taken, with about one hundred other officers, to Macon, Georgia, and there my imprisonment commenced; our number presently reached 1,600, being augmented by prisoners from Richmond. We were taken during the summer to Savannah and Charleston and in October to Columbia, S. C. I was more successful than most prisoners in being able to retain some money with me, and with this I each day added slightly to my confederate ration, and maintained an excellent degree of health. And in general our whole camp, which never exceeded 1,600, did, but we had abundance of air. We were outdoors nearly all the time and were not crowded, and we had an abundance of pure water.

In escaping from prison, which I did early in November, I had a varied experience in the use of food. Sweet potatoes and corn from the ear we could easily eat raw when we had no means of cooking them. Pumpkins from the field we could eat by cutting them in halves and cooking them by making a little fire in the woods in the dead of night, inverting the halves over some coals and making a fire over them Persimmons we found on trees at night by the roadside, and after they were thoroughly frosted they proved a most excellent article of food. Meats we only got on a very few occasions on our journey; raw beef was given us by a colored man at one time when we were too nearly famished and the situation was too critical to attempt to cook, and so we ate it raw. Our strength increased over what it had been in prison; we had not an hour's headache or sickness during the thirty-three nights that it required to finish our journey of over 200 miles, although we suffered greatly at times from hunger, weariness, cold, exposure and anxiety.

I cite these facts to show how easily the body is

nourished and how much our ideas are apt to become exaggerated regarding the necessity for and the regularity with which we obtain our food.

I am a great advocate of abstinence from food and an abundance of exercise, and the oxygen that it implies, in the treatment of colds.

What I regard as a curious incident in the use of food occurred to me recently.

On a holiday I sat down in the morning to write an article on a subject in which I was greatly interested and which called out all my powers of thought and expression. I was called from my work about one o'clock to take dinner, and did not intend to resume it for some hours. After dinner, however, I found that I wanted to complete an expression, and took up my pen again. I found to my surprise that my thought flowed as freely as before dinner, and continued to write. The result was that my article was finished before rising, and following this came an attack of indigestion that was not recovered from for a week.

From the pangs of a disordered stomach, Carlyle has said to us, "Take care of your health continually." Sweet morsels may be good but they are not to be run after with an excess of ardor.

> "Ruby wine is drunk by knaves,
> Sugar spends to fatten slaves."

Abernethy, the witty court physician of the early part of the last century, said to one of his patients, as the best advice he could give him, "Live on a shilling a day—and earn it." Emerson has told us we don't need to be coddled and to eat too much cake. And it is well to put on the lintels of our door posts that other phrase of his: "Plain living and high thinking: these are imperative conditions of survival, in the circumstances of our modern life."

Dr Robert G. Eccles:—

The lecturer of the evening has supplied us with an excellent repast and one that has proven to me exceedingly interesting.

I have no criticisms to offer upon it and will merely

supplement it a little in the direction of our main thesis, that of the relation food bears to survival in the struggle for existence. First let me call your attention to the fact that as we recede backward in geologic time the products of the earth become less and less fit for the food of man. At last we reach a point where it would be impossible to find a single plant producing material fit for human food. A little farther back and grasses as well as grains, legumes and starch-producing tubers disappear, so that herbivorous plants of the present type could find nothing fit to eat. Go still farther back and there is nothing that even carnivorous animals could relish. Then recede beyond this and there is nothing but a bare earth, with no food for any living thing. Through all these countless years plants and animals have been mutually evolving material each for the others' food. Change after change has transpired to make conditions fit for life and to make life fit for its conditions. Forever and ever it is one incessant compromise amid the balance of opposing strains. The history of these adjustments is a most intensely interesting one, but too long even to outline at present. The powers of adjustment of an animal's stomach to its environment are always considerable; so that the strain of adversity has to be relatively very great to kill. Geo. Francis Train showed what civilized man could live on when he restricted himself to a peanut diet of five cents per day. The Digger Indians around Walker Lake, Nevada, can exist during the winter on clay. It is an infusorial earth, containing some protoplasm. The character of a climate has also much to do with the kind of food required. The Esquimau prefers blubber to rice and the Chinaman rice to blubber.

The speaker of the evening referred to the fact that the very poor were the most extravagant livers we had among us when their purses would at all allow of it. This fact is true of Brooklyn, as well as of other places referred to. Some years ago Science called upon me to make some inquiries on this subject in my neighborhood. I found from provision dealers that their most tender and dearest meats and their rarest fruits and vegetables were bought by the very poorest.

The middle classes were more saving and bought cheaper but equally wholesome food.

Professor Atwater, in reply, referred to the recent wide interest among scientific investigators in the study of micro-organisms, and the importance of this investigation upon the question of food-material. Properly considered, the microbe is to be classed among the most beneficent agents as affecting the health of the human race. It is an agent of life as well as of death. Microbes enter into the composition of all things serviceable to man.

It is of the utmost importance to check the excessive waste which takes place in the preparation of food and in the use of it. Many of the poorer classes, as Dr. Eccles says, purchase the most expensive food; the middle classes, food of medium quality almost invariably. One reason, doubtless, is the fact that whenever they can, poor people strive to emulate their richer neighbors in some one or two respects if they cannot in all. It is another symptom of the discontent with existing conditions everywhere prevalent. It is, however, an encouraging circumstance rather than otherwise, for it is an indication of progress and is itself caused by an increase of education and a consequent enlargement of wants and desires, by the satisfaction of which men gradually rise to points of yet higher advantage.

We must seek to perfect the educational system, not to repress the desires. The Pratt Institute is a noble example of what should be done in this direction, and is directly in line with what is now most needed—scientific aid in the rational development of the things which will help the industrial classes.

THE ORIGIN OF STRUCTURAL VARIATIONS

BY

EDWARD D. COPE, Ph. D.

Darwin's *Origin of Species, Descent of Man, and Animals and Plants under Domestication;* Haeckel's *History of Creation;* Lyell's *Principles of Geology;* Mivart's *On the Genesis of Species, and Man and Apes;* Cope's *Origin of the Fittest;* Wallace's *Darwinism;* Romanes' *Scientific Evidences of Organic Evolution, and Darwinism;* Huxley's *On the Origin of Species, Manual of the Anatomy of Vertebrated Animals, and Manual of the Anatomy of Invertebrated Animals;* Carpenter's *Nature and Man;* Powell's *Our Heredity from God;* Kemper's *Animal Life as Affected by the Natural Conditions of Existence;* Schmidt's *The Mammalia in their Relation to Primeval Times;* Henslow's *The Origin of Floral Structures;* Nicholson's *The Ancient Life-history of the Earth.*

THE ORIGIN OF STRUCTURAL VARIATIONS.

BY EDWARD D. COPE, PH. D.

I. PRELIMINARY.

If we view the phenomena of organic life from the standpoint of the physicist, the first question that naturally arises in the mind is as to the kind of energy of which it is an exhibition. Ordinary observation shows that organic bodies perform molar movements, and that many of them give out heat. A smaller number exhibit emanations of light and electricity. Very little consideration is sufficient to show that they include among their functions chemical reactions, a conviction which is abundantly sustained by researches into the physiology of both animals and plants. The phenomena of growth are also evidently exhibitions of energy. The term energy is used to express the motion of matter, and the building of an embryo to maturity is evidently accomplished by the movement of matter in certain definite directions. The energy which accomplishes this feat is, however, none of those which characterize inorganic matter, some of which have just been mentioned, but, judging from its phenomena, is of a widely different character. If we further take a broad view of the general process of progressive evolution, which is accomplished by successive modifications of this growth-energy, we see further reason for distinguishing it widely from the inorganic energies.

In considering the dynamics of organic evolution, it will be convenient to commence by considering the claims of Natural Selection to include the energy which underlies the process. That Natural Selection cannot be the cause of the origin of new characters, or variation, was asserted by Darwin;[1] and this opinion is supported by the following weighty considerations:

(1) A selection cannot be the cause of those alternatives from which it selects. The alternatives must be presented before the selection can commence.

(2) Since the number of variations possible to organisms is very great, the probability of the admirably adaptive structures which characterize the latter having arisen by chance is extremely small.

(3) In order that a variation of structure shall survive, it is necessary that it shall appear simultaneously in two individuals of opposite sex. But if the chance of its appearing in one individual is very small, the chance of its appearing in two individuals is very much smaller. But even this concurrence of chances would not be sufficient to secure its survival, since it would be immediately bred out by the immensely preponderant number of individuals which should not possess the variation.

(4) Finally, the characters which define the organic types, so far as they are disclosed by paleontology, have commenced as minute buds or rudiments, of no value whatsoever in the struggle for existence. Natural Selection can only effect the survival of characters when they have attained some functional value.

In order to secure the survival of a new character, that is, of a new type of organism, it is necessary that the variation should appear in a large number of individuals coincidentally and successively. It is exceedingly probable that that is what has occurred in past geologic ages. ›We are thus led to look for a cause which affects equally many individuals at the same time, and continuously. Such causes are found in the changing physical conditions that have succeeded each other in the past history of our planet, and the changes of organic function necessarily produced thereby.

II. BATHMOGENESIS.

It is customary to distinguish broadly between inorganic and organic energies, as those which are displayed by non living and living bodies. This classification is

___
[1] Origin of species, Dd. 1872, p. 65.

inexact, since, as already remarked, nearly all of the inorganic energies are exhibited by living beings. A division which appears to be, with our present knowledge, much more fundamental, is into the energies which tend away from, and those which tend toward, the phenomena of life. In other words, those which are not necessarily phenomena of life, and those which are necessarily such. And the phenomena of life here referred to are the phenomena of growth and evolution, as distinguished from all others. I have termed[2] these classes the Anagenetic, which are exclusively vital, and the Catagenetic, which are physical and chemical. The Anagenetic class tends to upward progress in the organic sense; that is, toward the increasing control of its environment by the organism, and toward the origin and development of consciousness and mind. The Catagenetic energies tend to the creation of a stable equilibrium of matter, in which molar motion is not produced from within, and sensation is impossible. In popular language the one class of energies tends to life; the other to death.

That the Catagenetic energies, whether physical or chemical, tend away from life is clear enough. Thus molar motion, unless continuously supplied, or directed by a living source, speedily ceases, being converted by friction into heat, which is dissipated. And were we to suppose a case where friction is non-existent, motion would remain molar, and no phenomena of organic life would result, and sensation could not arise. The same is true of molecular movements under the same conditions. Chemical reactions, which are fundamental in world-building, result in the production of solids and the radiations of heat. The most familiar example, that of oxidation, presents us with the case of a gas becoming a liquid or a solid with the evolution of heat. The endothermic reaction, where matter undergoes a change of molecular aggregation the reverse of that just mentioned, with the absorption of heat, as in the case of several hydrogen compounds, is rare in nature, where free from organic complications, and is generally soon reversed by further reactions. Finally cosmic creation involves the perpetual

2 The Monist, Chicago, 1893, p. 630.

radiation of heat into space, and the gradual reduction of all forms of matter to the solid state.

In the anagenetic energies, on the other hand, we have a process of building machines which not only resist the action of catagenesis, but which press the catagenetic energies into their service. In the assimilation of inorganic substances they elevate them into higher, that is more complex compounds, and raise the types of energy to their own level. In the development of molar movements they enable their organisms to escape many of the destructive effects of catagenetic energy, by enabling them to change their environment; and this is especially true in so far as sensation or consciousness is present to them. The anagenetic energy transforms the face of nature by its power of assimilating and recompounding inorganic matter, and by its capacity for multiplying its individuals. In spite of the mechanical destructibility of its physical basis (protoplasm), and the ease with which its mechanisms are destroyed, it successfully resists, controls, and remodels the catagenetic energies for its purposes.

The anagenetic power of assimilation of the inorganic substances is chiefly seen in the vegetable kingdom. Atmospheric air, water and inorganic salts furnish it with the materials of its physical basis. Then from its own protoplasm it elaborates by a catagenetic retrograde metamorphosis, the non-nitrogenous substances, as wood (cellulose), waxes, and oils, and the nitrogenous alkaloids, and it may take up inorganic substances and deposit them without alteration in its cells. Many of the compounds elaborated by plants and animals have been manufactured of latter time by chemists. The discovery that the living organism is not necessary for the production of these substances has led to the hasty conclusion that the supposed distinction between "organic" and "inorganic" energy does not exist. But the elaboration of these substances is not accomplished by anagenetic or "vital" energy, but by a process of running down of the higher compound protoplasm, which is catagenesis. No truly anagenetic process has yet been imitated by man.

All forms of functioning of organs, except assimilation, reproduction and growth, are catagenetic. That is, functioning consists in the retrograde metamorphosis of a nitrogenous organic substance or proteid with the setting free of energy. The proteid is decomposed in the functioning tissue into carbon dioxide, water, urea, etc., and energy appears in the muscle as contraction, in the glands as secretion, and in all parts of the body as heat. The general result of physiologic research is, that the decomposition of the blood is the source of energy, while the tissue of each organ determines the character of that energy. That the tissue itself suffers from wear, and requires repair, is also true, but to a less extent than was once supposed.

In the anagenetic process of the growth of the embryo the case is different. Here the processes of functioning of organs are in complete abeyance, the nutritive substance is not entirely broken down in chemical decomposition, but it is in great part elaborated into tissues and organs. All the mechanisms necessary to the mature life of the individual are constructed by the activity of the special form of energy known as growth-energy or Bathmism. It is the modifications of this energy which constitute evolution, and it is these to which we will hereafter direct our attention. Its simplest exhibition is the subdivision of a unicellular protoplasmic body into two or more individuals or structural units of a multicellular organism. Further division of the latter does not abolish the individual, but extends it, and we now observe the elaboration of different structural types to become a conspicuous function of this form of energy. In other words, a once simple energy becomes specialized into specific energies, each of which, once established, pursues its mode of motion in opposition to all other modes not more potent than itself. Besides the evident truth of the proposition that a mode of building is a mode of motion, we have another very good reason for believing in the existence of a class of bathmic or growth-energies. This is found in the phenomena of heredity. The most rational conception of this inheritance of structural characters is the transmission of a mode of motion from the soma to the germ cells. This is a far more conceivable method than that of the transmission of particles of matter, other than the ordinary material of nutrition. The bathmic theory of heredity bears about the same relation to a theory of transmission of the pangenes of Darwin, or the ids of Weismann, as the undulatory theory of light and other forms of radiant energy does to the molecular theory of Newton. I have therefore assumed as a working hypothesis the existence of the bathmic energy, and will inquire how far the facts in our possession sustain it. In doing so it will be necessary to elaborate the theory so as to render clearer its application to specific cases. The fact to be accounted for is its specialization into so many diverse specific forms.

A further indication of the existence of the bathmic energy is the quantitative limitation to which growth is obedient. Thus the successive stages of embryonic growth are limited in number in each species. The dimensions of many species are limited within a definite range. The duration of life, or of the functioning organic machine, has a definite limit in time. All this means that a certain limited quantity of energy is at the disposal of each individual organism.

In "The Origin of the Fittest," I have endeavored to show what causes have been and are efficient in the production of different types of organic life, through the modifications of the bathmic energy. We will now briefly consider the question of the origin of the living substance, protoplasm or sarcode, which exhibits bathmism.

On this subject Professor Manly Miles remarks:[3] "Omitting subordinate details, which represent the separate links in the chain of events, the processes of nutrition may be summarized in general terms as follows: In plants the chemical elements and binary compound on which they feed, are built up by successive steps of increasing complexity and instability into protoplasm, with a storing of the energy made use of in the constructive process, which is derived from the heat and light of the sun. The constructive processes are expressed by the term anabolism, and the products of the different upward steps are called anastatic. Protoplasm, the most complex and unstable

3 Proceeds. Amer. Assoc. Adv. Sci., 1892, p. 203.

of organic substances, is the summit of the ascending
steps of anabolism; and katabolism, which represents
the succeeding downward steps of metabolism, then
follows, and its products or katastates are starch, cellulose, proteids, etc., or what we recognize as the proximate constituents and tissues of plants."

If the tendency of the catagenetic energies is away
from vital phenomena, it is impossible that they, or
any of them, should be the cause of the origin of living matter. This logical inference is confirmed by the
failure of all attempts to demonstrate spontaneous
generation of living organisms from inorganic matter.
Further, the principle of continuity leads us to infer
that the energy which produced organic matter must
be identical with or allied to that which is the efficient
agent in progressive evolution of organisms, and is,
therefore, anagenetic. Such a conclusion may seem
to lead to a dualism which is itself opposed to the
principle of continuity or uniformity, and which is opposed to experience of the phenomena of energy in
general. How is uniformity to be harmonized with
the hypothesis of two types of energy acting in different directions, apparently in opposition to each other?
Since facts and logic do not support the derivation of
the anagenetic from the inorganic energies, can the reverse process, the derivation of the catagenetic from
the anagenetic be and have been the order of nature?
In support of this hypothesis, we have the universal
prevalence of the retrograde metamorphosis of energy
in both the inorganic and organic kingdoms. Phenomena of structural degeneracy are well known in
the organic world, and purely chemical phenomena in
both organic and inorganic processes are all degenerate.
It appears, then, much more probable that catagenesis
succeeds anagenesis as a consequence, and does not
precede it as a cause. In other words, it is more
probable that death is a consequence of life, rather than
that the living is a product of the non-living. I have
therefore given to that energy which is displayed by
the plant in the elaboration of living from non-living
matter the name of antichemism.[4] Thus, while the heat
of the sun is necessary to the building of protoplasm,

4American Naturalist, 1884, p. 979. Origin of the Fittest, 1887, p. 431.

within a certain range of temperature, this form of energy has its opportunity.

In order to present more clearly the views enunciated in the preceding pages, I give a synoptic table of energies.

I	Anagenetic	Organic	$\{$ Antichemism Bathmism.

II Catagenetic	$\{$	Exclusively organic	$\{$ Neurism. Myism.
		Inorganic and organic	Radiant Energy Chemism. Cohesion. Gravitation.

The innumerable structures which are due to the activity of Bathmisms may be supposed to result from the composition of the inherited form with energies which are derived from sources external to the germ plasma, whether within the soma or external to it. These interferences produce new and specific types of energy. The inherited Bathmism I have termed "simple growth force" and the modified forms I have termed "grade growth force." [5] It appears that these types of energy should be distinguished by special names. Hence I propose to restrict the term Bathmism to the modified or "grade" growth force, and term the inherited or "simple" type of growth force, Emphytism. [6] As a matter of fact pure emphytism can only be observed in the embryos of sexless or parthenogenetic origin and in the repair of tissues.

Ryder has called the exhibition of growth energy Ergogenesis, and he calls attention to the fact that it appears under two aspects. In the first, Ergogenesis is due to mechanical causes resident in the organism exclusively, and consists of the physical tensions inherent in protoplasm under all the conditions of growth. With these the growth energies have to reckon, as they are the conditions which underly them. They are not, however, strictly speaking, growth energies, but would be exhibited by any similar colloid under similar conditions. To the movements due to physical causes under these circumstances, Ryder gives the

5 Proceeds. Amer. Philosoph. Society, 1871, p. 253.

6 I have supposed in a late paper American Naturalist, 1894, p. 212) that this is the Statogenic energy of Ryder. This mistake is now corrected.

name of Statogenesis.[7] The second aspect of the en ergies necessary to growth is present under the two forms already referred to, as Emphytism and Batnmism. The latter class, or interference energies, are natu rally differentiated into those which are due to physical (or chemical) external agencies (molecular move- ments), and those that are due to molar movements, as expressed in tissues, as impact, strain, etc. To the former I have given the name of Physiobathmism, and to the latter, Kinetobathmism.[8]

The relations of these forms of energy may be rep- resented in tabular form as follows:

Ergogenesis

Catagenetic *Statogenesis.*

Anagenetic $\left\{\begin{array}{l} \text{Inherited,} \quad\quad \textit{Emphytogenesis.} \\ \text{With interference} \\ \quad\quad\quad\quad \textit{Bathmogenesis} \left\{\begin{array}{ll} \text{Molecular } \textit{Physiogenesis.} \\ \text{Molar} \quad\quad \textit{Kinetogenesis.} \end{array}\right. \end{array}\right.$

Emphytogenesis I shall hereafter endeavor to show is an automatic (catagenetic) product of Bathmogen- esis.

I believe that the above table is simply a classifica- tion and formulation of the innumerable well known facts of organic growth and evolution.

The first step in the order of Bathmogenetic action is the effect of stimuli on an animal which is no longer protected by the parent or by parental products (egg- shell) as an embryo. Changes may be effected in the weight, color, and in functional capacity by temper- ature, humidity, food, etc., thus exhibiting physio- genesis. Or changes in the size and forms of parts of the body may be produced by movements of the organ- ism, or of its environment, so displaying Kinetogen- esis. So long as these modifications of structure should be confined to the individuals thus modified, there would be no evolution. A second generation, if not subjected to the same stimuli, would not possess the modifications; and their possession of them would depend entirely on the amount of stimulus. In other words, there would be no accumulation of modifica-

7 Proceeds. Amer. Philos. Society, 1893, p. 194.

8 American Naturalist, 1894, p. 214. The two types of growth are then Physio- genesis and Kinetogenesis. (Origin of the Fittest, 1887, p. 423.)

tion. It has, however, been generally believed that these modifications are inherited, and I think it can be shown that this belief rests on a solid basis. Meanwhile I call the Bathmogenesis which does not extend beyond the generation in which it appears, auto-bathmogeny.

The quantitative relation which necessarily exists between Bathmism and its sources may be expressed as follows, with due recognition of the fact that such expression does not rest upon any experimental tests. Emphytogenesis is work done in the construction of tissues like those of the parent and without interference. Here we have the molecular energy of the parent (either as protozoon or oösperm) temporarily converted in part into the molar movements observed to be concomitants of segmentation; to be represented in the completed tissue by the mutual tensions by virtue of which each structural element maintains its integrity. It is evidently a process of metamorphosis of energy in which there is less waste than in any other known to us. Embryonic growth is accompanied by a very slight dissipation of heat, though a slight rise of temperature is noticeable in the eggs of cold-blooded animals and in flowers, when reproduction is active. The products of breaking down are equally rare in embryonic growth, and both this and the dissipation of heat are evidently largely due to the changes wrought in non-cleavable nutritive substances with which the yolks are sometimes charged. It is probably to accomplish this process that the oxygen necessary for the embryonic growth is used. How much loss is due to cell division itself is not known, but it must be very little if any. We have here a nearly perfect conversion of energy. Theoretically we have anagenesis wherever the up-building exceeds the down-breaking.

The attempt to realize in the imagination the modus operandi of bathmic energy in embryo building takes the following form. It is to be supposed that movement which has been most frequently repeated, and for the longest period, is prepotent, and takes precedence of all others. This is clearly simple cell division, which follows the nutrition supplied by the spermatozoön, and which represents the first act of animal life. Hence, segmentation of the oösperm is the first movement of bathmism. Each subsequent movement appears in the order of potency, which is, other things being equal, a time order, or the order of record. The cause of the localization of tissues and structures is much more difficult to understand than the cause of the order of their appearance. The more energetic part of the process naturally requires the greater space for its products. The ectoderm, which becomes the seat of the nervous axis and its muscular adjuncts, occupies the superficial portions of the yolk. Hence, we may regard this expression of the structural record of these functions as more energetic than that of the record structure of the nutritive functions, which displays itself below the ectoderm. In microblastic and amphiblastic embryos, the segmentation which develops the nutritive tissues is evidently more sluggish, for the cells are larger and fewer in number than those of the ectoderm.

External stimuli modify the course of emphytogeny above described, and by producing new structural records cause a new form of energy, due to composition of the new with the old, and the process of growth then becomes bathmogeny. The external stimuli are molecular or molar, determining physiobathmism or kinetobathmism.

The effect of motion or use on the soma may be conveniently termed autokinetogenesis. Moderate use of a muscle is known to increase its size. Irritation of the periosteum is known to cause deposit of bone. Friction and pressure of the epithelium increases its quantity or changes its form. Increased activity of the functions of nervous tissues increases their relative proportions, as in the enlargement of nerves which replace others which are interrupted by mutilations, etc. On the other hand, it is equally well known that disuse produces diminution of muscular tissues, and through it, a reduction in the quantity of the harder tissue (bone, chitin, etc.) to which it is attached (as muscular insertions, etc.) It was the observation of such well-known phenomena as these that led Lamarck to advance his doctrine of evolution under use and disuse, and which has led many others to give their adherence to such a view.

Thus much for cell growth. Another class of modifications of a similar kind may be found in the parts
of an organism which consist of a complex of cells, or
tissues. Thus the lumen of a small artery is enlarged
under the influence of pressure when it is compelled
to assume the function of a larger vessel through the
interruption of the latter. A part of an internal or
external skeleton which is fractured will form an artificial joint at the point of fracture, if the adjacent
surfaces are kept in motion. Marey (Animal Mechanism, pp. 88-89) says, "After dislocations the old articular cavities will be filled up and disappear, while
at the new point where the head of the bone is actually placed, a fresh articulation is formed, to which
nothing will be wanting in the course of a few months,
neither articular cartilages, synovial fluid, nor the liga-
ments to retain the bone in place." I have given some
illustrations of this fact,[9] which have come under my
observation, and which have an important bearing on
the origin of the articulations of the vertebrate skeleton
as I have traced them throughout geological time. I
have, as I think, conclusively shown that these varied
structures have been produced by impacts and strains,
which are concomitants of the movements of the animals, acting through long periods of time.[10] I have also
proposed the hypothesis, that such kinetogenetic organic energies as are not under the control of the
organism, are the product of the catagenesis of energies
which were at one time under such control.

III. MNEMOGENESIS.

The above term is employed by Professor Hyatt[11] to
characterize the manner in which kinetogenesis is supposed to produce results in inheritance. I have suggested that the phenomena of recapitulation, characteristic of ontogeny (Amer. Naturalist, Dec., 1889),
are due to the presence of a record in the germ cells,
having a molecular basis similar to that of memory.
This view is adopted by Professor Hyatt. I have al-

9 Proceeds. Amer. Philos. Soc., 1892, p. 285.

10 Mechanical Origin of the Hard parts of the Mammalia, Amer. Journal of
Morphology, 1889. Origin of the Fittest, 1887, pp. 305-373.

11 Proceeds. Boston Soc. Nat. History, 1893, p. 73.

ready referred to it in the preceding pages. The stimuli which are thus recorded are those which produce growth effects in the body or soma, so that each stimulus may have a double influence. For this reason I have termed this theory of the distribution of energy, Diplogenesis (loc, cit.).

That acquired characters may be inherited is demonstrated by many facts. One class of these facts is derived from the study of the embryo of Mammalia. The characters of the articulations of the skeleton, I have shown to be the direct result of mechanical impacts and strains, persistently recurring during the life-time of the individuals, throughout the ages of geologic time. Now these characteristics are found in the foetus before birth, and are therefore clearly not due to causes acting at present on the adult during its lifetime. They have been acquired during earlier periods, and have now become congenital. This has been especially observed by Wortman. An equally remarkable case has been recorded by Von Brunn. The ancestors of the genus Mus are known to have had in past geologic ages, tubercular molars, whose cusps are covered with enamel. In the genus at present, the tubercles of the molars are not covered at the apices with enamel, but display areas of exposed dentine, which are surrounded with enamel, whose hard border is an important element in mastication. Von Brunn shows that in the dental papilla the enamel layer is complete over the cusps of the molar, but that prior to the eruption it undergoes atrophy at these points. The cells degenerate and no enamel layer is developed on the summits of the cusps, and they are so erupted. Thus the apparently worn condition of the cusps of the molars in the rat, is not due to wear during the life of existing individuals, but is born with them, being inherited from previous generations. But it is certain that this condition was originally produced by wear of the used crowns of the molars of species of past geologic ages, in which the enamel layer was complete at birth.

The first statement of the mnemonic theory of heredity which I can discover, is that made by Hering in 1870.[12] It is concentrated in the following paragraph:

12 Address before the Imperial Academy of Sciences of Vienna, May 30, 1870, by Edwald Hering.

"The appearance of properties of the parental organism in the full-grown filial organism can be nothing else but the reproduction of such processes of organized matter as the germ when still in the germinal vesicles had taken part in; the filial organism remembers, so to speak, those processes, and as soon as an occasion of the same or similar irritations is offered a reaction takes place as formerly in the parental organism, of which it was then a part and whose destinies influenced it." In explanation of this theory Hering says: "We notice, further on, that the process of development of the germs which ·are destined to attain an independent existence, exercises a powerful reaction upon both the conscious and unconscious life of the whole organism. And this is a hint that the organ of germination is in closer and more momentous relation to the other parts, especially to the nervous system, than any other organ. In an inverse ratio the conscious destinies of the whole organism, it is most probable, find a stronger echo in the germinal vesicles than elsewhere."

It is evident that evolutionists are reaching greater harmony of opinions on the question of inheritance, for both sides are adopting the doctrine of Diplogenesis. In fact, the discussion is beginning to be a logomachy dependent on the significance which one attaches to the term, "acquired character." Thus, Von Rath, who says he does not believe in the inheritance[13] of acquired characters, remarks: "There is nothing in the way of the opinion that by the continual working of such external influences and stimuli, the molecular structure of the germ plasma also experiences a change which can lead to a transmission of transformations. Above all, it ought not to be forgotten in this case that the somatic cells are in no way the first to be modified by the stimulus, and that then by some sort of unexplained process (pangenesis or intercellular pangenesis) this stimulus is transmitted generally by these cells to the plasma of the germ cells. The influence on the germ-plasma is rather a direct one, and if by continued influence a transformation of the structure of this plasma takes place and transmission occurs, we have then simply a transmission of blas-

13 Berichte der Naturforsch. Gessel. zu Freiburgi Baden; Bd. VI. H. 3.

togenic and by no means of somatogenic characters, and therein is not the slightest admission of the transmission of acquired characters."

This surprising paragraph contains an admission of the doctrine of Diplogenesis, and does not regard the phenomena as including a transmission of acquired characters. Nevertheless, the stimuli traverse the soma in order to reach the germ plasma. Such an energy is evidently, then, not of blastogenic origin, although it is such in its effects. Moreover, Von Rath omits to mention the fact that in traversing the soma, the stimulus frequently, if not always, produces effects on the latter similar to those which it produces on the germ plasma. I should call this process the inheritance of an acquired character, even in the case where no corresponding modification appears in the soma, since the causative energy is acquired by the soma, and is not derived from the existing germ plasma.

Romanes[14] says, in revising the opinions of Weismann, "(1) Germ Plasm ceases to be continuous in the sense of having borne a perpetual record of congenital variations from the first origin of sexual propagation. (2) On the contrary, *as all such variations have been originated by the direct action of external conditions*" (italics mine) "the continuity of the germ plasm in this sense has been interrupted at the commencement of every inherited change during the phylogeny of all plants and animals, unicellular as well as multicellular. (3) But germ plasm remains continuous in the restricted though highly important sense of being the sole repository of hereditary characters of each successive generation, so that acquired characters can never have been transmitted to progeny, 'representatively,' even though they have frequently caused those 'specialized' changes in the structure of the germ plasm, which, as we have seen, must certainly have been of considerable importance in the history of organic evolution."

Here the inheritance of characters acquired by the soma is admitted, and the process is after the method of Diplogenesis. According to Romanes, Galton origin-

14 An Examination of Weismannism, Chicago, 1893, p. 169.

ally propounded this doctrine. Galton's language[15] is as follows:

"It is said that the structure of an animal changes when he is placed under changed conditions; that his offspring inherit some of his change, and that they vary still further on their own account, in the same direction, and so on through successive generations until a notable change in the congenital characteristics of the race has been effected. Hence, it is concluded that a change in the personal structure has reacted on the sexual elements. For my part, I object to so general a conclusion for the following reasons. It is universally admitted that the primary agents in the processes of growth, nutrition and reproduction, are the same, and that a true theory of heredity must so regard them. In other words, they are all due to the development of some germinal matter variously located. Consequently, when similar germinal matter is everywhere affected by the same conditions, we should expect that it would be everywhere affected in the same way. The particular kind of germ whence the hair sprang that was induced to throw out a new variety in the cells nearest the surface of the body under certain changed conditions of climate and food, might be expected to throw out a similar variety in the sexual elements at the same time. The changes in the germs would everywhere be collateral, although the moments when any of the changed germs happen to receive their development might be different." This is the first statement of the doctrine of Diplogenesis with which I have met and it appears to me to furnish the most rational basis for the investigation into the dynamics of the process.

IV. THE FUNCTIONS OF CONSCIOUSNESS.

In the preceding pages I have endeavored to show that the factors of evolution are Ergogenesis corrected by Natural Selection. Ergogenesis embraces the two factors Emphytogenesis and Kinetogenesis, or the products of molecular and molar motion respectively. These two forms of motion have been co-extensive with the existence of life, neither one preceding the other in time. Statogenesis may be regarded as the function of persistent forms of energy which characterize inorganic matter, while bathmogenesis is entirely peculiar to living things. Kinetogenesis is the fundamental principle in organic evolution, since it determines the amount and kind of physiogenesis, because it creates the environment which furnishes the conditions of physiogenesis. Progressive organic evolution may then, be described as due to Kinetogenesis corrected by natural selection. At the basis, however, molar organic motion, *i. e.*, contraction of protoplasm, is probably molecular, but it is distinguished from other forms of molecular motion, in the vast aggregate of molecules which move simultaneously in one direction, as in an amœba or a muscle, thus effecting a change in the position of all or a part of an organism. Hence the distinction is a real one.

Molar motion being, then, of such fundamental importance as a factor in evolution, the cause of such motion is also a capital question. Contraction of protoplasm is caused by stimuli, such as currents of electricity, and chemical reagents; but such stimuli are not those which ordinarily produce the contractions to which the molar movements of living animals are due. In those animals which possess a nervous system it can be shown that contractions only follow stimuli which are conveyed to the contractile elements by nervous threads, and the internal energy which represents the external stimulus, is called nervous energy or neurism. In animals without a nervous system and in plants, external stimuli may be justly supposed to be converted into the same form 'of energy, which in such organisms has a general circulation throughout the contractile protoplasm. The important point about these movements in most, if not all animals, and in a few plants, is, that their direction directly subserves the attainment of some position which is favorable for the procurement of relief from some unpleasant sensation, or the acquisition of some agreeable one, or both. We have the best reasons for believing this to be true of the vast majority of animals, because their structure is fundamentally like our own, and the inference that the same is true of the lowest forms of life is justifiable until it is proven to be mistaken.

Lamarck has attributed the movements of animals to the necessity of satisfying their instincts, without entering into the metaphysical questions which this involves. I have regarded the question as a metaphysical one by asserting that the necessary preliminary to movement is "effort," of course referring to what are called "voluntary" as distinguished from automatic motions.[16] On this supposition I presented the relation of the development of mind to organic evolution in the following form.

"The influences locating growth force may be tabulated as follows:

Division.		Influence.
Plants	Physical and Chemical +- ? ?	
Plants with mechanical movements; animals with indeterminate movements.	''	+ use
Animals with determinate movements or will, but no intelligence.	''	+ effort under compulsion.
Animals with will and less intelligence.	''	'' + choice
Animals with more intelligence.	''	'' + intelligent choice."

This crude outline was intended as a presentation of the factors which lie behind Kinetogenesis, and to show the probable mode of origin of organs of motion. I have subsequently presented the subject in a form more in harmony with a correct psychology.[17] Without special organs of movement, a great part of the phenomena of Kinetogenesis would have no existence, precisely as natural selection cannot act unless the materials for selection (*i. e.*, variations) are already in existence. In explanation of the origin of organs of movement we have the general ability of the primitive animal, Protozöon, to project portions of its body-substance as pseudopodia, which become persistent

16 Proceeds. Am. Philos. Soc., 1871, p. 18. Origin of the Fittest, 1887, p. 194.
17 Origin of the Fittest, P. 390.

and more or less rigid, as flagella, cilia, etc.; which are the first distinct organs which subserve the transportation of the body from place to place. The causes which lead to these changes are as yet obscure, but that the use of these organs when once called into existence is due to stimuli similar to those which affect the motions of the limbs of the higher animals, is altogether probable. Whatever be its nature, the preliminary to any animal movement which is not automatic, is an effort. And as no movement is automatic the first time it is performed, we may regard effort as the immediate source of all movement. Now, effort is a conscious state, and is a sense of resistance to be overcome. When an act is performed without effort, resistance has been overcome, and the mechanism necessary for the performance of the act has been completed. The stage of automatism has been reached. At the inception of a new movement resistance is necessarily experienced. It is generally believed that a mental state, as a sensation, a desire, or an exercise of will, is concerned in overcoming this resistance.

ABSTRACT OF THE DISCUSSION.

Mr. Z. Sidney Sampson: —

It would be presumption in me to assume to continue the discussion of the topic of the evening along scientific lines, especially after its treatment by one who is an acknowledged master of the subject. It will be appropriate, however, to consider briefly one matter which is more closely implicated with the discussion of Structural Variations than with any other subject of the present course—viz.: the doctrine of Final Causes; to give it the more current name, the question of Design in Nature. Does the evolution of structural variations resulting in physical mechanism of bodily functions, and the psychical mechanism of brain functions, and the development of organs fitted to accomplish certain results, evince any proof that such organs were *designed* to effect such results? Because the eye has capacity of vision, was the eye made to see? Does the fact of sight prove a designing mind working through, or *evolving* through a given material for certain specific ends and objects?

To this question the philosophy of evolution answers distinctly and emphatically that it does not. Mere adaptability to perform a function does not prove any intentional creation by evolution of that organ to perform that specific function—and it denies it on sound scientific and metaphysical grounds.

First, to assert such doctrine would controvert one of the basic principles of the philosophy of evolution. That philosophy points, at its outset, as a first and immutable principle, that the Absolute One is unknowable—of which nothing can be asserted save that it exists.

Consider now, that if, for example, we were to assert that the eye was made expressly to see, and evolutionary design was thereby shown, this evolutionary design must be traced back to its primordial inception in the Unknowable Absolute. We must follow a regress from the organs of perfected vision to the minute and microscopic human cell from which it originated—thence back through the lowest animal to the lowest vegetable organism—backward farther through inorganic nature to the cosmic structure—still backward to the undifferentiated cosmic mass—still farther to the Absolute Unknowable in which the plan and design must have had its birth, and which in the course of countless ages, it has wrought out through processes of evolution, in the world-stuff and mind stuff, into determinate structures, through the long line of structural variations. But it will be seen at a glance that to ascribe such intentional unfolding into organs *for the purpose* of effecting certain recognized objects to an Absolute is to assert that we know this Absolute to possess a quality of the highest constructive mind and intelligence— and that would be to ascribe to it a quality and character and in fact, a function; viz., that of *intentional design*, which *ex vi termini*, we are forbidden to assert of the Absolute. To say that it is *Unknowable* and yet to assert that it possesses this quality of intentional design, would be a flat contradiction. All that we can know or assert about the Absolute is its EXISTENCE—beyond that, nothing. It would be no answer to this to say that we could claim that the eye was made for the express purpose of sight, although we were ignorant of the origin of the design—because as we have seen, this quality or characteristic of design must, on sound *evolution principles*, be traced back to the very edge of the material universeand back of that into the Unknown Absolute, if it is to have any logical or scientific basis whatever. It will never do to assert in one breath that behind all material phenomena there is an unknowable something, and in the next to allege that it possesses certain specific qualities, such as that of intelligent design.

The second objection to the doctrine of final causes, or of design in nature, is that it is unphilosophical, in that it implies 1st, a designer, 2nd, a design, 3rd, a material in which to work, and 4th, a finished product as the result. On this supposition we must ascribe all these distinctions to an Unknowable Absolute, as well as what I have called original intentional design—and this implies a separation in our conceptions of this Absolute One into the three or four distinctions which I have specified. But this the Evolution hypothesis will disown. When at the very first, distinctions appear in the region of the Unknowable, we are no longer, in fact within the Unknowable—we are at once in the realm of the knowable; that is we are already in the line of scientific evolution. But we have seen that the *idea of design* MUST, if it exist anywhere, exist before any scientific process evolved the idea into determinate material form. Hence *all that belongs* to the idea of design must have existed there in the first instance by parity of reasoning, or it does not exist at all.

The third potent objection arises from the evolution doctrine of the relativity of knowledge. The faculties of human perception, and the judgments based upon those perceptions are sufficient and true only for the individual perceiving and judging—but to leap from our limited conceptions of design, such as, for example, I may entertain regarding the struc-

ture of the eye, to conclusions that therefore the
entire range of infinite adaptations is the result of infinite design, is illogical, and thoroughly illogical. To
assert it would be to assert infinite knowledge in an
extremely limited human intelligence. This argument
is, of course, negative. It does not disaffirm or deny
the possibility of an infinite design—but it does emphatically deny that we are in any wise competent to
conceive it, or justified logically, in making it.

Still further, if we cannot admit that in a specific
case, now or heretofore existing, any particular organ
was made for the express purpose and end of accomplishing certain results, much less can we assert that
there is some ultimate and final design to be wrought
out through these temporary and particular designs.
Tennyson has thrown this idea into a single line when
he wrote of

"One far off divine event to which the whole creation moves"

But the idea of a far off event, that is, a summation
and conclusion of the entire scope and process of
evolution in one distinct, final and commanding purpose is foreign to the entire theory of evolution. Its
processes are infinite both in the direction of the
infinite past and of the infinite future. The assumption is wholly unfounded on strict evolution principles.

This denial of final causes, or of intention and design of any kind in the evolution process, is made
strenuously by those most prominent in evolution
thought. Says Mr. Spencer, "In whatever way it is
formulated or by whatever language it is obscured,
this ascription of organic evolution to some aptitude
naturally possessed by organisms is unphilosophical.
It is one of those explanations which explain nothing—a shaping of ignorance into the semblance of
knowledge. The cause assigned is not a true cause—
not a cause assimilable to known causes. It is a cause
unrepresentable in thought, one of those illegitimate
symbolic conceptions which cannot, by any mental
process, be elaborated into a real conception. In brief,
this assumption of a persistent formative power, inherent in organisms, and making them unfold into
higher forms, is an assumption no more tenable than

the assumption of special creations, of which it is indeed but a modification."

To the same effect Professor Huxley, in commenting upon Darwin in one of his "Lay Sermons, Addresses and Reviews": "That," says he, "which struck the present writer most forcibly on his first perusal of the 'Origin of Species' was the conviction that Teleology (the doctrine of Final Causes) as commonly understood had received its death blow at Mr. Darwin's hands. For the teleological argument runs thus: 'an organ or organism, A, is precisely fitted to perform a function or purpose, B; therefore it was specially constructed to perform that function.' In Paley's illustration the adaptation of all the parts of the watch to the function, or purpose, of showing the time, is held to be evidence that the watch was specially contrived to that end. Suppose, however, that any one had been able to show that the watch had not been made directly by any person, but that it was the result of the modification of another watch which kept time but poorly— and that this again had proceeded from a structure which could hardly be called a watch at all, and that, going back and back in time we come at last to a revolving barrel as the earliest traceable rudiment of the whole fabric—and imagine that it had been possible to show that all these changes had resulted first from a tendency of the structure to vary indefinitely, and secondly, from something in the surrounding world which helped all variations in the direction of an accurate time keeper and checked all those in other directions, then it is obvious that the force of Paley's argument would be gone. For it would be demonstrated that an apparatus thoroughly well adapted to a particular purpose might be the result of a method of trial and error worked by unintelligent agents, as well as of the direct application of the means appropriate to that end by an intelligent agent. The 'Origin of Species' is entirely and absolutely opposed to Teleology."

And again, Professor Fiske: "Not only is the teleological theory useless from a scientific point of view, but its claim to philosophic validity is open to serious doubt. Looking at it historically, we observe that its career has been that of a perishable hypothesis born of primeval habits of thought. As La Place says, Final Causes disappear as soon as we obtain the data requisite for resolving problems scientifically. The rejection of teleology by the most advanced sciences augurs ill for its ultimate chances of survival in any field of inquiry. The teleological hypothesis derives its apparent confirmation never from the phenomena which were explained yesterday, but always from the phenomena which are awaiting an explanation to-morrow. To represent the Unknowable as a person who thinks, contrives and regulates is simply to represent it as a product of evolution. The survival of the doctrine of Final Causes shows that a strong element of anthropomorphism is retained even in the latter conception. The doctrine of Final Causes ultimately reposes on the idea that an Infinite entertains intentions and purposes closely resembling in kind, though greatly excelling in degree of sagacity, the purposes and intentions of man. Everything that exists, it is said, has been created to subserve some design and as the means to the accomplishment of some end. A hypothesis which holds out such brilliant hopes may well be retained in our Cosmic Philosophy if it can be shown to be in harmony with the demonstrated scientific truths upon which that Philosophy rests. But if this cannot be done then the hypothesis must be discarded, even though it should carry with it all our hopes and wishes in indiscriminate ruin. It has been well said that we must follow Truth though it should lead us to Hades. In the present case we shall find reason to conclude that the hypothesis is likely to aggravate rather than to relieve, the mental distress of skepticism."

This paper is to be considered as limited to the statement that the doctrine of Final Causes, or Design in Nature, finds no justification in the evolution philosophy. If they exist, the proof must be sought elsewhere.

Dr. ROBERT G. ECCLES :—

I have been much interested and pleased with Professor Cope's lecture. I agree in the main with him rather than with Weismann. It is evident to me that consciousness is one of the most important, if not the most important factor in organic evolution. The highly specialized organs of the special senses appear to me to be positive evidence of this. The successive steps in the selection, through the evolution of such organs as the eye and ear demonstrate that they could have been of value to the animal only because of the con- - sciousness behind these, and for which they became available in higher and still higher degrees as they became more highly specialized. What is true of the organs of special sense is true of the whole body. Con- sciousness is usually assumed to be a unit. Careful analysis dispels this idea, and demonstrates that it is a complex instead. That general feeling of well being which is at the basis of a conception of self,--the so-called coenæsthesia—represents, in itself, myriads of minor conditions of sensation fused into one. It is an established fact that all, or nearly all, conditions of growth are conditions of comfort, and all, or nearly all, conditions of dissolution are conditions of discomfort, or pain. As this coenæsthesia was being built up it must have been the inner power of selection that held together advantageous changes, and so constructed the organism. From the simplest protoplasm up to man, the successive steps of selection must have been steps of comfort or advantage seized upon and maintained by this complex growing consciousness. The absorption of food was evidently the earliest effort of the organism. Do we know, or can we conceive of such absorption divested of desire? I cannot, with the lecturer, see the intensely radical difference between what is known as inanimate and animate nature. My mind being constructed as it is, I am compelled to believe, with Emerson, that

"Line in nature is not found,
Unit and universe are round."

The basic law of all science, the law of continuity, compels us to hold, with Darwin, "*natura non facit per saltum.*" Protoplasm is colloidal. Colloids and crystals are much unlike, but even they have their connecting links. Protoplasm is a reticulated colloid. The reticulations of protoplasm forcibly remind the chemist of the chains of atoms, with some of their higher complex molecules. In biology the law is, no egg without an egg   In crystallography the law is, no crystal without a crystal.   The growth of crystals often simulates the growth of ferns, as every one has seen on the window pane in winter.   Where there is so much in common, so far as appearance goes, there must be, fundamentally, some sort of resemblance in the laws that govern them.   While it is certain that the crystal possesses no intelligence such as we know, and while it is equally certain that we have no evidence that goes to prove the absence of intelligence, all analogy, and the law of continuity itself, on which all science is built, lead us strongly to infer that they must have something closely akin to that which we know as consciousness.   Natural selection, in building up the crystal, may have its subjective aspect here, as well as in the higher biological phenomena.   If this is so, it follows that the least part which consciousness can take in all evolution must be one-half, while the mechanical aspect can but cover the other half.

With reference to the question of 'final' causes, evolutionists should be extremely cautious either in their assertions or denials.   I hold that function precedes organism, however.   If this position be true, it implies the possibility of the existence of purpose and design in evolution.

Dr. Cope in reply:—

I agree with the position of the evolution philosophy that the doctrine of Final Causes is inadmissible.   There may possibly be a limited and relative design indicated by the fact that organisms seek to adapt themselves to their environment through a natural selection, but of Ultimate and Final Causes we have no proof.

As to Weismann's theory, I prefer to hold that the germ plasm is acted upon by impressions from without, in much the same way as impressions are fixed upon brain matter, and which, recalled under consciousness, give rise to the phenomena of memory.   In the same way, substantially, impressions are made upon the germ plasm, ineffaceably, and these are reproduced through the embryonic process at birth. The effects of these external influences are two-fold—first, upon the parent, and secondly, upon the germ plasm. I call this diplogenesis. Only the strong and vivid impressions are effective.

LOCOMOTION AND ITS RELATION TO SURVIVAL

BY

DR. M. L. HOLBROOK

Marey's *Animal Mechanism: A Treatise on Terrestrial and Aerial Locomotion;* Pettigrew's *Animal Locomotion;* Darwin's *Emotional Expression in Man and Animals,* and *Power of Movement in Plants;* Flint's *Source of Muscular Power;* Rosenthal's *General Physiology of Muscles and Nerves;* Warner's *The Anatomy of Movement,* and *Physical Expression: Its Modes and Principles;* McKendrick's *Life in Motion;* La Grange's *Physiology of Bodily Exercise;* Proctor's *Health and Happiness.*

LOCOMOTION AND ITS RELATION TO SURVIVAL.

BY DR. M. L. HOLBROOK.

We define locomotion as the simple act of moving from one place to another. This is accomplished in living things through the agency of the muscular system, guided and directed in the higher animals by the nervous apparatus which controls it. In the simplest animal organism, locomotion is very easily comprehended; all that is required is the contraction and relaxation of the muscle-fiber, or whatever stands for it. In the highest animals, it is a very complicated performance, as is seen in the wonderful feats of skill of dancers and sleight-of-hand performers, which can be witnessed by any one for half a dollar or less. Perhaps I cannot do better than to give a brief review of the evolution of muscle-fiber and locomotion as an introduction to the subject.

MOVEMENT OF WHITE BLOOD CORPUSCLES AND AMŒBÆ.

If any one who has a microscope with magnifying power of 1,000 or 1,200 diameters will take a minute droplet of blood, put it freshly drawn on the warm slide, and under the objective, he will see among the multitude of red blood corpuscles a few white ones. If he will find one of these white ones, removed a little from all others so as to have space and freedom to act, and watch it for half an hour, he will notice that it is constantly changing its shape. Sometimes a little flap or fork will be thrown out on one side, sometimes on the other. These take the place of limbs. A lively white blood corpuscle will change to a dozen or more forms in a minute or two. Now and then one may be seen to crawl along a little. This is the most primitive

189

form of locomotion, too slight almost to be given the name except to illustrate its low beginning in almost undifferentiated protoplasm. Now, how did this movement take place? The white blood corpuscle is a minute lump of living matter. It has a delicate structure visible only to long-trained eyes and under good microscopes. Heitzmann, the discoverer of this structure, calls it reticular. It is not dissimilar to the structure of muscular fiber, and has in a simple way the same power to contract and relax, and by virtue of this power to move from place to place. It performs, in other words, the act of locomotion.

For further illustration, if in summer time, when the water in stagnant pools is warm and filled with vegetation, we pull up the weeds and grass growing therein, wring the water from them into a cup, settle it and put a droplet from the bottom of the dish filled with the sediment on the slide and under the microscope, we shall no doubt see numerous amœbæ, simple unicellular bodies, and if we observe one of them we shall see it move across the field of the microscope in a very short time. Compared with the movement of the white blood corpuscle *its* movements are swift, but compared with those of the snail they are very slow, but it is locomotion as truly as in the fleetest race horse, or the fastest running man, or the fastest sailing yacht.

EVOLUTION OF MUSCLES.

Let us now see if we can trace the development of muscular fiber by the process of evolution from this simple structure seen in the white blood corpuscle of the blood and the unicellular body, the amœba—which has been used so much, in studying life, as the unit of living organisms.

"Multicellular animals must have arisen" says Eimer, "from colonies formed in consequence of the advantage of association of unicellular forms still at a low grade of development; of protozoa which had as yet developed no kind of permanent organs except perhaps the nucleus." But a multicellular organism, while it might have some advantage over a unicellular one, would stand a poor chance for self-defense and still higher development unless various groups of its cells should, by a division of labor, take on special kinds of activity, and relate themselves, some to one sort of external stimulus, and some to another. Locomotion would necessarily be one of the activities of these multicellular bodies, inherited, one may say, from their unicellular progenitors. It is very probable that some of these wrongly called cells, perhaps those most favorably situated, or those able to get most nourishment, would become larger and assume leadership in the direction of motion. As a consequence of this, movement would be more synchronous and regular than is necessary or possible in unicellular organisms.

The development of the muscle-plate would be the next step in evolution, and out of the muscle-plate by its activity, its ceaseless bendings and twistings, its contractions and relaxations, I think we may assume, would arise more complex organs adapted to the more perfect activity of the animal, or true muscle-fiber, from which lowly beginnings muscles would gradually appear.

In the monocellular organisms such a structural development would be impossible, since only a limited part of the body could be devoted to movement. This we see in the unicellular vorticella, where a part of it forms a rude muscle-fiber or its equivalent, which, however, is not to be compared with the typical muscle-fiber of a more complex creature.

Let us now consider how muscle-fiber arises from the indifferent or medullary tissue of the embryo. In this tissue the medullary corpuscles have the same general reticular structure as in the white blood corpuscles, and in the amœbæ. The change in the corpuscle is not so great as might at first be supposed, but it is an evolutionary one, that is, a change from a simple to a more differentiated structure. As I have observed it in the embryo of the chicken, with a magnifying power of 1,200 diameters, the first thing seen is a multiplication and crowding and lengthening of the medullary corpuscles. They also increase in size, some becoming as large as the white blood corpuscles, others still larger, some two or three times as large.

They also exhibit distinct nuclei and nucleoli. These corpuscles, bear in mind, are not structureless; they have, from the first, a distinct reticulation like all protoplasm (the amœba, for instance), and each corpuscle is connected with every other adjoining it by numerous threads of protoplasm which give unity to the structure.

The next step in the evolution of muscle-fiber is that the points of intersection of the medullary corpuscles enlarge, and, instead of being arranged around the nucleus, arrange themselves, or are arranged in rows vertical to the long axis of the corpuscles. Sometimes this arrangement in rows takes place first in the nucleus, sometimes first in the body of the corpuscle.

This simple transformation goes on in all the corpuscles. As I view it, the points of intersection of the reticulum of the corpuscles become the important sarcous elements of the muscle; no other change takes place except the elongation of the corpuscle, the enlargement of the granules of intersection, and their arrangement in rows as we find them in striped muscles. In the embryo of the chick, nutrition, no doubt, plays an important part in the change, and the change goes on quickly, there being abundant food stored up in the egg. Probably each corpuscle forms a fibrilla, and as all corpuscles are united together by threads of living matter, it is not difficult to see how a number of them may unite to form a fiber.

I have seen the same features in the embryo of other animals, especially the human embryo, but the order of evolution is not so easily followed as in the embryo of the chick. There is no more instructive sight than to observe muscle-fibers becoming evolved, so to say, from the simple medullary corpuscles of the embryo. It seems as natural for them to take on the structure of muscle-fiber as for mineral matters, in solution under right conditions, to take on the form of crystals.

I have here only given the first step in the evolution of muscle-fiber, which we find quite as perfect in animals low down in the scale of being as in higher ones. The muscle-fibers of some insects are as perfect as in human beings, so far as minute structure is con-

cerned. Those of the lobster, one of the crustacea, I
have worked out and found not essentially different
from those of the ox or man. When, however, it
comes to the evolution of a complicated muscular sys
tem, as in man and the horse, the problem is too great
for us to trace in all its details. We can only say it
probably took place by use, by struggle, by inherit-.
ance, by natural and sexual selection rather than ·
special creation. The everlasting struggle for existence
has no doubt contributed largely to this evolution.
What we often deem a misfortune has been the greatest of blessings.

EVOLUTION OF FLIGHT IN BIRDS.

We get, perhaps, some hints of the evolution of a
muscular system in the study of birds. We now know
that these creatures which astonish us with their feats
of flight have descended from the reptiles. The reptiles, of course, include the serpent, the turtle, the
alligator, the lizard, etc., a very large class of creatures which in the early age of the world were far
more numerous than now. They are vertebrates, ovip-
arous, air-breathing, and cold blooded, and they
crawl on the belly. Professor Marsh, of Yale University, has discovered a large number of their fossils,
many of which have the characteristics of birds and
reptiles combined. He thinks that our birds are descended from some of the smaller reptiles which lived
in trees and were probably able to leap from branch
to branch. The fore limbs gradually developed feathers which aided in this leaping, and by degrees, flying became possible. Probably the necessity of es
caping from the prey of other animals made this form
of locomotion desirable, and those reptilian birds
which could go into the air when pursued had a far
better chance of survival than those which could not.
At any rate locomotion by flying has become wonderfully developed in birds, and is so interesting that I
cannot refrain from spending a little time over it.

One of the first requisites for flying is that the bird
be heavier than the air, and it may be very much
heavier, as is the case with the larger ones. If lighter
than the air they would rise as steam rises, but they

could not fly. The balloon floats in the air, it does not
fly, nor can it even if alive and possessing wings, so
long as it is lighter than the volume of air which it
displaces. But this force of gravity acting on the
body of the bird to bring it down must be continually
overcome, else it falls to the ground. This requires
a muscular apparatus and wings suited to act on the
elastic air, and this is what evolution has given to
birds.

In order to overcome gravity, the extent of the wings
of birds must be great, but it varies with different
ones according to whether their flight must be rapid or slow, or whether they live almost constantly in
the air, as the albatross, or only a small part of their
lives, as the robin; also in proportion to the number
of times the wing moves per minute. A partridge,
whose wings move so fast you cannot count their
strokes—several hundred per minute, probably—and
which dwells in the air but little, requires less wing
surface than an eagle, whose wing movements are less
rapid—perhaps 150 per minute—but whose life is so
constantly on the wing. Lucy has calculated that the
Australian crane, which flies well, has half a square
foot of wing surface for each pound of weight. In
the same proportion a man, weighing 150 pounds, to
navigate the air no better than the crane, would need
wings 14 feet long and 3 feet wide ; and to fly like a
swallow its wings would need to be enormous, for a
swallow requires, the same authority tells us, about
5 square feet of wing for each pound of its weight.
This gives it its wonderful power in the air and a
speed equal, says Wilson, to 100 miles per hour.

The structure of the wing of birds, too, is very interesting. It is concave on its lower surface, and this
imprisons the air so as to give greater effect to the
downward blow. The wing is also so contrived that the
downward motion closes up the feathers and prevents
the air from escaping through it. In order, however,
that the upward movement of the wing may not counteract the downward movement, it is convex and the
air easily moves to one side. Still this is not sufficient, and the whole wing opens enough to allow a
portion of the air to pass directly through between the

feathers as it moves upward. These two conditions are absolutely necessary to give the downward blow of the wing greater force on the air than the upward one. The gain of power in the less resistance of the upward movement by this arrangement is sufficient to enable the bird to make all its wonderful gyrations—

"The scythe-like sweep of wings that dare,
The headlong plunge through eddying gulfs of air."

The amount of energy, however, required in flight is very great. Any one who has had a partridge fly against him can appreciate this, or one who has been struck by the powerful wing of a large bird, as many of us no doubt have been. It has been estimated as three times greater per pound weight than the force exerted by man in foot tons. The greatest output of force, however, is required in rising. Let any one observe the effort made by a wild duck or a seagull to rise from the water, and he will have a practical illustration of it. It takes at least twenty times the energy of a bird to rise a certain number of feet vertically as to fly the same distance on an even plane; the latter is comparatively easy, especially if the wings are large, and those birds which can soar have the added advantage of being able to rest themselves in the air. This explains why such a bird as the albatross, with its marvelous power of flight, can spend day after day in constant aerial locomotion without complete exhaustion. It is able to soar for hours and days at a time, during which little effort is required beyond keeping the equilibrium of the body adjusted to the currents of air Thus poised, the bird does not fall; on the other hand a soaring bird instantly falls if its balance in the air is not perfectly maintained. Occasionally one who watches soaring birds much sees this to be true.

ADVANTAGE OF FLIGHT FOR SURVIVAL.

In the evolution of flight in birds there has been a great departure from the simplest form, and this has been an almost perfect adaptation to different conditions of life. Take the partridge as an example. It lives mostly on the ground in thickets near open fields, and

does not migrate in winter. Its need of flight is
mainly to enable it to escape a foe quickly, and it has
short wings, round at the ends, not easily injured by
the brush and trees, which by powerful pectoral muscles are made to move with very great rapidity for a
short time. But this rapidity could not be kept up
for hours and days without exhaustion. Such wings
would be of little use to the swallow, which lives and
secures its food when flying. The swallow has many
times more surface to a pound of its weight than the
partridge, and far greater dexterity in flight. Probably in no bird has the evolution of aerial locomotion
been more highly developed than in this creature.
Wilson estimates that during the life of the barn swallow it flies over 2,000,000 miles. I think, however, this
is an over-estimate.

If we take the sparrow and pigeon hawk, or the
European variety, the merlin, fine specimens of which
can be seen in the Museum of Natural History in New
York, what a difference in them! The evolution of
flight in the merlin has reached a high degree of development. It is a small bird, about the size of the
pigeon, with long, narrow, sharply-pointed wings. It
is perhaps the most spirited of all the hawks. Its
surpassing powers of aerial locomotion enable it to
secure its food openly. It makes its attacks on its
prey in the air, gives it a fair chance to escape, and
prefers game which is some match for its own skill, to
call out its highest efforts. Other birds do not dare
to attack and worry it. If they do, it soon makes an
end of them. The sparrow-hawk has less perfectly developed wings. It cannot attack its prey in an open
field, but must get it under cover of hedges and near
borders of woods, where it may be partly hidden from
view, and so pounces on unsuspecting birds that in
an open field can outfly it. If it cannot do any better
it finds and eats mice and even insects.

The question may be asked, what are the advantages of survival for birds by flight over their ancestors, the reptiles?

Very great. They have taken on a higher development of the nervous system. By living so much in
the air, they have been able to breathe more oxygen

and have become warm-blooded. Cold-blooded animals have less nervous activity than warm-blooded, in
part because they consume less oxygen.

By flight birds have been able to escape many enemies. If we except man and woman, their greatest
foes, they have fewer than most animals, though they
have quite enough to keep them active and alert in
self-defense, and in procuring food. The ability to
migrate is also a very great advantage, in that when food
is deficient they can leave one locality for another at
a moment's notice. This all migratory birds do. From
some studies I once made from swallows, I found they
arrived at a certain place on exactly the same day of
the month for several years in succession.

This power of flight gives them greater breadth of
life, more fullness of life ; and is this not, as in man, an
advantage? We sometimes speak as if the power of
survival were the most important of all things, but if
not at the same time accompanied by a larger and
constantly more perfect life, of what use is it? Very
little, it seems to me.

It is very doubtful if the reptiles from which our
birds have descended would to-day exist if not by the
evolution of aerial locomotion, and we should now
have no feathered songsters. They have survived because they evolved flight. In the air they had a world
almost all their own.

EVOLUTION OF LOCOMOTION IN MEN.

Let us now turn to man. It is a long way from
birds to human beings. They came to their present
estate by different routes, birds by the way of the
reptile, man, as Darwin has pointed out, by way of
the *Simian*. They could not have reached the same
destination by these different routes. The causes
which have acted on one have brought forth the human race, and on the other the bird. Birds surpass
man in power of locomotion only in a few particulars.
Their apparatus for flying is simple, and there is only
one movement, the upward and downward of the wings
at right angles to the axis of the body. The young
bird learns it quickly. With man locomotion is compli-

cated and the movement of so many parts must be correlated into one movement, so that walking is not learned, like flying, in a day, and does not come by instinct.
Indeed, many of us never learn to walk perfectly in
our lives, but only awkwardly and with much friction
and loss of power. This is owing to the fact that evolution has not gone far enough to give perfection in
this function, and also to the fact that our locomotive
apparatus to a certain extent degenerates both by
excessive physical labor and by the sedentary and un-
hygienic habits of civilization.

Let us now turn to the evolution of the muscular
system of man from his ape-like ancestors. To a certain
extent we are in the dark and can do little more than
speculate—which is unallowed in science, unless one
can do nothing else. It will perhaps simplify the subject if we do not attempt too much. If we examine
the hands and the feet of those *primates* which are
accessible to us, and especially those which most of
us can see in our museums, we find them less differentiated than the same parts in man. The foot is still
to a certain extent a hand; the large toe is also a
thumb, and correspondingly is used with great effect
in grasping and climbing. There is, however, little
elasticity or flexibility in the foot when used in walking. The fingers and toes are of nearly equal length,
the inside toes not yet so prominent as in man, and
the small toe has not degenerated as we see it in ourselves; i. e., it is more of a hand and less of a foot
than the same parts in the human race.

By what process did this change take place? Mr.
Herbert Spencer has given a graphic picture of the
probable causes of the change, in his masterly answer
to Weismann, in the discussion as to whether acquired characters are inherited by offspring. Let me
quote a paragraph. He says: "If we go back to the
genesis of the human type from some lower type of
primates, we see that while the little toe has ceased
to be of any use for climbing purposes, it has not
come into any considerable use for walking and running. It is manifest that the great toes have been immensely developed since there took place the change
from arboreal to terrestrial habits. A study of the

mechanism of walking shows why this has happened. Stability requires that the line of direction—the vertical line let fall from the center of gravity—shall fall within the base and the walking shall be brought at each step within the area of support, or so near that any tendency to fall may be checked at the next step. A necessary result is that if at each step the chief stress of support is thrown on the outer side of the foot, the body must be swayed so that the line of direction may fall within the outside of the foot or close to it; and when the next step is taken it must be similarly swayed in an opposite direction, so that the outer side of the foot may bear the weight. That is to say, the body must oscillate from side to side, or waddle. The movement of the duck when walking shows what happens when the points of support are far apart. This kind of movement conflicts with efficient locomotion. There is a waste of muscular energy in making these lateral movements and they are at variance with the forward movement. We may infer, then, that the developing man profited by throwing the stress as much as possible on the inner side of the feet, and was especially led to do this when going fast, which enabled him to abridge the oscillations, as indeed we see it now in the drunken man. Then there was thrown a continually increasing stress upon the inner digits as they progressively developed from the efforts of use, until now the inner digits, so large compared with the outer, bear the greater part of the weight, and being relatively near one another render needless any swaying of the body from side to side in walking.

"But what has meanwhile happened to the outer digits? Evidently as fast as the great toes have come more and more into play the small ones have gone more and more out of play and have been dwindling for—how long shall we say?—perhaps 100,000 years."

We have here a graphic picture of the probable processes of the evolution of the human foot, so important in locomotion, from that of the lower primates. It can be made still more graphic by first observing the feet and the movements of some of these primates in our museums, and also studying the action of our own bare feet on a hard floor, in the movement of rising on the toes to take a step forward. It becomes at once plainly evident how important it was for the most effective walking or running—of which primitive men must have had much need, both in securing food and escaping from attacking foes—that the inner part of the foot should be changed, as it has been changed, and also that the degeneration of the little toe which has taken place in the human race is after all not a misfortune, albeit it may be a physiological error for us to hasten this process by badly constructed boots and shoes. The outer toe still has its use in giving sufficient breadth to the foot to make standing easier from a broader base, but beyond that it has little to do. Probably we shall never become four-toed, for it has just enough activity to keep it as well developed as it now is, but not enough to cause it to grow larger.

In a similar way we might trace the development of the leg of man from that of the ape; the greater calf, the larger thigh, the alteration in the attachments of the muscles and in the articulations of the knee and hip joints, and its straightness compared with that of the ape; but I will not attempt to do this here. During untold ages the process has been going on by constant adaptations to new and more complicated uses, and we now have man with a muscular system of wonderful perfection in many ways, and as a whole far surpassing that of the bird, which can neither fly backward nor sidewise, but only forward; or of the ape, whose movements are well enough suited to arboreal life, but which on the earth is awkward and clumsy, and which cannot make a long journey on foot with anything like the celerity man can.

For real usefulness, no animal, as a whole, equals a well developed man in the perfection of the locomotive organs, and no one can doubt but this perfection has contributed in a high degree not only to his survival, but also to his enormous multiplication and spread over the earth. Some of these advantages, as they appear to me, I will now enumerate.

Man's first want for which he must provide is and always has been food. The air comes to him unsought,

but food must be sought in a great variety of places
and ways. In the present stage of civilization, with
our perfected agriculture, a large part of our time is
consumed in procuring it. How much more was that
the case when there was only a crude agriculture!
Even those sessile plants and animals whose bodies
are attached to a fixed spot, send out their rootlets or
other parts of their bodies in search of food. Primitive man, we know, often had a very hard struggle to
obtain enough to eat. Especially was this the case
in cold climates in times of scarcity. Then without
the power of locomotion in a high degree he must
have perished—often did perish, and only those most
highly gifted or most enterprising or with best powers of locomotion, or most fortunate, were able to survive. We must, however, not give all the credit to
locomotion, but a full share to the intellectual development of the early man, to a brain sufficiently unfold-
ed and experienced to learn quickly that if food was
scarce in one place there might be abundance elsewhere by going there for it. His organs of locomotion were only the servants of his mind.

Another advantage of locomotion for survival, and
especially for human improvement, has been to bring
the different races into contact so there might be
intermarriage between different varieties rather than
too much interbreeding. Interbreeding, no doubt, has
had its uses, even among human beings, but too long
continued, especially if it be close interbreeding and
without knowlegde of its laws, the results are likely
to be disastrous. We see this in our own time when
any small community becomes isolated from others,
and its members intermarry for a few generations.
The result is likely to be a lowering of the physical
and mental characteristics, unless there are counteract-
ing conditions, as is sometimes the case. · We sometimes point to the Jews as a race which by continual
intermarriage has developed a high degree of physical
and mental vigor; but the Jews are a composite race,
made up of several races, Aryan and Semitic, and
considering their persecutions, it is very doubtful if
they could have survived had they not been able by locomotion to disperse themselves to all parts of the

world to escape persecution and to seek those countries where they might be free, and to come in contact with other freedom-loving races.

Another advantage for survival would be to relieve
over-crowded parts of the earth by emigration. We
have a good illustration of this in the discovery and
settlement of America; and still another in the movement of races now going on from one continent to another, or one part of a continent to another part of
it. By it, man is able to find the most healthful climates and most fertile regions—very great advantages;
to seek new opportunities where there is less or different kinds of competition, which brings into play and
developes other less used faculties; and finally to pop-
ulate the whole habitable globe with the most progressive races.

To this end, however, the movement of man from
place to place by his own muscular system has not
been sufficient, and he has been compelled to use his
brain to develop means of transit by sailing vessels,
by ships and railroads, and by the use of animals as
beasts of burden. This, however, he could not have
done without excellent powers of locomotion to seek
and bring material together from which to construct
these contrivances. No animal but man has done it.
Without these, if he had his genesis in one region of
the globe only, as is pretty certain, he must forever
have been confined there—or at least to those continents which he could reach by walking. In this respect he is inferior to the bird, which is capable of
flying over a wide extent of water, or even to the seeds
of many plants, which are wafted by winds or carried
by streams or currents to all‐continents and islands.
The railroad and the steam and sailing ship have made
survival possible for countless multitudes who otherwise could not have existed, and their work is not
perfected yet. To-day, in China and India, if famine
prevails in one department, a very large number suffer
or starve to death, when there may be abundant food
in another department near by, but with no means to
either bring this food to the people or carry the people to the food. For the relief and survival of the
people of those countries, better means of transport

are, it seems to me, of the highest importance to prevent overcrowding and loss of life from famine. Even in our own country, where there is little or no overcrowding and where intercommunication between all parts of the land is so easy, we have much to learn. By our high duties on certain raw materials we prevent the building of ocean steamers or the buying of them from abroad. The result is we have given over most of our carrying trade to foreign nations; and, still worse, we have such a high tariff on steel rails—which can be made cheaper at home than in England, and at a good profit, too—that there can be no foreign competition, and then by means of trusts we limit production and keep the price so high that far less rails are used than otherwise would be, that far less men are making them, and many thousand less making tracks and laying down rails. The result is many of the least profitable roads are imperfectly constructed and accidents often occur. How many men, women and children have failed to survive, or have become feeble and diseased and will die or have become tramps, or *locomotive perverts* who might be employed in producing and laying down new roads or mending those which need repair, none of us will ever know.

Locomotion by means of artificial methods has been of almost infinite benefit to man in yielding those pleasures which come from visiting lands not our own, and learning the habits and customs of other people. Indirectly this promotes health and enjoyment and also human progress. Many of those changes of opinion which have been beneficial may be traced directly to intercourse thus promoted. If such intercourse has also carried evils as well as blessing, as the spreading of the use of intoxicating drinks among temperate nations, this is to be regretted. Everything beneficial may become a source of harm, as is the case when primitive races are subjected or destroyed by foreign invasions only possible by artificial means of locomotion, to gratify the wishes of those who claim to be more enlightened.

PHYSICAL CULTURE.

I pass on to another part of my subject—the train.

ing and development of the organs of locomotion and the whole muscular system by means of special physical culture.

The muscular system of man and of animals was not developed by special training, but by exercise in supplying those wants which were imperative. Youthful sports were indeed always the spontaneous outbursting of a surplus of energy in all races, probably even in primitive men, if they were at all like their primitive ancestors, the ape; but these spontaneous exercises were, first, I believe, reduced to a system and applied to the perfection of the body by the Greeks. Their course of education embraced two very important branches—music and gymnastics. Music had a direct relation to mental culture, and embraced the liberal arts and sciences, including architecture, sculpture, language, poetry, eloquence, philosophy, and history. Gymnastics, on the other hand, had relation to the perfection of the body, both in form, and in grace and perfection of movement. The gymnasia of the ancient Greeks were their schools, and hardly an important city or town but had one or more of them. The most beautiful and healthful part of the city was chosen as a site. The grounds embraced often ten or more acres, with groves for philosophic study and reflection, enclosures for out of door exercise in pleasant weather, halls for lectures, baths, anointing with oil, boxing, running, wrestling, ball playing, quoits, and many other games. A special teacher had charge of the training, and adapted it to the youth. From an early age the boys were taught music and grammar and the easier games and exercises. From sixteen to eighteen they spent most of their school hours in practicing their exercises; at eighteen they were fit for war, for leisure, for the study of philosophy, or entered the field of professional athletes and devoted their lives to prize running, wrestling or fighting. The professional athlete did not live to be old. The intense strain of excessive bodily development weakened his hold on life and made his brains dull and heavy. Those who devoted their lives to philosophy or science, or art, took only the lighter and more graceful exercises, producing a more harmonious development of the whole man, and lived often to old age. The Greeks had a saying that "it takes a philosopher to live long and well." Plato spoke of the athletes as a sluggish set of men with dubious health and short-lived. "A more elegant kind of exercise," says he, "is required for our military wrestlers, who ought to be wakeful, to see and hear acutely, to be able to endure changes of food, heat and cold, and not to fail in health."

In Sparta the training was more for war. The girls had equal bodily training with the boys, often in co-education with them. The object was to produce strong mothers who could bring into the world strong children to become soldiers, able to defend the government from external foes. While it no doubt produced masculine women, who often forced their way into politics to no advantage to themselves or the state, yet, if we may believe history, the training was of great value, promoting both health and national longevity. In Athens the training was less severe, and inculcated manly bearing, grace and bodily vigor. No means were thought so valuable in preserving and restoring health as exercise. I have often thought that if the Grecian method of bodily development and the use of gymnastics had prevailed in Christian civilization, the more Arabic system of drug medication, partly at least, the outgrowth of chemistry, would not have gotten such a hold on western races, but we should long ago have had what we are now beginning to have, a system of hygienic medication. Perhaps it is stating it too strongly to say that we should have had a medical system free from drugs; but as nine-tenths of our medication is by drugging the sick, often with poisons, often also with useless nostrums, and less than one-tenth by means of hygienic medication, so might not the figures have been reversed; may they not yet be reversed and we finally have a system nine-tenths hygienic and preventive treatment and not more than one-tenth devoted to internal remedies, the action of which we still know very little?

Fortunately or unfortunately, however, the early Christians, with all their zeal and earnestness, had not the scientific spirit of the Greeks, and they were too much absorbed with their souls to care for their bodies and train them for the highest service of the mind. The long series of centuries of the history of primitive Christianity in which the body was almost despised and neglected, produced most disastrous effects. We are now coming back to the Grecian idea, and it is to be hoped the results on the future will be of the highest value. Nearly every Young Men's Christian Association has adopted, imperfectly, it is true, their ideas of physical culture, and while they do not yet do their work as well, they are doing much to save and perfect the bodies of the young.

It is a long story to go into, and I can only say here that the physical education in Greece had two effects, one good and one evil. The good effect is seen in the fact that it aimed to produce perfect men and women for the higher duties of life—for philosophers, statesmen, soldiers, scholars, poets, artists, sculptors. It is generally believed that sculpture among the Greeks was only possible in the high degree in which it existed because of the physical perfection of the people. The love of beauty was so conspicuous in the Greeks that they would never have cared to perpetuate in marble an imperfectly developed and homely set of men and women. Their perfect bodies inspired the artists to produce an equally perfect art.

The effect of this physical training—especially among the Spartans—on national survival would require a volume to fully illustrate, but that it did have an important bearing on this subject no one can doubt. Men in Sparta lived for the state, and were trained with the severest rigor to endure calmly and passively every hardship, to feel perfectly at home amidst perils and trials. "Come home with your shield, or on it," were the words every Spartan mother gave to her son when he left home with his shield to fight for Sparta. All the Spartans, both the wealthy and the poor, submitted to the same rigorous discipline. The love of home which we so highly prize was perhaps less to them than to us; the love of the state everything. No doubt that was a serious error, the effects of which were felt later.

The necessity of good power of locomotion is important in war for attack and retreat. If an army is beaten, it must fly before its pursuers. We read of Socrates once as a soldier in the ranks of a retreating army carrying on his back a wounded friend. Without locomotive ability in a high degree in him, we might not have had his influence on the world as a moralist. Still this experience has its ludicrous side, and happening to-day would have furnished material for many cartoons.

EVILS OF ATHLETICISM.

The evil side of Grecian physical culture grew out of athletics for the sake of contending in games, for prizes, or in other words, for exhibition. The games of contestants, the boxing, the wrestling, running, and Grecian athletics were in the end a positive evil. The gymnasia became finally the place, not for perfecting men physically and mentally, but for idle loungers, for pleasure, for dissipation. Little by little these evils crept in as wealth increased and the young had leisure; and finally, the degeneration of Greece and her national downfall grew, in part at least, out of the misuse of the means devised for her survival.

A somewhat brighter picture is found in Germany and also in Sweden. In the early part of the century Europe was overrun by the armies of Napoleon, and Germany was a great sufferer, for German soil was the battlefield for all Europe. The German people had not been trained and developed in the arts of war by special physical culture, and they were unable to drive out the foreign foes that were despoiling their land. In the emergency arose Frederich Ludwig Jahn, a pupil and disciple of Johan Christoph Fredrich Guts Muths, whom we may call the father or grandfather of modern physical culture, who formulated a system of physical training for the people which, crude as it was, enabled them to expel the French. He excited unbounded enthusiasm and the spirit of patriotism, and established throughout Germany Turnhallen for training which accomplished wonders. It was to him that we owe the revival of modern physical culture in Germany; and indirectly also in other countries, even

our own.   There was at one time a fear on the part
of the Government that the German Turnhallen would
become places for political intrigue, but that danger
really never did exist, and to-day they are the centers
where meet the best, the brightest and most progressive young men of Germany.

It has been due quite as much to the adoption of
the Grecian idea of physical culture that the German
nation has become great, as to any one cause, and it
is due to lack of it that France has in late years been
so far behind Germany in war.   Whatever others may
think, I do not doubt but the greater fecundity of the
German race as compared with the French, is largely,
though not altogether, due to their training, which
has given them stronger bodies and intellects more
alert.   Here we see as a result of physical training,
not only national survival, but race multiplication of
superior men and women, which favors survival.

Much also might be said of the great progress made
in physical culture in Sweden. Ling, who has done so
much for rational physical training for both sick and
well, was also a pupil of the same Guts Muths, if not
personally, at least through his works.   Steadily during this century have his methods been developed until
now the state has adopted them and educates a certain number of teachers every year, who, in turn, educate others in all parts of the world.   The system has
been introduced into all hospitals, and the people who
crowd the clinics usually receive medical gymnastics
in place of medicines. Patent medicines are unknown,
being prohibited by law.   It seems as if the Ling system was gradually supplanting drugs.   Eighteen drug
stores are considered sufficient for Stockholm, a city
with a quarter of a million inhabitants, and 289 for all
Sweden.

PHYSICAL CULTURE IN AMERICA.

Forty years ago we had not established physical
culture on a scientific basis in any of our colleges, and
they were turning out far too many lop-sided men, with
brains overweighted with Greek and Latin, often with
bent forms, debilitated stomachs, maimed lungs and
flabby muscles. Had it not been for the fact that so

many of our students were farmers' sons, with strong bodies through manual toil, this evil would have been still greater. A real danger threatened us. Many youths of high promise failed to survive because physical education did not accompany mental training, and numerous families of promise became extinct. Common-sense parents often preferred that their sonsshould educate themselves by alternating study and labor in shop and on farm, or out-of-door life combined with books, as Lincoln and Franklin and many others were educated, and well educated, too. In this emergency a few men like Professor Hitchcock, Dr. Dio Lewis, and more recently many others, came to our rescue, who have changed all this, so that, to-day, our boys and girls who go to college and the university, stand as good, often a better chance of developing strong, well-disciplined bodies than those who stay at home. One evil, however, yet threatens us, and that is the danger of turning our gymnasia into schools for developing only athletes, foot-ball players, men who can win at the games and public exhibitions. These public games are in the main only an evil. Many parents feel that their sons have gone to the university, not to develop their whole manhood, but only a part of it, the physical. This would indeed be an evil, the same evil the Greeks fell into; but I believe it will be averted, and that we shall have at last a standard in education for perfect manhood and a perfect womanhood, so far as we can grasp this idea, or men and women with good bodies and well trained minds.

Those who cannot steer between the evils of excessive mental development and excessive physical development, or those who will not make themselves fit, will run the risk of not surviving.

There is still a very large portion, however, of our people debarred from wise and systematic training. First are the youth in our public schools.

With few exceptions the physical training they receive, in our own country at least, is a mere apology for what they should receive. A few movements in a school-room behind desks in dry, dusty air, are not physical culture. At least one floor in each public school in a large city should be a gymnasium with a trained teacher, a gymnasiarch, as the Greeks called them, whose duty it should be to show each pupil his or her bodily defects, and give the proper training to correct them, and inspire him with the idea of ideal physical perfection.   We can well afford to leave out of our curriculum of education many things now in it, especially history which, as taught, has almost no value and is only an incumbrance to the mind; also much of geography which, important as it is, can be learned later in life to greater advantage.   No doubt other studies could be curtailed to find abundant time for one hour daily for physical culture, and as I know from experience in this branch of education, the better discipline of the school and the better health of the pupils far more than compensates for the time taken from other studies.

Another class of persons who also need the advantages of bodily training is that very large class whose work is mainly in offices and stores, in badly ventilated rooms, and under circumstances very certain to produce bodily degeneration.   No matter how well equipped with physical health they are when they enter their vocations, a few years' time thins their blood and takes away half their muscular force.   It is not so much gymnastic work such need as more out-of-door life, together with such special exercises as will counteract the evils of their occupations.   This class needs an inspiration of some sort to keep up healthful exercise all through life, not the exercise of the athlete, but a modified form which gives bodily health without danger of over-doing.   "The wise for cure on exercise depend," said a great poet, and this should, so far as it can, be the motto of all sedentary people. Their survival depends largely on it.   There are thousands on thousands of people laboring under the delusion that they are overworking, dosing themselves with all sorts of drugs and patent medicines for debility which more oxygen brought into their blood by out-of-door exercise would in great part, if not wholly, remove.   There are few of us city people who do not suffer in this way.

Another class who are serious sufferers from the life they lead are the laborers in factories.

Ours has chosen to become a manufacturing as well as an agricultural country. To a certain extent this is necessary; but our cotton and woolen mills, the pride of many of us, and a great source of wealth to others, are deteriorating more bodies than our gymnasiums and all our athletics are creating.

It is on such material that socialism and anarchy thrive. A human being weakened in body and mind by a life such as is led by workmen and workwomen in the air of factories is a fit subject to receive the crude ideas of these doctrines. Surely if we wish to promote Individualism as a prevailing system, we must have brave, proud-spirited, independent, truth-and justice-and-liberty-loving men and women, who can stand on their own feet and take care of themselves without infringing on the rights of others, and not weakly ones clamoring ever for help. What the methods may be to counteract these evils, I have not time here to indicate, and so, thanking you for your indulgence, I will close with the words of Tyndall, who says in a lecture to students:

"Take good care of your bodies! There have been men who, by wise attention to this point, might have risen to eminence, might have made great discoveries, written great poems, commanded armies, ruled states, but who by unwise neglect of this point have come to naught (failed to survive). Imagine Hercules as an oarsman in a rotten boat; what can he do there, but by every stroke expedite the ruin of his craft? Take care, then, of the timbers of your boat, and avoid all practices likely to introduce either wet or dry rot among them. And this is not to be done by desultory, inter-mittent effort, but by the formation of habits. The will, no doubt, has sometimes to be put forth in strength in order to strangle or crush some special temptation, but the formation of right physical habits is essential to our permanent security. They diminish our chances of falling when assailed, augment our chance of recovery when overthrown."

ABSTRACT OF THE DISCUSSION.

Mr. Henry Nichols:—I shall consider briefly some

of the relations of improved methods of transportation and artificial locomotion, to the social order.

The transportation system has become a controlling factor in each one's private business. It shapes the public policy of the nation, as well as the opportunities, the opinions and the standard of living of each one of us. The present generation has seen this great social and economic factor pass under the control of a few families or individuals, who have also acquired the greater part of the wealth of the nation. Fifty men, it is said, have it in their power, by reason of the wealth which they control, to come together within twenty-four hours, and arrive at an understanding by which every wheel of trade and commerce may be stopped, every avenue of trade blocked, and every electric key struck dumb, and thus paralyze the entire country; for they control the circulating currency and create a panic whenever they will. It is shown that two and one-half per cent of the people of this country own eighty per cent of the property, and that, including their families, they do not, at the most, represent more than twelve and one-half per cent of our population. And this accumulation of wealth in a few hands, beyond precedent in human history, is due to the fact that all the profits arising from improved transportation facilities, have been conferred on a few individuals.

Now, I believe it to be a fundamental principle in political economy that it is not upon the mass of wealth, but upon its distribution, that prosperity depends. It is certainly true that the prosperity of this country is the direct outgrowth of a social system in which there were few very poor and some very rich, whose opportunities were open to those who exercised foresight and industry. "Opportunity," said Emerson: "America is another name for opportunity." But we are living in a period of changing economic conditions. Great organizations of capital having been made possible, combination has driven out competition, and a wages system has grown up by which one set of men run the tools and implements of industry, and another set use them in producing wealth. These enormous corporate bodies have frequently shown their power for mischief, and have proved able to override law, custom and restraint without scruple. They have enacted the laws, elected their own judges to construe them and the executives who administer them. Strikes, once so potent, no longer protect the labor organizations. There has not been a successful strike against a great corporation in ten years, nor will there ever be another successful one. On the other hand, the tendency of recent judicial decisions is to go back to the villenage of the Middle Ages, and attach the laborer to his task, and, if he protests, to treat him as a conspirator.

While the mass of men seem to be blind to the fact, we are well on the way toward a new feudalism, founded, not upon strength of body or skill at arms, but upon mere money accumulations, acquired mostly through public franchise, owning fealty only to an overlord who is the prefect of the feudatories, elected by their money and registering their will.

It is a matter which interests all as well as the poorest laborer, for our children are threatened with the same loss of opportunity, and with finding all avenues of occupation closed, except on condition of becoming servitor of some wealthy oligarchy. The danger is not imaginary; for, given a decline in the standard of living and in average comfort, which is certain to come from such concentration of wealth, and it is possible to have a gross anthropomorphism, the Salvation Army, the mediæval synagogue and the voodoo charm, side by side with the Brooklyn Ethical Association.

Dr. Robert G. Eccles: —

I wholly disagree with the position assumed by Mr. Nichols. In the evolution of locomotive systems there is but little to fear from the economic aspect of the subject. In a general way it may be stated that accumulations of wealth are dangerous when the people cease to be vigilant; but as long as the American people watch capitalists as closely as they are watching them now, it is absurd to anticipate any great amount of danger. The control of railroad and telegraph systems by a few has proved a benefit and not an injury to the many. When the transportation and telegraph business was divided we had to pay far more for their service than at present. When I say far more, I do not mean a few per cent more, but much more than double. With every concentration into fewer hands comes greater economy of working, because of reduced friction; and the lion's share of this benefit comes to the public and not to the capitalist. Let Mr. Nichols compare our railroads with those of Germany and our telegraph system with that of Great Britain, and he will be compelled to acknowledge that these men he complains of are making their fortunes out of what would otherwise be squandered and lost. The English telegraph, run by the Government, charges a greater average per mile than the Western Union, and instead of dividends there is a deficiency every year which the tax-payer has to make good. The population where the English telegraph goes is much more dense, so that the profits should be even greater than those of the Western Union. If our government ran the telegraph we should have precisely the same condition here, or even worse, for our politicians are greater squanderers than those of England. Our railroads supply us with comforts not dreamed of in Germany, and at practically lower rates. The speed is greater, the roadbeds are better kept on the trunk lines, the cars are more luxurious, the heating facilities are perfection itself as compared with those of Germany, and with all these improvements capitalists are getting rich, while roads owned and run by government rarely, if ever, take in more than their running expenses. Why should we denounce the capitalists for getting rich? The more rich men we have, the better for the poor. While the contrast may be greater between the rich of to-day and the poor of to-day, change your point of view and compare the poor of to-day with the poor of seventy-five years ago, and you will find that our lowest depths are paradise compared with those of that time. The more riches men own, the more money they have to pay in wages. Every cent spent by a rich man is spent on some poor man. He cannot spend for anything but it goes to the poor. When he spends it on personal comforts he spends it well, for the poor, but when he spends it to make himself richer, viz., in building more railroads, telegraphs, etc., he spends it better. In the first case he is like a farmer who grinds his wheat to make flour; the flour does good. In the second case he is like the same farmer scattering it on the soil, so that it multiplies. In concentrated wealth there are fewer persons to grind an excess of flour for themselves and more of it is sown to make flour for others.

To be successful in any business, the one in charge must have self-interest. The greater that interest, the more efficient his action. This is the secret of the success of private enterprise, and of the failure of public enterprise. The public servant has no compunction in spending others' money, whereas if it was to be his own loss he would look after it more carefully. As the tax-payer is the loser and not himself, he doesn't feel as keenly the loss of a few dollars and doesn't look as sharply after the danger of such loss. In business the successful man is the man who has survived in the struggle for existence. Generally he has a special adaptation for his work. The place found him; he did not find the place. The place selected him, he had little to do with the selection of it. Put the matter into politics and we make it impossible for the place to do the selecting, since in that case the man survives on popular votes, whether he brings in money or not. Let every one ask himself whether or not he feels as keenly another's loss as he does his own, especially if he does not know that other, and he will perhaps see the danger that inheres in governmental control of any line of business.

Dr. Lewis G. Janes:—

Dr. Holbrook has given us one of the most interesting and profitable lectures, thus far, of our present series. In emphasizing the bearing of his topic on survival, at every point, he has carried out the main intention of this course of lectures. I fully coincide with what he has said about the use and abuse of athletics. All men, and particularly all city dwellers, need a systematic culture of the body as well as of the mind. The early breaking down of brain and nerves, the premature decay of faculties, the extreme susceptibility to disease, observable in the city dweller, are largely due to the lack of this desideratum. On the other hand, the excesses of athleticism often resulting from the competitive contests undertaken by our young men, are productive of great evils. Any form of exercise which results in the exclusive and abnormal development of the superficial muscular tissues is an injury to the health. It depletes the nervous forces and robs the vital portions of the system to create mere brute strength. All culture, whether physical or mental, should aim at symmetry and true proportion in development, and not at abnormal excess.

We are indebted to Dr. Holbrook for coining a new phrase—the "locomotive pervert." We have recently had our attention called to one specimen of the "locomotive pervert"—the prize-fighter. If you will conquer your disgust and read the account of the brutal contest in Florida, in a recent number of the *New York Tribune*, you will see that a spirit of barbarism still survives in this free and enlightened country which is almost incredible. We have heard much of late concerning the alleged savagery of the natives of the Hawaiian Islands; but I will guarantee that no such exhibition of savagery has occurred there for seventy-five years as that reported in the *Tribune*, countenanced by our own "millionaires," gloated over by thousands in our cities before the bulletin-boards and in the columns of the daily newspapers, and educating our young men in a taste for such brutal exhibitions. The Hawaiian may well pray to be saved from the contamination of our boasted "civilization." As teachers of ethics, our condemnation of such brutalities should be positive and emphatic. The press which panders to this depraved appetite with columns of descriptive glorification of such contests is equally guilty with the participants. We are painting the picture of our civilization for the future historian to exhibit and for future generations to peruse. Let us not hide its fairer features with human gore, shed for the amusement of alleged men and Americans in this last decade of the Nineteenth Century!

LABOR AS A FACTOR IN EVO-LUTION

BY

DAVID ALLYN GORTON, M. D.

COLLATERAL READINGS SUGGESTED.

Carpenter's *Principles of Mental Physiology;* Grant Allen's *Physiological Æsthetics;* Becquerel's *Traité Elémentaire Privé et Publique; Labor as a Means of Human Improvement* (Popular Science Monthly, 1891, p. 571); Carlyle's *Critical and Miscellaneous Essays;* Hamerton's *Intellectual Life;* Fothergill's *Diseases of Sedentary and Advanced Life;* Galton's *Hereditary Genius,* and *English Men of Science: Their Nature and Nurture;* Froebel's *Education of Man;* Kindergarten and Manual Training Literature; Gladden's *Man and his Tools;* MacArthur's *Education in its Relation to Manual Industry.*

LABOR AS A FACTOR IN EVOLUTION.

BY DAVID ALLYN GORTON, M. D.

EVOLUTION has won a place in the literature of every language. Even those who, from pride of lineage or fear of heterodoxy, decline to accept the doctrine of man's descent from the ape, will admit that he is being evolved from darkness to light,— from barbarism to civilization.

Evolution is stamped on every page of history and on every leaflet that flutters in the breezes of heaven! Even the rocks attest its truth. Not only is it observed in the awakening faculties of the child, in the unfolding of childhood into manhood or womanhood, but it is apparent in his subsequent career. In him are treasured the experiences of the past, which he enlarges upon and sends, ever augmenting, down the line of posterity.

The subject is strikingly illustrated in the growth of language and literature, science and art, industry and invention. It is illustrated in a manner equally striking in the mechanical arts. Every schoolboy knows the humble origin of the plow, mower, reaper and other implements cf the farm and garden, and can trace back, step by step, the modern harvester or threshing machine to the humble flail and the horses' tread. The steim-engine has been perfected by countless inventions superposed upon Watt's original idea. The simple canoe has become a palatial steamship; and the common wheelbarrow has grown into a commodious express wagon; the gig has become a stately brougham, and this, again, a palace car, with all the luxuries and conveniences of the modern drawing room.

Nothing is created or was ever created, but everything is evolved. The organic forces are evolved from the physical; the psychic or spiritual forces are evolved from the organic; the celestial forces are evolved from the spiritual. Evolution is as true of man and the earth as it is of the humblest invention, or the tiniest flower. It is equally true of nations and peoples, institutions, religions, art, science and philosophy. What is called education is but the process of evolution. Teachers, preachers, books, schools, colleges, universities and the manual arts and industries are means, to which evolution is the end. And when we speak of education, we imply the application of means and methods by which to unfold dormant faculties, or of evolving the mind from a nascent state to that of intellectual and moral supremacy. Let us note briefly, at the outset, the failure of education, in the popular sense, to effect this purpose.

One has been wont to look upon the common school as the hope of the race. Every parent, ambitious for his son's advancement, and in these days, that of his daughters, too, turns to the school as a means to that end. Education is supposed to begin and end with the school. The reformer and philanthropist have regarded the school as a nursery of morality. Statesmen and politicians have likewise based their hopes on the same institution for bettering the condition of the masses and the prevention of pauperism and crime. To this end, the public school has been instituted in the enlightened centers of christendom, and attendance upon it made compulsory. It is a wiser policy, it is said, to tax for the support of schools than for the poorhouse and penitentiary. This sentiment, which was advanced by Horace Mann, one of America's most prominent educators of the last generation, assumes that if we are not taxed for schools, we shall of necessity be taxed to support paupers and criminals. But it is an assumption resting upon a questionable basis, for pauperism and crime keep even pace with the extension of the common school system, and the increase of thieving and over-reaching, with the number of college graduates, showing that vice and ignorance do not sustain the relation of cause and effect,— no more than do knowledge and virtue. Nay, it shows more than that: it shows that education, in the popular sense, is not a specific for the evil of crime and pauperism. We must awaken to the fact, therefore, that intellectual culture is no shield against corruptions of the moral nature, which find expression in the evils of the times. The most atrocious murder in the annals of Massachusetts was committed by a Harvard graduate, while the most wise and virtuous statesman, since Washington, had scarcely the rudiments of a common school education.

The great crimes of the day are not committed by the working classes. The man who lives by the sweat of his brow scorns to live by the sweat of another's brow. He has no disposition to despoil his fellow. He does not steal railroads nor wreck corporations. He does not embezzle, hypothecate, nor run away with trust funds. He knows nothing of the tricks of trade, or methods by which profits may be trebled without increase of costs. He does not sell his opinions or influence by which to rope in the unwary into schemes nefarious. Nor is he a candidate for bribery. He is neither a "bull" nor a "bear;" nor does he form "combines" nor make "corners" to fleece the public. The strongest search-light would fail to find in the "American Colony" on the other side of the St. Lawrence, a hardy son of toil—a working man. The men who prey on society, who reap where they have not sown, who rob and cheat their neighbors, and do all the other wrongs, not to say crimes, which we have enumerated, under forms of law and otherwise, are mostly men of education, many of them college bred. And, be it observed, it is not the wrongs done against law, that Society has most to fear. A thousand-fold more dangerous to society are the wrongs committed in the name and under the sanction of law.

It may appear strange to you that I should stand in this place, consecrated as it is to the service of education and morality, before an audience that owes so much to letters, and speak in terms not altogether laudatory of the influence of books and schools. Do not misunderstand me. The school has its place, and a very large one, among the agencies of evolution. It is as dear to me as it is to any man. But it has its limitations in this direction, as at present constituted, and we insist its influence is as a means and not as

an end. A little French, a little music, a little drawing and painting, and a smattering of Latin and
Greek, boxing and fencing, are empty accomplishments. Of what avail is it if one be master of the
learning of the world and can do nothing? Such an
one is as a leech on the body politic. But for the
labor of others he would starve. Development of
character is of vastly more importance than the possession of the learning of the schools. Genuine education begins where the learning of the schools leaves
off, and the pupil is brought in contact with men and
things, and takes an active part in the world's work.
Mere knowledge does not make character, nor does
it afford any adequate discipline of our faculties; nor
does it civilize us, or affect our moral status. Knowledge is as likely to sharpen the wits of the vicious
and wayward, making them more successful in schemes
to outwit or despoil their fellows, as it is to sharpen
the wits of the virtuous and well-intentioned. It is
to the conflict of mind with mind that we must look
for an education worthy of the name, which means
active participation in the affairs of life—in the world's
work.

Let us now speak of the place of Labor as a factor
in evolution. The subject is so large that we shall
have to confine it to the individual.

Do we sufficiently appreciate the intrinsic beneficence
of labor in the evolution of character? There exists
a tendency to degrade labor, especially if it be manual,
and to put a small value on the man or woman who
is compelled to do it. Public opinion has made it
odious. The aim is, therefore, to gain a living by
other means—to seek to live by the sweat of other
men's brows instead of one's own brow,—to secure the
rewards of labor without incurring its opprobrium.
The spirit of Mammonism which despotically rules
the age, has put a money valuation upon a man's time
and sense alike. Character and success it estimates
by the same unequal standard. The youth who depend upon their wit, or the work of their hands for
a subsistence, are impelled by the force of circumstances and the influence of the time-spirit to do that
which they must, and only so long as they must,

merely as a stepping-stone to something that can be done easier or better, or that pays better. They take no sufficient interest in what they do, and consequently too often fail to attain to excellence in anything.

The same anomaly may be observed in our schools and colleges. The struggle of the student is to get on, to attain position, rather than to build character; to acquire, rather than to possess. In his haste he overlooks the substance and contents himself with the semblance of learning. We all know what a bugbear examinations are to the student and how he is crammed and coached for them, that he may have a better showing than he deserves and reap rewards which he has not earned. The inevitable result on the student is superficial accomplishments, pretense in place of performance, and defective scholarship; on labor, industrial disturbance, bad workmanship, adulteration and shoddy. The real dignity and nobleness of labor are lost sight of, and the chief benefit derived from labor, the physical and moral benefit, is lost altogether.

Now, the influence of labor is two fold, subjective and objective:—on the laborer himself, and on those for whose benefit labor is performed — society. Unless a man loves his work, takes a lively satisfaction in its performance, he fails to reap the blessing it would otherwise confer on him; yes, more; the loss is two-fold. The work fails to bless him, and he fails to bless his work; for it is impossible to do any service, however humble, honestly and faithfully, when the heart is not in it. Besides, society suffers immeasurably from work indifferently done. Lord Derby, in his "Advice to Young Men," has well said, and the idea cannot be too often repeated, that "what a man really takes a keen interest in, he is seldom too dull to understand and to do well; and, conversely, when a man does not care to put the best of his brains into a thing, no amount of mere cleverness will enable him to do it well if it is a thing of real difficulty, or else it is one which he has trained himself to do easily by much previous practice, in which latter case he is really repaying in present ease, the fruit of past exertion; living, so to speak, upon capital he has accumulated by early industry."

While there is such a sentiment in human nature as altruism, the fact should not be overlooked nor disregarded that self-interest is the natural incentive to labor, and that its highest rewards cannot be obtained under a régime that disregards that incentive. Under the existing abnormal order of things, labor is enslaved. The industries are carried on chiefly by organized companies and corporations whose agents pay the least possible price for the greatest possible amount of labor. Such profits as may be made from it go into other men's pockets. The condition that is thus imposed on labor is unethical, not to say unjust. It is a condition that destroys a man's true interest in what he does. Every man who would be free should—yea, must, be his own employer and a sharer in the profits and losses of his own industry. In so far as he is compelled to work for another, on terms and conditions imposed on him, or in the making of which he is not consulted, he is a slave, and sooner or later must lose his manhood. Since one evil hatches another, this one has led to a counter organization of labor, which demands that the least possible amount of labor shall be rendered for the greatest possible amount of money. A more demoralizing state of things it is difficult to imagine, since it causes the direst injury to labor, and clogs the benefaction which the individual would otherwise reap from it. A thousand times better is it that a man should remain poor, struggling for himself, than to become rich under the orders of another. The welfare of the State has a vital interest in this problem, for on its equitable solution hang social order and permanency.

In our nearsightedness we are too prone to regard the money-equivalent as the chief end of work. It is no doubt a very important desideratum, and one not likely to be either overlooked or undervalued; but we submit that the material compensation for one's labor is altogether secondary, compared with the spiritual benefactions which come to a soul wholly devoted to a congenial calling. These cannot be measured or weighed like merchandise; nor can their value be set down in figures and reckoned up in dollars and cents. Good health is among the rewards of honest work. Who shall estimate its market value? So likewise, are a clear head and an honest heart. Who could compute the money value of the delights which they bring? Can any one give the exact equivalent in currency of the raptures which come with a new idea; a beautiful thought; a noble consecration; an elevated sentiment, or a tender, reverent emotion? Probably not. Yet these are some of the delights which well up from the Infinite within one as a reward of work well done, of trusts faithfully discharged. He who does honor to his work is enlarged and ennobled by it, in his whole being, body and soul. Such an one does not suffer from debility, weak back, ennui, insomnia, nervous prostration, or other ills which spring from idleness and pleasure seeking. Nor does he know anything of the hell of unrest and discontent which engulfs so many idlers of the human family. Nature cares for the honest toiler precisely as she cares for every good being or thing that is true to itself and to her, and that fills its appointed sphere, and does her bidding, saying all the time, so distinctly as to be almost audible: "Well done, thou good and faithful servant." Such a soul reaps the choicest fruits of living—the joy that comes to one whose every fiber and faculty thrill with life and emotion—born of the love of his task and the consciousness of its faithful performance. What more could a rightly constituted individual ask for than this? What more, indeed, could he have? His existence is an overflowing fountain of delight which money might detract from, but could not add to. If he were indeed mortal, having nothing to hope for, or to expect beyond this present life, the pleasure of well-doing would make life worth living. One should remember that some acknowledgment is due to the claims of self-respect and the dignity of human nature, without regard to ulterior hopes or fears. Every man is in duty bound to be a man, or at least to try to be a man: act his part on life's stage *like* a man; do his work like a man, with compensation or without compensation, though it were for even three score years and ten without hope of reward in a Beyond, and trust the Providences for the rest. Nature holds him or her, on whom she has conferred the high dignity of manhood or womanhood, to fearful responsibilities in this matter, which neither can in any wise disregard.

It is work for work's sake that puts a crown upon man. Work that enlists the energy of arms and brain is a developing power of unlimited proportions, an educator that has no superior. He who brings such consecration to his task is rewarded for his pains, though the money consideration be barely sufficient to keep body and soul together. There is a law in the constitution of Nature which apportions deserts to her subjects with a justice that is absolutely even handed, depend upon it, and he who fails of his meed, whether of rewards or punishments, in one way, is sure to get it in another. It may come in the form or manner which we least desire or expect; unobserved, invisible as the dew, or the gentle zephyrs; imperceptible as the approach of dawn, the flight of time, or the pulse-beat; mysterious as a providence or a pestilence; but come it must and does, for Providence is no uncertain paymaster, be assured. It is our blindness that conceals the fact, and obscures a power as certain and as unerring in its results as the growth of a flower, or the justice and benignity of God.

The query has often risen in my mind, whether a man is made by his task, or his task by him. The point is by no means so easily determined, if his task be a congenial one, as it at first sight appears to be.

Cromwell is described by Macaulay as a restless, uncouth, purposeless man, until the occasion came that was to awaken his genius. The same is true of our own General Grant. We have known grown boys too stupid to learn their spelling lesson, become, by contact with the world and devotion to congenial pursuits, capable men and useful citizens. Many of them developed all the graces of manner that distinguish the best college bred. Henry Clay may be cited as an example of this type. Mechanics, merchants, bankers, brokers, farmers, business men of all sorts, and statesmen, even of noble records, comprise the long catalogue of men of that description, which my memory recalls. Very dull minds may be awakened, quickened into activity, by work that fully engages their sympathy and commands their minds. We have in our memory a stupid lad, born of semi-idiotic parents, too dull in fact to learn anything at school, whose experience is apropos of our subject. Having been born in abject poverty, he was compelled to work for his bread, or starve, or become a pauper. His was a docile, plastic nature, submitting readily to whatever lot befell him. In the course of events he happened to become apprenticed to a village blacksmith. The blacksmith's shop proved to be a school *par excellence* for him; the smith, his natural schoolmaster. His progress, however, was slow. For a long time he seemed incapable of mastering the minor details of the shop, and was retained to do little else but blow the bellows and swing the sledge, keeping the alternate stroke with that of his master's hammer. In the course of a few years his faculties began to grow, expanding, as it were, under the blows of his heavy sledge, until he finally became a good blacksmith and a respected citizen—thanks to the benign potency of the sledge hammer.

This case is by no means an exceptional illustration of the power of even rude labor to educate a man when kept to his task. The great and good Lincoln acquired the rudiments of his education at rail-splitting and completed it on the platform. Elihu Burritt studied language and worked at blacksmithing at the same time; and Robert Collyer, an eloquent clergyman of the Unitarian church, began his career in the blacksmith's shop. Many of the names that do most grace the pages of American history never saw the inside of a college. Among the more conspicuous of these may be mentioned, Franklin, Patrick Henry, Henry Clay, Lincoln, Chief Justice Chase, "Squatter-sovereignty" Douglas, General Jackson, General Grant and Horace Greeley; while among the more conspicuous of those who have disgraced and are disgracing those pages have been and are college bred.

All effective work is the product of energy inspired by love; and it is certainly high art when it is thus inspired, whether the plane of industry be high or low; whether it be with the sculptor's chisel or the blacksmith's hammer; the pen or the plow, and whether the work itself be the masterpieces of literature, scientific discovery or invention, or the products of mechanical skill, the industrial arts, or common manual labor, faithfully done—done with both hand and heart. The power that directs the hand with certainty and integrity, in any case—in all cases—is the mind. And surely the skilled hand could not exercise its cunning if the mind, whose bidding the hand obeys, were uneducated. "It is by action," says John Stuart Mill, "that the faculties are called forth,—more than by words,—more at least than by words unaccompanied by action."*

The remark, although a truth founded upon the experience of individuals, is likewise a truth founded upon physiological observation. The loss of an arm or a leg results sooner or later in atrophy of the brain on the opposite side of the body from which such loss has occurred, and consequently impairs the mental powers of the brain on that side. This fact has been verified in numerous autopsies. The reason of it is self-evident. The brain depends for its healthy stimulus to action upon the activity of the body. The brain needs the hand no less than the hand needs the brain. If the brain be deprived of such normal stimulus, it ceases to perform its functions, and according to an organic law of all growth, becomes, in consequence, dwarfed and enfeebled, in the same manner precisely that a muscle not used becomes impaired and finally useless. In all sound development, therefore, action must supplement thought. The child that should sit and reason upon the theory of walking would never walk.

Would that we could impress upon every one of you one great truth in this connection, the full significance of which no mind untrained in natural psychology can fully comprehend, namely: the unity of man—the monism, oneness of mind and body, the psychical and the physical. The mind is not distinct and separable from the body. It does not have a local habitation in this organ or that, as taught by the earlier phys-

*The Claims of Labor.

icists. It does not reside exclusively in the head.
It comprehends the body and the body comprehends
the mind .That is to say, mind occupies the whole
body ; permeates every organ and member; ramifies
every tissue; energizes every cell. For this reason,
one cannot take physical exercise without at the same
time, using and stimulating the mental or psychic
powers.

What more effective stimulus to mental action
can there be, therefore, than the employment of
the hand in honest work? the mind in useful
industry? It may never teach one the alphabet, to
real and write, or the multiplication table; the
nomenclature of one's mother tongue, the meaning of
conic sections or other technicalities, useful only as
a means of knowledge; but it does discipline the
faculties of mind and body; it does make one a more
strongly conscious and better-centered man or woman ;
puts one more in harmony with nature and nature's
methods and processes; and brings one nearer the secret of God, the divine, and, therefore, the most
skilled worker. He only can work as does nature,
ceaselessly, with perfect adaptation of means to an
ideal,—the perfect attainment,—who has the perfection of nature in him, working in him and through him,
the will of the divine Workman. It may seem com-
monplace enough, this following a plow or using a
chisel or hammer, but to him who is in harmony with
the life of things, this putting forth the hand and
operating on nature, is full of profound significance.

We have heard common mechanics say that the delight which came to them upon the successful completion of some simple mechanism, over which they had
labored long and diligently with might and main, exceeded their power of expression. It could only be
compared to that exhibited by Archimedes, who, upon
discovering the law of specific gravity, ran naked from
his bath, crying: "Eureka! Eureka!" oblivious of
everything but the supreme joy of his discovery.

The delight that thus overpowered Archimedes like
a flash of light from the Eternal upon his discovery,
is no other than the inspiration which waits upon, cheers
and warms every successful worker; no other than

that which the divine Architect himself experienced, one may suppose, as day by day He reviewed His work, and said, with infinite satisfaction, "It is very good."

Watt was by no means of an enthusiastic temperament, but Dr. Black, one of his eminent biographers, says that he was filled with rapture when the grand discovery of the improvement of the steam-engine first "flashed across his mind." The great composer, the late Gounod, found in his task not only the highest reward but his greatest pleasure. He wrote: "Woe to him who finds not his highest reward in the act of creating! The composition of 'Romeo and Juliet' has filled my soul night and day for years—filled it with pleasure, filled it with pain; I am indebted to it for the happiest hours of my life, and have found therein my reward. That which follows the completion of the work—rehearsals, performances and success—all this is weariness and disappointment. If a god were to give me the power to create a masterpiece, whole and imperishable as Shakespeare's, on condition that no mortal should ever know the author's name, I should be a thousand times happier than over the success of my works and my knowledge of their imperfections." But Gounod is no exception in this respect to other workers in the world's laboratory.

The successful worker needs not to be told of the joy which attends the birth of a new idea. We have known students of literature to become as happy as a child with a toy, over the writing of an exceptionally fine paragraph. Such joys are not unknown to the lower grade of work, or workers. Many a poor, starved soul has forgotten his wretchedness in the inspiration of his task. Every good cook or devout housekeeper, we venture to say, can appreciate the comfort which possessed "Aunt Chloe's" heart when the family and their guests relished her cooking. What a pleasant pride and satisfaction she took in her pies, which Mas'r George liked so well! Her soul was in her pies; and we feel sure that they were indeed good, since flour and water were by no means the most essential elements that entered into their composition.

The Greeks live in the works of their hands even

more than in the works of their brains, immortal as are the latter. What people ever equaled them in sculpture, painting and architecture? For fine originality, idealistic conception, and exquisiteness of workmanship they give us models, the attempt to improve upon which would be presumption the most idle. The exquisite cunning of their hands disclosed the profound genius of their minds; one supplemented the other, and, as might be said, they mutually educated each other. Yet, comparatively few of the Greeks could either read or write. Many of the greatest minds that ever helped to shape the course and destiny of life on this planet, have been developed through honest toil, unaided by the knowledge of letters. The traditions of the divine Jesus must have perished but for the memories of unlettered men. Jesus himself was an apostle of work, a carpenter by trade. The apostle Peter was a fisherman, unfamiliar with letters. And if the others of the Twelve were superiorly educated it does not appear in the record.

It was wise that they were selected from the ranks of the simple and lowly. Their mission was to the poor and unfortunate, falsely so regarded then as now, because of poverty. Faith was the instrument they used, not knowledge; faith was the element they appealed to, not the intellect. Hence it is not at all strange that the Christian Church discredited learning, and that for more than a thousand years but few of its votaries could read or write ; nor that the Christian clergy, for the same period, were unlettered. "In almost every Council," writes Hallam, "the ignorance of the clergy formed a subject of reproach. It is asserted of one, held in 992, that scarcely a single person was to be found in Rome itself, who knew the first elements of letters. Not one priest in a thousand in Spain, about the age of Charlemagne, could address a common letter of salutation to another."*

And yet what mighty trusts were reposed in those early Christians, and with what remarkable fidelity did they execute those trusts! Moreover, the Emperor Charlemagne, himself, could not write his name. And the wise King Alfred was not master of

* History of the Middle Ages, VIII , p. 288.

the Latin language, the almost exclusive language of literature in his time. And yet he could found a great University, if tradition is credible. The most famous and powerful of the Ostragoth kings of Italy, Theodoric, could not write his name; while the Emperor Frederick Barbarossa, King John of Bohemia, and Philip the Hardy of France, could not read, much less write. Hallam says that signatures first began to appear in the fourteenth century, before which seals were used to authorize state papers; and before these, the sign of the cross was in common use for the same purpose.

It is the life which a man puts into his task, however humble it may be, that enables his task to put life into him—paradoxical as it seems. Hard work seldom kills any one. There is, on the contrary, more work killed by men, than men killed by work. Worry may cause death, and idleness kill, and damn while it kills; but honest work never killed anybody with age and strength proportioned to his task.

It is pleasant to have our views on this subject, which may be regarded by many as extreme, confirmed and supported by that indefatigable worker and student, the late Sir Andrew Clark, who, it is well known, inherited a feeble and infirm constitution, but who, by temperance and hard work, managed to live to a good old age. We quote from *The Lancet* of recent date, these words spoken at a clinical lecture at the London Hospital:

"Labor is life," said Sir Andrew, "but worry is killing. It is bad management that kills people. Nature will let no man overwork himself unless he plays her false—takes stimulants at irregular times, smokes too much, or takes opium. If he is regular and obeys the laws of health and walks in the way of physiological righteousness, nature will never allow him to work too much."

The interdependence of genius and the medium of its exercise is so reciprocal that neither can subsist independently of the other. Action is the condition of development in any direction. Did the arm find nothing to act upon it would never round out and ma-

ture. The muscle or the tooth that is not antagonized
withers away. An eye isolated from light loses its
power of vision. So genius, unemployed, deprived
of its natural stimulus, labor, would inevitably die,
for it is as dependent upon exercise for its unfolding,
as the arms of the smith on the hammer, or the tint
of the rose on the sunbeam. To him with special
mental defects—and who of us is without them?—we
would say : "Find them out and work them into fruition.
Give the weak faculty something to do, that indo-
lence may be helped into activity; poverty into plenty.
The weakest faculty in us may thus be developed into
respectable proportions."

Genius and the works of genius go, therefore, hand
in hand, and mutually supplement each other. From
this point of view it may be said, for example, that
the "Birds of America," that incomparable work of
genius, immortalized Audubon, and that "The Animal
Kingdom" created a Buffon and a Cuvier. Those distinguished naturalists live in their works, and it is
difficult to dissociate their own history from the Natural History they so ably wrote. The degree of patient, painstaking toil that all of them gave to their
task almost justifies Goethe's declaration that "genius is patience." They possessed the genius of taking
pains. Of Buffon it is said that he wrote his great
work, "The Animal Kingdom," consisting of twenty
volumes, eighteen times over ! What manner of man
must he be with so poor a genius that he could not
produce a respectable piece of literary or other work
after eighteen earnest trials ! Bishop Butler's celebrated "Analogy" is said to have been re-written
seventy times. It is such a complete exponent and
exemplification of the author's thought, that not a
word could be added to or taken away from it without injury to both author and book. Each has a re-
nown inseparable. The work is certainly a masterpiece of industry; and as a theological text-book
Protestant theologians are deeply indebted to it ; but
not more so, it is believed, than was the Bishop
himself for the genius which so greatly distinguished
him.

The ancient Greeks, to whom we have already re

ferred, have set the world incomparable examples of
diligence in their work without which, it is reasonable
to presume, they never would have attained acknowledged excellence.   Their students took pains.   Their
artists could never do anything too well, and accordingly, each had his specialty in which he excelled.
In painting, for example, some were distinguished for
high finish, as Protogenes; others for fancy, as Theon;
others again for composition, as Pamphiles; still
others, for depth of expression, as Aristides; while for
grace, Apelles is said to have been unrivaled; and
"Euphranor was in all things excellent."   We read,
too, that Protogenes spent seven years on his most
excellent work, the figure of "Ialysus with his dog."
So excellent was this work of art, indeed, that Apelles,
the most celebrated painter in point of grace in all
Greece, and probably the foremost painter of all time,
stood speechless in astonishment when he first saw
it, finally pronouncing it wonderful.*

Apropos of Greek industry and love of application,
it is instructive to note the course pursued by Demosthenes to enable him to become the world's most
celebrated orator.   Though studying rhetoric in his
youth with a master, his first attempt before a popular assembly was a failure, according to Plutarch.
The people laughed at his awkward manners, ungrace-
ful gestures and defective periods.

The ridicule which was poured upon him would
have dissuaded many men from repeating the effort
of public speaking; but in him it served rather to
kindle renewed energy, inflame ambition, and to stimulate perseverance.

He shaved one side of his head, it is said, that he
might not be tempted to go into society. Returning into
subterranean seclusion, he practiced before a looking-
glass the art that was to distinguish him, and that
he was to distinguish.   With him, as chief companions, were the rhetorical works of Grecian masters,
which he studied unremittingly.   The most famous of
these for depth of thought and energy were the writings of Thucydides, which Demosthenes is said to

*See an excellent article on Painting in Anthon's *Greek and Roman
Antiquities.*

have transcribed no less than eighty-eight times! That
was indeed taking pains. But how well did the gods
reward him for it! "Of all human productions," says
Hume, "his orations present the models which approach the nearest to perfection." And Macaulay, himself a master of speech, speaks of him as "standing at
the head of all the mighty masters of speech."

All truly excellent work is the outcome of painstaking thrift, for the intrinsic love of it, and is not the
product of an hour, or the momentary spasm of an exceptional genius. Mushrooms may be produced in a
night, and the white mycelium of fungus in an hour;
but the hardy, wholesome grain condenses within its
cells the sunshine of months; the stately oak or elm,
that of a century. So it is with the masterpieces of
genius. They are evolved by slow process, by dint
of hard work. The trash that costs the least, that is
soonest produced, the soonest dies; but that which
grows the slowest, maturing by slow process under
the strong rays of brilliant genius, the longest lives.
We are well aware that many so-called masterpieces of
literature were produced with great rapidity. Thus
Dryden is said to have written "Alexander's Feast" in
a day and a night; Johnson, his "Life of Savage" in
thirty-six hours; and Mrs. Browning, her "Lady
Geraldine's Courtship" in twelve hours. But it would
have been exceedingly unwise in these eminent au-
thors to entrust their literary immortality to these
little pieces, chiefly remarkable, we make bold to say,
for the ease and rapidity with which they were produced.

No, no, these are not "masterpieces" of literary
excellence that are begun and finished in a few hours,
but the mere foam of exceptional genius, and are as
unlike the real masterpieces of art as shadow and substance. The real masterpieces, we repeat, either of
literature, the fine arts, mechanics, or of invention,
have come through the throes of hard and prolonged
labor. They are not the productions of a day, a
month, or a year. They are often the growth of a
decade, a generation, a lifetime—sometimes of a century, and even a decade of centuries. Shakespeare's
plays occupied the best part of a rare lifetime. "Par-

adise Lost" was forming in the busy brain of its illus-
trious author for many years ere it took definite form and
shape. It is said of a certain college professor that
he spent five minutes over every sentence he ever
wrote. That seems like slow work; but it had one
advantage over most literary work—that of needing
no revision. One may well be suspicious of the quality of hasty literary productions. He who is sparing
of his pains in letters, no less than in other work,
never attains to a high degree of perfection in them.
There can be no great excellence without great labor.

Newton blew soap bubbles in the sunlight for years
before he dared to announce his discovery of the laws
of refraction. So with Hahnemann and Jenner; each
plodded and experimented year after year for a decade, before either had the courage to declare to the
world that he had made a discovery, the one in ther-
apeutics, the other in prophylaxis. Robert Fulton
dreamed and worked, worked and dreamed, for a generation, over the invention of the steamboat; and the
despondent Watt, his predecessor, plodded amid most
discouraging and vexatious difficulties, also for a generation, to get his improvements of the steam-engine
recognized and accepted. Morse, though dying at a
green old age, barely lived long enough to perfect his
life work, the electric telegraph. Professor Grove was
not less fortunate, living to see a discovery in physical philosophy, the unity and mutual convertibility
of the forces, the truth of which was demonstrated by
him at the age of maturity, universally accepted by
men of science. That was glory enough for him.
Grove, poor, is a greater man than Gould, rich. Time
will brighten the name of one; it will tarnish that of
the other.

The experience of these painstaking workers, selected promiscuously from the long catalogue of industrious heroes who have given their lives to labor,
who were evolved by labor—is that of the innumerable throng of men and women who claim it as a
grateful privilege to do the world's work, just for the
sake of doing it. These "Captains of Industry," the
leaders of the world, as Carlyle declared, in any field
of labor, or any department of thought, have found no

royal road to success—rarely a money compensation. Anxious, laborious days, sleepless nights, vexation of spirit, disappointment, self-renunciation, privation and sorrow, have been their chief companions from beginning to end. Their course has been up steep and craggy pathways—the pathway of the gods, as Porphyry declares,—beset with difficulties which, but for patience to wait, the spirit to animate, and the courage to preserve, would have proved insuperable.

And what have been their rewards? Simply, the consciousness of well-doing and the joys of fulfilling the trusts reposed in them by the Supreme Author of their existence.

ABSTRACT OF THE DISCUSSION.

William H. Maxwell, Ph. D. :—

The lecturer has devoted his time to the establishment of three propositions:

1. That education in the popular sense of the term does not rouse the mind from a dormant condition to what he calls "a state of intellectual and moral supremacy."

2. That all the faculties of mind and body develop only through exercise.

3. That labor is an essential condition to high moral development.

He has, unfortunately, not given us a definition of labor. This omission is much to be regretted. While I am prepared to admit the second of the propositions, I can admit the third only with very considerable modifications. There are kinds of labor which do not tend to intellectual and moral development. Does the burglar, who toils with intense concentration over the problem how to break into a bank-vault and burst open a safe, develop his moral sense? Did Mr. James Corbett, who recently worked very hard to "knock out" Mr. Charles Mitchell, develop in the operation the virtues of gentleness, kindness and brotherly love? Had the primeval savage, who sharpened his wits by fashioning, within the recesses of his cave his rude weapons of flint and bone, and by contending with them against the brutes that disputed his right to existence, been compelled to devote his brain and his hands to doing just one thing, say making heads for pins, or eyelets for shoes, as in a modern factory, is it not very doubtful whether he would have advanced far beyond the condition of the anthropoid ape, whether he would ever have become in action like an angel, in apprehension like a god? Or think you that labor such as Thomas Hood describes is the labor that develops the moral and intellectual faculties?

> "With fingers weary and worn,
>   With eyelids heavy and red,
> A woman sat in unwomanly rags,
>   Plying her needle and thread.

> "Work—Work—Work!
>   Till the brain begins to swim!
> Work—Work—Work,
>   Till the eyes are heavy and dim.

> "Seam and gusset and band,
>   Band and gusset and seam,
> Till over the buttons I fall asleep
>   And sew them in a dream.

> O men with sisters dear!
>   O men with mothers and wives,
> It is not linen you're wearing out,
>   But human creatures' lives.

> "Stitch—Stitch—Stitch!
>   In poverty, hunger and dirt;
> Sewing at once, with a double thread,
>   A shroud as well as a shirt.

> "But why do I talk of death?
>   That phantom of grisly bone!
> I hardly fear his terrible shape,
>   It seems so like my own.

> "It seems so like my own,
>   Because of the fasts I keep;
> Oh, God, that bread should be so dear
>   And flesh and blood so cheap!"

And there is many a woman, aye, and man too, in this very Brooklyn of ours at this very day, who is working only to starve. And does this labor make men moral? Where, under such conditions, man retains his honesty, and woman her virtue, it is not because of labor, but of something within that raises the soul above its surroundings, that preserves honor and virtue in spite of grinding, degrading toil. Robert Burns compassed the whole argument of Kant for the immortality of the soul into a single stanza:

> "The poor, oppressed, honest man,
>   Had never, sure, been born,
>   Had there not been some recompense
>   To comfort them that mourn."

And what sort of training do the moral and intellectual faculties of young children receive who are shut up at ceaseless, grinding labor in mines and factories?

> "For oh, say the children, we are weary,
>   And we cannot run or leap;
>   If we cared for any meadows, it were surely
>   To drop down in them and sleep."

John Fiske, it was supposed, had made an original contribution of great value to philosophy when he showed that the evolution of the species becomes more extended as the period of infancy is prolonged. In other words, high development is possible only when the period of labor for a livelihood is long deferred. If Dr. Gorton is right, Mr. Fiske is all wrong. Instead of devoting years to the careful training of a child, we should set it to labor, and it will reach all attainable heights of intellect and morality. Fortunately for humanity, the civilized world does not adopt this view. Fortunately for humanity, the enlightened state endeavors to prevent the destruction of the child, and to preserve it from toil that debases the body and degrades the soul.

From these considerations it is evident that, before accepting the proposition that labor is a means of cultivating the moral sentiments, we must throw many safeguards around the term. I am loath, in the brief period at my disposal, to attempt the task. I shall

not try to do more than throw out two or three suggestions, tentatively.

1. The term "labor" must include intellectual as
well as manual labor.

2. Labor, to be a means of moral and intellectual
advancement, must be adapted to the intellectual as
well as the physical capacities of the laborer.

3. The work must be of such a character as to employ actively the intellectual powers in the direction
of the hand.

4. The work must be inherently interesting.

A volume might be written in the expansion and
illustration of these four propositions, but even without illustration, I doubt not that they will commend
themselves to the common sense of every thinking man.

I regret exceedingly that Dr. Gorton should have
thought it necessary to his argument to make an attack on popular education, and on college education.
The colleges of this country need no defense from
me. I shall not dwell, therefore, on this part of the
subject further than to say that every really great
statesman of the country from Alexander Hamilton
down, with the single exception, perhaps, of Lincoln,
that is every statesman who has added something to
the political knowledge of the world, has been a man
of college education; and, further, that this country has
never yet elected to its Presidential chair a common-
place man, of inferior education, that it did not have
bitter cause to repent its choice.

With regard to popular education—the education of
the common schools—I desire to add a single word.
Dr. Gorton tells us that "pauperism and crime keep
even pace with the extension of the common school
system." It is unfortunately true that, so far as the
Eastern and North Atlantic states are concerned, the
common school system has not grown in proportion to
population. In 1850 over twenty per cent of the population of these states were in the common schools.
In 1890 only a little over seventeen per cent were in
the schools. Whether permanent pauperism and crime
have increased in proportion to the population during
the same period, I must confess myself, in the absence of the statistics of the subject, unable to say;

but if they have, the cause might be traced, with some plausibility, to the diminution of the attendance at the public schools in proportion to population. However this may be, the argument usually urged in favor of the lecturer's position, which, by the way, he asserted, and did not attempt to prove, is that which was set forth with a great array of statistics in the *Popular Science Monthly* about three years ago. The writer had collected the statistics of many penitentiaries and reformatories, and had found, as well as I remember, that about seventy-five per cent of the inmates were persons who could read and write, while only twenty-five per cent were illiterate. From these facts he argued that education and crime advance hand in hand. In doing so, he neglected one of the most elementary principles of arithmetic: that, when comparing fractions, we must consider their denominator as well as their numerator. The writer, in this instance, neglected the basis of population. In our population, about ninety-five per cent read and write; only about five per cent are entirely illiterate. Now, if the ninety-five per cent who read and write produce only seventy-five per cent of the criminals, and if the remaining five per cent of illiterates produce twenty-five per cent of the criminals, it is at once evident that the conclusion to be drawn from these statistics is diametrically opposite to that which was drawn. It is this—Education is the great preventive of crime. That there are great and glaring defects in common school work, no one is more ready to admit than I am. Nay, I go further and say that this admission is, necessarily, the first step toward the remedy of these defects. But *on the other hand* I believe, with all its faults, public school education is the great safeguard of liberty, the best defense of the commonwealth.

Mere labor, in itself, counts for but little. Mere knowledge in itself, counts for but little. When knowledge is so imparted and so employed as to exercise faculty, and train the moral sense, and when the trained mind directs the trained hand, and both work together for a noble purpose, then, and then only, does labor become a factor in evolution.

Dr. Lewis G. Janes:—

Carlyle has well said that work is worship. It is more than that: it is salvation. Action, rational exertion toward noble ends, is life. Stagnation and quiescence are death. No honorable labor should be drudgery. However humble, it should interest the mind and arouse a high ambition to render the best possible service Herein, it seems to me, lies a radical defect in our present methods. Among mechanical workers, there seems to be a jealousy of one who aims at superior service, or who accomplishes more than the average laborer, at his allotted task. A dead level of mediocrity seems to be aimed at, rather than superiority and perfection of results. Work in this spirit does not tend to survival ; nor do the shoddy garments and Buddenseick buildings which it produces.

The differentiation of labor, which is so marked a feature of our modern life, tends to lessen the hours of employment and open opportunity for the cultivation of the higher faculties. But we should remember that spare time is only opportunity. It is not of itself necessarily a blessing. The old adage is still true in spirit. Satan finds mischief for idle hands and idle brains. If the "eight hour law" results in a mere disuse of faculty—if it sends men to the saloon instead of to the library or the home—it is an evil rather than a benefit.

The speaker has treated the subject almost exclusively with regard to the effect of labor on the individual. Much might also be said of work as a factor in national development and survival. There is time only for a hint in this direction. In tropical climates, for example, where, it has been said, all that a young couple have to do when they start in life is to plant a banana tree and sit down under its grateful shade for the rest of their existence, we find no high development of character—no inspiring sense of nationality or community of sentiment. The contest with nature and competition with our fellows are required to bring out the highest that is in us. This very competition which the socialist deprecates, it might easily be shown, has worn off the rough edges of individual idiosyncrasy, and rendered possible a deeper sympathy and more perfect co-operation.

The question of the Sunday rest is also fruitful in this connection. I believe it highly essential to have this stated relief from daily avocations, but I most seriously question whether absolute rest or disuse of faculties one day in seven is of advantage to man, either physically or spiritually. Let this time be sacred to high uses—not dissipated by idleness of mind and body. Sunday has often brought me the severest work of the week—but it has been life-saving and life-prolonging in its effects. Sunday work of this high character is the best prophylactic for "blue Mondays."

I did not understand, with Dr. Maxwell, that the speaker eulogized the influence of all sorts of labor, indiscriminately, on the formation of character. On the contrary, I thought he made a very clear distinction between those kinds and conditions of labor which are ethical and those which are unethical in their effects. It was "honest work," "useful labor," "the congenial calling," which he praised, I think not too highly. While no one values more highly than myself the opportunities for education in our schools and universities, their methods are not above criticism, and I agree with the spirit of Dr. Gorton's teaching that they are only the primary stages in our education, which is continued in the faithful attention to our subsequent life-work. I am glad to believe that our methods of study are becoming more practical, as more intelligent attention is given to the psychology of our educational methods. I am glad to testify as to my own appreciation of the good work which Dr. Maxwell is doing in our Brooklyn schools. Let us take to heart the lessons of intelligent criticism, and strive for the highest utilities, both in our schools and in the University of Life.

PROTECTIVE COVERING

MRS. LIZZIE CHENEY-WARD

COLLATERAL READINGS SUGGESTED.

Spencer's *Sociology*, and *Illustrations of Universal Progress;* Hulme's *The Birth and Development of Ornament;* Balfour's *The Evolution of Decorative Art;* Flower's *Fashion in Deformity;* Starr's *Dress and Adornment* (Popular Science Monthly, 1891, pp. 488, 787); Carlyle's *Sartor Resartus.*

PROTECTIVE COVERING; ITS EVOLUTIONARY HISTORY AND MEANING.

By Lizzie Cheney-Ward.

Next to what we eat, no other topic ranks in importance with what we wear. It is what we wear that makes us largely what we are to others. In one of its great aspects dress is a disguise. By it popular standards would have us believe that we improve upon our defective physiques. Among the conscious uses of clothing it is probable that that of beauty-producing stands now and always has stood preëminent.

> "To dress the maid the decent graces brought,
> A robe in all the dyes of beauty wrought."

This phase of it (the ornamental) has come to occupy a very considerable portion of the thought of mankind. Whether true or not, it is believed now to exercise a most potent influence on our lives and doings. Mrs. Pryor says: "Well-dressed, according to her own standard, a woman is always more agreeable, apart from the pleasing impression she makes upon the eye. She is brighter, wittier, more sympathetic, and in her own inner consciousness experiences a sense of serene content which can not be attained by the consolations of religion." No less a man than Bulwer wrote his first novels in dress suit. A considerable portion of the clergy hold robes and vesture as indispensable to religious service. And every servant regards himself or herself as not quite happy and successful unless he or she has on a uniform or dresses in the style of master or mistress. Altogether, the appertainings of dress probably cost humanity more than food. For the majority of the race, the two fill up nearly the whole of life.

In an hour's discourse it would be manifestly impossible to give a complete account of so momentous a question. In general, detailed accounts of special fields are more interesting. However, bird's-eye views also have their value, and at the risk of obscurity I shall undertake to direct attention to the principal phases and stages in the evolution of the protective covering of living forms from lowest to highest. I do this the rather because I am unable to anywhere find such a survey, and because the modern bias is such that a cause is not put in the way of rational progress till its evolutionary aspects are comprehended.*

PLANTS.

In the plant world we see many and wonderful instances of naturally developed protective covering. No one, of course, will need prompting to think of the enormous varieties in the types of bark which cover the trunks and main branches of trees and shrubs. The thick, spongy bark of the pine protects it against excessive sun-heat, and therefore preserves its blood (the pitch) from over-evaporation. And so the epidermis of every plant protects it against one or another of the influences of heat, air, insects, etc., which would otherwise beset it. Then the calyxes are modified leaves which serve to guard the flower, and the corollas are the underclothes or a finer protection for the more delicate stamens and pistils. Besides these are numerous other characteristic coverings and guards. The wool on the mullein leaves prevents sudden changes of temperature from too vital effects. The spines of thistles and thorns, though not exactly a covering, are an effective guard against grazing animals. It is on this principle that rose bushes and berry bushes and berry patches thrive so abundantly. The stinging hairs of nettles and the cutting edges of many sedges and grasses, the leathery character of flags, cattails and rushes insure for these long life and prosperity. Those many characteristics of nauseous, pungent odors (as skunk cabbage and mint), or the acrid,

* I wish to add by way of foot note, that this lecture is a coöperative effort. It will represent the standpoint of a man as well as a woman. At every step in the preparation, I have consulted the wider knowledge and insight of my husband, Dr. Ward.

bitter, or resinous tastes of smart-weed, tansy, scrub pine and milk-weed do not belong under the head of protective covering. Perhaps within our special field are those sticky exudations found occasionally at the joints, which act as a sort of trap to catch pillaging insects. A very curious sort of protection is related by Sir John Lubbock:— "In South America there is a species of Acacia, which if unprotected is apt to be stripped of its leaves by a leaf-cutting ant, which uses them not directly for food, but to grow mushrooms on. The Acacia, however, bears hollow thorns, while each leaflet produces honey in a crater-formed gland at the base, and a small, sweet, pear-shaped body at the tip. In consequence, it is inhabited by myriads of a small ant, which nests in the hollow thorns, and thus finds meat, drink, and lodging all provided for it. These ants are continually roaming over the plant, and constitute a most efficient body-guard, not only driving off the leaf-cutting ant, but rendering the leaves less liable to be eaten by herbivorous mammalia." Plants sometimes afford themselves protection by bending over, to keep out the dew at night or the rain in time of shower. Some close the flowers entirely.

ANIMALS.

If we pass now to the animal types of existence we observe that even the very lowest forms are provided with some protective covering. A cell, to be a cell, must have a sort of epithelial film to hold the fluid part in place. Of such character are the protozoön coverings. In the next stage differentiation of covering is much higher.* Star fishes and sea-urchins are covered with a more tenacious and relatively harder limy coating imbedded in the skin, or covering it as a plate. The myriad forms of these strange creatures inhabit for the most part the ocean beds.

> "There the sea-flower spreads its leaves of blue,
> That never are wet with the falling dew,
> But in bright and changeful beauty shine,
> Far down in the green and glassy brine."

*There are also single-celled creatures some of which have developed a limy and others a flinty cell-like covering. The sponges have flinty points or spicules forming a sort of projecting skeleton and protecting the softer cell substance

Here they are not subject to the dangers which beset the creatures of land and air. To have a hide ill-suited to the mouths of the swimming swarms of the vertebrate order is all-essential. An even temperature and quiet water makes life for them of a tranquil character.

> "There, with a light and easy motion,
> The fan-coral sweeps through the deep, clear sea;
> And the yellow and scarlet tufts of ocean
> Are budding like corn on the upland lea;
> And life, in rare and beautiful forms,
> Is sporting amid those bowers of stone,
> And is safe when the wrathful spirit of storms
> Has made the top of the ocean his own."

With each higher stage the type of protection changes, as does the mode of life. The harder shells of the snail and oyster afford a better retreat, while they allow a certain greater freedom of action to the inmates. Sometimes, alas, this freedom is indulged in at peril. The Roman poet Oppian, 1500 years ago, graphically describes these struggles:—

> "The prickly star creeps on with fell deceit
> To force the oyster from his close retreat.
> When gaping lids their widening void display
> The watchful star thrusts in a pointed ray;
> Of all its treasures spoils the rifled case,
> And empty shells the sandy hillocks grace."

If he cannot do this, he clasps the shell till the poor bivalve dies from suffocation, and then his relaxed muscles give up his soft body as easy booty. Again, these apparently effective coverings prove most ineffective under the operations of the insidious Drill (Fusus Cinereus), which punctures their shells by thousands and millions, and thus sucks out their life juices. Still more varied in characteristics are the types of covering among the crustaceans and insects. Lobsters and crabs are provided with limy over-lapping plates, forming an external skeleton. In insects the material is chitine, a peculiar nitrogenous substance which is neither horn, lime, nor flint. Than these many types of protection nothing can be more perfect. For example, the armor of the beetles and the hard encasement of their bodies and limbs. Insects often have something imitating the feathers of birds covering their antennæ, wings, and sometimes their bodies. Others are clothed with hair resembling that of the quadrupeds but of infinitely fine and silky texture and brilliant and delicate color.

In the vertebrate the bony parts are located in the interior of the body and hence do not serve for protective covering, as was the case with the crustaceans and insects. To begin with the lowest, this is offset in the eels and lampreys by an excessively tough and slimy skin. In the fishes the skin is covered with horny scales. The batrachians are exceptional for their lack of protection, depending more largely upon the seclusion of water and other hiding places, or their superior powers of locomotion. A few of the reptilia have a sort of dermal skeleton, consisting of horny plates over-growing a tough and wrinkled skin. Of these the alligator and crocodile form the best examples. The turtle, the slowest of its race, has developed a horny armor into which it draws limbs and head, for safety against attack. This must also prove an effectual shelter against cold.

When reptiles began to spring from bush to bush, and from tree to tree, natural selection had a new task on hand, namely the evolution of hair and scales into the lighter, more helpful material, feathers. Lightness, warmth, and sustaining power were the elements to be accomplished. The success to which during ages these have been achieved is past understanding. Compare in these respects the jumping toad or tree-frog with the gull or stormy petrel. The perfection of quality in the covering of birds, like the frigate pelican which is found far out at sea, where it probably remains for days, in any and every kind of weather, battling with the fiercest storms, is something to excite the keenest admiration. Contrast again the coarse, hair-like, cylindrical stalks of the almost wingless cassowary in the Eastern Archipelago, or the fluffy hairs of the Australian emu, both clad, so to speak, in the flowing garbs of tropical regions, with the compact and densely downy covering of the Arctic puffin or the king penguin of Patagonia,

Of the land animals, the varieties of covering are still greater. Beginning at the tropics with the tough-hided rhinoceros and elephant, with the sleek-coated zebra and leopard, the coarse and loose-haired llama or paca, we find their antitheses in the ancient woolly mammoth of Siberia, the shaggy Shetland or Cossack pony, and the thick-furred seal, Arctic fox, or Polar bear. It is interesting to note the work of climate in the difference between the naked Mexican dog and his muffled Eskimo brother, or between the hairy-coated Wallachian or Astrachan sheep and the fine-wooled merinos of Northern Europe. In the temperate zones there occur many curious compensatory climatic adjustments. The snake sloughs his skin and comes out in summer clothing. The horse and the ox shed their hair in large patches on the ground where they lie and roll in the spring. Birds moult their thick winter feathers on approaching summer. We have before seen instances where covering has served the double purpose of protection against changes of temperature, as well as the attacks of enemies. The most curious intance of this is the quill covering of the porcupine, a defensive armor of very effective character. This uncouth and stupid creature survives with out speed, caution, or ingenuity, in various parts of the world. From time immemorial the story of its power of shooting quills at its enemies, has been handed down. Aristotle, Pliny, Ælian, Oppian, Claudian and many modern writers have helped to propagate the illusion. At most, the excited and attacked porcupine raises his quills by subcutaneous muscles at nearly right angles to the body, and lies curled together like a bristling ball; in which condition this otherwise inoffensive little creature becomes a dangerous victim. The Quadrumana have remained inhabiters only of tropical regions. Some of them have little covering, but generally they are coated with a coarse, loose, thin hair, varying in length on the different species

Whether primitive man had such covering as his present nearest of kin, is not known. If he originated in the warmest climes, it might have been from ancestry with naked skin. (Compare the naked dogs, ele-

phants, hippopotami.) On the other hand, it is possible that his ancestry were hairy. On this basis such
natural protective covering has under the wearing of
ornament and clothing, nearly disappeared, natural
covering thus giving way to artificial. The hairiest people now extant are the Ainos of Yesso of the Northern
Japanese Islands, and the North Australians.

These peoples may have remained nearer the primitive type, or their hairy covering may be a development occasioned by emigration to colder regions.

SKIN.

With animals or men, the primary natural protective
agent is the skin. The appendages of hair, fur, wool,
quills, feathers, bony substance, scales, and shells are
secondary developments, to meet special rigors of circumstances. They are peculiar formations of the epidermis. Man during historic times not having had
any of these natural coverings, has been obliged to
make up for them by artificial means, when circumstances have compelled him to live in temperate or
frigid zones. The uncivilized man of the tropics still
goes covered almost solely in this basic natural garb.
Had mankind emigrated northward slowly enough it
is probable that the secondary appendages would have
grown to meet the needs of the gradually encountered
climatic rigors. But such was not the case. With
enemies behind and relentless cold before, his survival
depended upon his adjustment to the new conditions.
His own skin, too thin, must be supplemented by
those of the animals he has slain. And dire necessity
must teach him how to dress their hides.

We shall shortly see that the donning of clothes did
not arise in quite so simple a manner. Meanwhile a
word or two on this marvelous fabric, the natural
skin. Steele says of it: "A protection from the outer
world, it is our only means of communicating with it.
Insensible itself, it is the organs of touch. It feels
the pressure of a hair, yet bears the weight of the
body. It yields to every motion of that which it wraps
and holds in place. It hides from view the delicate
organs within, yet the faintest tint of a thought shines
through, while the soul paints upon it, as on a canvas,

the richest and rarest of colors." The blood brings replacing material continually to the surface, so that we are all the time growing out and growing off. This keeps an outer scale, the cuticle—the not yet grown off particles—as a sort of protection for the more delicate and sensitive membranes beneath.

Protective covering may include also those phases of mimicry in the exterior of living creatures which enable them to avoid capture through being unobserved. This aspect of it refers only to color and form. As, for example, the grayish green tone of the female of the so-called Virginia red-bird is a mimicry of nest surroundings brought about by natural selection; while the bright red plumage of her mate is the result of her taste through ages of sexual selection.

ORIGIN OF CLOTHING.

We must now consider the problem of how in man there arose the practice of artificial covering. How did people ever get into this bothersome habit of making so much trouble for themselves? To primitive minds the pains, the fussing and botherings of civilization are incomprehensible. This point is illustrated by the experience of a clergyman who was stopping at a fishing hamlet on the coast of Maine. While finishing his toilet one morning with a comb, the story runs, a little native of ten stood looking on in amazement. With hands on his knees, mouth and eyes wide open and face upturned before the minister, he stood it as long as he could, and then burst out in inquisitive amazement: "Say, Mister, do you comb your hair every day?" "Certainly," said the minister, "of course I do."

Lifting his hands from his knees and dropping his head with a sigh, the boy exclaimed: "Wal, don't it seem to you sometimes as if you was an awful sight of trouble to yourself?"

In seeking for the motives and influences in which the fact of artificial covering had its origin, we naturally think first of those concerning which our consciousness is keenest. If we examine our present consciousness we find that clothing serves for comeliness, comfort, and covering; or for ornament, protection, and modesty. With enlightened nations among the three objects, that of covering nakedness rises first in the mind as most essential, that of protection against heat and cold, insects, rocks and branches comes second ; that of ornamenting and beautifying the person is last, and least consciously necessary. But a study of the history of civilization and the condition and notions of primitive mankind, leads us to a literally reversed conclusion as to its origin. We discover that the desire for display has from the first been the strongest motive in dress. Ornament is universally prevalent among human races ; while nakedness, aside from sparse ornamentation, is frequent. Primitive man had no scruples of modesty. Even some of the primitive races having the art of clothing highly developed, go naked when temperature permits; as, for example, the Eskimo in their over-heated huts. The idea of shame of nakedness is one relatively very advanced, while that of ornament is more primitive than even the race of man. Many animals and birds possess it. Modesty is the outcome of a relatively high moral development And moral development has resulted from the pressure toward social organization, and the maintenance thereof. With every increasing complexity in the methods of life, and with the increase in numbers of the roving hordes and of the hordes themselves, there necessarily grew apace ideas regarding questions of individual right. The promiscuity of sex relationship which may to a greater or less extent have previously prevailed must necessarily become more and more restricted as the social organism advanced in completeness. The dependent condition of females during gestation and nursing and the individual responsibilty of males in providing for their mates and offspring must end in the insistence upon monogamic and chaste relationships. As soon as ornament had made a considerable advance and had become to some extent a covering, the consciousness begotten by the moral social relationships insisted upon the continual wearing of such ornaments as tended to prevent temptations to sexual unchastity. This is, in brief, the genealogy of clothing for modesty's sake. I shall have occasion to refer to it again shortly,

ORNAMENT.

Just how the notion of ornamenting the person arose, it is not necessary here to discuss. Whether from mere fancies, from notions of exhibiting game secured, booty plundered, trophies of war or otherwise, the fact of the actual wearing of ornament having begun, its later results in the history of the race are secured.

Ornaments may be *hung* on head, neck, arms, wrists, fingers, waist, and ankles. These are the natural places of support.

They may be *bored through* the ears, nose, lips, and breast.

They may be *painted on* by stains or greases in stripes and spots of various kinds.

They may be *cut in* by a process of gashing the forehead, cheeks or breast.

They may be *pricked* in with pigments, with a greater or less degree of art. The latter is known by the name of *tattoo*.

They may be used as *æsthetic swathing* or clothing, after the arts of skin preparation and weaving have been learned.

The most primitive decorations are merely the result of the desires of the individual to make himself attractive and conspicuous. This he does by attempts to exhibit his bravery or skill, to create the feeling of his terribleness, or produce admiration as to his beauty. Sometimes that which serves as ornament, serves also as protection. For example, the colored earth mixed with lard which the Andaman Islanders use as paint serves also to protect them from heat and mosquitos. Some of them line it with finger marks, others add stripes of color, while a real dandy will paint one-half of his face red, the other olive green, and make an ornamental border where the two colors meet down his chest and stomach. The practice of painting has been very universal, and is even still to be met with in the streets of highest civilized lands. I have heard of some tribes whose mourning costume consists of a coat of black or white paint all over. Most of the smearing of primitive peoples is impermanent and has to be frequently done over. It is probably something of a

protection against changes of temperature. Tattooing
is permanent painting. It is accomplished by a very
delicate process of pricking the pigments into the skin
under the epidermis. It has the effect of doing away
with the naked appearance, especially with the yellow
and tawny races. It might be remarked in passing, that
dark-skinned races show and feel less nakedness than
others. The German traveler Bastian says of his experiences among the naked Youma Indians in Arizona,
that he came to regard this as natural and proper for
them.

It scarcely comes within the compass of protective
covering, to speak of cutting and gashing. Yet this
is one of the phases belonging to the natural history
of dress. Scars are an evidence of hardship and bravery
that have been experienced. Everywhere in primitive
life, courage and endurance are prize virtues. Little
wonder, then, that some primitive and barbarous peoples
have cut and gashed the skin purposely. Sometimes
they did this as a test of the young warrior's mettle.
Sometimes as a tribal mark. Sometimes again, out of
mere fancy and taste for the odd and ornamental.
Trophies taken in war or the chase, are naturally
among the earliest ornaments. Every one likes to be
admired for his courage and expertness. The North
American Indian hangs the scalps of his enemies upon
his belt with cruel pride. It is hard for us to understand the unfeeling and apparently fiendish yearnings
of the head-hunters among the land Dyaks of Borneo.
And the grotesqueness of the New Zealander's exhibit of hunting skill by sticking birds in his ears, is
only equaled by the American or European woman's
thoughtless but cruel fancy of wearing them on her
hat. When nations come to call themselves civilized
so that they cannot wear the scalps of those they kill,
their queens and rulers pin medals on their soldiers'
breasts as more æsthetic evidences of their murderous
depredations.

Beads and shells are types of ornament dating from
the very earliest period of known human existence.
Prof. de Mortillet (Le Pre-Historique) cites instances
of stone beads in the early Quaternary if not Tertiary
period. And in these, as in all other phases of dress,

the fashions have changed from red to blue and so on.

Rings are also very old. They perhaps had their origin in beads by the drilling of larger holes. Sometimes they have been very profusely worn. One traveler relates the finding of seventy-one on one woman. Being mere ornamentation, they have lingered longer as a female adornment. Among some peoples, rings are a method of preserving wealth. Gold, silver and other valuables are stored up in this way. Four-fifths of the relics of the ancient Swiss Lake Dwellers are ornaments, and of these a considerable portion are rings. Rings are not confined to the fingers alone, but have been worn on the waist, arms and legs. They become useful also for carrying knives, warding off blows, and in other ways.

This kind of ornaments, trophies, beads, shells, and rings, easily and gradually blends into broader orna- ment. Teeth, tusks, and the like, are substituted for beads. These in turn, give place to leaves, strips of bark, tails of animals, feathers, bunches of grass. These again to skins, furs, and woven fabrics. The longer, more tassellate, and dangling neck gear, forms a sort of cape; while that hung around the waist, becomes a little skirt. What we call "dress' is thus seen to be on the advance, while what we call ornament, *per se*, declines Yet the savage is not dressed in such a stage as this, nor have the civilized peoples, as we have seen, left off that which is merely and distinc- tively ornament. As there are savages who know noth- ing of clothes, so there are yet civilized people who bore their ears, band their fingers in metal and wear plumes and feathers on their heads.

As a rule the most painful methods are the first to disappear. Among the earliest to be left off are the painful and inconvenient mouth and teeth ornaments; then would follow those of the nose, the bandaging and flattening of the head, the piercing and gashing of the chest, the boring of the ears, and finally the bandaging of the waist and pinching and distorting of the feet. All stages, however, are yet to be met with, here and there upon the globe. The Botacudos of Brazil, Kolushes of the Aleutian Islands, and certain Central American Indians wear huge plugs and ungainly ornaments in their lip. In New Guinea and Australia (as well as among the ancient Jews, according to Ezekiel and Isaiah) are found the nose-ornaments, attached by holes through the septum or wings of the nostrils. In some tribes the teeth are filed sharp, or into the forms of crescents and crosses. Among others they were filled with brass nails or inlaid with mosaics; and perhaps the most unaccountable of all is that of breaking them off. The flattening and bandaging of the head had its most conspicuous illustration among the old Peruvians who sought to form round and cylindrical crania, and the modern Quatsino Indians who pressed them into conical or sugar-loaf form. Strange as it may seem to us, these processes do not seem to have affected the mental power in any marked degree. Bandaging the arms in order to make the hands large, is a custom in the Philippine Islands. The bandaging of the hands in leather encasement to make them small, prevails in Europe and America. In China the feet of girls of high rank are kept in wooden shoes from childhood on, to prevent their growing large. In Europe and America leather is used.

If we look for the reasons for these customs, we find that the notion of beauty is everywhere at the bottom. As secondary and later motives those of individual distinction, social standing, family, clan or tribal designations, as for example, coats of arms, follow later.

PROTECTION.

The extension of ornament till it becomes abundant develops it into a protective covering. Especially is this the case with neck and waist ornaments. The necessities occasioned by living in changeable climates and by rough exposure made that which at the first was merely a fancy become later a necessity. Early man undoubtedly lived in warm regions and might have been protected from the slight changes to which he was subject by hairy covering. As the increase of population and the scarcity of food caused emigrations to less hospitable temperatures, and as his simple primitive necklaces and waistbands of trinkets increased their length and quantity, they came to serve a most important but unintended purpose. From these in course of time have been derived all capes, shawls, coats, shoulder garments, and skirts, drawers, petticoats and trousers.

After the art of weaving had been invented it gave to ornament a more extended character, and became an indispensable aid when ornament came to take on the feature of protection. Its most primitive forms were braided strands of leaves, grasses, thongs, and twigs. Then came the tying of these together in more extended surfaces, and the sewing of them upon barks and skins. The karose or feather-cape of the Kaffirs is an example of this, and is said to be the finest type of needle-work in the world. The spinning and braiding of threads of wool and hair marked a great advance, and made possible wider and wider braids of closer and closer texture, till the stage that we call weaving was reached. Thereafter the possibilities both for ornamentation and protection were unlimited by this immense step in the improvement and development in the means.

Ornament after ornament adding element after element of protection were easily and naturally extended till the whole body was covered. An illustration or two may help our imaginations in carrying out the process by which this has been brought about. A square piece of cloth of any attractive color could easily be worn over the shoulders, by cutting a slit in the center large enough to insert the head through. This is actually extant in the Spanish-American *poncho*, a pretty and useful article of clothing of the simplest possible character. They are often wrought with beautiful designs. By pinning the *poncho* together under the extended arms and down the side it becomes a smock, shirt, or coat. So, too, a straight piece of cloth pinned round the waist and reaching to the knees or lower, is a skirt. Inclement weather, cold climate and convenience at labor, gradually necessitate the pinning and tying of the skirt around the legs. Finally it is divided. Instances of these last stages are to be found among the Javanese, Chinese, and Japanese; and so far as the skirt is concerned, the undeveloped primitive stage still survives upon European and

American women. It is interesting to observe that among peoples considerably advanced in the art of protective covering, there occur occasionally curious intances of reversion to the primitive costume and features of old-time dress. Thus the Monbuttos in Central Africa dress in skins during certain great religious festivals. In some regions of India the Hindoos dress in leaves and go to the woods for celebrations. The gowns of the Catholic and Episcopal clergy are survivals of the ancient robes of Roman and Jewish times.

It will help us to understand the origin and grounds of present customs if we spend a moment or two in consideration of two widely-diverging types of dress. The Mediterranean and Southern races of ancient times were clad in what are called flowing garments. Both sexes draped themselves with large pieces of variously cut cloths hanging from shoulder to ankles. Among the simplest and least artistic of these were the Ancient Eygptians. The men wore a short kilt which hung nearly to the knees, and was gathered full in front, and had a girdle round the waist. Over this the higher classes wore a large, long, full shirt or gown of fine linen, reaching almost to the ankles. This was tied in various forms. Both were usually white and the outer was transparent. The lower class men wore only kilt and girdle or went naked at labor. The women wore a tight shirt or gown skirt reaching to the ankles and supported by shoulder straps. It had a girdle at the waist, with the long ends hanging in front. Over this was a full shirt or gown extending to the ground. It had wide sleeves coming below the elbows. The whole dress was light and cool, and served well the purposes of taste and warm climate.

The nations of the North who lived in the inhospitable regions of Germany, Scandinavia, and Northern Asia, were very differently covered. Cold and storm compelled the tying in of their garments to insure greater warmth. A description of the modern Eskimo clothing will help us to picture to ourselves its contrast. Men and women dress almost upon the same plan. The men wear a jacket with a hood hanging on the back used for the head in cold weather. The jacket has no opening except at the neck. The women's jacket has a fur-lined hood for carrying a child. It has no collar. Trousers are sometimes tight, more often loose. They are fastened into boots made of seal-skin. The women's trousers are usually ornamented with necks of the eider duck, or with an embroidery of native dyed leather. Their white leather boots reach over the knees. The jacket and trousers are laced together. In winter they wear two suits, one with hair inside, the other with hair out. Carefully made bird-skin shirts are also sometimes worn. Stockings are of dog or young reindeer skin. The fine clothes have the hair out, and working clothes have the hair in. In wet weather both sexes wear an over garment, a sort of cloak made of seal's intestines. It is waterproof and very light. On sea voyages, they draw on a smooth black seal-skin, which sheds water. Their clothes are neatly made, being sewn with sinew thread and bone or steel needles (if the latter is obtainable). They often fit beautifully. They are profusely decked with ornaments, rings, feathers, pearls, shells, worn on the clothes, in the ears, lips and sometimes nose. Bands of leather on the legs, arms and forehead are often set with pearls. Among the women tattooing is almost universal. That value is a matter of latitude and longitude, we may realize when we know that "the every-day clothes of the commonest persons," as Mark Twain says in the *Eskimo Maiden's Romance*, "are worth twelve or fifteen hundred dollars." He says he is not acquainted with any one at home who wears twelve hundred dollar toilets to go a-fishing in.

The general types here described serve to illustrate the general characteristics of clothing, in warm and cold climes. In the early centuries of the Christian era they were represented by the tunics and togas of the peoples composing the Mediterranean portions of the Roman Empire, and the *braccæ* Gauls and Teutons on its Northern border. When the loss of faith had morally undermined the Empire, and luxurious indulgences had enervated the rich and enslaved the poor, there swooped down upon them these trousered hordes of stalwart Germanic origin. Rome and its boasted civilization became their booty. Their chiefs

sat in the place of the Cæsars, and their men became
the captains and rulers of the realm. The man in *toga*
took orders from the man in *bracca*. The party in
power always sets the fashions for the realm. All men
who aspired to place or influence or even respect,
gradually shortened their skirts and donned the trousers. The new style of dress was found to be far better fitted to the exertion of existence. The more conservative elements of society, namely the women and
the priests, still continued to be clothed in the flowing
Southern draperies.

Thus arose a differentiation which has lasted to our
day, and which has become one of the most deep-
seated prejudices known to history. It has been an
inconceivable power in keeping the female sex from
the progress which it would naturally have made in
these later centuries of greatest human advancement.
Dressed in the swaddling-clothes of primitive ingenuity, a widely active and successful paticipation in the
fields of human effort has been impossible for woman.

It will of course be understood that within these
main lines of tendency there have taken place many
important changes. The fancies of mankind, though
by no means so strong as the environing natural forces,
are always at work accomplishing modifications. The
history of modern fashion is an interesting chapter of
sociology. There is time to notice only two or three
of the most meaningful tendencies.

To begin with the *male* side, the gown forms worn
in classic times became gradually shortened under the
influence of the Teutonic garb on the men who held the
power, swayed the realm, and commanded affairs. In
the fourteenth century this shortened gown had become a mere tunic or shirt which, under the improving
processes of weaving and tailoring, was lined and orna-
namented. Thus transformed, it became a sort of
coat buttoned in front—the celebrated doublet. To
begin again at the feet, the short hose worn with the
long gowns, gradually increased in length as the
skirts ascended. And when in the fourteenth century
the togas and gowns had been reduced to doublets,
the hose had extended to the hips. Fancy, ever at
work, shortened the doublet still more, till it reached

that most awkward length, just below the top of the
hips.   The uncouthness thus produced, before and behind, in the then-reached drawer-hose, necessitated
the invention of a new garment, a so-called "trunk."
For a century or more the shortening of the doublet
went on, till it became a mere waistcoat.   The movement now tends downward again, by the lengthening
of the trunks to trunk-hose, then to knickerbockers,
to small-clothes, and finally, in our century, to panta-
loons.   Thus the modern trousers are the lineal des-
cendants of the Middle Age trunks extended downward.   It is claimed that the modern vest is all that
is left of the doublet.   The coat and overcoat are developments from ancient capes and cloaks.

In *female* dress the change has been less radical, although considerable.   The female flowing garbs of
classic times were little modified by the Teutonic in-
cursion upon Southern Europe.   During the Middle
Ages there was a plainly observable tendency towards
closer fitting garb.   By the middle of the fourteenth
century this had reached the notion of distinctly out-
lining the curves of the waist, bust and hips.   In the
pictures of the princesses in England and France about
the close of the fourteenth century there is indicated
a distinct intimation toward the separation of waists and
skirts.   When this process had actually come about,
the weight of the lower garments had to be sustained
by bands and belts which impinged upon the soft parts
of the stomach, and hung from the hips.   The discomfort arising from this was sought to be relieved by
an under body shield in the form of stays, the predecessor of the modern corset.   In the sixteenth century,
the time of Catherine de Medici and Queen Elizabeth,
there was worn a case or sheath of nearly solid metal;
sometimes, however, of ivory or wood.   So little do
people realize the purpose for which this or that is
worn, that many men put on these "corpses," as
they were called.   This buckling and lacing went on
to an alarming extent.   "To make their forms thin as
a Spaniard's," says Montaigne, "what hell will not
women suffer, strained and lashed to the very quick?"
Amboise Père tells of a *sectio cadaveris* on a patient
who died from this cause and in whom the lower ribs

actually rode over one another. "Stays," in our sense, came in at Paris in the winter of 1809; although costing one hundred francs, they soon became widely used, and great excesses again followed. Not seldom did women die in direct consequence. Charles X. said of them, "Formerly it was not uncommon to see Dianas, Venuses or Niobes in France; but now we see nothing but wasps." They have remained in vogue till now, and will continue to do so till the radically evil principle which they were invented to offset, is clearly seen and removed. Since, however, humanity rarely or never learns anything except from necessity, it is probable that the change will come about only through the practical requirements of large masses of women in active and commercial life. The puffs and ruffles and flounces, the hoops and bustles and panniers, together with the numerous under and outer trappings ever changing their variety, are but accompanying paraphernalia. They occupy no fundamental place in the development of the main features of woman's dress. They are simply excrescences, and are in no sense a constructive or a necessary part of the lines of conformity or development.

Armor is a special type of protection which requires passing notice. Clothing guards against injuries from temperature, rain, briers and rocks. Armor is designed to ward off the attacks of human enemies. Under this heading come shields of all sorts, carried in the hands; then they can be worn on the body as breastplates, helmets, greaves, and the like; by taking a hint from the fish, the shields are greatly reduced and hinged together in clumsy articulation. A further refinement occurs when the shields are diminished to small scales or links which conform more or less to the movements of the body. First the shields are external and partial. Finally they become closely woven and form a complete defensive covering. The earliest stages may be likened to the mollusk, the intermediate to the crustacean, and the final to the fish. The scientific development of the arms of attack has rendered defensive personal armor practically obsolete.

MODESTY.

The third object of clothing, that for modesty's sake,

demands here but brief attention. Ornaments worn all the time beget habit. Without them the wearer feels uneasy. This is the subjective side. Each person in society, having experienced a similar feeling, naturally demands for himself and others the satisfaction of this uneasiness by the invariable wearing of his accustomed ornaments in the presence of others at least. Thus is begotten public opinion. It becomes a binding necessity; each person feels ashamed unless he has on what both his own consciousness and that of others expects. This is the sense of shame. Observe that it has *at first* nothing whatever to do with the hiding of the organs of sex. There are tribes yet extant who are punctilious as to the covering of the back upper portion of the head, or the wearing of neck ornaments, who are otherwise entirely naked. And there is doubtless suffered in fashionable society in Christendom, pangs quite as deep from the absence of dress suits, proper gloves, bustles and hoops, as were ever occasioned by the absence of clothing. Who can measure the difference between the Mohammedan woman's anxiety to scrupulously keep her face covered, and the American belle's mortification should she appear at a ball without the customary display of neck and bosom? Perhaps the greatest excess of this modesty feature is found among the Aino women, who will not change garments except alone and in the dark. The stress which the higher civilizations now lay on sex covering had its origin, as before stated, solely in the requirements of a developing society. Every impediment must be placed in the way of promiscuity of sex-relationship. Thus clothing becomes a negative help toward higher social organization.

THE ETHICS OF COVERING.

Inseparable from this phase of the problem of covering are the other features of its ethics. Dress has become an artificial necessity in each of the three primitive and fundamental purposes. It has come to have an almost omnipotent power of influence. It therefore becomes a moral question of the gravest import. We cannot ask too loudly, *what dress will look best, protect best, and hinder least.*

Two or three axioms may be stated :—
Dress should reach the maximum of its ends with the minimum of bulk and weight of goods;
Dress should be adapted to the occupation;
Dress should enhance and be conformed to the person, and not the person to the dress ;
Dress should insure against indecent exposure.
To the extent that these principles are violated, to that extent is violence done to human life, and insult heaped upon Nature. It would be out of our province to do more than suggest here the ways in which prevailing customs are ignoring these essentials of progressive life. Many kinds of cloth woven tight, unyielding, having nap, and shoddy-like in character, as also the cottons spoiled by alkaline preparation, are not adapted to meet these ends. The recent improvements in knitting processes and cotton preparation have in them great possibilities. Wool is more elastic, and when used in the form of knit goods (which are now being. made in all grades and qualities), leaves almost nothing to be desired as under clothing, and for many features of outer clothing. Silks and other woven fabrics may have a place, but used alone never entirely reach the true ends where good fit and freedom of movement are desired. If they fit, then violence is done to health and freedom. If they are large enough for these, then the æsthetic sense is offended. One demand is fairly well satisfied in men's clothing to-day, the other less well in woman's. The clothing of man is as ungainly as that of woman is unhealthy. Man's cylindrical trousers and coats, consisting of three bags each, are an emblem of the inartistic, sordid, utilitarian end of nineteenth century life. Drapery is an emblem of leisure, luxury and dignity That on the modern woman of fashion is historically a degradation, and symbolizes the inanity of much female life in "upperten-dom." It does not retain the simple artistic elements of its prototype ; but, since the Elizabethan Age, lingers only as a survival mid innumerable incongruities which deviate so widely from the original type as to be almost unrecognizable. To what a plight has uninformed vanity driven the modern woman in her search for beauty! Where is he who hath the skill

to discover the remnant of the graceful *chiton* of the Greek lady amid the busks, corselets, bodices, corsets, kirtles, farthingales, hoops, panniers, bustles, petticoats, basques and skirts that have for three centuries violated the laws of freedom, health and art?

Clothing may bring out the general outlines of form in two ways; either by loose drapery which takes the shape of that which it covers, or by shaped clothes of yielding material cut to fit the form. This is already accomplished in ribbed jersey-fitting underclothing. But the art of combining drapery and shaped clothes in garb appropriate to the advancing needs of both sexes, has only begun to be learned. A hint in this direction may be taken from male attire in the Renaissance period. The principle of the Dutch Knickerbockers, now being so widely adopted in ladies' gymnasium suits, is another lesson in the adaptation of drapery to practical ends.

The increasing economic independence of woman is pointing unmistakably to the adoption of practical, comfortable, and, what goes without saying, artistic clothing. The unparalleled interest in this question at the Woman's Congress during the World's Fair; the wide spread use of knickerbocker suits by cycling women; the daily wearing of the Syrian suit by eminent women, such as Mrs. B. O. Flower, Miss Laura Lee, Mrs. Rachel Foster Avery, and others; the prophetic introduction of this custom by wide-awake writers, who are picturing the future, as Mr. W. T. Stead's recent social study, "Two and Two Make Four;" the numerous published articles by men and women, especially the noble work of the *Arena*, as well as the Symposium of Women on Improved Dress held in Madison Square Garden the past week,—these, one and all, are indications of an evolution which has passed its beginning stages.

Many men and many women are coming to have the eyes of science, which in sociology means the observance of fact, the discovery of law and the application of it to the improvement of life. It is clear that the dressing of humanity has been conducted on lines and principles which are not to-day rational. An impenetrable century-long conservatism has dictated the main

lines, and a freakful vanity has been the only relief.
The two in partnership have made "fashion," and
fashion has been a tyrant. It has always damned individuality, and has always tried to crush it. But a
curious thing is happening in these our days. Science
itself is becoming a fashion, and its very nature is to
foster what the spirit of authority strangles. Science
grows by experiment. Hence it encourages reasonable
variations from the standard. Under this chance, wom-
en have made progress enough to see some things
that stand in the way of their further progress. They
perceive that it is futile to hope to take an active part
in this busy modern life while continuing to be clad
in the swaddling-clothes descended from unbusy ages.
They see that the practice, maintained since the sixteenth century, of cutting gown forms off at the waist
and sustaining skirts by belting the abdominal region,
results in prostration of its muscles and the distortion
of the form, together with a lamentably absurd difference between the agility of the sexes. They see that
a garment suspended from the waist and hanging loose
and free at the bottom is an incalculable check to activity and therefore a wicked prevention of development and opportunity. They see that genuine drapery,
artistically arranged, for the parlor and platform and
other state occasions where every surrounding is clean
and where activity is suspended in repose and dignity,
has a use and a beauty which no other apparel can
equal. They see that it is a foolishness indescribable
which causes women to go about with their right hands
behind them, occupied in keeping useless drapery out
of nameless filth. They see that the ineffectualness
of this attempt causes them to wipe the streets, plat-
forms and steps everywhere, to stir up the decaying
organic substances with their myriad bacteria, and either
to carry them home or set them floating in the air for
those near by to breathe and take into their systems.
They see that the wearing of skirts for the sake of
so-called modesty is an ignorant inversion of the truth.
They see that skirts, no matter how long nor how
short, are an insecure and partial covering, keep wom-
en in a condition of oft necessitated immodest exposure, and provide a constant method of cultivating

the lasciviousness of men so inclined. They see that the aggregate daily crime committed by society in its prudism and ignorant insistence upon this utterly indefensible mode of raiment exceeds the combined damage done to humanity in a year by the so-called criminal class. And finally, they are anxious that the world shall soon see the irreparable injustice which its unnecessary blindness is doing to womankind, and through them to humankind, in these ways. In the race for life, woman has more at stake than man. What a humiliating shame that men should show sham chivalry to the women who are trying to remove the chains of their own slavery!

> "Men whose boast it is that ye
> Came of fathers brave and free,
> If there breathe on earth a slave,
> Are ye truly free and brave?
> No! true freedom is to share
> All the chains your [sisters] wear,
> And, with heart and hand, to be
> Earnest to make others free."

And is not growth in civilization mostly release after release from the bondages established in times of lesser knowledge? To let Lowell speak again:—

> "New occasions make new duties,
> Time makes ancient good uncouth."

A new freedom is demanded because new ideals have come. "Adaptability or utility is the first law of beauty in costume," says the apostle of the beautiful (Ruskin). And what can be our excuse for living,— unless "to conspire with the new works of new days?"

ABSTRACT OF THE DISCUSSION.

DR. FREDERIC COOK:—

I have been much interested and instructed by the lecture, this evening. I can only add a word, as invited by your President, about my own experience in the higher latitudes. When the expedition of Lieut.

Peary, with which I was connected, set sail for the Arctic regions, we carried with us a great variety of clothing recommended for protection against the rigors of the climate, heavy underwear, some of wool, some of cotton and wool, some of silk, in various degrees of thickness and proportion. As a result of our experience, we discarded all except the thin all-wool underwear, and an external covering of skins, practically three close skin bags, which retained a layer of air outside the underwear, and this proved to be the best protection from the cold. Thus clad, we did not suffer at all from the cold, with the thermometer at forty degrees below zero. At night, we disrobed completely and crept into skin bags, retaining the hair inside, which were brought up close about the neck, and in which we slept comfortably.

Any admixture of cotton in a garment absorbs the moisture and renders it cold and clammy. The heavy woolen fabric also absorbs too much moisture. Two qualities are essential to proper clothing for the colder regions; the material must be capable of confining air-space, and it must be as far as possible incapable of absorbing moisture. The skin garments universally worn in the Arctic countries are made from the skins of the reindeer, Arctic fox, dogs and seals, without buttons or seams. These most perfectly confine the air-space and secure warmth for the body. Knit fabrics will not do, as they do not confine the air-space. Even the closely woven, thin underwear will contain some moisture at night; hence it became necessary to remove it entirely before retiring. As may be inferred, this change of clothing in a temperature of forty degrees below zero required rapid adjustment.

With proper care, however, we passed through the winter season comfortably, without scurvy, disease or suffering. The result of our experience seemed to show that persons temporarily living in the Arctic regions can not do better than adopt, substantially, the customs as to clothing which have been adopted by the inhabitants of those regions, and which have been found to conduce to their survival.

DR. LEWIS G. JANES :—

I am sure we have all recognized and heartily enjoyed the completeness and excellence of the lecturer's treatment of the topic of the evening, admirably in line with the object of this course of lectures.   One or two points, though certainly not in the way of criticism, occurred to me as she was speaking.

An ingenious writer, in apparent seriousness, has recently argued that man's pre-historic ancestor was doubtless a hairy animal, and that every successive stage of progress has been accompanied by increasing depletion of the hirsute covering.   In the modern tendency to an increasing prevalence of baldness, he sees a prophecy that the coming man will be an absolutely hairless animal.   Though this may be regarded as a complimentary suggestion to some of us who are not gifted with a sufficiency of this natural covering for the head, it is to be hoped, for aesthetic reasons, that this theory is not correct.

The lecturer has noted the fact that the assumption of dress by man has been a very gradual process. This is further emphasized by the deleterious influence which clothing sometimes has when worn by races which for generations have been unaccustomed to its use. Among the Hawaiian Islanders, for example, the use of clothing has been followed by a marked increase of pulmonary disease, almost unknown to them in their savage state. This is doubtless aggravated by carelessness in exposure to the elements—they never carry umbrellas, and are not careful to change their clothing after a wetting—but it seems to be due in a large degree to the necessary interference of the clothing with the free excretory action of the skin, and the deprivation of the body of the stimulating influence of the sunlight and air.

I am impressed, also, with the fact that the sentiment of modesty is in a high degree conventional as to the mode of its manifestation, and that we are liable to do injustice to people whose education has been different from our own, by condemning them for violating our standards of propriety when we are equally liable to condemnation from their point of view. I am convinced, for example, that the Japanese are as modest and decorous in deportment as ourselves; yet with them the promiscuous bathing of the sexes in a state of nature is not deemed improper, while the public kissing of one's wife, or the contact of the sexes and exposure of the body which is familiar to our best society at the ball or opera would be regarded by them as highly indecorous and immoral. In judging of the customs of other people, we should endeavor to put ourselves in their places, and do them no injustice by assuming the infallibility of our own conventional standards.

Dr. Duren J. H. Ward briefly replied to the remarks of the preceding speakers, and thanked the audience and the speakers for their cordial reception of Mrs. Ward's paper.

SHELTER, AS RELATED TO THE EVOLUTION OF LIFE

BY

Z. SIDNEY SAMPSON

COLLATERAL READINGS SUGGESTED.

Darwin's *Origin of Species*, and *Descent of Man;* Wallace's *Darwinism;* Joly's *Man before Metals;* Lyell's *The Antiquity of Man;* Lubbock's *Prehistoric Man;* Tylor's *Primitive Culture,* and *Anthropology;* Spencer's "Sources of Architectural Types," in *Illustrations of Universal Progress;* Le Duc's *Story of a House;* Eassie's *Healthy Homes;* Lubke's *History of Art;* Articles "Anthropology" and "Architecture" in *Encyclopædia Britannica;* Gerhard's *Architecture and Sanitation.*

SHELTER, AS RELATED TO THE EVOLUTION OF LIFE.

BY Z. SIDNEY SAMPSON.

In what relation does Shelter stand to the development of life, and how may it further or hinder survival? In the discussion of this topic it is of the first importance that we have a satisfactory definition of life. Many have taken this in hand, with more or less success, but we shall not err if we accept Mr. Spencer's conclusions as being at the same time more comprehensive and scientifically exact than any of those yet presented. Mr. Spencer, in his Biology, after testing various preliminary definitions of life reaches the following as being inclusive of all its processes, viz., "the adjustment of internal relations to external relations." Internal relations are the total of all relations between and among the several organs, which, in their manifold mutual interactions, constitute what we term the vital organism. External relations are the sum of all influences external to the organism, which, in their manifold variations and combinations, impress upon the vital organism changes either simultaneous or successive. These external influences are, themselves, either simultaneous or successive in their occurrence, and in their effects upon the body. Influences like gravitation and atmospheric pressure upon the same level, are instances of simultaneous and permanent influences. Meteorological changes are examples of influences which are successive, while they are also simultaneous with the former. And further, the changes and alterations induced by these external factors produce within the organism affected, alterations and changes which are heterogeneous in their character, and essentially diverse, from the fact that they act upon localized and specialized organs and functions, each of which has its individual and peculiar service in the vital economy

277

—and herein differing from the effects upon inorganic nature, upon which they are substantially uniform, so far as they extend.

The total of these ever acting and ever varying incident external forces we call the environment—a word which has passed into such common and extensive use, that the greater number, by far, of those who use it, do so without any sufficient knowledge of the complex ideas which, to the mind of the scientist, are involved in it, from the point of view of Scientific Evolution.

Now, life is the adjustment of the vital organism to the environment—the constant endeavor upon its part to secure and maintain, as nearly as possible, equilibrium with these exterior and antagonistic forces. Wherever what has been appropriately termed a moving equilibrium is obtained and held, life exists. It exists wherever and whenever the organism can hold its own with the surrounding cosmic energies—for the entire universe here comes into play. Under the doctrine of ever widening correspondences, first of the lowest forms of life with its immediate surroundings, through all gradations of the evolution of sentient beings, establishing, in time, infinite correspondences in time and space, through touch, sight, hearing, speech and concomitant intellectual, moral and religious development, to its highest consummation, man's spirit, there is no atom of cosmic dust, or vibrations of the ethereal medium, now traveling towards us from worlds yet invisible, which does not, in and through the grand sweep of infinite energy, record its influence upon all that lives and moves and has its being thereby; so true is it, not alone in the moral and intellectual life, but in the merely physical as well, that the sentiment of the poet has full meaning, that each is bound to each in natural sympathy. "Hitch your wagon to a star," says Emerson —but in truth and scientific fact all our wagons are hitched to all stars, whether we will or no, and we are one with all the constellations.

But this equilibrium of the organism with the environment is at no time perfect. We are always more or less out of joint with it; and this holds true throughout the entire range of plant and animal life, as well as in man. Yet it is in and through this very fact that advance becomes possible, and that slow but certain improvement is ultimately assured. For observe, that it is only through the constant strife of organism with environment, and this constant and persistent endeavor to attain adaptation to it, that has been induced, and is now continued, that ceaseless struggle for existence whereby arise, in the organism, variations which are favorable, in the successful contestants, to survival. Were it not for this endless search and contest for adaptation to surrounding conditions, there would, in due time, eventuate that complete equilibrium which would be paralysis and death. This is the famous principle so revolutionary for both science and theology which is forever associated with the name of Darwin —the doctrine of Natural Selection—to which Mr. Spencer subsequently applied the phrase, "survival of the fittest." In this strife peace is secured only through war. It is not only organism against environment, but organism against organism; though the latter phrase is included in the former, since, to each individual organism, all other organisms are part and parcel of its environment. The weakest go to the wall. Disaster takes the hindmost,—not alone man, but all lowest creatures "rise on stepping stones of their dead selves to higher things." Favorable variations are further strengthened and made permanent in species by use, and valuable qualities of survival, both for offense and defense, are transmitted by Heredity. New species originate—thousands disappear. The Geological and Palæontological records are Bibles of Science, wherein we may read both warnings and prophecies.

In this preliminary survey we have not lost sight of our topic, but have been moving directly towards it. For observe that, in a state of nature, favorable variations cannot possibly arise except through this warfare of species and varieties. Those which are hindered from entering and taking part in this contest, or are protected unduly from it, lose their ground of advantage. In order to secure that adaptation which means progress, they must be placed directly in touch with all those external relations, which, though they may destroy, yet will alone develop in the organism a higher life.

Shelter, therefore, is a positive disadvantage to the lowest forms of life, except in those rare instances where the shelter is so complete as to give opportunity for the development of other favorable variations; and by the lower I mean all organisms below man. The ways of nature are adapted to this circumstance. The lowest organisms are the most completely exposed. The amœba, the mere jelly-like substance which first exhibits a nucleus, is capable of subdivision by fissure, and, by repeatedly turning itself inside out, as we may say, will expose every portion of its structure to its environment. As organisms develop we note the gradual appearance of correlated structure—the cartilaginous and bony skeleton and thicker outer covering, both of these being serviceable for protection. But still, exposure to the environment is imperative, in order that the increasingly complex nervous systems which are evolved may have unrestricted course for development by contact with adverse forces. Animals unduly weighted with defensive structures have succumbed to the more virile and active genera. They were so burdened with shelter as to forbid their entering into successful competition with their smaller and more agile enemies. Says Mr. Kimball in his excellent lecture on "Arms and Armor" read before this association in our course upon "Sociology," and which I cordially recommend to the reading of students of this subject, "Nearly all the races and orders that were provided with massive external defenses have been overwhelmed, and those equipped with finer forms and textures have survived. Orthoceras and Dinicthys, Megalosaur and Megatherium, Ichthyosaur and Iguanodon, monsters armed with shell and scale, enormous and terrible, have all, without exception, gone down in the great life battle, while those whose weapons were the finer skeleton, the keener sense, the quicker nerve, the larger brain—are the races that have been victorious and have survived."

And, in this connection, it is to be remarked in passing that even now the Lords of the British Admiralty are in serious consultation as to whether there should be any considerable further building of immense armor-plated Megolosaurs and Dinosaurs for the navy. The

unfortunate and unwieldy Victoria went to the bottom
in fifteen minutes after one shock from the Camper-
down, where a dozen smaller craft would have avoided
the blow.

Again, late researches indicate that all such favorable
variations as have resulted in the evolution of sense
organs have been wholly the consequence of free exposure to the environment; that organs of touch, vision,
hearing and smell are all localized modifications of the
dermal membranes. If this be so, our doctrine is powerfully reinforced, for we see that if the higher life is
to be realized at all. it is only through the slow increment upon increment, through vast cycles of time, of
modifications superinduced upon the organism by free
interplay with the environment, and made permanent
by use and inherited dispositions. To these considerations add our common experiences with plants, the
necessity of constant exposure to light and moisture,
the decay which results from unreasonable and unnecessary shelter, against which even the vegetable forms
dumbly remonstrate, by turning from the shelter of
shade to seek the sun. Plant forms of various kinds
growing in shadow. will. for a long time, bring forth
no foliage; only in exposed situations will the tree
develop sturdy branches and heart of oak. Fishes.
in sunless caves, are blind. The account could be extended indefinitely, from our common knowledge and
observation. To the vast majority of species and varieties shelter is. therefore, unfavorable to the development of such variations in structure and function as
will assure survival.

And now let us turn to man. Somewhere, and through
processes never probably to be fathomed by the most
acute and painstaking psychological research, the germs
of a true, self-conscious human intellect were evolved.
Man, though heavily weighted, and for ages to be
weighted, with brutal appetites, and instincts merely
animal, yet came to his own, and knew himself, though
blindly and gropingly at first, to be truly man. If. as
Darwin claims to be probable, he descended from some
species of anthropoid, arboreal in its habits. and if. as
later anthropologists assert, he was himself arboreal,
yet he descended from his tree at a period so immensely

remote that it defies even approximate computation.
But, for ages, it was a hand to hand fight; with beasts,
with wastes of snow, with torrid heats, barely holding
his own, gaining some slight advantage here, some
slight advantage there. If the morning stars sang
together and all the sons of God shouted for
joy at creation's dawn, how should they not have
wept thereafter at the ferocious strife through
which man's intellectual and spiritual mastery was
thereafter won? I know not how it may seem to others,
but I cannot without emotion look over, in one of our
museums, the collection of roughly chipped flints which
are to us the sole relic and reminder of primeval man,
and of the ages during which, in direful exposure and
privation, hunted by the elements, in savage conflict
with cave lions, cave bears and cave hyenas, he made
possible for us the broad ways of culture and civilization. Not to theological Adams and Eves, whose
frail virtue falls in pieces at the first touch of temptation, but to prehistoric man, savage though he was,
warring and starving, let the full praise of all that we
have achieved be gratefully ascribed. To him we owe
it, to his rude handiwork and patient toil, that we sit
here this evening under goodly architecture and
in friendly converse. But note here again, that it was
only in this age-long strife that rested the hope of his
future. It was through and by this prolonged and
ceaseless struggle, through this free exposure to elemental and savage forces that he secured and held that
slight advantage which won for him ultimate superiority over contending forces. Free action and interaction with the environment was, with him, as with the
lower animal orders, the prime necessity.

Probably at the earliest prehistoric period, man discovered that he could destroy animal life, and thereby
secure food better, with the use of some weapon than
with the unaided hands, even were it only, as it probably was, at first, by throwing rough stones; for savages of to-day do the same, and become expert at this
practice. Before long it would occur to him that these
would be far more effective if pointed and so made
penetrating—hence all devices of the old palæolithic
or old stone period, of which we turn up hundreds in

the course of nearly every year—knives, axes, hammers, arrow-heads, spear-heads. In time also he would see the advantage of giving these weapons smooth surfaces, securing greater adaptability for wounding and piercing. Hence his chipped flints become polished flints —we have the neolithic, or new stone age—and along with this, rude attempts at decoration. Hereby man differentiates finally from the brute creation; he becomes a tool-using and tool-producing being. These, with the added advantage of manual dexterity, acquired by the use of weapons, give him the survival in the struggle, and make him lord and master of the animal kingdom.

But observe that further and still further improvement in weapons and tools, and the frequent use of these, puts primitive man at a certain disadvantage in the matter of physical development of brawn and muscle. Relying more and more upon weapons and less and less upon unassisted physical prowess, he begins to lag behind the lower animal in respect to perfection in physical activity. But this is an imperative condition as well as consequence, of intellectual advance. The necessary means of support are obtained, but in securing these the skill of the eye and hand are brought into play, and this, by slow degrees, relieves the struggle between man and brute of that aspect of mere brutality which its earliest stages exhibit; and, in gaining the first step, the ultimate mastery of mind over brute force is assured by the principle which is found to work in the intellect as well as the physical organism, of the accumulation of favorable inherited variations.

But the growing inferiority of man to the animal creation, in these physical relations, entails another consequence—and that is the necessity, steadily increasing, for improved shelter, not alone as a means of defense, additional to his use of weapons, but as a protection against all other external conditions, unfavorable to survival, to which he becomes more and more sensitive, the more he is relieved from the necessity of a merely physical struggle for existence;—conditions of atmosphere, climate and soil. Shelter of some sort primitive man, from the remotest period possessed. Prehistoric science has explored his cave

and subterranean dwellings, wherein, with the aid of
his rude flint weapons, now found buried beneath remains of extinct animals, and again beneath deposits of
stalagmite incrusted slowly upon them through ages,
he cut or hacked his food, and existed as best he
could. "Who does not remember," says Thoreau, "the
interest with which, when young, he looked at shelving
rocks or any approach to a cave? It was the natural
yearning of that portion of our most primitive ancestors
which still survived in us." Cave dwellings, or mere
pit excavations, seem, from the geological record, to have
sufficed for man during at least two tolerably well defined
geological epochs, viz., the pliocene, or latest period
of the tertiary, and post-pliocene, or earliest period of
the quaternary, called also the diluvium or drift, and
including the glacial period. But something better had
to be discovered, some more complete and effective
shelter. Nature had done her best for him, when, by
upheaving the earth-crust, and tossing aloft the mountain ranges, manifold nooks and crevices were thereby
formed, wherein, for a time, he might prepare for improved conditions. Observe now how surely necessity
forces. on the one hand invention, and how, at the
same time it ordains that the inventive faculty shall
attain success. That intellectual advance should be
assured, man was led to the invention of tools. Thereby he was placed in physical inferiority to the animal
kingdom, or to such of them as were to be most dreaded,
and forced into shelter and protection. By slow degrees the faculty of intelligence developed, and finally,
when cave shelters and excavations no longer sufficed,
he had so far improved that the ability of intelligent
construction came to his help, that he became not only
a tool user, but an intelligent constructer and builder;
and, what was of surpassing importance to us here,
as well as to him, possessed of what we may term a
deliberative constructive faculty. The animals build
from inherited instinct; their constructive faculty is
inherited reflex action. From age to age it is the same,
without conscious attempts at improvement. Man,
with conscious deliberation and selection, adapts his
buildings to his various necessities and environments.
This meant nothing less than the ultimate supremacy

of man throughout the habitable globe—it meant the colonization of every zone, security to civilization, and the possibility of existence in every climate. But the advance was painfully slow. Perhaps even yet we have not succeeded in attaining the economy of space which the bee exhibits in its cell arrangements. "The chimpanzee," says Sir John Lubbock, "builds a house or shelter quite equal to that of some savages." It was long before man ceased to imitate nature and the lower orders of life, and became an original and intelligent designer. At first he burrowed, like some of his animal congeners, in subterranean or semi-subterranean excavations. He lived in dug-outs, and threw the earth in a circle around it for defense—in bee-hive mounds, in weems, in the so-called Picts' houses, in barrows of stone, with coverings of earth, in crannoges—in all ways which were possible for him with his low intelligence. Yet this ability to construct and adapt shelters reasonably sufficient for protection wherever he might locate, and in whatever seasons he might encounter, made man a world-traveling species, and enabled him to fulfill the prime condition of life, viz., adaptation to the environment wherever placed. He was delivered from the bondage of waiting upon the tardy and age-long processes of natural selection, and supplied by artificial invention that which unassisted nature would have given to him only after the lapse of geological periods. Hence in physiological characters, man has not varied to any marked extent since, as we may say, he reached man's estate. "As long," says Mr. Alfred Russel Wallace, "as man led an animal existence he would be subject to the same laws, and would vary in the same manner as the rest of his fellow creatures, but, by the faculty of clothing himself, and making weapons and tools, he has taken away from nature that power of changing the external form and structure which she exercises over all other animals. As an animal he would remain almost stationary, and the changes of the surrounding would cease to have upon him that powerful modifying effect which it exercises over other parts of the organic world."

Geographical distribution enters as one of the most important factors into the question of race develop-

ment. So far as this implies the influence of the
presence or absence of shelter, we can state only the
most general and obvious conclusions. In arid wastes
and torrid heats shelter, if desired at all, is of the lightest both in quantity and texture. The temperate and
cold zones force shelter upon man. Doubtless we find
in the colder climates, as a consequence, greater individuality, such as Tacitus records of the Germans. Here
we find liberty-loving peoples who yet know how to
subordinate individual activity to the welfare of the
tribe. Yet it is not historically true that shelter has
established a relative superiority of northern over
southern races. The southern races hold their own.
The wave of conquest has been from south to north
quite as frequently as otherwise. To this we can except only a certain portion of the interior tribes of
Africa, where under torrid heats, enervating miasmas
enfeeble the indigenous races. The question is one of
acclimatization as well as shelter. Exposure to the
environment in Arabia produces as hardy a manhood
as the driving snows of Norway. If, in either case,
there is established that sufficient equilibrium with the
environment which conserves life, it is other factors,
either of superior invention in arms for offense or defense, or superiority of organization, or the enthusiasm
of a common purpose, which secures survival in the
conflict of races. With the cessation of nomadic life
and the arrival of the agricultural stage, comes fixity
of habitations, and a more compact social environment.
Families coalesce into tribes, clans and gens—these
into the nation. Everywhere appear the integrations
of social structure. All this means the development
of national spirit, improvement in shelter, and after
no long period, architecture on the grand scale. Architecture is the earliest form in which the growing art
tendencies of a people find free expression. Some may
claim this for sculpture, since the fashioning of rude
idols is of an antiquity to which we can assign no definite limits in the past of the race. But it must be
allowed that, from the very moment when man left his
cave dwellings, and first betook himself to pit excavation,
or mound and barrow construction, the primary elements of art were, though unconsciously to him, brought

into application; for, to whatever of surpassing beauty art has attained or may attain, it has depended and will depend upon just relations and proportions in construction. There will be no cloud-capped tower or gorgeous palace which will survive faulty construction. Figure, line and weight are first in order. Early man was obliged so to build as to meet certain exigencies of climate, having in view at the same time preservation of life and property. The more permanent the habitation, as in advanced society, the greater care to secure this permanency in the proper adjustment of material. In the very oldest of the so-called bee-hive houses and weems, as also in the Indian tent and negro hut, the problem of so constructing the shelter as to leave an opening at the top for the escape of smoke, was one which demanded considerable ingenuity. In the case of the lake dwellings of Switzerland the question of sufficient subaqueous foundation leads to ingenious pile construction. All this means the slow development of man's nascent ideas of structural proportion, the support of superincumbent masses, and the strengthening of weak points, until finally earth, stone and metal become plastic to his touch, obedient to his art-ideals, and serviceable for beauty.

Of architectural types much has been written, and well written. It is clearly impossible here to go into detail. To name these types, instantly brings to mind the familiar illustrations—the terraced mounds of Syria and Chaldæa, the shadowed temples and pyramid tombs of Egypt, the finely chiseled Lycian architecture, Greece with its horizontal lines and exquisite proportions, the more complicated and therefore less beautiful composite of Rome, the Christian Basilica, the Romanesque, the superb and aspiring Gothic, the florid Renaissance, the graceful involutions of Moorish architecture; the Russian with its bulbous domes, China with its tinkling pagodas, and India with its fantastic and irregular but wonderfully effective masses; all these are born of the environment. The race inevitably speaks in its architecture, for the environment fashions both, the workman and, through his ideals, the product. Think of a Chinese pagoda in Northern Germany, or a Gothic temple in Arabia, and the intimate and necessary relations of architectural types to locality become self-evident. But observe also that in early periods of the nation it is devoted to the expression of those ideas which are the most powerful and controlling in the national life. They are founded and dedicated to the spirit of religion, to the shelter of the god viz., the temple, or of the demi-god (the god that is to be after death), the chieftain or the king, viz., the palace. Not until a late stage of culture do there appear any considerable improvements in the dwellings of the common people. This is attained only with the advent of the industrial stage, partially superseding the stage of militancy, when the worth of the individual and the dignity of citizenship become large actors in the social economy. In the meantime, and for a long period, the magnificent proportions and lavish decorations of churches and palaces emphasize the wretchedness of the dwellings of the poor clustered at their bases. But this also we should say, that the cathedrals of mediæval Europe were not only the religious but also the social homes of the people, and their common pride. Whatever of the best and richest art of the time was denied them in their poor and often squalid homes, was there freely displayed and was their common possession—statue, sculptured tomb, effigy and painting, all glowing under the rich and varied hues of gorgeous windows and oriels, which emblazoned the legend of saint and martyr, whereby were fused into a common experience the religious and social life of the community.

But, contemporaneous with this growth and improvement in constructive art, man has been building himself up into a rational manhood. The grosser impulses, the purely sensual in which he had rivaled the brute, yielded to the domestic impulses, and to the gracious sentiments of duty to the family, to the tribe or the State. With the evolution of these shelter has much to do; for now that which served merely for protection against beasts, floods and enemies, becomes invested with a higher interest. It becomes under the law of association, and of inherited associations, the home. In the wandering tents of nomadic life the true home sentiment is but nascent. Not until the agricultural stage is reached, and considerable permanency of nationalities is attained, does it fully appear; in fact over four fifths of the world it can hardly be said to exist to-day, with the full significance which it has for us. For observe, that to the existence of the true home the idea of individuality, the worth of the individual, is essential; for that idea includes also the worth of whatever belongs to him—family, property and reasonable liberty. The stronger is this idea, the more efficient solidarity does the nation possess; and, as a consequence, the better are its chances for survival in the contest of nations. The successful nations are the nations of homes—since it is a fact that greater individual freedom if intelligent, co-exists, invariably, with the greater compactness in the social structure, and therefore, with the deeper and more resolute patriotism, that wider affection which regards the nation as the larger home and the State as the larger family. A true reverence for the State exists, therefore, only when based upon individual love of home. The loosely aggregated tribes of early history are aggregated mostly if not wholly for self-defense; and submission to authority within the tribe is secured by fear of offense to the semi-god, to wit, the chief. True patriotism is a late product, and its highest energy is secured only where a national solidarity co-exists with a flexibility which permits a reasonable freedom of the individual. Not till then is the home as we know and appreciate it, truly founded; the shelter for the domestic affections, the object for which to labor, and the refuge for declining years. It is unfortunate that the nomadic tendencies which prevail so extensively among the people of our own land should have weakened, materially, the home-loving instinct which our English ancestors so carefully cherished, and which the English of to-day so carefully preserve. "It is time," says Prof. Marsh, "for some abatement in this restless love of change which characterizes us. It is rare that a middle-aged American dies in the house where he was born, or an old man even in that which he has built. This life of incessant flitting is unfavorable for the execution of improvements of any sort." And still more effectively writes Ruskin: "There is a sanctity in a good man's house which cannot be renewed in every tenement that rises on its ruins; every good man would be grieved that all they had ever treasured should be despised, and the places that had sheltered them dragged down to the dust. There must be a strange dissolution of natural affection, a strange unthankfulness for all that homes have given and parents taught, a strange consciousness that we have been unfaithful to our father's honor, or that our own lives are not such as would make our dwellings sacred to our children, when each man would fain build to himself, and build for the little revolution of his own life."

The home is peculiarly the shelter of infancy. It has been ordained that in the processes of social evolution the home should be adapted to further the intellectual development of man by affording that constant protection which insures the care of parents and friends over the infant during a prolonged period. This point has been admirably presented by Prof. Fiske as one of the most important factors in the sociological problem. The animal at birth is already completely adjusted to its environment. Its physical life is as complete (except in the case of some of the higher animals, and for a short period) as its life of reflex action will ever require. But the prolonged infancy of man insures that constant and watchful devotion which is the source of the domestic affections, and therefore of those permanent differentiations into separate families, the social units which finally integrate into the nation. To this result the home is essential. To the familiar sentiment "there is no place like home" none so fully respond as those with whom the word is indissolubly associated with memories of infancy and the gracious influences of parental love.

In the meantime, while the intellectual and moral life is thus furthered by the home, man's innate love of beauty in color and form asserts its claims to culture. The home should be the House Beautiful, and with permanency of habitations, and improved architectural tastes, it is possible that it should be such. In this connection we may observe, also, that the higher art becomes attainable only when the hand has become sensitive to a finer touch, the ear to more refined musical harmonies and sequences, and the eye to increasingly delicate perceptions of variety in color and shade. But this refinement of sense perception is possible only upon a refinement of the entire physical system, inasmuch as the improvement of all bodily organs is intimately correlated, each being dependent upon the improvement of all; and such result is secured only where shelter has brought it to pass that the nervous system has become more highly developed, and more immediately responsive to outward impressions. Shelter does, in fact, not only enhance delicacy of sense perception, but, owing to the same doctrine of correlation, the brain texture is notably refined. We are obliged to confess to this much of materialism at least, that the brain of no savage is ever racked by ceaseless strivings to realize lofty ideals. He is conversant with nature in her pleasant and gusty moods, but to suggestions of higher and spiritual import he is impervious. Shelter replaces the coarse fiber of primitive races with the susceptibilities of the modern brain and physique. Thus, through art, the family relations, and the wider sense of social relationship, the individual comes to his larger self—that larger self which recognizes as part of the *myself* not alone the immediate circumstance of body and a vital organism, but as well that which he takes into himself through his environment, and more especially the constant environment of home life. Your household books are your friends. The pictures on your wall are constant, though voiceless teachers of the beautiful. How sacred even is the old furniture! You give up none of these without a pang, for they have entered into your larger life, and are as much a part of your moral and spiritual existence as are the thoughts which they stimulate. Read Mr. Gladstone's delightful essay on "The Housing of Books, " and you will the less wonder at the superb energy which his ample life has developed and which has made it possible for him, through a half century, to devote his wealth of physical and intellectual resources to his country, and inscribe upon the pages of English history that extraordinary record of public services which but recently he closed at Windsor. For Gladstone has always lived the larger intellectual life, and has forcibly illustrated the principle of Emerson that a man should not be a politician, but a Man in politics, taking to himself, through wide and varied study, whatever was serviceable for furthering a progressive national life.

Pass now from individual to social life. We have seen that shelter, except in few instances, was a disadvantage to animal species, and to prehistoric man, but with the advent of tool using and buildings, shelter becomes indispensable to man, especially if he is to be a world-colonizer. The conditions are reversed. The struggle for survival continues, but it is transferred from the physical to the emotions and the intellect, and ultimately, to the sphere of morals and religion. But the same law of variation persists here also. It is the law of individual life, and the law of nations. "We pray to be conventional," says Emerson, "but the wary heavens take care that you shall not be if there is anything good in you." In more prosaic language, wherever a community develops a favorable intellectual variation, it gains that advantage which leads to mastery over other communities, even on the low plane of material warfare and conquest. In a state of universal warfare, intellect has small chance at first, but in the slow evolution from militant to industrial conditions of society, it finally secures its coign of vantage. A state of chronic warfare, such as primitive man must have exhibited, which savage races still exhibit, and which persists into late periods of history, even among cultured nations, means going from home and staying from home. The industrial aspect means staying at home; it means the strengthening of family and domestic associations. Industrial conditions again mean wealth. It does not occupy for immediate and temporary purposes; it owns. The idea of land ownership, and of exclusive occupation of the soil arises. Whatever may be the ethics of property in land, it is historically true that individual ownership of land has played a part of fundamental importance in the social economy. Agrarianism is for a future millennium, possibly a millennium where the wolf shall lie down with the lamb, and individuality be extinguished. Be sure, however, that for centuries yet to come man will fight for at least as much exclusive possession of the soil as will preserve for him the benefits and associations of home. Observe that the highest civilization exists with the largest number of private holdings of land. There state ownership is reduced to a legal fiction; in despotisms state ownership prevails. In societies of low development, private property is held by the right and favor of the sovereign, which means by the "grace of God." State ownership co-exists with conditions of slavery—the slavery of those who are not permitted to hold land, or the feudal slavery of semi-civilized Europe of the middle ages. Brook Farms will invariably come to nothing. Swamp property rights and you swamp the nation. You so far diminish, or take away altogether that sturdy individuality which alone gives promise of social variations favorable to national life.

What we have seen to be true of the disappearance of the cumbrously defended monsters of palæontological eras, viz., that they have yielded to the superior activity of the smaller and more active orders, prefigures the history of those massive defensive structures whose ruins picturesquely ornament the mountain sides of Europe. These, together with the unwieldy armor of chivalric knights, remain but for the curiosity of the tourist and the antiquary. With the invention, or at least the introduction of gunpowder, the lighter and more portable weapon supplanted the ponderous battering-ram. The heaviest armor could not withstand the shock of artillery. The arquebusier supplanted the archer. Intelligence of invention gained the mastery. Feudalism lowered its banners, and the advance guards of the hosts of industrialism marched in. Each man's home now became his castle. The gross inequality between Lord and serf slowly disintegrated, for, thereafter, unless Earl, Duke and Marquis would venture into close quarters without the walls, and upon the levels of the open field, fate had written the epitaph of his family. Exposure to the environment was the only remaining safety of the military aristocracy, and the future problems of European policies and civilization were to be solved at Marston Moor and Dunbar, at Blenheim and Austerlitz.

And this law of shelter holds good in the matters of intellect, morals and religion. There are intellectual, moral and theological shelters; and this not by any figure of speech but in truth and fact— and it is well that

there are such. The law of evolution demonstrates
these to be indispensable. We are what the ages have
made us, and with what we are we have had nothing
whatever to do. But it earnestly behooves us to look
into these wisely, to examine whether they are upon
stable foundations, lest when the floods of doubt come
and the winds of criticism blow and beat upon those
shelters, they fall. To be conventional is the spirit of
every age, from the newest fad in dress up to the latest
fad in religion. Conservatism is the mighty force which
eternally threatens death to every favorable variation
which the social organism evolves, in any direction, for
its health and beauty. But let us speak well of conservatism—a wise conservatism is the indispensable
centripetal force which holds the social and religious
system within the radius of its influence, and will see
to it that the unwise fancies and excessive aberrations
of impetuous reformers shall also, in due time, be
brought within the circle of its law. There is to my
mind no more valueless individual than an illiberal
liberal, who cannot relate his present thought or his
pet theory to the past evolution of man, or who would
carry the torch of anarchy through every fair edifice
of past or present faith. Yet we should recognize that
conservatisms are but shelters; if necessary yet, to be
occupied with discretion, and that one window should
always be kept open towards the east, whence new in-
spirations may come. If man looks for intellectual
growth he must expect that the old social, moral and
theological shelters shall ultimately dissolve and he
must be looking out for new. But he can move from
the old shelter into the new without any convulsions or
earthquakes attending the operation. He will find his
new home as does the Chambered Nautilus in Holmes'
exquisite poem:

> "Still as the spiral grew
> He left the past year's dwelling for the new,
> Stole with soft step the shining archway through,
> Built up its idle door,
> Stretched in his last found home
> And knew the old no more."

In reference to all such shelters let us bear in mind

the lesson which we have been taught by the lower orders of nature, viz., that favorable variations occur only from free exposure to the environment. Shut ourselves within the walls of a creed, whether orthodox or unorthodox, and we invite paralysis of the religious life, and a weakening of the moral fiber. Take up with a philosophical or social theory as a finality, and progress in such directions is doomed, for us. We must open the windows, court the atmosphere of free and tolerant discussion, and expose ourselves to the environment of the latest thought and most strenuous current of intellectual activity, else we surely lose our faculty of continuously better adaptation in the mental and spiritual life, and the result is torpor.

In modern industrial and social life the sheltered recluse counts for much less than a social and industrial unit, unless his seclusion be the soil wherein he meditates something of value and inspiration to his fellow man.

When many in this audience were young, no question was raised among the vast majority of thinking men, but that all existing species were separately created, to serve some occasional purpose, and then be thrown aside as fossil ornaments to geological strata. But it happened that there arose in the convolutions of the brain of Charles Darwin variations favorable to the development of a theory of natural selection which, in the struggle of conflicting theories, held its own and survived. But was this theory thrown out as a possibility merely, for naturalists to toy with? Not at all. It was the outcome of prolonged and patient research, and it was brought by him directly into the environment of scientific fact, and, tested by that criticism, it stood. Tyndall will teach us the scientific use of the imagination, and the necessity for working theories; but he will bring both imagination and theory to the crowning test of fact and experience; that is, he will prove them by exposure to the crucible and the polariscope, which will soon advise him whether or no they are in touch with the environment of cosmic energy.

And not otherwise is it with the political life. Going to the primary is the necessary exposure to the political environment which secures a healthy civic life. Slippers and the evening paper satisfy many an honest citizen—but in the meantime the slaves of the ring are busy at the foundations of his political house, and only when the bricks begin to fall about him will he rush out to prop up what may remain to be propped.

The rule is universal—from the amœba to man there must be this incessant action and reaction. There is no progress apart from the constant stimulation upon the vital and intellectual organism of the immensely varied and constantly variable forces of the vital intellectual, moral and spiritual environment. Only that person and no other is virtuous—possesses the virile quality—is *vir*, the man, who has successfully antagonized the temptations which are pressed upon him by circumstances. The wealthy who have never been tempted to peculation are not virtuous in the matter of stealing, nor are they truly honest. Those who have never experienced in any direction and resisted the incentives to a lower life, or who have never fought with any of the greater or lesser Apollyons, are nobodies, under all moral aspects. Hegel works out, in manifold forms, as the basis of his entire philosophy, this rising by successful and repeated antagonisms of the outer by the inner life, and therein anticipates the entire subsequent systems of evolutionary science. As Prof. Royce has eloquently stated it: "As the warrior rejoices in a foeman worthy of his steel, * * as courage exists by the triumph over terror, and as there is no courage in a world where there is nothing terrible; as strength consists in the mastery of obstacles * * so, in short, everywhere, in conscious life, consciousness is a union and organization of conflicting aims and purposes, thoughts and stirrings. There is nothing consciously known or possessed till you prove it by conflict with its opposite, till you develop its inner contradictions and triumph over them. This is the fatal law of life. This is the pulse of the spiritual world."

From the cradle to the tomb the history of civilized man is a history of adaptations of shelter. The other-world idea is still the idea of home—resting place—security. Memorials to the dead invoke the noblest conceptions of architecture. Among savage tribes the other-world spirits become invested, to their minds, with exceptional forces for good or evil. Fear of the ghost makes sacred the sheltering structure of the tomb. The tomb expands into the temple; nay, the tomb itself becomes the altar. The other world spirit must be fed, and supplied with articles for use and service, as when living. Hence the universal custom of oblations and offerings to the dead, growing eventually into a formal religious service and ceremonial at the grave of the departed. In Egypt, on stated occasions, it was the custom among the wealthy classes to partake of a banquet in the ante-chamber of the rock-cut tomb, and a portion of the viands was placed upon the table at the seat reserved for the dead, who it was fully and reverently believed were present, and assisted at the ceremony. So also journeys to the tomb with gifts, became pilgrimages to the shrine. It is evident how love and veneration for the shelter for the dead, reacts upon and intensifies the idea of family, the basic social element. Quaint Sir Thomas Browne does indeed have it, in his Urn Burial, that "pyramids, arches and obelisks were but the irregularities of vain glory and wild enormities of ancient magnanimity," but this is a retrospect of an after civilization. To the Oriental, death is the supreme circumstance; of a future exist-ence or of many such he has no shadow of doubt, and the shelters which he consecrates to the dead were not, as they are with us, simply memorials of the earthly life, but habitations, as necessary for the use and shelter of those who have passed from view as are dwellings to man.

And now let us recall our definition of life, and see whether we have kept in touch with our topic—life, as we saw, is adjustment of organism to environment. In the struggle for adjustment, variations here and there arise favorable to continuance of survival. The race pro-gresses by slow increments of advantage gained by the evolution of favorable variations. And this principle we find operative in the intellectual as in the physical life. With greater necessity for shelter, owing to loss of physical strength, arises the faculty of intelligent adaptations in structure. Here again, the better adapted the structure, the greater the security for the preservation of favorable intellectual variations. Not only so, but with the greater intelligence comes an ever widening area of social sympathy. Again, the better the home life and the more gracious and beautiful the domestic relations, the better integration will there be of the social structure, which is the nation. The whole question of success in the struggle for existence among the nations relates back, therefore, to permanence in home life, as one of the controlling factors so far as sociology has to do with the problem. Survival is secured by the intelligent co-operation of free individuals. Both the original differentiations of man from the animal and the subsequent integrations into social masses are made possible by the necessity for shelter on the one hand and that further necessity for the preservation of that shelter which leads to social aggregation for purposes of defense. So that we discover no breach of continuity in our law. Adaptation, not always (nor at all at first) intentionally sought, but forced by necessity, is *life*. The person who adapts himself, not only to the house as a mere shelter, but to all those suggestions of beauty which are possible in home architecture, or in home life, either in outer construction or, in its inner economics, to books and art, such an one enjoys that fuller life which secures survival. We stated at opening that we were to inquire not only how shelter might further but how it might hinder survival, and we have found that wherever it might prevent free exposure to the environment, it is thereby deleterious, as hindering the development of variations favorable to survival and, therefore, a hindrance to progress. Exposure to the environment is therefore the prime condition—constant action and interaction—the free and constant interplay of vital, social and economic forces. But it is to the shelter of home that we bring our hardly won acquisitions, and thence issue again, with energies restored, to wage the battle anew; and thus, though contending with our disadvantages, not seldom oppressed by unfavorable conditions, yet constantly reinforced by withdrawal into the sympathetic circle of home, we secure in large degree that progressive adjustment of external to internal relations which constitutes life. So that after all it is the home which is the central thought of our subject, to which all our reflections bring us back. For this is the center of gravity for society—the center of life for the individual; it may be the inspiration for all high enterprise, and, in hours of discouragement and disaster, like the shadow of a great rock in a weary land. Who can teach us better than our own Emerson, himself one of the best of home lovers?—"Not aloof from homage to beauty, but in strict connection therewith, the house will come to be esteemed a sanctuary, the progress of truth will make every house a shrine. These are the consolations—these are the ends to which the household is instituted and the rooftree stands. If these are sought and in any good degree attained, can the State, can commerce, can climate, can the labor of many for one yield anything better or half as good? Beside these aims society is weak and the State an intrusion. He who shall bravely subdue the gorgons of convention and fashion, and show men how to lead a clean, handsome and heroic life amid the beggarly elements of our cities and villages, whoso shall teach me how to eat my meat and take my repose and deal with men, without any shame following, will restore the life of man to splendor and make his own name dear to all history."

ABSTRACT OF THE DISCUSSION.

Mr. George E. Waldo:—

I shall not criticise the lecture, for, in the main, I agree with speaker and feel that he has covered quite fully and satisfactorily the topics of which the limited time would permit him to speak.

I should like to have heard some more extended discussion of the actual growth and development of the habitations of men, and the influence of such development upon different races and nations. This, however, would be more than a subject for one lecture in itself.

So, too, it would have been of great interest and benefit to have some inquiry made into the limitations of development and growth, which in some respects make our dwellings little improvement upon the most primitive abodes of man.

To one of these limitations I desire to call your attention. It is of the utmost importance, as we all know, that we should at all times have the greatest abundance of pure fresh air, and yet that is a provision that is never contemplated in our dwelling houses, and rarely in the large and more pretentious buildings.

It is true, we have windows and doors, which can be opened, letting draughts of cold air in upon us. This, however, is practically little change from the primitive method of rolling away the stone that closed the mouth of the cave-dwelling of aboriginal man.

Architects and builders, with the greatest skill and perseverance, have expended ages in bringing our dwellings and edifices to the highest degree of beauty and stability, but have almost totally neglected to give us proper ventilation.

It is true that some schemes for ventilation have been suggested, but practically none are applied.

In these two great neighboring cities, having a population of three millions, there is not, so far as I know, a single dwelling-house that has a proper system of ventilation. This, however, is not so surprising as is the fact that among all the great hotels and public edifices, the enormous office buildings, costing millions, built without regard to expense, so far as stability and beauty of style and ornamentation are concerned, not one of these great palaces has a proper and practical system of ventilation. If there be one such building in either city that has any systematic provision for ventilation, it has not come to my notice.

It seems strange that owners and tenants do not insist upon air, as well as upon light and warmth.

The additional expense in building would be slight, and the increased cost of heating could and ought to be gladly borne by tenants.

A proper ventilation of the working rooms in which the denizens of cities spend nearly all the hours of their lives, would mean not only greatly increased and better product from their labors, whether physical or mental, but also much comfort and years added to their lives.

It is to be hoped that this subject will have such continued and public discussion as will rouse the people to the necessity of a constant supply of fresh air in their dwellings, offices, school-houses and factories, and that in the not distant future unventilated buildings may be as rare with us as properly ventilated ones are now.

Mr. James A. Skilton:—

Whether the word *shelter* is derived from the word *shell* or not, the idea of shielding is common to both words. While protection and survival may.be, among animals, as among men, the primary or immediate objects in the construction of shelter, the greater, if at first unconsidered results are growth, development, association and eventually most of what society and civilization stand for. Shelter is the occasion and opportunity for the growth of the spirit of man. And where, within reasonable limits, shelter is most needed for protection against climatic and other foes, there civilization becomes most powerful.

As shelter becomes more and more assured, more and more are the senses called in from the picket line of duty and subordinated to employments that have for their results, if not for their recognized objects, the development of the inner man.

Shelter is related not only to the prolongation of the period .of infancy among men. with its important implications, but also to many other nascent things.

In order, however, to promote survival, shelter must . be planned and managed according to evolutionary principles; otherwise it will promote non-survival.

But as the shell, after becoming a cover and protection to the animal by which it has been secreted, may become a hindrance and an obstruction to further growth, so the architectural shelter produced—we might almost say it is the product of secretion—may become limiting and injurious in its later effects.

Consequently mere examination of the buildings produced by any race or civilization may enable the competent, without other aids, to determine not only the character, but the destiny of such races and civilizations.

Inspection of the buildings produced by modern civilization shows the faults of its educational systems, in the extreme subordination of the senses. Even book-taught science—so-called—in these days leaves many college graduates inferior to savages and to many animals in their appreciation of what makes for survival or extinction.

Compared with nomadic life, the fixed life of modern cities, while producing more children, also kills more of them.

Defects of ventilation have been mentioned. Modern language seems to have no capacity of expression and the modern mind no capacity of comprehension of what is taking place in modern cities in consequence of imperfect ventilation. The annual loss of life due thereto is many-fold greater than that of all the battle-fields of the world, with all the murders thrown in. And yet it seems impossible to arouse public attention to the fact, or to find a single properly ventilated building anywhere.

In one of the finest office buildings in New York City, during a recent winter, eighteen employees, lawyers in the prime of life, were so poisoned with foul air that four of the eighteen died within a year in consequence. The physician of one of them, finding his medicines had no effect, instituted inquiry and concluded it was due to poison in the blood resulting from bad ventilation of the room occupied by the eighteen young men, who were thus more than duo-decimated thereby in a single winter.

But this is only one of many faults of the aggregated shelter system of modern city life. The foods even of city people are nearly always injured and often infected, in transit from the places of production to the city and the tables of city dwellers. The sizes of modern cities and the separation of residences from places of business are causes of enormous cost of time, waste of life and wear and tear of nerve, muscle and brain tissue, of which we take little or no account, although they constantly tend to reach the limit of endurance.

These results are due in part to the misuse of shelter and to the misunderstanding of its true function in a progressive, evolutionary civilization.

And they are also symptomatic evidences of the constitutional disease at the very heart and core of modern civilization.

Mr. Franklin S. Holmes:—

I must differ with one of the speakers when he states that no building in New York is to-day well ventilated. Good and scientific ventilation can be had if paid for. The Metropolitan Club building, corner of Sixtieth Street and Fifth Avenue, which was opened a week or two since, is an instance in point of a building artificially ventilated throughout. To accomplish this work power machinery, fans and ducts have been provided throughout, without stinting cost. The Carnegie Music Hall is another building similarly ventilated. Here one of the assembly rooms is entirely below ground, and without a window of any kind. The capacity of the ventilating apparatus is entirely adequate to the removal of the air from the hall in a few minutes. I agree with what has been said as to the indifference of people in general to the matter of ventilation, but differ with the speaker as to his wholesale denunciation of all modern ventilating practice. Suitable ventilation can be obtained, but it requires the employment of a specialist and the outlay of considerable money.

I am tempted to say a word concerning the modern office building. As we cross the Brooklyn bridge on a cold morning the silver clouds of exhaust steam everywhere rising from the New York buildings are a silent witness to the enormous energy consumed in operating elevators; while we almost mistake the roofs of the four and five story buildings for the ground, so high do the tall office buildings forming New York's second story rise above them. This new class of architecture was brought in by the steam elevator. Formerly a builder was his own architect and engineer, but this is so no longer.

Construction is becoming specialized. The modern architect may design and arrange and supervise construction, but, to be successful, he must call to his aid a variety of professional help—a mechanical engineer to arrange foundations and iron construction, a steam engineer for the power plant, an electrical engineer for lighting. The creation of a well-equipped twenty story office building is no insignificant feat in modern engineering.

HABIT

BY

REV. JOHN WHITE CHADWICK

Spencer's *Principles of Biology*, Sections 302-303, and *Principles of Psychology*, chapter on "The Physical Synthesis;" Carpenter's *Mental Physiology;* Maudsley's *Physiology of Mind;* Sully's *Sensation and Intuition;* Huxley's *Animal Automatism,* and *The Physical Basis of Life;* Proctor's *Hereditary Traits;* James's *The Laws of Habit*, in Popular Science Monthly, February, 1887.

HABIT.

BY JOHN WHITE CHADWICK.

In his declaration that conduct is three-fourths of
human life Matthew Arnold may or may not have made
an accurate calculation. Four quarters would, perhaps, be nearer to the mark, but, three or four, the
major part of it is habit, good or bad. Proverbially
"we are creatures of habit." That we are equally the
creators of habit seems not to be proverbial, but happily it is no less true. Whether we submit to habit
as a fate or make it the means of our self-conquest and
our social help, is a matter of first rate importance.
As for the individual so for the community, the state.
The subject is one which has many and various implications. Concerning some of these I have read and
thought too little, or too much, to speak of them with
the authority of personal conviction.

Habit is not monopolized by man, nor by him in
conjunction with his poor relations of the animal world.
Nature has her orderly arrangement and succession.
How many of our habits are conformed to hers! Our
very life depends on such conformity—the adjustment
of our organization to her environment. "The stars
have us to bed," as Herbert quaintly sings. Our plant-
ings and our reapings are in unison with her spring-
time and her autumn weather. The waters run down
hill and seek their own level with infallible fidelity.
The attraction of gravitation is always inversely to the
square of the distance. The radius vector of a planet
always describes equal areas in equal times. Ordinarily, we speak of these uniformities of coëxistence
and sequence as laws. By calling them habits we
should better express our meaning and be better understood; so many understand by laws something anal-
agous to the statutory laws of kings and parliaments.
The uniformities of nature are the habits of the mighty

mother, the eternal God. Some of these habits are fundamental and instinctive, like our human habits of breathing, eating, sleeping. But others, like the majority of our human habits, have been acquired. The story of their acquisition will be found in Darwin's chapters and those of other writers, under the head of natural selection in the vegetable and inorganic worlds. In truth there is no break. By imperceptible degrees the habits of the inorganic world become those of the vegetable, those of the vegetable are succeeded by those of the animal and human world. The sun knoweth his going down; seed-time and harvest do not fail; the young lions roar and seek their meat from God; man goeth forth to his labor until the evening.

But not only have the habits of mankind their analogue in nature's uniformities, they have their roots, or at any rate, their concomitants in our physical organization, our nervous system. So intimate is the relationship, so invariable the concomitance, that we have men of great authority in science and philosophy affirming that there is no psychology but physiology, that what we call mind is only the rattle of the cerebral machinery. Queerly enough, the rattle hears itself. This is the theory which would have it that animals are automata, a theory that Descartes applied to the animals below man, but which Huxley and Clifford and others more courageous and consistent than Descartes have applied to man as well. Sometimes we are assured that it is a matter of indifference whether we express one and the same thing in the terms of matter or of mind. Now, I have held in my hand the naked brain of a great mathematician and philosopher who cordially assented, I believe, to this automaton theory. If I could have seen into it and seen all the wriggles of its neurotic substance while it was agitated with his highest thoughts, I do not think it would have been quite the same as reading these thoughts in a book. But that might be because I could only see the motion and could not hear the rattle of the wheels. Take, then, a treatise of psychology, that of Prof. Wm. James, the brightest one at our command, as fascinating as "The Raiders" or "A Gentleman of France." Much of it is expressed in terms of the material organization.

But if all had been so expressed, how different would
have been the grand result! It would have been anything but grand. Yet even that expression would
have been infinitely removed from the cerebral concomitants of the Professor's vivid thought. His own
reasons are as good as any that I know for rejecting
the automaton theory. And they are reasons that hold
equally against the amiable but silly compromise which
suggests that in conscious thought and nervous action we
have two parallel lines that never touch, so completely
insulated that they have no effect upon each other,
absolute concomitance and absolute mutual independence. "Having firmly and tenaciously grasped these
two notions," says a distinguished writer, "we shall
have surmounted half our difficulties at the start." But
Prof. James thinks he should not have said "surmounted"
but "ignored." It is to his mind quite inconceivable
that consciousness should have nothing to do with a
matter to which it so faithfully attends. What *has* it
to do with it? It seems to have a veto power, a casting vote. The more habitual the act, the less conscious. But given a moment of hesitation, a crisis in
which action is imperative, and the consciousness becomes intense. Here is the suggestion of a selective
power, a loading of the dice, Prof. James would say,
before the fatal throw. That habit is the brain a-making
does not admit of any doubt. Dr. Carpenter's phrase
that "our nervous system grows to the modes in which
it has been exercised," is one which no dread of materialism can set aside. Were not this so, Dr. Carpenter never would have given us the formula, for there
could not be any one less of a materialist than he. The
plasticity of the brain is the element in which habit
works. Nowhere else in the body does the process
of waste and repair go on so vigorously as in the nervous system and especially in the brain. The reproduction of a section of the spinal cord which has been
destroyed is only, we are assured, a marvelous illustration of what is always going on in nervous tissues.
But in virtue of this "incessant regeneration" the tendency of every part to form itself after the manner in
which it is habitually exercised finds in the brain a
very special illustration. Those grooves are fixed, into

which impulse runs as naturally as the swelling stream
into the channels which the summer's drouth makes
dry.   As these channels interlace each other, so do the
channels of the brain, and hence we have the association of ideas. And as "more water glideth by the mill
than wots the miller of," so more thoughts glide
through the brain than what the owner knows of, and
we have the phenomena of unconscious cerebration
and the memory of things to which we have never
consciously attended.

If one finds this statement of the case repulsive, as
conceding too much to the materialist, he has the al-
ternative of suspending his judgment altogether for the
present in regard to many things which the brain
grooved by habit would explain.   In regard to others
he can have all the moral implications of this doctrine
while still withholding from this his assent. For it is as
clear as possible, apart from any considerations of cerebral psychology, that the repetition of certain acts, or
courses of action, makes them more easy, natural and
inevitable.   It is equally clear that the mind, however
it may be with the brain, is more plastic in youth
than at any later time, and that therefore this is
preëminently the habit-forming time.   Moreover, the
means by which bad habits may be inhibited, and
good habits confirmed and strengthened, are just the
same whatever psychological theory we hold.

The relation of habit to instinct is an important one,
which may as well receive our attention now as further
on.   To define instinct as congenital habit is clearly a
mistake, seeing that many instincts do not develop till
maturity or some earlier or later period long after birth.
Prof. James defines instinct as "the faculty of acting
in such a way as to produce certain ends without foresight of those ends, and (the heart of the whole matter) without previous education in the performance."
Omit the final clause, "without previous education,"
and we should have a very good account of a great
deal of habit, not only that which furnishes our subject with illustrations that are very humorous and absurd, but that which is the staple of our daily life and
which we could not easily forego.   Surely habit is wonderfully like instinct when it proceeds with the min-

imum of consciousness and volition, as where a gentleman winds his watch at whatever time of day he happens to put off his waistcoat. Others have gone
further, even so far as undressing entirely and going
to bed when they had set out to dress for dinner.
Many a time have I, after concluding that I would pass
a friend's house without calling, been brought to my
senses by finding that I had rung the bell. An endless catalogue could be made of such freaks of habit,
but they do not impeach its ordinary service to the individual and the community. The shoemaker or other
artisan will work for hours without thinking of his
work. And it is wonderful how the nervous system
treasures up the habits that have once been impressed
upon it. Once upon a time when I had not made a
shoe for several years, I set out to make a pair for a
young lady in whom I was very deeply interested.
She wore the smallest size of children's ankle-ties. I
wondered if I could remember my lost art. I did not
have to remember it. There it was in my hands, in
my finger tips, as if I had left my bench only the day
before to become "a mender of bad *souls.*" The second nature that was then so serviceable to me was of
a piece with the whole web of our domestic life. A
household without habitual order and recurrence is a
spectacle in which neither the angels nor the men,
who are a little lower, can take rational delight. It
means an enormous waste of time, and for that reason if for no other "miserable beyond all other forms
of wretchedness are those who must deliberately settle
before hand the details of each domestic day."* There
are a thousand little things which can be done as naturally, as unconsciously, as we breathe, if once relegated
to the sphere of habit, leaving the body of our time
and strength for fresh experiences of labor, thought,
and love.

The instinctive character of many habits lends itself
heartily to the doctrine that instincts are the products
of habits long persisted in, and inherited from one generation to another. The doctrine of Weismann that
acquired traits cannot be transmitted is opposed to

* A free quotation from Dr. Samuel Johnson.

this derivation of instinct from persistent and hereditary habit. Out-Darwining Darwin in his faith in
natural selection, he would look to that and to that
alone as the author and finisher of the instinctive element in man and the lower animals. However it may
be derived, it has a part to play of wonderful significance through all its range. Each set of instincts is
appropriate to the particular creature to which it belongs. Each set has its appropriate stimuli, furnishing the required impulse upon which they act. The
empty nest or single egg furnishes "the meek birds"
of Emerson with the stimulus to oviparation; a goodly
number of eggs the stimulus to setting. Take some
away, and the hen goes on laying more. The cuckoo
is guilty of no conscious meanness when she finds a
particular nest with one or more eggs in it and tumbles
them out to make room for her own. Nor is she actu-
ated by any desire to preserve the cuckoo species. But
the sight of the nest and eggs furnishes just the impulse needed to excite her egg-laying function to perform its work.

The popular understanding of these things is too
favorable to the animal and insect races, and too de-
preciatory of mankind. The instincts of the lower
creatures are neither so blind nor so infallible as we
commonly suppose. A hen, for instance, that has reared
one brood of chickens, remembering the joy she had
in gathering them under her wings and listening to
their tiny "Cheep!" certainly does not altogether "go
it blind" when she again becomes broody. Her broodi-
ness is reinforced by the remembered joys of motherhood. The animal instincts are not so infallible as
we have imagined, for one reason, because they are
always liable to be inhibited by other instincts and so
partly or entirely neutralized. As animals rise in the
scale of being this happens oftener. The lower and
the lowest "always act in the manner which would be
oftenest right." Thus "there are," says my much-
quoted Professor, "more worms unattached to hooks
than impaled upon them; therefore, on the whole,
says Nature to her fishy children, bite at every worm
and take your chances." But the higher animals have
many other impulses playing at cross purposes with

their instinctive greediness, so that they lose their instinctive demeanor and "appear to lead a life of hesitation and choice, and intellectual life," "not," we are reminded, "because they have no instincts,—rather because they have so many that they block each other's way." The animal that has the most is man. If his instincts do not act with the regularity of the lower animals, it is not because they are fewer or less powerful, but because they are oftener mutually inhibited; also by habits formed in a more or less rational manner and by impulses of the imagination which the reason has evoked.

The inhibition of instincts by habits has a suggestiveness requiring something more than a mere passing reference. The rule in this matter is "first come, first served:" i. e., the first object of a kind usually reacted on awakens the usual instinct to the exclusion of those following; the instinct is inhibited by a habit that keeps it from acting on any but the habitual object. The instinct of new-born chicks to follow their mother as the first moving object they see, betrays them into following any moving object they first see, dog, child, or man. So a hen that has several times hatched ducks, afterward hatching chickens, tries to drive them into the water. Another hen sat patiently upon a brood of ferrets that had been substituted for her expected chickens, and another nursed a young peacock eighteen months, not laying an egg for all that time and taking a ridiculous satisfaction in her infant phenomenon. Now, this inhibition of instinct by habit has no inconsiderable part to play in human life. It does much to insure the stability of domestic happiness. It explains, perhaps, why good men are devoted to bad parties. With the instinct of justice, they have attached themselves to one of these when it appealed to that instinct. From force of habit they have stuck to it when it has dragged Astræa in the mire.

That many instincts are very transitory and have their time to come and go is another circumstance of much importance. Much that we call instinct is really habit. An instinct acted on becomes a habit, and remains potent and imperious when the instinct exists no longer. "A chicken that has not heard the call of the mother till it is eight or ten days old hears it as if it heard it not." Children are born hungry for the mother's breast, but it only takes a brief denial to destroy the instinct altogether. It would seem as if habits were, as Wellington said,"ten times nature." If only we could wean the drunkard from his bottle as easily as we can wean the suckling from the mother's breast, how happy we should be! The various human instincts have their fixed times, and it is the part of a wise education to avail itself of them to make them habits of the mind. Otherwise they tend to atrophy and at a rapid rate, and we have men who were never boys, who do not care for play or adventure or travel, for study or business enterprises or married life. "There is a happy moment," we are told, "for fixing skill in drawing, for making boys collectors in natural history and presently dissectors and botanists; then for initiating them in the harmonies of mechanics and the wonders of physical and chemical law." The tendency of bachelorhood to prolong itself indefinitely is undoubtedly an illustration of this law of transitory instinct.

No creature has so many and such powerful instincts as a man, and no animal's instincts serve him better. It would be an easy matter to spend all my time with these, but if I am going to say something on each of the seventeen different heads which Doctor Janes has grafted on my subject, I must be wise in time. But a few things in this kind cannot be tacitly ignored. Thus, if it be true that children do not have to learn to walk, that they will walk anyway when their nerve centers are ripe enough, it seems a pity that the fact should not be generally known. Professor James proposes an experiment, a small blister on each baby foot, during the usual learning time. Of course he knows that it would be impossible for maternal fondness ever to make so cruel an experiment. What he hopes is "that some scientific widower, left alone with his offspring at the critical moment, may ere long test this suggestion on the living subject." That the habits of the primitive man were "mainly arboreal" afforded Matthew Arnold when he was in this country food for inextinguishable laughter. Such habits are instinctive with children about three years old. If, then, the young Romeo is encouraged, he may be a climber all his days. John Tyndall must have been encouraged, and James Freeman Clarke, or the first would not have been the Alpine climber that he was, and the second would not have gone up 404 feet to the top of Salisbury spire and stood beside the vane. Maternal fear for the piano or the banisters frequently prevents the child's arboreal instinct from becoming a life-long habit, and sometimes it is inhibited by the consequences of a too daring feat.

The fighting instincts of the animal world have been bequeathed to man to a remarkable degree, and they are encouraged by an extensive sanguinary literature of war enjoyed by young and old, and by the generous amount of space allowed by journals of repute to the prize-fighting interest. To all intents and purposes the mercenary editor joins "the ignoble crew that escorts every great pugilist—parasites who feel as if the glory of his brutality rubbed off on them, and whose darling hope from day to day is to arrange some set-to of which they may share the rapture without enduring the pains." Does not the same instinct declare itself in the polemical habit of the clergy? Surely Dean Stanley was the mildest mannered man that ever engaged in controversy, but that he dearly loved a row we are not left in doubt. That there should be a good ecclesiastical scrimmage, and he not be in it, was a thing that he could not endure. The instincts of fear, curiosity, constructiveness, play, sociability, secretiveness, cleanliness, modesty, shame, sexual and parental love, furnish innumerable examples of the wealth and force of human instincts, and of their frequent mutual inhibition, as when the most timid mother dares anything for her endangered child. Puss hates the water, but throw in her kitten and you would think her to the aquatic manner born. Speaking of cats, if it is an instinct of cleanliness that induces them to engage in such everlastingly recurrent attention to their glossy coats, it is surely strange that the instinct has no preventive character. In short, why does our own cat, whose disposition to "wash up and brush up" is phenomenal, have such a predilection for the coal-bin and the ash-heap? I have found myself wondering whether her ablutions had anything to do with cleanliness;

whether they were not a survival of the ancestral satisfaction in the incidents of the bloody fray.

All habits, we have heard, are bad habits, but there
could not be a sillier notion. For every human instinct there should be a corresponding habit, or one
inhibiting its excessive action, if we would not have
a maimed and thwarted life. The extent to which instinct can be inhibited by habit proves that the latter
is the greater force in human life. Who has not heard
of prisoners who, set free, pleaded to be sent back to
the familiar cell? What hardship can it not enable men
and women to endure? When the Englishman was
gently expostulated with for eating the white end of
the asparagus, he made answer, "I always eat this
end." Then, of course, he liked it better. Habit can
make the most disagreeable thing delightful, the most
painful thing agreeable. That he might neither lose
his life nor caste, a Hindu accepted for his punishment
a bed of spikes on which he was to do all his sleeping
for a term of years. At the expiration of the term his
skin was like the hide of a rhinoceros, and he had no
inclination to exchange his spikes for feathers. "What a
fearful example," do you say, "of the power of evil habit
to harden those who are subjected to its sway?" Say
rather, "What a fine example of the power of any habit,
good or bad, to make over the individual!" And for
one habit that is bad there are a dozen or twenty that
are good. And the problem for the individual and for
society is not to narrow the sphere of habit, but to
widen it and make it the ally of virtue and the common-
weal. "Habit," says Professor James, "is the enormous
fly-wheel of society, its most precious conservative
agent. It alone is what keeps us all within the bounds
of ordinance, and saves the children of fortune from
the envious uprising of the poor. It alone prevents
the hardest and most repulsive walks of life from being deserted by those brought up to tread therein. It
keeps the fisherman and the deck-hand at sea through
the winter; it holds the miner in his darkness and
nails the countryman to his log-cabin and his lonely
farm through all the months of snow; it protects us
from invasion by the natives of the desert and the
frozen zone. It dooms us all to fight out the battle of

life upon the lines of our nurture and our early choice,
and to make the best of a pursuit that disagrees with
us, because there is no other for which we are fitted
and we are too old to begin again. It is well for the
world that in most of us. by the age of thirty, the
character has set like plaster and will never soften
again."

I am myself a standing illustration of the thing
which I am setting forth. Do not imagine that I am
going, for no extra charge, to make an exhibition of
my personal habits, good or bad. I only mean that I
have quoted Professor James so much that the habit of
quoting him is getting to be easier than to refrain.
And now I have come to a point from which onward
I should like to quote him right along, what he has
written for us is so very fine and good. But always,
you will notice, the best people to quote are the quoters
—Plutarch, Montaigne, Emerson. Professor James is
himself a famous quoter, and that makes him the more
quotable, and would make me sure of his forgiveness
if I had not sinned in the same way before and got his
blessing. "The great thing in education," he assures
us, "is to make our nervous system our ally instead of
our enemy." If you prefer to say "our habits" rather
than "our nervous system," you probably have his
permission. And to make our habits our allies we must
go about to make as many useful actions as may be
habitual—physiologically speaking, automatic—and at
the same time defend ourselves at every weak place
in the line against the assault of actions which, once
grown habitual, would be the ruin of our usefulness
and happiness. Some of Professor James's best maxims
for our guidance in the formation of habit and the conduct of life are taken from Professor Bain's chapter on
"The Moral Habits." The best thing about them is
that they are not far off and strange, but in singular
agreement with the judgments of our ordinary common
sense. Thus, for example, one of the maxims is that
when we are trying to acquire a new habit which we
are convinced would be serviceable to us, or to break off
one which we know to be detrimental, we must *launch
ourselves with as strong and decided an initiative as
possible.* We must "accumulate all the possible cir-

cumstances which shall reinforce the right motives,
put ourselves assiduously in conditions that encourage
the new way; make engagements that are incompatible
with the old." Many a character might have been saved
from moral wreck that has drifted to it like a ship
upon the breakers by the rigorous following up of a
device as simple as the last. That would be praying
in good earnest, "Lead us not into temptation." For
it is of little use to pray thus with our lips and then
deliberately or carelessly walk into it with our legs.
The best way to conquer temptation is to keep out of
it. It doesn't act so powerfully at a distance as it
does close at hand. It has its appropriate stimuli, and
we can muster strength to keep away from these when
we couldn't muster strength to withstand these if we
came close up to them. Tennyson's Northern Farmer
understood perfectly the philosophy of this business
when he said to his son: "Don't y' marry for money,
but go where money is." If you don't want to marry
money, or drink, or gambling, or licentiousness, or any
obvious departure from the line of rectitude and truth
and purity, don't go where such things are. The wise
Ulysses, coming to where the Sirens sweetly sang, bade
his companions lash him to the vessel's mast. So
ever the wise man, coming to where the Sirens of temptation sweetly sing, will, if he can, *tie himself up*, or
get his friends to tie him until the danger shall be
overpast. But how shall he tie himself, and how shall
he be tied? Well, with the strong cords of affection,
surrounding himself with those who expect him to be
good and true. With some good book, with some ex-
acting task, with some frank confession—in no priestly
ear, so by a cheap repentance getting a new lease of sin,
but in the ear of some beloved friend whose eyes are
too pure to look upon uncleanness, and whose confidence would be as inviolable as God's. Hundreds that
tread a dangerous way know that they have a friend
with whom five minutes' honest talk would mean the
old life ended and the new begun. The ice once broken,
bitter chill would be the plunge, no doubt, but it would
be a baptism of regeneration such as never was the
sacrament of priestly hands.

The second maxim of Professor Bain is, "*Never suffer*

an exception to the new habit to occur"—the habit
that you wish to graft on your old stock—"*until it is
securely rooted in your life,*" and Professor James comes to
the confirmation of this maxim with a very happy illustration. He says, "Each lapse is like the letting fall
of a ball of string which you are carefully winding up:
a single slip undoes more than a great many turns will
wind again." "The peculiarity of the moral habit,"
says Professor Bain, "is the presence of two hostile
powers, one to be gradually raised into the ascendant
over the other. *It is necessary above all things in such a
situation never to lose a battle.* Every gain on the
wrong side undoes the effect of many conquests on the
right. The essential precaution, therefore, is to so
regulate the two opposing powers that the one may
have a series of uninterrupted successes, until repetition has fortified it to such a degree as to enable it to
cope with the opposition under any circumstances."
This would seem to rule out entirely the whole system
of "tapering off" with any such evil habit as that of
drink or opium-eating or the use of tobacco, or with
the indulgence in illicit pleasures of any kind whatever.
In the conflict of opinions among experts on this head,
Professor James's opinion is very much after the manner
of the farmer's in the matter of planting potatoes: "You
can't plant them too deep unless you plant them a
little deeper that you oughter." You can't break off
the evil habit too sharply unless you attempt more than
you can possibly perform. "We must be careful not
to give the will so stiff a task as to insure its defeat
at the very outset; but, *provided one can stand it,* a
sharp period of suffering and then a free time is the
best thing to aim at, whether in giving up a habit,
like opium, or in simply changing one's hours of rising or of work." And then we have this sentence, which
every man encountering habitual temptation should
bind as an amulet upon his wrist: "It is surprising
how soon a desire will die of inanition if it be *never*
fed." Says Bahnsen, a German psychologist, expounding
the psychology of habit, "One must learn first, unmoved, looking neither to the right hand nor the left, to
walk firmly on the straight and narrow path, before one
can begin 'to make one's self over again.' He who

every day makes a fresh resolve is like one who, arriving at the edge of a ditch he is to leap, forever stops and returns for a fresh run. Without *unbroken* advance there is no such thing as an accumulation of the ethical forces possible, and to make this possible and to exercise us and habituate us in it, is the sovereign blessing of regular work." That is to say, there is such a thing as a habit of habit, and those who have not this, but live habitually feeling "the weight of chance desires," will find it much more difficult to form any habit which may seem to be desirable either for their body's health or their soul's peace. As for Professor James's advice not to attempt too much, we should, I think, remember that it is easier oftentimes to tempt the will with an heroic course of action than with a timid, halting one. The ancient rule of whist, "When in doubt play a trump," may not be a good rule in whist any longer, but it is still a good rule in habit. When in doubt whether you can initiate the new habit that shall inhibit the old one, *make a trial of your strength.*

There is a third maxim for which I do not know to whom I am indebted: "*Seize the first possible opportunity to act on every resolution you make, and on every emotional prompting you may experience in the direction of the habits you aspire to gain.*" John Keats's line, "A moment's thought is passion's passing knell," is too good to be believed. Any amount of thinking and feeling that does not materialize in definite volition may do nothing but confirm the habit we despise and make the one we crave less possible of realization. For

> "thus the native hue of resolution
> Is sicklied o'er with the pale cast of thought,
> And enterprises of great pith and moment
> With this regard their currents turn awry,
> And lose the name of action."

The good intentions with which hell is proverbially paved are the good intentions which have been content to remain unrealized. There are good intentions rushing into action which pave hell with adamant for the victorious car of the triumphant will, sternly resolved upon escape out of its bondage into the glorious lib-

erty of the children of God. It is interesting here to
see John Henry Newman clasping hands with the physiological psychologist in a fellowship of fruitful
thought, the psychologist saying, "A tendency to act
becomes ingrained in us in proportion to the uninterrupted frequency with which actions occur, and the
brain grows to their use. Every time a resolve or a
fine glow of feeling evaporates without bearing practical
fruit, is worse than a chance lost; it works so as positively to hinder future resolutions and emotions from
taking the normal path of discharge;" while Newman
sings:

> "Prune thou thy words, the thoughts control
>   That o'er thee swell and throng;
> They will condense within thy soul
>   And change to purpose strong.

> "But he who lets his feeling run
>   In soft, luxurious flow,
> Shrinks from hard service to be done,
>   And faints at every woe."

And the antiphony goes on with the words of the
psychologist, "There is no more contemptible type of
human character than that of the nerveless sentimental-
ist and dreamer, who spends his life in a weltering sea of
sensibility and emotion, but who never does a manly
concrete deed."—"There is reason to suppose that if
we often flinch from making an effort, before we know
it the effort-making capacity will be gone." And hence
we have offered for our consideration and urged on
our acceptance the further maxim, *"Keep the faculty
of effort alive in you by a little gratuitous exercise
every day.* That is, be systematically ascetic or heroic
in little unnecessary points; do every day or two something for no other reason than that you would rather
not do it, so that when the hour of dire need draws
nigh it may not find you unnerved and untrained to
bear the test." I find myself disposed to doubt the
wisdom of this particular advice. It does not seem to
me that in the most ordinary lives there is likely to be
any real scarcity of opportunities to do the hard, the
disagreeable, the painful, the heroic thing. If any man

or woman finds himself or herself afflicted with such a
scarcity, they would do well to question whether they
have taken a correct account of stock. We have the
assurance of Emerson that difficult duty is never far
off, and those who do not find this to be true in their
own experience should seriously suspect themselves,
and overhaul their spiritual stock. If a man cannot
find plenty of natural channels for his ascetic and
heroic will, then he may very well make artificial ones.
But first let him be sure he has not overlooked some
obvious opportunity for "looking on the things of another" and "pleasing not himself."

Given an evil habit that we must throttle and destroy
if we would not be ourselves destroyed by it, nothing
is more fatal to the strong initiative and the accumula-
tive energy required for our salvation than the tacit
expectation of some ultimate reprieve, the anticipation
of some happy day when we may "treat our resolution"
as a reward for our enforced denial. Poor Hartley
Coleridge looked into his own heart, no doubt, and
wrote the sonnet which is black as thunder with the
doom of those who go this miserable way.

"If I have sinned in act I may repent,
If I have erred in thought I may disclaim
My silent error and yet feel no shame.
But if my soul, big with an ill intent,
Guilty in will, by fate be innocent,
Or being bad yet murmurs at the curse
And incapacity of being worse,
That makes my hungry passion still keep Lent
In expectation of a carnival,
Where, in all worlds that round the sun revolve
And shed their influence on this passive ball,
Abides a power that can my soul absolve?"

Where but in such a flash of terrible illumination as
we have in such a cry from this poor wanderer's heart;
in response of our own latent good to such a cry; in
the resolve to look for no reprieve, no carnival, but
taking no step backward, to go on, go on, putting the
bad things underneath our feet, seeking the better and
the best with an unconquerable will.

The moralist is apt to fear the Greeks of science

bringing gifts unto his treasury of ethical motive, sanction, inspiration, but except in George Eliot's Romola, which, by the way, is nothing more than the same laws that we have been considering written large in the imagination's golden light, I do not know of any moral teaching more impressive than that which I have found in the psychology of habit, as set forth by the masters in this kind, and especially by Professor James. When we used to foregather in Divinity Hall some thirty years ago, I little thought that I should ever owe to him so large a debt. "Let no youth," he says, "have any anxiety about the upshot of his education, whatever the line of it may be. If he keep faithfully busy each hour of the working day he may safely leave the final result to itself. He can with perfect certainty count on waking up some fine morning to find himself one of the competent ones in whatever pursuit he may have singled out." But there is thunder upon this horizon as well as rosy light. Its long reverberations tell us that by these habits of ours which we are tolerating or making, "we are spinning our own fates, good or evil, and never to be undone. Every smallest stroke of virtue or of vice leaves its never so little scar. The drunken Rip Van Winkle, in Jefferson's play, excuses himself for every fresh dereliction by saying, 'I won't count this time.' Well, he may not count it and mankind may not count it; but it is being counted none the less. Down among his nerve cells and fibers the molecules are counting it, registering it and storing it up to be used against him when the next temptation comes." "Everything has two handles," says an ancient proverb; "beware of the wrong one." The wrong one here means such self-wounding that the life-blood ebbs away. The right one means a sword to hew all hateful opposition down and bring us to our own. If a good deal of this seems to you very much like preaching, again I furnish in my own preaching an illustration of the laws with which I deal. The habit of preaching is one of the most inexpugnable and irresistible of all habits. When Coleridge asked Lamb, "Charles, did you ever hear me preach?" the stammering humorist made answer, as you know, "I n-never h-heard you d-do anything else, Sam."

The great controversy between Spencer and Weismann as to the inheritance of acquired traits has evidently an important bearing on the doctrine of habit. The difference between them is that while Spencer thinks that we inherit from preceding generations the capital of their character with the accumulated interest of habit, Weismann contends that the accumulated interest is not inherited. The argument in favor of Weismann from the non-inheritance of malformations and abridgments of parts and functions may be conceded to him for what it is worth. There is a variation of Mother Goose's three blind mice who all ran after the farmer's wife; a continuation of that tailless tale which is, upon this head, "significant of much." The experimenter took twelve white mice, five males and seven females, and having cut off their tails, began breeding with them in Oct., 1887. By January, 1889, there were three hundred and thirty-three, and a little later nine hundred and one, and there was not one that showed the least shortening of the tails, though the tails of each successive generation had been lopped in turn.* But the inheritance of mechanical injury is one thing and that of acquired habit is quite another. Mr. Spencer is perfectly willing to allow that the discouragement of the little toe by boot-pressure has nothing to do with the increasing insignificance of that part. Signs of its progressive degradation are found in barefoot tribes. But he is not convinced that its disuse, sympathetic with the change from climbing to walking habits, would not in some hundred thousand years have caused the degeneracy of which we are aware. But it is a far cry from these considerations to the doctrine of Weismann that the germ-plasm of successive generations leads a life of absolute seclusion and independence, i. e., that general bodily conditions have no influence whatever on the development of the prenatal life. It may be conceded that a great deal has been passed to the credit of heredity which has come another way. Weismann no less than Galton believes in hereditary genius. What he does not believe in is hereditary talent, i. e., the inheritance of any special ability. His

*The failure of three thousand years of circumcision to leave any inherited trace might, it would seem, have rendered this experiment unnecessary.

argument on this head is full of interest, and it is most persuasive and convincing to my personal mind. A man is not born a physicist or a botanist, however great a physicist or botanist his father may have been before him. How, then, do we account for a line of musicians, or botanists, or artists in one family? By the force of the environment and example. "A great artist (or thinker) is always a great man, and if he finds his talent closed on one side, he forces his way through on the other." We may allow all this, and still we are far away from Wesimann's doctrine of the complete isolation of the germ-plasm, its complete independence on the general bodily character. There are many facts which do not look this way, resemblances of the off-spring of a second union to a previous sire. The conflict of domestic with wild instincts in domestic animals is quite unaccountable if acquired habits cannot be transmitted. If, as Darwin believed, the families of drunkards become extinct in the fourth generation, something very different from the seclusion of the germinal life from all general bodily conditions has got to be supposed. Hereditary senility is not uncommon. It is a striking fact that nearly fifty-three per cent of all murderers, according to certain careful tables, were begotten by fathers who had reached the period of decadence. That early marriages are those which produce health, strength, power, genius in the offspring is a conviction fortified by many illustrations, with Michael Angelo and Goethe and their fine girl-mothers marching in the van.

But indeed the original vigorous and rigorous statement of Weismann's doctrine has received quite as many notches from his own grinding and regrinding as from any blows of his opponents in the lively fray. As gradually modified by himself, his doctrine now bears a very close resemblance to that of Galton, which involves the exertion of a certain amount of influence on the germ-substance by the general substance of the body, and consequently the possible transmission of acquired habits, traits, and talents in some very slight degree. That the transmission of such habits, traits and talents, is much less general and important than Spencer has conceived, would seem to be the outcome of the

long discussion up to the present time. But even supposing that Weismann had made good his original
contention—that the material of heredity is absolutely
stable and continuous—our doctrine of habit would not
be cast down and utterly destroyed. We should have
to look to natural selection alone instead of to that and
the transmission of acquired habits, traits, and talents,
as the secret of development. We should have to reform our grandparents and the earlier generations to
improve our progeny. A clean sweep would be made
of all those lovely sentimental notions as to the habits
and environment of the mother on the life she nourishes
within her own. The books she read, the pictures and
the natural scenes delighting her, the lofty thoughts
she cherished, would be of no account as influencing
the unborn child. Even as it is, these things are
evidently gone. But do parental habits therefore cease
to be a matter of importance? Evidently not. Weismann has ventured no such heresy. Rather has he
given to the force of habit a more important character
than it had before. According to his doctrine, it is the
child's association with the habits of its parents that
gives that direction to his faculty or genius which we
call talent. He negatives the influence of hereditary
habit, but he makes the influence of personal and associated habit a factor of immense importance. Buckle,
who did not believe in hereditary character or talent,
would have rejoiced to see his day. There is abounding
comfort in his thought for those who have in charge
the education of children and the reform of criminals.
For given the doctrine of Spencer in full force, and the
dead weight of heredity is depressing to the last degree.
The modifications of Weismann give the matter more
completely into our own hands. At least they deepen
our responsibility, and if they do not take off the curse
for our shortcomings from our immediate ancestors altogether, they distribute it over a much wider field. In
losing the transmission of parental habits, traits, and
talents, we lose much less than we have generally imagined. It is true that before the birth of children
from a normal marriage the personal habits of the parents are generally fixed, but those deeper habits of
thought and action which make the full-grown charac-

ter are not. But it is not as if human parents were like so many of the insect world, and like the mother of Aurora Leigh, who "could not bear the joy of giving life; the mother's rapture slew her." We generally live on, and if our children have not inherited our habits, traits, and talents, they will fast enough contract them from association with our own, or in their plastic substance receive the impress of our moulding hands. Henceforth the mother's occupation is not gone. Not only while her child is yet unborn, but through many years before she has conceived the blessed hope, and through many years after its fulfillment nothing that she can do to store her mind with lovely images and noble thoughts will come amiss, nothing that she can do to make the habits of her life as calm and sweet as she can make them with assiduous and loving care. And what is true of the mother is not less true of the father. In despite of Weismann's doctrine, they can still say to their children present and future, For their sakes we consecrate ourselves. For what they are is the most potent influence under heaven in determining what their children shall become.

The application of these principles to the social structure is perfectly obvious. Mr. Benjamin Kidd, the writer of a recent book called *Social Evolution*, which sides with Weismann in a somewhat reckless manner, has some very interesting pages on the comparative values of the savage and the cultivated brain. He finds the difference so little that it does not suggest much accumulation of intellectual ability either by hereditary transmission or natural selection. And what, then, makes the difference between the savage and the civilized man? Answer: The accumulation of social advantages by infinitesimal increments from generation to generation and from age to age. There is inheritance, but the wealth which we inherit is hoarded not in the convolutions of the brain, but in the continuous tradition of the arts and habits of the race. The inheritance is along the social, not along the physiological and cerebral lines. There seems to be much truth in this. But why, then, does the savage remain savage? Because he has not broken that "cake of custom," as Mr. Bagehot called it, that bond of early habit which is a necessity for all primitive societies, but which must be broken if there is going to be indefinite advancement. It is what the shell is to the chicken, absolutely necessary to the early stage of its development, absolutely fatal to its larger life if it is not broken in due time. It is evident that the influence of habit on the successive generations is a less imposing factor if its transmission is entirely, or almost entirely, upon social lines, and not on both social and physiological. But the transmission of habit is not less of a reality in the former case than in the latter.

This Easter Sunday is the Church's Resurrection Day, and our coming here this evening to consider the subject of Habit may appear to some a strange, incongruous sequel to the morning's festival of flower and song. But were I disposed to make out a connection between the sentiments appropriate to the day and my particular theme, I should have no difficulty in doing so. The nexus would be ready for my hand. For what but putting off the old man and putting on the new was the phrase by which the great apostle of the resurrection indicated the reality which the resurrection represented to his mind. Putting off the old man and putting on the new: as if each in time were a garment, a *habit*; as in Shakspere's phrase—"In habit as he was." To-day as eighteen centuries ago, this is the most important business that we have in hand. How the old habit sometimes clings!—like Dejaneira's fatal shirt to the unhappy Hercules. It often clings the closer because it has been woven on some loom of noble aspiration, because its warp and woof are the associations and the memories of some heroic time. That is the trouble with the worst social habit of our time, that of partisanship in politics. That is the reason why it has taken so many of the noblest spirits in its snare. The party earned their allegiance by devotion to some principle of equity, and it keeps it from the force of habit, no matter how it drags its garlands in the mire. But while this habit of political partisanship is the most baleful habit of our time, fatal alike to personal character and the public weal, there is not on the horizon any gleam of happier light than that which heralds the incoming of a habit of political independence.

"When the tale of bricks is doubled, then Moses comes."
When the McKanes and Pratts and Hills become
insufferable,then good citizens break their "cake of custom," their partisan habit, and quit themselves like men.
And, once rejoicing in their new-found freedom, some
are recruited for the future to the ranks of those who
hold the doctrine that parties were made for men and
not men for parties to be sound and good. But the
habit of political partisanship, although the worst, is
only one of many that press balefully upon our social
life, and there are other habits that press not less balefully upon us as individuals. To break the force of
these, and to establish others in their places is, as
Abraham Lincoln said of his special task, "a big job."
But like that,it is one that sounds a note of joyous in-
vitation to all those who are not yet given over to believe a lie.

FROM NATURAL TO CHRISTIAN SELECTION

BY

REV. JOHN C. KIMBALL

COLLATERAL READINGS SUGGESTED.

Spencer's *Principles of Sociology*, and *Principles of Ethics;* Darwin's *Descent of Man;* Graham's *Creed of Science,* and *The Social Problem;* Ward's *Dynamic Sociology;* Greg's *Enigmas of Life;* Savage's *Morals of Evolution;* Huxley's *Social Diseases and Worse Remedies,* and *Ethics and Evolution;* Crooker's *Problems in American Society;* Hobbes's *Leviathan;* Malthus *On Population;* Keene's *Art in Evolution and Ethics* (Dublin *Review,* July, 1893); Haeckel's *Evolution of Man.*

FROM NATURAL SELECTION TO CHRISTIAN SELECTION.

BY JOHN C. KIMBALL.

When Darwin's and Spencer's doctrine of Natural Selection and the Survival of the Fittest was first set forth—two names, as you know, for essentially the same thing—its novelty and philosophic aptness and the discussions it provoked as to its theological bearings, drew attention away for awhile from its deeper moral implications. But now that its truth has been in a measure established and leisure found for examining more carefully the prize so brilliantly won, the glow of delight excited by its scientific beauty has gradually given place to a feeling of deep depression over its awful destructiveness and its apparent evidence of an absolute disregard in nature of all ethical and humanitarian principles. It lets us into the world's workshop as no other discovery has ever done; but reveals its magnificent walls more stained with blood than was ever any wild beast's cave: gives us a hero to worship such as no other kingdom ever saw, but one with a Cyclopean greatness that even a Carlyle would hardly offer incense to; takes life on from its unorganized protoplasm to its Richmond of civilization, as no other principle ever has, but does it Grant-like through a wilderness where its uncounted armies are heaped up on battle-fields of uncounted slaughter. Even such an advocate of its truth as Mr. Huxley can see in it no ethical or philanthropic import. "The cosmical process," he says, "has no sort of relation to moral ends," is rather "the headquarters of the enemy of the ethical nature." And in its attitude especially to the poor and weak its contrast with Christian selection is so great as to give, with many persons, new strength to the argument that Christianity could not have come from nature and must, therefore, be a supernatural religion.

Before giving it up, however, as utterly hopeless for these higher things, it is well to remember that one of the most striking characteristics of evolution, as exhibited in other fields, is its habit of producing its richest fruits up above from what lower down are its most unpromising stems—unity from differentiations, the sky-seeking flower from the earth-seeking root, the rattlesnake's tail and Plato's skull from the same vertebrate skeleton, and Jephtha's sacrifice and that of Jesus from one religious sentiment. The real thing needed for getting out of the moral difficulties into which at first it so thickly plunges us is not less of it but more; the word of the Lord it speaks to the Moseses and peoples who in starting out of their old Egypt for a better land are confronted first of all with its Red Sea, "Go Forward." And obeying such a command, I want to take this doctrine of the Survival of the Fittest, so terrible in its beginnings, and try whether following it right through its blood-red seas will not lead us now, as of old, to a Canaan flowing with all the milk and honey of religion's and philanthropy's most loving care for the unfit poor and weak.

Starting with its operations in the physical world, it means there, beyond question, the preservation of only those animals and plants in each species and of only those species and genera in the organic world as a whole, which without any regard to their ethical character, excel in such qualities, whether of size or smallness, skill or stupidity, courage or cowardice, generosity or meanness, often the worst ones even physically, as best fit them for their environment; and the crushing out and crowding out, without any mercy or honor or justice, of all their unfit brethren. Nature provides herself with plenty of material to select from by having her creatures produce an immense number of offspring, more than are needed or able to grow up— is a mighty hunter who loads her gun not with a single ball, making everything depend on her accuracy in firing that—which was the old idea of Providence— but with a multitude of small shot, many more than she wants to hit the mark, so many that if they all did hit it, there would be no mark left, intending only two or three to take effect—which is the modern, scientific idea of Providence. Her shot are seeds, eggs, children, species, nations, possibly worlds. And it is the tests they are put to in reaching the mark of fitness which make her famous struggle for existence and constitute what is figuratively known as natural selection.

It is a struggle in which really the first round takes place before birth. Only the strongest and most attractive males are allowed to become parents. The whole vegetable world is an Oklahoma territory into which seeds carried on all manner of vehicles are vying with each other to get corner lots and promising sites on which to plant themselves. With eggs a favorite diet the world over, it is only those which get shielded and sheltered by the shrewdest devices that escape tongue and bill and boiler. Of the myriad germs which are called up to the gates of life in viviparous animals how few are chosen to pass through them into actual existence! The whole embryonic world is a battle of the pigmies against the giants, a battle in which the odds are so great it seems a wonder that any of the little folks survive even to the extent of getting born.

Victors in this preliminary contest, the outward elements,—heat, cold, moisture, dryness, earth, sky and the like, constituting the very home into which they are born, these fall upon them with their tests, giving a welcome and shelter only to those which can withstand their onslaughts, and giving to their weaker comrades sooner or later only a grave. The numbers perishing in this way even after they have reached maturity are enormous. Darwin estimated that the cold winter of 1854-5 destroyed in his own estate four-fifths of all its birds. With no extra wraps to put on and no warm fires to get before, every change of climate which affects man, affects the feeble among animals a vast deal more. Fifteen thousand hides were sent east awhile ago on a single freight train, taken from the cattle out on a Western prairie that had died in one of its blizzards. Who shall count the frail mosquitoes and the aged flies that have their song hushed forever with the first autumn frost? Even the little tough, grip-making bacteria, resisting all the devices of man to prove their unfitness to survive, seem to have been compelled by the past winter's thermometric hard times to join the ranks of the unemployed. And going back to the geologic ages, we find that not only individuals, but whole species and genera both of animals and plants have been killed off in a like manner by their ever changing elemental environments. So far as Nature is God it is all fiction that she tempers the wind to the shorn lamb. She tempers it to the lamb which is not shorn, provides wonderfully for the well and strong of her children, provides well for the weakest and smallest so long as they are well and fit; but she has nothing which corresponds with human care for any of them, large or small, when they are hurt and sick,—never folds the little suffering bird in her loving arms, never makes any warm gruel for the chilled-through rhinoceros and tiger, has no soothing syrup for the restless cubs of the distracted wolf and bear, provides no surgeon for the broken-limbed deer and bone-choked fishhawk, and builds no asylums for consumptive lilies, mashed mosquitoes, and aged sharks.

It is pitiable sometimes to see how little her creatures expect such a thing from any one as disinterested, individual kindness. Visiting an unused room in my Ipswich home awhile ago, I noticed that a solitary bird driven from its flock apparently because of its feebleness, had been in the habit of creeping for shelter at night between the window pane and the closed half of the window blind. Seeing how the bitter wind was whistling through the open slats and remembering my own sensitiveness to drafts even inside the room, I was moved altruistically to fit a stray shingle over the open space so as in some measure to break off the wind. The little creature with the evening shadows came as usual to the sill, peered at the ᵟ improvement on this side and that, with evident surprise, and then, concluding apparently that it was too good to be true otherwise than as a trap, flew away into the night shadows, preferring their certainty to any, even clerical, Greeks bearing gifts.

The care which nature does take of them is itself a sifting process, what are blessings to the strong being banes to the weak. Every farmer's boy who has tried to raise chickens, has noticed how the mother hen, as

soon as they are hatched, begins leading them for food
through the wet June grass and off on long journeys
such as only the strongest can stand, and that with all
her diligence and self-sacrifice in providing for their
wants as a whole, scratching the earth for their meat,
covering them with her wings from the cold, and de-
fending them from foes at the risk of her life, she herself kicks over the foolish ones which get in her way
as ruthlessly as she does the clods their food is among.
Nature is such a hen. The food of her creatures is
always in some kind of June grass. She leads them off
in migrations where even her wild geese grow weary,
and her grasshoppers their own burden. And the very
suns and showers which scratch the earth so wonderfully for their sustenance, kick over into its dust the
witless ones which get in their way.

Nor is any exception made in the case of her human
children. Three-fourths of them die of her blows before they are five years old. She wades with her boys
into green apples and snow water ponds, and with
the girls into slate pencils and corsets and colored
candy. "Don't strike him when he is down," is the
rule enforced in even the most brutal prize rings; but
in the struggle for existence it is when a man by reason of some weakness or misfortune gets down, that
she rains upon him her fiercest blows. Nero used to
select his victims for the wild beast conflicts of the
amphitheater by taking all from a file of prisoners marching before him who came between two bald heads.
Nature, fortunately for some of us, is not so particular
about the bald heads; but, if she sees a person having
anything the matter with his lungs, or liver, or stomach, or heart, he is handed over with equal indifference
to her fiercer, elemental wild beasts. The old Burial
Ground at Plymouth, into which one-half of the May-
flower's passengers were carried their first New England winter, is a witness to the rigor with which her
sifting process is applied in finding out of man's migrations, the fit founders of a new nation. And the
earth is everywhere full of graves warning her human
broods who wish to survive, that it will not do for
them, any more than for her brute ones, to get in the
way of those mighty legs of hers, the earthquake, tor-

nado, thunderbolt, with which she is scratching for them the earth's deeper soil.

Escaping the elements, however, does not end their struggle. Her scratching, vigorous as it is, supplies them with only a fraction of their needed food. The greater part of it they have to get out of each other's bodies; and that, too, by a system of "mutual murder" arising not through a fall from Eden, but instituted to begin with as a fundamental principle of the organic world, by which alone life can exist.

> " Then marked he
> How the lizard fed on ants, and snake on him,
> And kite on both; and how the fish hawk
> Robbed the fish tiger of that which it had seized,—
> The strike chasing the bulbul. which did chase
> The jeweled butterflies till everywhere
> Each slew a slayer and itself was slain."

Several years ago, before I knew as a Darwinian that the fish is my elder brother, and that piscicide is no more justifiable as sport than homicide, I caught a cod, in the stomach of which, on dressing it, I found a pollock, in the pollock a young lobster, and in the lobster several fine protozoa, all fresh. It was a good representation of the whole organic world. Its highest beings holding in them as food everything down to the protozoa, are a genuine "codfish aristocracy." And in the struggle to see which shall be the eater and which the eaten, the well fitted not only get the prize sought for, but get with it as side dishes all their weak and witless competitors. Some of you may remember one of Punch's famous cartoons some thirty years ago, entitled "Misplaced Sympathy," in which a pious mother who has taken her heedless Sunday School boy to a picture gallery to be impressed with a painting of Daniel and his companions in the lion's den, is horrified by his exclaiming, "O, mother, mother, see that poor little lion down there in the corner; he won't get any!" I have always had a great respect for that boy. He was evidently a true lover of animals, thought vastly more of them than of any old Bible prophets, and became afterwards, I doubt not, a genuine member of some Anti-Cruelty Society. But nature is no such boy.

What she is concerned for is not lest the poor little lions in a corner should not get a share of her Daniels, but that the fierce big ones should get them all. She has not only too much company at her table, as the Hebrew host explained the difficulty in his case, but too few chairs and too little food, so she ekes out its scantiness by setting the guests to eat each other up. It is indeed

" A rage to live, which makes all living strife."

Then while their struggle is bad enough even in the best of seasons, it is aggravated by drouths and famines ever and anon into scenes of unspeakable horror, as for instance during the dry seasons of Central Africa, when all the animals of the country for miles around, driven by their intolerable thirst, come to the few stagnant pools here and there into which what little water there is has sunk, the larger and fiercer ones taking possession of them entirely and lying in wait for the others,—huge hippopotami wallowing in their depths, long glittering snakes reaching out over their surface from the trees, ferocious beasts of prey watching with fiendish shrewdness their every avenue of approach, and on the outer rim rabbits, antelope, deer, scores of weak herbivorous creatures, looking with longing eyes and parched tongues for a chance to get one sip of their black, slimy, putrid, yet how precious drops, and having to choose at last between the ferocity of sharpened teeth and the fierceness of desert sands.

So with man: a large part of his struggle in all ages has been for the means of life, air, light, water, food, even ground; a large part of his social differentiations those between the big lions with a plenty of Daniels to eat and the poor little ones down in a corner with hardly a Daniel's bones to pick—on the one side Astors, Goulds, Rothschilds, Vanderbilts, millionaires ten fold over, on the other millions without a mill; on the one side corporations and coal mines, on the other families and freezing. And ever and anon there comes along some great financial drouth in which eyes as thirsty as those of the desert deer look on pools of wealth, some of them wallowed in by creatures as foul and circled around by teeth as sharp as those of the African

waste. Men complain sometimes of the Church, the
State, the whole social fabric as responsible for these
awful inequalities,—think, perhaps, with Rousseau,
that if society were only abolished and everything left
to nature, everything would be equality and peace.
Delusive thought! The trouble is that the original
source of these inequalities and hardships is not Church
or State or Society, but nature herself. Poverty, cold,
hunger are a part of her ways for sifting out the poor,
cold, hungry. And to go back to her primitive reign
would be only to go back from the ferocity of cities to
the ferocity of desert sands.

Then worse from the moral standpoint than even
their struggle with each other for food, is the tendency
of animals to war against those in their own ranks
which are simply different from themselves, and to do
so especially against such as are disabled and weak,
the object being apparently only to assert their superiority. If there is a lame or sick chicken in the
brood, or a stray one from another nest, everybody has
noticed how the strong and at-home ones will peck at
the unfortunates till they are either killed or driven
away. "When I was a girl," said a lady, "and now
and then got into little childish squabbles with brothers
and sisters, I used to have quoted to me Dr. Watts'
familiar hymn, 'Birds in their little nests agree,' to
my shame and confusion. But after trying in later
years to raise a brood of canaries and seeing how
readily they made each other a funeral,—especially after
leaving four of them in a cage one Sunday while I went
to church, and finding on my return three hanging by
their heads out of the wires, executed by their own
brother, I began to think that bird nature was not
after all so very much better than human nature." One
of the most pathetic sights the animal world affords
is its wounded members trying to get away from the
well ones, even of their own species, to suffer and die
alone—monkeys who carry off their disabled comrades
from the battlefield, anthropoids, therefore, in something more than bodily form, being almost the only
exception. It is notorious that no two roosters or
bulls can be put together in the same locality without
a fight simply to determine which of them is smartest;

and no matter what the affections lavished upon them beforehand, there is not a hen or a cow which does not turn from the beaten ones as promptly as ever a society belle did from a poverty-stricken beau.

Nor is it a kind of struggle which is left behind when nature comes to man. What are nine-tenths of the world's great historic wars but the fights of its larger barnyard roosters to see which is smartest? what the huge armaments all the governments of Europe are sporting to-day but the spurs to try sometime again the old question which of them shall crow the loudest? Big nations as regards little ones are all bullies, our own no exception, as witness its dealings with Mexico, Chili and the Indians. How ready all the different social classes are to set their feet on the necks of the ones that are in any way below them! What are the competitions of the business world but a crowding of the weak to the wall as mercilessly as any that ever ran with blood? If a man gets a new idea, or a woman a dress out of style, who does not know that they are pecked at and driven off by themselves exactly as a bird is with a new feather, or a beast with a strange form? And even in the church what are the martyrdoms, persecutions, anathemas and rivalries of sect against sect, things of which in all ages it has been so fearfully full, but the efforts of the strong to crush out what to them have been its unfit weak?

Such are the various ways by which natural selection is carried on.

Turning now to Christianity, Christianity not as an institution half realized, but as an ideal and aim, how transcendently different from all this is the new principle, new atmosphere, with which the inquirer is at once brought in contact! Its fundamental idea, as Mr. Huxley says, is beyond question exactly the opposite of that on which physical nature is carried on—is love, not hate, self-sacrifice rather than selfishness, and pre-eminently caring for the weak, poor, sick, unfit, instead of crushing them out. Its founder declares explicitly that he came to seek and save that which is lost; that to love thy neighbor as thyself, the wounded man everywhere being the neighbor, is one of the two greatest commandments; that whosoever shall give a cup of cold water only to one of these little ones shall in no wise lose his reward, and that he who is least among you shall be greatest. It was the poor, lame, halt, blind, that were invited especially to his gospel supper; the sick and sinful that his life was spent in healing, not crushing out. And in the same spirit his great apostle declares that not many wise, not many mighty, not many noble were called to be his followers, but the foolish things to confound the wise, and the weak things to confound the mighty, and the base and despised things and the things which are not to bring to naught the things which are. Then with and by itself, in spite of all its alliances with pride and power, and all its subserviences to wealth and fashion, it is historically along this line and among this material that for 1800 years it has won its victories and done its work. It has built hospitals for the sick, opened churches for the sinful, scattered bread to the hungry, demanded freedom for the slave, championed the cause of the poor, and lifted up to a new level the weak and despised—has had a kind word even for animals themselves, recognized their rights, denounced cruelty in their treatment, established societies, newspapers, laws for their protection. And in the final building up of its kingdom its principle is to work into it every weakest, wickedest, meanest, poorest, unfittest soul, rejected of nature and despised of men, there is on the face of the earth.

How now, with this immensity of difference, this apparent utter antagonism between them, are these two things made under evolution the gracious parts of one majestic whole, and in the larger cosmic process the natural outgrowths, one through the other, of a common love-planted root?

The first step of the answer is to recognize the adaptation of each agency to its own especial part of the work. Looked at as simply the means for attaining what is physically best, and for laying at least the foundation of what is morally best, there is no difficulty in seeing, even with Christian eyes, that the principle of the survival of the fittest through a struggle for existence is one of immense practical wisdom. If a man is going to build a first-class house, he naturally puts

his fittest timbers into its walls and his unfit ones into
its waste.   Every farmer aiming to improve his cattle
and corn, has to pick out the most perfect of them to
breed from and the others for his table and common
work.   And in all wars, wars for liberty and right as
well as for tyranny and wrong, the general who wants
to win victories enlists in his army not weak and
sickly men, saints though they be, but the soundest
and toughest ones the land affords, without asking for
their standing in the church.   So when nature wanted
to build a first-class universe, improve her original
protoplasmic cattle and corn, and win victories for her
great final cause, how could she do otherwise than act
on the same principle?   Suppose that in her physical
realm the opposite course had been adopted—that of
preserving the sick and weak, what would have been
the result?   We have tried it to some extent with human beings, have for centuries been keeping alive the
lame, halt, poor. blind,thousands of persons whom nature at a very early date would have put in graves; and
the answer is—society overrun with tramps, the dangerous and criminal classes more numerous than ever
before, and the unemployed poor mounting up into
the hundred thousands.   And if nature had been doing
the same through her million centuries, how many more
than now would have been, not her human, but her
sub-human darkest Londons—her animal tramps, her
Juke fishes, her sickly cornfields and her unemployed
vegetable poor!   Call it mercy to the weak and poor
themselves to have them saved, what is it to their de-
scendants, what lesser cruelty to have the myriad offspring of a crippled creature suffer and live than to
have the one creature itself suffer and die?   A well
managed saw-mill is run by its waste, run by using its
slabs and sawdust, valueless themselves for lumber, as
the engine fuel with which to turn out its straight and
beautiful sticks. Nature's life-mill, in its system of
having the weak eaten by the strong, is only acting on
the same economic principle—utilizing its slab-animals
in producing its straight and smooth organic timber.
And what are their struggles with each other, and with
the elements to get their food, but one of the factors
in developing their strength, the exercise as needful

for species and genera as it is for muscles and minds? Suppose that all of them had been so amply provided with sustenance that there would have been no need of their struggling for it, what would have been the result? The succulina has answered—a creature beginning life well organized, but which after fastening itself as a parasite on the hermit crab, where it gets safety and support without effort of its own, loses its higher organs and degenerates into a mere jelly-filled sack. Without this awful struggle for existence every animal would in time become a succulina. Starvation has been a part of the world's food. Our first stage in becoming angels is necessarily to fight like devils. Cruelty to the individual has been kindness to the race; selfishness in the realm of physics has done the same uplifting work as unselfishness in the realm of morals. And horrible as the struggle seems from our Christian standpoint, out of it—out of only the bare and cindered rock and the organless and senseless protoplasm to start with, has come our Christian standpoint itself—come the beautiful, organized, intelligent world which is here to-day, the fragrant flower, the singing bird, the stately tree, the marvels of the brute creation and the race of man.

But physical perfection and an animal world are not the whole of nature's aim. She has had other things in view, a moral and spiritual being and a social, civilized, religious world. How were these to be attained? Self-seeking, eating each other up, trampling down the weak and poor, agencies so potent in her physical realm, were powerless for this higher work. Others were needed, those which involve love, justice, mercy, self-denial, self-sacrifice. And it is at this point and for this purpose that the principle of preserving the weak and poor, the physically unfit, comes in, the stone rejected by the animal builders, which is made the cornerstone in the temple of soul.

It is a principle which operates as a factor of this higher evolution in two ways. The first is by bettering the poor, the sick, the weak themselves, making them the fit, lifting them up into health, strength, morals, self-support. While nature was working chiefly on bodies, and could use the unfit ones as food, it did not pay to spend effort on what was imperfect; but

when she came to soul, it would seem as if everything
had been brought along so far and had cost so much
that it began to be precious—paid better to be improved and kept on with than to be broken up and
used over. Then, too, having the one do for the other
brought in gratitude, allayed antagonism, helped bind
the two classes together, and so evolved the higher social world. It is a kind of work which the hard times
of this past winter have been the occasion of on a grand
scale. They have brought the fit and the unfit into
such kindly relations with each other as not all the
preaching in the world could have brought about, have
compelled, too, a study of their problem such as it
never before has had—have done it, also, just at a crisis when the two classes were getting dangerously wide
apart, a benefit which more than pays for their money
loss. There is nothing else which can do it so well—
love, not law, which is needed to put down social discontent, the loaf of bread thrown one way which stops
as no gallows can the dynamite bomb thrown the other,
capital's wives and daughters basket-armed and love-
sent who have been going every day this past winter
into quarters of our large cities unharmed, where capital's police, bludgeon-armed and law-sent, could have
gone only through blood. And though in the past
such service has aimed chiefly at relief, it is being
gradually found that it cannot stop there, but must go
on, helping the dependent to become the independent,
and the unfit to be in all respects the fit.

Better still, lifting up the unfit operates as nothing
else can to lift up the fit themselves into being more
fit. Bodies grow by self-seeking and by what they take
in; souls by self-sacrifice and by what they give out.
When a tiger meets a sick and wounded traveler, he
is made the stronger and larger by eating him up.
When a man meets a sick and wounded traveler, he is
made the stronger and larger by saving him from being eaten up. All qualities which are put forth to help
others—love, sympathy, kindness. justice—react and
help the helpers; all the downward things which called
them forth—weakness, want, sickness, sin—become the
world's uplifters. Who has not seen families where
the little crippled boy's feet have been the ones on

which the strong, rough brothers have reached heights
of gentleness and self-denial into which not all the
physical vigor of the world, nor all the teachings of its
Sunday Schools could have carried them alone? The
live babies of the household may unlock for their parents the joys of earth; but it is the dead ones who
open for them the heavenly gates. Look at the dark
side of a great city, at its white faces, bleared eyes,
brutal passions, bloody crimes, and you exclaim what
a drag on the world's progress is their preservation.
Look at the bright side of a large city, the white souls,
pitying eyes, angelic graces, heroic deeds, which the
struggle to save them has called forth, and you ask
what other agency in all this world is aiding progress
so much. Count the tramps who are walking the earth
as the result of 1800 years of Christian care for their
survival, and you question where is its wisdom. Count
the saints who walk the skies as the result of 1800
years giving them that care, and you have a hundred
fold the question's answer. 't is the unfit who are the
food of the fit in the new dispensation as truly as in
the old, only now it is by their saving instead of by
their being destroyed. The imperfections of nature
are the raw material out of which are made the per-
fections of spirit. None of the shot with which Providence loads his gun really fail. Those which miss the
animal hit the man—go astray of the mark at the distance of a generation, lodge in its very bull's eye fifty
million years off. Reformers stand aghast sometimes
at the immensity of our age's problems, those especially of poverty, vice and crime. They are the most
precious commodity there is on this earth to-day, are
worth more to it than all its mines and manufactures,
are a grander field for its science than any sun or star,
for they mean the mining and making of men, and are
a shop where the things made make, also, the makers.
What if the material is so large and so constantly increasing as to preclude all hope of its being all made
morally fit in this life? That only adds new need, new
meaning for a future life, suggests that its hell instead
of being the mere refuse heap of the universe, as so
many have thought, may be the quarry out of which
new stones are to be forever wrought for heaven's

walls, its sinners more material out of whose saving its saints are to be continually more saved. And surely it is no unworthy thought, is in keeping with what is the divinest element of Christianity here, is what we have a hint of in the story of Jesus going down the first thing after his crucifixion to preach to the spirits in prison, is better than any endless psalm singing, that through all the eternal years souls are to lift themselves up by lifting up their weaker brother souls.

There is one vital question more—how this tremendous change in nature's use of the unfit has been brought about, what the forces and processes by which the principle of their preservation has been evolved from the exactly opposite one of their destruction. It was no gift of a supernatural world, no message brought to earth on angel wings. It began back of all religion, back even of man, back among the animals themselves, began in that source, as worthy always of scientific as of filial reverence, mother love.* The first old hen,—speaking metonymically,—that scratched the earth for a brood of chickens, scratched it up along with the worms, kicked over with her clumsy legs some of the chickens, but kicked over with them the old self-centered universe, gave at any rate the blow which is to end with its toppling over. And it came directly out of the old system. The chickens being the offspring of her own body, care for them was at the start simply care for her own larger self, an outgrowth, therefore, of selfishness. But care is in its turn the natural nurse of love—what costs us something, that is, what is dear, becoming dear. The feebler, therefore, the offspring were, costing, as they would, more care, the dearer they became, the stronger the impulse to keep them alive; and this care which at first extended only to the brood as a whole, gradually differentiated to individuals, as everything under evolution does, till in humanity everywhere, savage and civilized, the weak, puny, physically unfit child, needing most the mother's anxiety and care, is the one to which naturally she gives the most,—the first cosmic step how easily, yet how wonderfully taken

*This lecture was written and delivered last spring—May, 1894—before the publication of Professor Drummond's "Ascent of Man;" but it is a great satisfaction to find him emphasizing the same truth.

across the apparently impassable chasm between care
for the fit and care for the unfit! The Christian house-
wife, when she cuts off part of the old hen's coarse,
tough legs in preparing it for dinner, does not think
of any connection between them and the subtle, sacred
ties which bind her to her sick babe upstairs, or the
Christian minister, as he eats the other part, a guest
at her table, of their relation to one of the sacredest,
grandest elements of his religious faith; yet not less
certainly they have all been evolved in nature's factory
out of one primal stock.

Another factor helping on the change is the underlying solidarity of all life in one grand organic whole,
one vast and all-embracing self. The reason why animals prey on each other is not hate but hunger; why
the strong prey on the weak, not tyranny but facility in
satisfying the hunger; and why the weak and odd ones
of the same family, even when not needed as food, are
pecked at and driven off, is because difference from the
common size and look has been so long associated with
what is to be feared as predatory that the sight of it
raises at once and blindly the instinct of self-defense.
Just as likeness makes liking, for we like at first only
what is like us, so unlikeness makes dislike. With
savage and nomadic tribes, also, surrounded with foes
and often pinched with want, care of the old and feeble is a source inevitably of tribal weakness; putting
them to death, therefore, a condition of tribe survival,
done with filial love and endured with patriotic submission. And thus it is that care for the original,
larger, homogeneous self is overcome and held in abeyance by the necessity of providing for the smaller, differentiated, individual self. But the original oneness is
not lost, any more than universal gravity was in the
evolution of suns and planets; and as the world pro-
gresses and tribes become larger and more settled, it
reasserts itself in a higher form. The differentiations of
labor under the industrial stage of society give the
weak kinds of work to do, and a tribal value that are
impossible in war. Patriotism and pride come in, covering with their ægis every citizen, however humble,
as a part of the common whole. And out of the original life-unity there emerges at last the mystic tie of

sympathy reaching out with its nerves finer than those of flesh to everything which lives, even the feeblest creature, and making all others a sharer of its joy and pain, and so interested for their own sakes to secure its welfare—the subtle scientific truth which underlies the great command, "Thou shalt love thy neighbor as thyself," not as much as but *as* thyself.

Allied with this solidarity and growing out of it, the union of the weak with each other for mutual help and protection has contributed not a little to the general principle of their being cared for and preserved. Animals which individually were unfit, very soon learned that collectively they might have the highest degree of fitness; and driven off by themselves, their misery not only developed a love of company, but with it a strength of company which in securing food, building shelter, and fighting foes was the very thing needed for their survival. Misery, however, could not thus receive aid from its brother misery without giving aid back, could not have company at all without its being mutual; so care for the individually weak and poor became a necessity for the existence of the flock and herd; and when the weak and poor differentiated out of themselves the strong and well-off, what began as a necessity was inherited as a principle. The golden rule is a law of nature. Eons before it was taught by Jesus, it was acted upon by animals and plants. It is the underlying principle to-day of all trade-unions and labor organizations,—the association and united protection of the weak individual laborer against the encroachments of capital; benevolence organized as business; good wages and good treatment insisted upon by all for the weakest and poorest because it is the only way in which they all can secure for themselves good wages and good treatment. The church preaches it and too often that is all; labor practices it. And thus how wonderfully and beautifully the trampling down of the weak has pressed out of them the wine of care for their survival, and the iron hammer of ferocity driven home and clinched the golden nail of fraternity.

The unfitness has had, also, in its contagiousness, a powerful goad driving on the fit to its relief. It has been learned after many terrible lessons that no man can be sick or ignorant or vicious to himself alone; and that if we do not want him to make us all sick, ignorant and vicious, we must all go to work and make him well, educated and virtuous. ·Why have all our large cities been so anxious this past winter to vaccinate the poor at the public expense? Because the disease of which it is thought to be the preventive, is so "catching." That word catching grows in very humble soil, but it has on its branches a vast amount of very precious fruit—one-half at least of all our asylums, poor laws, schools and churches. What we don't do because we love our neighbor as a part of ourself, we have to do because we fear him as a part of ourself. I knew of a woman down in Arkansas, the daughter of a cowboy, and inheriting her father's pluck and pistols, whose lazy, domineering husband tried to impose on her all the work. One day when the baby was sick and she needed some water for its washing, matters came to a crisis. Setting down the bucket on the doorway and drawing her revolver, she said, "If you don't start with it for that water before I count three, I'll shoot." He laughed in her face. "One." He laughed again. Bang! And he rolled over in the dust never more to get up. "Two, three," she counted, as leisurely wiping the weapon with her apron, she went back to nurse the baby. That is what nature does with her husbands when they refuse to bring to her sick babies the water of life. It is One as a warning; then Bang; and not till after they have rolled over, the Two and Three. We call her severe when she deals with the babies herself in her animal realm; but it does not begin to equal her severity to those in her moral realm who won't deal with them at all. Plagues and black deaths have been some of her "bangs." The French revolution was another. We shall have one in our own land, if we neglect things too long. And counting the husbands sneering at reform who as a consequence have bitten the dust, what wonder that the rest of us are gradually learning to seize its bucket with her first word Go, and no matter how unfit the babies are, faithfully fill it up to the brim!

Another potent factor in the evolution of this higher

principle has been trade. The fearful competitions of the business world driving the weak and poor to the wall, so opposite apparently to any survival of them, are only one of its aspects. What is it the real interest of all great trading houses to bring about? Not the poverty of the world. With everybody else poor, who is to buy their goods? No; it is the real interest of all trade, whether of one person or of one people, that all other persons and all other peoples should have something to trade on; and it is this really which trade tends to give them. Whatever may be accomplished by rascality, there is honestly no such .principle in this universe as the rich growing richer, and the poor poorer at the same time. It is like electricity. The rubbing which develops it at one pole has to develop it at the other also. It was business which abolished slavery at the North; the best business operation that even white men ever had done for them, its abolition at the South; business that in every direction has given the weak and poor a thousand luxuries that without it would have been only their vain wish. I congratulated a large manufacturer once on the interest he took in bettering the condition of his workmen. "Oh," he said, "that isn't goodness, its only goods; there's no machinery it pays so well to improve as the human machinery." The first vessels sent by Christianity to heathen shores carried rum and missionaries. It was a mistake only in the kind of merchandise. The more gospel, the more goods. And even as a business transaction the best investment civilization could make of its money would be the lifting up the whole savage world into moral and religious fitness.

Finally, on these lower things as a basis, religion itself comes in—love, altruism, conscience, the sense of right, all the highest and best sentiments of our human nature, to complete the work. We care at last for the unfit because we like to. Weakness appeals to our gallantry. We shrink with instinctive horror from stamping out any creature simply because it is feeble and sick—"would not needlessly set foot upon a worm." The Vision of Sir Launfal becomes our favored poetry. The trumpet calls of reform thrill our blood as the bugle's blast did our sires. A mighty nation finds its

inspiration for four years of war in the freeing of a
slave. And when the world's greatest and best man,
a Jesus, sacrifices his life to save its meanest and worst
—a thing so utterly at variance with nature's old economy, eighteen hundred years unite in honoring it as
humanity's crowning deed.

It is thus that I find a passage from nature's Egypt of
destroying the unfit, right through its awful wilderness
and Red Sea on to religion's promised land of their
preservation and lifting up. The old way of writing
a novel, as you know, was to get its characters and
incidents all involved in a hopeless snarl, the lovers
parted, the hero knocked senseless, the heroine in the
villain's clutches, wickedness and wealth everywhere
triumphant, modesty and merit everywhere trampled
down; and then to unravel the snarl, have the hero
saved, the villain shot, the maiden rescued, lots of
other killing done, and somewhere about the fortieth
chapter the mystery all cleared up, the lovers happily
married, poetic justice done to everybody, and in the
distance several fine children. Evolution is a novel
more full of intricate snarls, dramatic surprises and
thrilling incidents than any ever written by a Scott or
a Sue, one also with killing enough to satisfy the most
bloodthirsty schoolboy appetite, but which unravels at
last all entanglements, overcomes all brutal villains,
brings heroic virtue up out of all defeats, and does
everybody and everything full poetic justice. It is to
be noticed, also, that it is all accomplished by strictly
natural laws, without any bringing in, or need of bringing in, any *Deus ex machina* to untie the cords in
which the Deity within had become wound up. Instead
of its being true, as Mr. Huxley says, that the cosmic
process is the enemy of the ethical nature and with no
sort of relation to moral ends, it is directly and inevitably out of the cosmic process and by the simple
continuance of it that the ethical nature and the moral
ends have been evolved. "The ruthless self-assertion,"
"the trampling down of all competitors," and the survival of only the physically fittest, so conspicuous and
so revolting at the beginning of the work, were engaged
after all in laying, as nothing else could, the founda-

tions of the structure on which alone its ethical part could be raised; and if there is anything which argues the height of the pinnacle in the coming ethical sky as a part of the original design, it is the depth and breadth of its base in the physical earth. It is a process, to be sure, which is yet very far·from being completed. Nature never makes her changes all at once, never lets go the old till her creatures have got a good grip on the new. We are now in the transition stage between the two—indeed have been so ever since civilization began—are partly under the old law of the survival of the fittest, and in part under the new law of saving the unfittest; and it is this fact which explains not a few of the difficult problems of our time—our tramps, our Juke families, our cut-throat business competitions, our military conflicts, our evils of democracy and our aristocratic churches—explains the conflict between the cosmic and Christian with which Mr. Huxley and others are so deeply impressed—is what makes philanthropy and reform, a reaching for the ideal and yet never a cutting loose wholly from the old real, one of the most difficult of all arts. But it is a stage of the work which is full of hope. The shuttle in nature's mighty loom, the same as in that of man, is shot back and forth two opposite ways, but it carries only one thread and weaves only one piece. Egoism at the animal end does the same work as altruism at the spiritual end, serves the race by serving self; altruism at the spiritual end the same work as egoism in the animal, serves self by serving the race. And as out of the two there has come already a being who has not only the inner desire to lift out of their death stream his unfit brothers, but, what is equally important, the bodily strength and the solid shore of flesh to stand upon which make it possible, so out of them both there shall come at last a world in which the unfit, never, perhaps, so long as life is progress, ceasing to come, shall everywhere be developed into the fit, a realization of Tennyson's splendid trust—

"That not a worm is cloven in vain;
   That not a moth with vain desire
   Is shriveled in a fruitless fire,
Or but subserves another's gain;

That nothing walks with aimless feet;
That not one life shall be destroyed,
Or cast as rubbish to the void,
When God hath made the pile complete."

ABSTRACT OF THE DISCUSSION.

MR. A. EMERSON PALMER:—

The evolution of philanthropy has been so exhaustively treated in Mr. Kimball's admirable paper that it seems almost presumptuous in any one to add even a word—much less to criticise or discuss it. A few words, however, may not be out of place in reference to one phase of the subject which has long appealed to me with especial force. I refer to the development of Sympathy, which has been called by some one the finest flower of civilization. It is certainly one of the noblest fruits which evolution can display as the outcome of its long and laborious processes. Sympathy is one of the things that differentiate man most broadly from all other animals. In the animal world, so called, it is scarcely to be found at all. There the rule is that the wounded animal shall be left to perish, or shall be devoured by his robust companions. The chief exceptions to the rule are in the cases of mothers caring for their injured young, but here it is the maternal instinct—not true sympathy—which comes into play.

Doubtless the first crude beginnings of the altruistic feelings of man are to be traced in the affection of a bird or animal for its offspring. The development of this tendency has gone forward more or less steadily until the truly immense results we see around us have been achieved.

But every student of human nature will promptly admit that the development of the sympathetic side of man has not gone hand in hand with the development of his intelligence generally. The reason for this is not far to seek. Among primitive men warfare was universal. The first notion of regard for others was concerned only with the members of one's own family. All other men were to be preyed upon, robbed, and murdered. The sense of family relationship slowly broadened until the tribe and the clan grew up, and from these have come nations as we know them. So general has been the desire to fight that the world has not yet outgrown it, and we have to-day the spectacle in Europe of nations staggering under the heavy burdens they are forced to carry in order to maintain their huge standing armies. We are still in the military-camp and powder-cart stage of civilization—to a very large extent at least. It would seem as if these nations had taken as their motto the saying of Jesus, "I came not to send peace but a sword."

Of course I do not undertake to deny that a good deal of the progress which the human race has achieved has been the result of war; but I am convinced in every fiber of my being that the time has come when wars and rumors of wars should cease from the face of the earth. Every right-thinking person must look hopefully for the time when this happy condition shall be brought about. And I am among those who hope that the day when the nations shall not learn war any more is to be hastened by the perfection of the implements of war. So smokeless powders, and Krupp guns, and heavily armored battle-ships, and the invention and use of more and more powerful explosives, are not without a hopeful and encouraging side.

It is because the warlike spirit has prevailed so long and been so predominant a factor in the history of the race, it is because the advancement of man in civilization has been so largely brought about by fighting, that the development of sympathy has been slow. And yet, as I have said, the results as we see them to-day are indeed immense. We see the results of applied sympathy in our hospitals, in our asylums for the insane and other feeble folk, in our charitable institutions generally, in some of our prisons and reformatories. But if we say with the poet,

"Look backward, how much has been won!"—

we are constrained to go on with redoubled emphasis to the next line,—

"Look round, how much is yet to win!"

We have only made a beginning as yet. But it is a beginning big with promise.

If we take a broad survey, glancing over the history of the last three or four thousand years—going back, indeed, as far as history permits—we can see vast progress in the elimination of strife. But man is slow in casting off what Mr. Fiske so well describes as the brute inheritance—the only "original sin" which science recognizes. "By the time warfare has not merely ceased from the earth," says Mr. Fiske, "but has come to be the dimly remembered phantom of a remote past, the development of the sympathetic side of human nature will doubtless become prodigious."

Even so may it be! But it will not be enough to eliminate merely actual fighting. The same spirit manifests itself in the fierce competitions which are going on in trade and business and the whole industrial world, where the doctrine seems to be, Every man for himself, and the devil take him who is not sharp enough or shrewd enough or unscrupulous enough to keep up with his fellows. Here is a survival from the primitive ages of brutal warfare, and most emphatically *not* a survival of the fittest. When the prodigious development of the sympathetic side of human nature has come, surely there will be no room for the spirit of bitter competition in which at times all sense of human brotherhood appears to be lost sight of.

But there is a more personal sense in which the idea of sympathy appeals to us. What is sympathy but the power of putting ourselves in others' places? In connection with this phase of the subject Mr. Fiske speaks of the power of imagination, or ideal representation, which underlies the whole of science and art, and "is also closely connected with the development of the sympathetic feelings. The better we can imagine objects and relations not present to sense," he says, "the more readily we can sympathize with other people. Half the cruelty in the world is the direct result of stupid incapacity to put one's self in the other man's place. So closely inter-related are our intellectual and moral natures that the development of sympathy is very considerably determined by increasing width and variety of experience. From the simplest form of sympathy, such as the painful thrill felt on seeing some one in a dangerous position, up to the elaborate complication of altruistic feelings involved in the notion of abstract justice, the development is very largely a development of the representative faculty. ' The very same causes, therefore, deeply grounded in the nature of industrial civilization, which have developed science and art, have also had a distinct tendency to encourage the growth of the sympathetic emotions."

Let me add here that this power of putting ourselves in others' places is a power which we ought all to strive diligently to cultivate. It is one of the highest developments of altruism—a word, by the way, which we owe to Comte, so recently did it become needful to have a term to denote the benevolent instincts and emotions of man. How vastly greater would be our charity for the faults, the blunders, the follies and frailties of other people, were we able to see things with their eyes, to transfer ourselves to their environment, to put ourselves in their place! Burns longed for the power to see ourselves as others see us. But such a power would have far less practical value to us than the imaginative power to see others as they see themselves.

The old Mosaic law laid down the doctrine, Love thy neighbor as thyself, and it was repeated by Jesus with warmest approval, being declared by him to be one of the two commandments on which hang all the law and the prophets. But have we here the highest development of the altruistic feelings? Nay. For that let us turn to the great poet of human nature who sounded all its depths and heights. We shall find it in the injunction of Wolsey to Cromwell,—"Love thyself last."

SANITATION

BY

JAMES AVERY SKILTON

COLLATERAL READINGS SUGGESTED.

Gardiner's *Longevity;* Gerhard's *Architecture and Sanitation;* Shoemaker's *Heredity, Health and Personal Beauty;* White's "From Fetich to Hygiene" (Popular Science Monthly, 1891, pp 493, 600), and "Miracles and Medicine," (Ibid., pp. 1, 145) in *Chapters in the Warfare of Science;* Corfield's *Health;* Teale's *Dangers to Health;* Johnston's *The Chemistry of Common Life;* Richardson's *A Ministry of Health,* and *Diseases of Modern Life;* Oswald's *Physical Education;* Tyndall's *Essays on Floating Matter in the Air;* Smith's *Health;* Martin's *The Human Body.*

SANITATION.

BY JAMES A. SKILTON.

Our topic has two distinct, clearly definable and separable aspects, one practical and suited to the present imperfect and faulty stage of human and societary development, and the other suited to all normally progressive stages of development to whatever attainable, theoretical, or evolutionary extent. The promises and prospects of the first are the decay and ruin of men and society; those of the other are their progress and prosperity continued from age to age.

Not only in the minds of individuals, however, but also in the public mind generally, and even in the dictionaries, there seems to be confusion and misunderstanding as to the true meaning of the words sanitation and sanatory. The same is true as to the scope, relations and applications of the topics they are used to characterize and define.

To the large majority, both of these words and their subjects are believed to have to do with cure, remedy and disinfection after infection, rather than with prevention. This implies that in our world unsanitary conditions are to be accepted as absolute, normal, inevitable and eternal or æonic. Consequently, we have at the outset the disadvantage of dealing with a state of mind that erroneously takes it for granted that the race is afflicted with conditions that it must necessarily and always have with it, to the end of time and things.

This raises the preliminary question whether the human mind is not the first and most important object of disinfection and sanitation.

Pity it is that this is true, notwithstanding it has been the function of the gospels of the ages, and is the essential function of the evolution gospel of the present age, to banish that error from the human mind. Still it not only lingers, but remains dominant, everywhere blocking the way of all progress. Nevertheless, unsanitary conditions represent only human blunders and ignorance, and are therefore neither normal, inevitable, or æonic. But still they are the symptoms of widespread organic disease in the social body in which they exist, that is certain to be fatal in time, unless the unsanitary conditions are removed by the restoration of organic health through obedience to cosmic law.

The root idea of both these words, relatively considered, refers to soundness, health, sanity, saneness, wholeness, and covers soundness, wholeness or health of body, mind, function, and all the action of organic life. The confusions of understanding seem to have arisen in part from the fact that the word sanatory is derived from the verb meaning to heal or to make sound, to cure; while the word sanitary is derived from the adjective *sanus*, meaning sound, by the way of the noun *sanitas*, meaning health, soundness, wholeness.

But a larger and more persistent cause—one that has had an active part in producing these confusions—is to be found in that theological poison, born of ignorance, limitation and despair, which has been handed down to and still powerfully infects and affects the modern human mind, seemingly almost beyond any power of disinfection, that nature is everywhere vile, destructive, and to be either conquered and suppressed, or safely ignored as well as despised and discouraged.

Thus the very words come to us with effects as if they still reeked with the slime of the sewers and cesspools they seem to be relegated to and to make use of as their fit places of abode.

Nevertheless, sanitation relates, among other things, to the atmosphere, earth, water, food, clothing, shelter, structural variation, work, gravitation, solar energy, and even human labor; each and all of which have to do with and are affected by sanitary principles and practice, not only, but also have an automatic and characteristic system and capacity of sanitation constantly working in and with them as a part of their very natures and methods of action, independently and without human intervention, and, indeed, in spite of the unwise and negligent human interference and in-

difference which in fact produce the unsanitary conditions to be complained of.

Doubtless, that branch of the subject which deals
with sewage, all manner of feculence, plumbing, and
the like, may be interesting and at any rate necessary
as a subject for immediate consideration and action, at
proper times and places. But it is rather to the larger
meanings of the word that consideration should be here
given, in this forum of evolution, since it does not
accept unsanitary conditions as inevitable and permanent and proclaims the law and philosophy of their
permanent removal or gradual and continuous improvement.

It is here our peculiar purpose and function to apply
evolutionary principles in teaching Life—meaning
thereby sound and healthy living—in all their proper
fields, relations and domains of application, including society, as being an organism, and therefore subject to the laws of life.

It has been said heretofore that where in the earlier
beginnings promise and potency of life were discerni-
ble in matter, there might be found the promise and
potency of a system of ethics or of conduct of life.
So, from the very beginnings of life, and constantly
therewith from the earliest stages, are to be found evidences of adequate sanity and sanitation in the conduct of life.* In fact, a principal factor, instrument or
means in the process of natural selection is to be found
in natural sanitation and its laws, as a part of and in
the whole of physics back to its beginnings, even in
gravitation, the effect of which sooner or later is to
destroy all life that will not conform to the laws of
health, considered from the preventive point of view,
and to strengthen, enlarge and develop that which does
conform thereto.

It is not, of course, to be understood that the curative function is not one of the expedients of nature.
But the curative function of nature never is performed
in such a way as to cultivate, repeat and perpetuate the
thing sought to be cured and the process of curing. This
last is the method of ordinary sanitation and therefore has in it an element of criminality, in view of the
perpetuated reign of sickness and death that follows.

*The Land Problem. Man and the State, B. E. A.

Concealment and obliteration, or complete restoration,
are parts of the plan or method of nature's curative
processes.

A study of the life and history of all plants distinctly
shows sanitary action and function co-ordinated everywhere in their lives, and in their self-conduct,
infinite almost as those lives are in variety
of conditions relating to air, temperature, seasons,
moisture, elevation, and other matters of environment, and also in possibilities as already disclosed to our feeble vision. Trees rupture and throw
off the outer bark when it becomes useless and an
incumbrance, or retain it when needed; they protect
their buds from the injurious effects of severe cold
and too much moisture; they protect themselves from
drought by sending their rootlets by the way of cracks
made in the earth by drought, deeper down into
the earth where water may be found; taking advantage of the effect of the wind upon their branches,
they rock to and fro and loosen up the earth, thereby
enabling their roots to penetrate still further and
further, and securing increased stability, and protection from overthrow by severe winds. They send out
lateral and tap roots as required by conditions of soil,
strata and water below the surface, furnishing models
for lighthouses and other structures subject to stress
of all kinds. They respire, that is, take in and
throw out air, voiding and disposing of excreta
in such ways as not to poison themselves. Ever-
green trees protect themselves from climatic
severities by appropriate variations in form,
structure, condition and location of branches
and leaves; they deposit their leaves over the
ground beneath them, thereby protecting their
roots as with a mat in winter as well as fertilizing the
earth, aiding the production of humus, which performs the office of nitrification, and preparing their
food for other seasons to come, with sanitary
economy and avoidance of waste. Shading the
ground thereby and keeping it cool, they make of
the earth about them a condenser and an absorber
of moisture and injurious gases from the atmosphere,
to be later appropriated by their roots and digested

as tree food. They in fact purify the air, supply
it with oxygen, make it fit for respiration by higher
orders of animal life and set a fine example of sanitation
to men and boards of health. In fact, plants and trees
seem not only to adopt preliminary sanitary expedients,
but to almost if not quite make inventions for self-pro-
tection and development that not even a Patent Office
Examiner could reject, either for want of invention or
because they would work injury to things, men or society. Deciduous trees wisely give up the unequal
contest, shed their leaves, retire and store their sap
or circulatory fluid below the earth's surface, and
make ready to meet winter cold and avoid its disastrous effects, relying confidently upon the promise of
a returning spring.

Animals intelligently and persistently search out infinite preventive sanitary ways of living and of conducting themselves under myriad variations of conditions, habitat and other surroundings; and when left
alone by man, they not only find out ways that are
conducive to longevity and enjoyment of life, but those
that are conducive to fullness of development and to the
highest possibilities in the direction of beauty and
grace, as well as of efficiency and preservation. Cata-
clysmic destruction may overtake plant and animal life,
but in few instances, if ever, do they poison themselves to death, or create diseases and pestilences by
their own unwise conduct of their lives. Such follies
they seem to leave to man.

Both plants and animals perform with perfect fidelity their correlated parts and functions with man and
society, from lowest to highest stages of development.
With such fidelity is this done, that where they seem
to fail and go wrong the implication immediately
arises in positive force that somehow, somewhere, man
is himself the culprit, and not these his truest friends.

Attempts have been made to give a definitive description of man, as by calling him a two-legged animal without feathers, and in various other ways, some
satirical, some serious; but perhaps as accurate a description as any would be to define man as the one
and only unsanitary living thing, the one who alone
destroys himself by filth of his own creation, serenely and

stupidly poisoning the water he drinks, the air he breathes, the food he eats, the clothing he wears, the houses, cities and country in which he dwells, and, in fact, every material element that goes to make up his substance, life and surroundings, each with its own special poison. That work being thoroughly done, his home and surroundings having been made unsanitary and uninhabitable, he straightway sets himself to puzzling over problems of divine malignance, particularly when his children, and other dear ones, die of disease he has himself promoted; frequently ending with the unctuous but sad worship of a deformed deity, the creation of his own ignorance and folly so great as to show that, unlike the ox and the ass, he knoweth neither his master nor his master's crib. Such is his perverse wrongheadedness, that when he sets himself to seek and produce prosperity and wealth he goes about and pursues his plans for it in such a way as inevitably to produce poverty and all that poverty implies, either for himself or for his children.

However much of a pathetic or criminal burlesque artificial and curative sanitation that promotes and perpetuates unsanitary conditions may be, it is instructive, consoling and restful to watch in all directions the operation of preventive natural sanitation. By the aid of solar energy, the water of the swamp and the cesspool is vaporized, purified, transported, distributed and eventually deposited where it will do the most good on the face of the earth. Being deposited, it finds out myriad plants and their rootlets, following down the leaves, the branches, the stems, the trunks, into the earth, where it furnishes the plant with its medium of circulation and life development; and in co-operation with soils of different characters produced by geologic action, it percolates and purifies, and even when thrown upon the absorbent earth in a filthy condition, it facilitates absorption of impurities by the earth and thereby becomes purified and again fit for use, while enriching the soil with supplies of plant food, and conserving the elements of life used again and again and then still handed down through the cycles of time by and through myriad generations of lower forms of life, for eventual repeated use by those of ever higher and higher forms. In so doing the very humblest forms of life have their parts to perform in the preservation of empires, races and civilizations; and they do perform them with absolute fidelity.

The atmosphere also has its own sanitary methods of action, under the influence of solar energy and otherwise. There is an action of the outer air something like respiration. The very earth itself breathes, teems and lives. Not only does the action of the sun expand the air and give it motion around the earth as it revolves, but under the same influence, when the earth cools at night it draws in air to very considerable depths and throws it out when warmed by the sun, with respiratory effects; and it probably does so even where the surface is composed of stratified rock, since rocks are porous and there is a pressure of atmosphere thereon of something like fifteen pounds to the square inch.

The word *pneuma*, meaning air, breath, also signifies the spirit, the principle of life, and it is a means of life to the earth as well as to man, animals and plants.

When the functions of life cease, alike among animals and among plants, air, water, heat and the soil unite in a natural system of disinfection by oxidation, nitrification, absorption and in other ways, immediately and without the aid of any alleged sanitary functionary or board of health whatever.

If nature, or cosmic law and process, were allowed to have their way and our obedient co-operation, sanitation would be perfect, disease and premature death would disappear, along with all dire misery in all forms of life, human, animal and plant, and also with all war and vice.

But the moment we approach and inspect human life and its operations we detect a marked change of attitude and action, and a distinct failure of comprehension, fidelity and performance permeating them throughout.

From the laying of the keel of a ship to its final stranding on some lone foreign shore or its dismantlement on some mud flat in distant years, not a single moment of watchful care, seeking to keep the water of its element out of the ship, can be safely missed, without sending the ship to the bottom; and even then every ship leaks more or less.

But when it comes to houses, schoolhouses, churches, public places of assemblage of all kinds, located in the temperate zones, with marvelous success our architects erect structures, submerged in air pressing all surfaces with an energy of fifteen pounds to the square inch, provided with carefully contrived systems of alleged ventilation, into which it seems practically impossible to get the fresh air in which they are immersed to penetrate, and out of which it seems equally impossible to drive the foul air, however foul it may become. Buildings that would themselves breathe if they were only permitted, are practically asphyxiated, and poisoned, together with the people who occupy them. Facts heretofore presented from this platform show that people who live and work in the finest buildings in our cities are sometimes more than deci-mated in a single year without attracting public attention or private remark, and without correction when remedy is shown to be practicable and at hand, one such case being known to have occurred in an elegant building built, owned and administered by a leading life insurance company. Sewer pipes are, however, abundantly provided so as to introduce foul air to our sleeping and living rooms, with diphtheritic and other poisons from the top to the bottom of the list; and this also without effective protest or remedy.

In those modern towers of Babel, the ten to twenty-four or more story office buildings, by which men are now striving to climb into the financial heavens, all attempts to supply fresh air to occupants are absolutely abandoned. In churches, even, where men mouth and mumble the saying that cleanliness is akin to godliness, worshipers are universally and unnecessarily compelled to breathe and rebreathe air containing atmospheric excreta of the most offensive kinds. And the moment some brother member more intelligent or more sensitive than the rest rises and meekly asks for air more decent and less stercoraceous, then the powers of darkness in the shape of vested interest and vested ignorance rise up and veto all attempts to find remedy and fresh air.

And so it goes everywhere in every department of life, the poisoning of men being only an accompaniment of a gigantic system of waste of highly organized matter, the product of ages of energetic sanitary and preparatory effort on the part of the lower forms of life, through which the capacity of the earth to further support human life on sound sanitary and evolutionary lines is diminished or destroyed beyond recovery by any human power that can be practically applied.

In fact, our entire modern civilization seems at this moment to be in the greatest need not so much of reform as of universal treatment by a process of evolutionary disinfecting sanitation in the nature of avoidance or prevention. And any system of sanitation which proceeds on the mere theory of cure has in it the elements of a crime, since it implies acceptance, continuance and recurrence of conditions that should be prevented *ab initio*. But this is the system now everywhere in vogue.

In fact, the whole of modern civilization seems to be permeated and dominated by some mysterious influence deceiving and deforming the human intellect almost beyond rectification or sanitation.

It is evident that in most if not all the essentials of life our ancestors in the arboreal or animal stage enjoyed and themselves secured conditions as to sanitation superior to our own of to-day. They did not willfully poison their air and water as we do. They had one great advantage of us; being nomadic and untrammeled with too much property, they could move on, and leave necessary sanitation of their habitations to nature's more perfect methods. Fresh air our later ancestors always had until window glass was invented. Then foul air and trouble began to afflict the race.

It is not now simply that things are seen as through a glass darkly, or men as trees walking, but men as trees walking on their heads, with their feet in the air, and everything else reversed as though we were all afflicted with a form of intellectual strabismus, and received all rays of knowledge so crossed and confused as to make what is absolutely false seem to be the absolutely true and only fact and knowledge.

Just here lies the beginning of the work of honest evolutionary Sanitation—its field of exploitation the human mind, its means an evolutionary education and an evolutionary religion that will restore the human mind to its true and normal relations to the cosmos and to all the cosmic energies and processes, their comprehension and application in the work of individual and societary progress and development.

Take, for instance, our dominant medical system. Under the influence of environing conditions we, even the wisest of us, wait until the invading disease is in possession before we summon the physician—just as we summon the fire brigade after the house is on fire —and we pay our doctors for service in proportion to the duration of our sickness, amusing ourselves with idiotic hilarity at the expense of the antipodean who gauges the pay of his doctor according to the duration of health only, and puts upon him the penalty for his sickness. Our lawyers we employ and reward for the most part according to a similar method, paying in fact a premium in large fees to the court lawyer for burdens we should seek in advance to avoid and might avoid by seeking ourselves to deal justly with all, or employing less pretentious and less expensive office counsel in the first instance in order to prevent litigation. And it may be doubted if there is a single, crying, active reform, political, social, economic, religious or other, that is not thought about, planned and worked for in a similar manner; that is, in a way exactly the reverse of the normal and logical; the characteristic purpose and limitation of all being, not prevention *ab initio*, but cure *ad æternitatem,* or in eternal succession.

The other liberal professions, commerce, politics, education, governmental administrations, societary reforms, religion, business, mechanics, even, and the greater of all the activities proceed upon the same false and unsanitary plan.

It is not so much the fault of medical men as of the public that empirical methods have so long held the field against scientific methods. But the reproach that there is no such thing as medical science is being rapidly removed by the application of evolutionary principles in the development of prevention and its substitution for curative medication. The opportunity for applying the same principles in the domain of law and in other professions and branches of sociological activity are at least in sight.

It becomes now a question of choice at what point in the chain or series of life-activity the attack on the subject should be made. At almost any and every point of approach unsanitary conditions and results can be observed, but, for the benefit of the unskilled or unobservant, there is a choice to be made. In the Old Testament account, the entrance of evil into the world is associated with food and its method of growth and appropriation. And even at that time thorns and thistles were accepted as evidence that evil was common to men and plants, as well as that man was responsible for both. Not much later the first murder is said to have occurred in a quarrel over the products of the earth and labor, being in fact the original "labor trouble." And it is to be noted that the murderer, the perpetrator of the first attack upon human life, was the first man to build a city, the field of so much unsanitary sacrifice of human life since that day. In the New Testament account, food and raiment are pivotal matters of consideration. And in the Lord's Prayer the express and emphatic limitation of request for "daily food," to be bestowed for "this day" only, exhibits a sublime confidence in the adequacy of the supply according to nature's laws, as an integral and essential element in the religious system promulgated by Jesus.

In the Malthusian theory, which has had much to do in preparing the way for an evolutionary sociology, food is a prime factor. The food producing function of the earth correlating with its function of producing other supplies needed for the development and employments of human life, may be considered as the point where the whole action and interaction may best be observed, studied and criticised. In fact the Theory of Population, and, perhaps more directly and simply speaking, a true Theory of Food are the best tests of the goodness, wisdom and power, in human terms, of the organizing energy of the universe.

While speaking from this platform on prior occasions and particularly when dealing with the Land and Race questions in our Man and the State book and

series, I have prepared the way or laid the foundation
for that with which I am to here deal and for the
present method, at least in part.

In speaking of land impoverishment and barbarization as the cause of the barbarization of the people
who bestow their labor upon such land, and of the
entire society of which they may form a part, only a
portion of the results are more than indicated. The
controlling factor, in sociological effects, is the continuing diminishment of the return for the labor
bestowed thereon and particularly of the resulting
food supply. From the Sermon on the Mount down
through all the thinking of men, including the thought
of Malthus, to the last writer on economics, the
food supply has had to do with questions of misery
and moral restraint not only, but with æonic life
and survival; and food supply depends upon the
method—sanitary or unsanitary—pursued in treating
land. But we have not certainly always realized that
it also has, and has had, to do with the causes at work
in producing vice, crime, disease and premature death
or decay of individual men, as of nations, and in
hindering and preventing all proper societary growth
and control over human life and destiny, as well,
through resulting conditions of the unsanitary order.
In fact, wasting fields imply and correlate unsanitary
conditions in the city and also the vice, crime and
unmoral conduct to be found there; since, according
to cosmic law, the fields furnish the only means of
maintaining true sanitation, and true cosmic life in
both city and country, with weal and wealth at both
ends of the line.*

It is possible to spend much time and show much
interest in contemplating the houses tumbling into
ruin among the old worn out fields, as well as the return again of wild animals, including serpents, and of
the trees and vegetation of a more coarse and

*The scientific details and supporting evidence held in mind and
implied during the preparation of this paper, but not set forth, may
perhaps be found stated in the best and most conclusive form in the
book of Dr. George Vivian Poore, Essays on Rural Hygiene, Long-
mans, which has come to hand since the essay was read. This book
makes it clear that the canker of unsanitary practice is already seen
to be at its fatal work in that center of modern civilization—London.

rank kind which alone can there live, to their old haunts in the growing, re-encroaching wilderness, all faithfully setting on foot nature's processes of repair and restoration in the midst of the desolation wrought by the boastful man of the modern civilization, without realizing all that is thereby implied. A complete study involves consideration of the long and slow process of declining prosperity and diminished return for labor by which these conditions have been reached, the grinding struggles and history of individuals and families in resisting the inevitable, and particularly the following of the outcasts from these deserted fields into the wilderness life of new lands again like their forefathers, or into cities where they may have taken a worse refuge; and it also involves the investigation of the resulting effects upon them and their associations there.

It is among the necessary consequences of the action and interaction of biological, physical, psychological and sociological laws, that as the product of the labor bestowed upon the land had diminished, the severity and strain of that labor had told upon the worker, not only in his physical and nervous systems and constitution, but also psychically, morally, intellectually and socially, in the form of resulting deterioration; as also that in case of a steady increase of return in products from fields growing richer, instead of poorer, there would have resulted effects directly the opposite. As nature, and wilderness tendencies under conditions of diminishing return and food supply reassert themselves, malaria and other unsanitary external conditions follow as necessary results of diminished human intelligence, capacity and control, producing peculiar types of disease inevitably accompanying the same, due to unsanitary conditions that prepare the way for final judgment of incompetency and extinction. But abandoned farms and diminished population in such a region imply, for a time, a period of mere delay of the plunge of final extinction, together with the concentration of population elsewhere, and a constant tendency thereto throughout large areas. Observed from the point of view of the consequent increase of city population and lot prices, such movements may even be, and often are, mistaken for evidences of prosperity instead of impending ruin and decay.

But on examination, the unhappy, as well as the seemingly happy, coördinate and contemporaneous city conditions will be found to be alternatively related to the wilderness conditions more or less as effect to cause, and again as cause to effect, particularly in the matters of sickness, disease, misery, vice and crime and their causes operating through effects of centralization. All of which would be ameliorated and eventually removed in case a true sanitary policy of land enrichment, increased return and food supply were adopted in time to prevent concentration of life in cities. The true nature of such a policy may be indicated to those who accept the view that society is an organism, by calling attention to the requirement for the health and development of all known organic life, plant or animal, that the circulatory system of each must be kept in proper action, and that congestions on the one hand and anæmic conditions on the other, are to be avoided if an active life or even survival are to be expected, either one of them in excess presaging death or decay.

There are those, some of them reformers, and even evolutionary sociologists, who, in the presence of resulting increased activity and seeming development that is to be found in modern cities coördinated with diminished fertility and return for labor on farms and their consequent abandonment by laborers compelled to seek refuge in cities and some share in the benefits of a civilization to which they belong and for which they have severely toiled, can neither see nor accept the necessary inference that these movements and conditions mark and indicate a process of decay that must result in destruction, unless changed for a system and practice, conforming to cosmic law, that will inevitably turn the current the other way and send people from cities into the country, not as mere pleasure or rest seekers, but as workers who are prepared to coördinate themselves, their lives, their bodies, and their work with cosmic law and process there by obedience thereto. But this must be a movement in which men are pulled by opportunity, not pushed by dire emergency; drawn by interest, not forced by necessity.

Such persons not only refuse to accept the situation for themselves, but they frequently decry and cry down those who see and accept the cosmic scope and meaning of the conditions and movements referred to, and would obey their laws; and they thereby join themselves, as *participes criminis*, to those who are for their own selfish ends bringing upon civilization an inevitable destruction with all its appalling accompaniments. And these conditions, whether in field or city, are the infallible symptoms of an overmastering and disobedient selfishness somewhere at work, and at work in violation of cosmic law and ethics as well as of psychological, or revealed law and ethics, or those of "the law and the prophets." The naturally associated intellectual stupor and calloused understanding that accompanies and only makes these conditions endurable being already great, such action on the part of alleged reformers therefore becomes doubly criminal in thus preventing intellectual awakening and helping to perpetuate them. These are the people who would decry the deluge until they were themselves submerged and not even avail themselves of a broom to keep back the ocean, imagining that they could do so with words—mere words—of negation.

So far the resulting increase of vice, misery, disease and crime have been considered as consequences of diminished food supply. But there are two factors in the Malthusian Theory and also in the correlated cosmic problem of vice, crime, misery, disease and premature death, viz., food supply and increase of population. When diminishing food supply is accompanied with increase of population, the pace of vice and misery is necessarily still further accelerated and their dominion enlarged. But these do not necessarily stop when population ceases to increase. Of such conditions I have recently had abundant opportunity for study in the States of Ohio, Indiana, Illinois and Missouri, as also in the cities of St. Louis and Chicago, and in smaller Western towns. The coincident and most striking features to be noticed along the railroad lines have been the poor housing of the farmers, small villagers,

crops and animals, among the farms of those four
States that are supplying the world with food, the
magnificent housing of certain seemingly prosperous
but not relatively large business classes in the
great cities, the number and persistent importunity of
the beggars on the streets of those cities, the constantly menacing crowd of lounging, unemployed but
lusty occupiers of the lake front of Chicago at all
hours, and the flagrant dominance of vice and crime in
that city.   This in large degree in one and only
somewhat smaller degree in the other of the two great
food centers of the continent and the world.

I find also in the current discussions of political and
social problems in the South and West further evidence of the importance of food supply and management in their bearing upon all political, social, sanitary and hygienic problems of the time, and the aspects
of the same that are here and now under consideration.   Somehow, strangely enough, and yet not strangely, fifty and sixty cent wheat and nearness to great
sources of food supply, do not relieve the situation.
For, everywhere we find evidence of violated sanitary
law, in its larger and smaller aspects, made conspicuous
in the condition of thousands, and in some respects or
other of all.   And this evidence is to be had in rural not
less than in city precincts.

Poverty, degradation, vice and misery exist not only
in cities where people flock in crowds, but also in the
country, over large areas where unoccupied land is
abundant and people are few and widely scattered;
and they are all traceable to violations of sanitary laws
of the large and evolutionary types. In other words, too
many people for the food supply they can rightfully
earn may be found in both kinds of habitat.

What, then, is the solution?   Mr. Spencer shows
that when men live sanely, according to cosmic
morality and process, the excessive increase of population and pressure upon subsistence will be normally diminished until the actual rate of reproduction will become as low as two children for each
husband and wife, thus relieving the tension of this
strain upon life and food supply progressively as conformity increases and spreads among the members of

the race. And here he finds the true law and solution of evolutionary progress, as did the man of Galilee before him when dealing with the problem of food and raiment.

The gospel solution of this problem may be even more briefly stated in the terms of the Sermon on the Mount, declaring, "Seek ye first the Kingdom of God and his righteousness; and all these things shall be added unto you." We have only to understand that the Kingdom of God and the kingdom, or democracy, of the Cosmos are one and the same, and that righteousness and obedience are the same, to discover that the gospel and the synthetic philosophy agree, if they are not identical in their solutions of this problem, the stumbling block of progress during the ages.

In dealing with land exhaustion and Southern conditions generally, including slavery, and with their coincidents and consequences, I have heretofore shown that they were caused primarily and mainly by an insane infatuation for freedom, in violation of cosmic laws, particularly for a free market for the produce of the land, and that under the influence of railroads in cheapening transportation similar consequences were extending into new regions and even into the northern portions of our own country, resulting in impoverishment of the soil, diminishment in capacity for food production and increase of all kinds of unsanitary conditions considered in the broadest sense of the words. The events of the last twelve months have tended strongly to confirm the views so presented, and also to show in a way almost startling how much need there was two and three years ago for the thorough consideration by our whole people of the topics presented in our Man and the State series of that time, and to which only one politician, Mr. Clarkson, gave due attention.* But at best our Man and State series could only have been a mere beginning, opening out in many directions and particularly in the direction of the present topic considered in its widest aspect, including dis-

---

*And the further experience of the country, through the railroad strike and other occurrences located chiefly at Chicago during the summer of 1894, that took place since this paper was written and read before the Association, add still further confirmation.

ease, vice, misery and crime in their proper order, and also considered as affected by great public policies and particularly by the egoistic and warlike or militant commercial policies and, practices of our Western civilization.

The question is, What and where is the clew to the situation and to all the situations? To which my reply is that the clew is still the same. Slavery and its serious accompaniments and consequences were due to an insanity of freedom,—freedom not earned by obedience, but forced in spite of disobedience; and so are these conditions with which we are now dealing. And this, too, it is that without any regard whatever for the duty of cosmic obedience, like a virus poisons the entire body and substance of what is known as the Western Civilization, and marks it for speedy destruction or slow decay, as unquestioning and therefore unprogressive obedience it is that constitutes the virus that stagnates and paralyzes what is known as the Eastern Civilization.

This being true, that can be no true sanitary system in the large sense of coextension with life and society, that does not properly deal with or coördinate the problems of freedom with the problems of obedience to cosmic law in such a way as to bring them into co-operative harmony throughout life and society and all their functions and activities.

In order to see how that may be done, we must make further study of their past history and learn why and how it has not been done in the past.

Ages ago it was the boast of the law of the Medes and Persians that it was fixed and unchangeable, demanding only implicit obedience. Of such has been the type of all Asiatic law ever since, resulting in the evolution of a peculiar type of civilization in which progress and freedom have been made impossible, indeed, but in which stability and survival on a low plane have been secure. This, too, notwithstanding the law so obeyed was imperfect, particularly on its objective side, its saving factor in the main consisting in the fact that the religion of the East, as well as its law, was largely of natural or cosmic derivation and character. Thus we have the

evidence of the history of man for ages, or at least
the probability, that societies in which the system of
divinity includes the physical as well as the psychological will survive those in which it does not include it.

As to the Western civilization, an extract from a
political platform promulgated or repromulgated during the current week sufficiently indicates its character
for ages past as well as now.

It reads as follows: "Everywhere let Democrats
determine and proclaim that this freedom's battle once
begun, shall not end until every citizen of our repub-
lic shall be secure in the untrammeled right *to buy
what he will, where he will, and of whom he will; ex-
changing without let or hindrance the products of his
labor for those of his fellow laborers anywhere in the wide
world.*"

Out of the very fields at this moment undergoing
desolation and impoverishment because of this freedom of the *citizen*, without regard for the interests
of the society of which he may be a member, to
sell, and its unsanitary consequences, comes this
agonized voice,crying,not like that in the wilderness of
bygone ages to make the paths straight, but demanding
that they shall be made still more crooked. For here
is no hint or dream that there is any such thing as
natural, cosmic or sociological law concerned and demanding obedience, but instead the vociferous assertion
that the individual human will and not the divine, cosmic, national or societary will shall be made supreme.
And here we have the resulting vice of Western civilization in all its avenues of thought and action, first
producing uncosmic and therefore unsanitary conditions and degradations that not only promise but
enter upon its destruction, and then a suicidal call
upon them for salvation.

Can anything be more clear and self-evident, in
this forum at least, than the fact that what we need,
not merely to save Eastern and Western civilizations,
but to save man and society universally, and to establish enduring freedom, is accepted cosmic law
and applied cosmic process, with the independent individual human will held in check or brought to the

point of voluntary obedience thereto? All of which
may be summed up in the words: Sociological and
Religious Reform combined, and of the cosmic and
evolutionary order.

Certainly American practice, and at least seemingly
American law, both take it for granted that legislative
bodies can make adequate laws for the government of
men and society, if only the individual legislators are
consecrated and selected by a majority vote cast
by ignorant voters, who are themselves without any other consecration except that of life on a
plane little above the animal. The incongruity can only
be eliminated by turning legislatures into sociological
schools and laboratories for the study of the divine
law established from the foundation or formation of
the earth. This, however, brings human law and divine
law, the secular and the religious, the State and the
Church, into what many will consider a dangerous
proximity if not a foreshadowing of Theocracy as the
true form of Government. The union of corrupt
religions and churches with corrupt States begotten
of the original corruption and their joint corruptions,
can furnish no grounds for objection to the union
of a cosmic religion and church with a cosmic State.

Certainly in an ideal State there must be found
obedience to cosmic law as the final sanction. And
in such a State the unity of the cosmic Religion and
Church would be an inevitable result.

Particularly at Chicago, and in and about the
Columbian Exposition, but also throughout the world
at this time, evidences have accumulated tending to
show that changes if not revolutions are already imminent, if they have not already begun in both civilizations, that may dominate the future ages and produce civilizations of a higher type than any the world
has yet seen, through the intelligent modification of
the controlling features of these older and manifestly
imperfect ones, particularly in the matter of obedience
and freedom.* For a proper education and a true re-

*Since these words were written and uttered, two events have oc-
curred, one in each civilization, of deep corroborative significance.
First, the railroad strike in Chicago, resulting in the turning of the
Art Building where the Congresses and Parliament of Religions were
held in 1893, into the citadel of law and obedience by General Miles
and the United States Army. And, second, the emergence of Japan

ligion represent the only possible sanitation of human life through restoration to true cosmic relations. It was, however, a similar opportunity that was lost some eighteen centuries ago, when the last Golden Age blossomed in Judea; and this opportunity may also be lost as was that one. Rigid, unprogressive law had for ages forced the freer and more uncontrollable spirits, men and peoples, in successive streams from Western Asia into Europe, which was the wild and free West of the times. At last the whole of Europe had been occupied—leaving no more new land—and under effects of internal pressure, and reactionary influences generally, adjacent portions of Africa and Asia had consequently fallen under the control of one power—Rome—which brought to all these regions the benefits of a brief, unstable peace—peace of the armed or military order—the wilder sorts of freedom having been checked and brought, by arms, under the temporary control of Rome as the center of the system. Rome thus became not only the military and governmental center, but the commercial, the art, the social and eventually the religious center of the system, for all these accessible countries and regions, toward and in which all their power, wealth and opportunity gravitated, and by which it eventually and necessarily became corrupted, through unsanitary conditions affecting life in all its activities and manifestations, while the outlying regions and peoples became impoverished, and destroyed or barbarized through the loss of power, wealth and opportunity. These unsanitary conditions, especially those of the religious order, which drew their characters from poverty, ignorance and other unsanitary physical sources, have been handed down to us with the same power to destroy that they exercised in the stronger civilization of Rome. Intercommunication was of

as a first-class power, capable of protecting Asia from the rapacity of European destructive commercial methods. Here are to be found two opportunities for both sanity and sanitation. And still later we have, even in the streets of Brooklyn, charges of infantry and cavalry, with bayonet and saber, interspersed with cannon, gatling guns, and platoon firing at mobs organized and inaugurating civil war as a direct consequence of the same teaching. These occurrences begin a new epoch in which it must be decided whether the unsanitary conditions that have brought them about are necessary, inevitable and permanent, or only the temporary results of violated cosmic law,

course an essential feature of the system, as it is
of that of to-day, and while the drift of all the
materials of weal and wealth drawn from the land,
toward Rome, impoverished the provinces, it facil-
itated the spread of ideas far and wide, and then
as now the more men suffered the more they thought
and asked the reasons why. Borne on thistle-
down wings, along the currents of commerce, under
the protection of temporary, armed peace, certain moral
and social ideas, most of them of Greek, Eastern and so-
called heathen origin, were caught and took root in a far
away and comparatively quiet region among the hills
of Judea, where they found a peculiar and fit soil for
growth and development, cross-breeding as they did
with the local ideas, religious, moral, social and other,
of the Hebrew race. Practically all the religions
of the time, including that of the Hebrews, were
natural and approximately normal and cosmic religions, with little or no controlling supernatural
taint of indirection or subterfuge, and related mainly,
as did the philosophies of the time as well, to Life
and its actual needs, and not to its fictions, its super-
stitions, or to its mere spiritual side. Business was,
when let alone by foreign influences and forces, close to
nature and nature's laws, and all of culture, whether
of man or of fields, as well. The polytheistic systems
of those ages, being cosmic, localized worship and
obedience and therefore hindered centralization. But
through some inherent defect, that civilization decayed
and hope for the continuous progress of the race was
lost so completely that it has not even yet been recovered or restored.

It is believed that this decay of civilization, and the
characteristic conditions and struggles of European and
modern civilizations, those of our own as well, are
traceable to the unsanitary impoverishment of outlying
regions and unsanitary enrichment of Rome and near-
by Italy, through soil exhaustion caused by the free
movement, over the improved roads built by Rome
throughout her domain, of the produce of the land
toward the center of political, social and financial
power of that day, under a system of organized selfishness. The unsanitary systems of those ages were

similar to those which in our time center in London, but now engage the entire globe in their toils and therefore must, unless in some way speedily counteracted and countermined, eventually bring again upon the whole world of our time and future time, what they brought upon the known and accessible world of that time. Since this would include the whole race of mankind, with no new worlds or continents to discover, conquer and destroy in turn, it is easy for the open eye to see that the coming disaster for which we are so energetically working must far exceed any that the race has ever before met.

And yet nature, science and cosmic process point us to a clear way of escape, but only as they have done in vain for ages past, the way of sane and sanitary obedience to the laws of life as related to and with the physical cosmos and its laws.

While the conditions of peace, intercommunication, seeming wealth and general hope for the race are now in some respects better than then, there are important respects in which they are not so good as in long past ages, and therefore may be considered to be only temporary. Then men had, almost exclusively, natural religions that brought them nearer to the laws of life and physics and to the possibilities of survival. We have only supernatural religions that practically ignore laws of life, physics and the cosmic process and leave us to destruction by them through our unsanitary conduct. Nevertheless the true principles are now practically the same as nineteen centuries ago, and they are stated by the leading thinker of each era in terms that are practically identical.

In the former age the instruments employed in producing the conditions of concentration leading to unsanitary developments, misery, poverty, vice and crime, were Roman Legions and Satraps, adding to militancy a system of robbery reduced to a working science by the effects of a centralized and centralizing commerce, all governed by organized and relentless selfishness, or unadulterated egoism. In our own time commercial Legions and Satraps are used, where they will avail, mainly to convert and persuade barbarous and weak peoples to consent to their own destruction by

accepting mere pottage for their birthrights. And
even then the missionary—Livingston, for example—
with his Bible, and with his church particularly, as a
kind of Trojan horse, is employed to open the gates
of the city, as it were, at night, or all unawares, for
the admission of the new Greeks on their errand of
plunder, devastation and destruction, under the euphe-
mistic titles of Religion and Commerce.

Among stronger peoples the so-called Christian minister and missionary is supplemented by the banker,
the professor of the dismal science, mistakenly called
political economy—better knowable as wealth waste—
all preaching, like the others, a bogus and treacherous
charity and freedom on behalf of an utterly selfish,
piratical and despoiling foreign commerce, as corol-
laries of an unnaturally supernatural religion.

In quite another way did one man (and he was not
without followers in his own time) find the perfect solution and the perfect remedy in the earlier instance.
The central proposition of his system was that the
power which had produced the earth in the midst of,
or out of, the heavens, was a beneficent power and not
only knew but acted on the theory that all men had
need of food, clothing and the proper opportunities of
life, and also that the proper and only way to obtain
them was to follow and obey that power as one would
follow and obey a father who was fatherly enough to
know and provide for the wants of his children. A
unique system was this, unlike any other known—in its
completeness—until that of Evolution appeared. Another principle was that the earth belonged to and was
intended, not for the strong, rapacious and selfish, but
for the meek, the unmilitant, the industrious, for those
who considered others as well as themselves, and must
do so from the very nature of the industrial system
according to which they must work and live. This
was the true land reform of that time and of all time.
Further, he offered as the balance wheel and governor
of this system, a rule the effect of which was to prevent over-centralization and over-dispersion, and to
establish harmony among men by balancing charity,
or consideration for others against selfishness, or consideration only of self, or in modern phrase altruism

against egoism as a foundation principle [of the world system, applicable to matter as well as to man. Having found that the world was—both as to man and as to nature outside of man—so made as to be controllable in the interest of all and without the necessity of sacrificing any, he thought it not improper, still following nature and cosmic process in dealing with life, to give the name of the Heavenly Father, or God, to the Maker of it, as a fit object for human worship, and the title of the Sons of God to the children of men whose privilege it was to coöperate with the Maker of all things. Here was a system that had in it salvation, survival, and eternal life for individual men and for society as well, and mediately the solution of the problems of sickness, suffering, vice, deformity of nature, physical or spiritual, in fact of all the problems of sanitation in the largest senses of the word.

The habendum clause and principle in the title deed of the earth according to this system was not strife and violence, but peace and good will to and among all mankind. That principle is still the only principle upon which true sociological progress and survival can be based or expected. No other can ever prevail.

This Man, living, thinking, seeing, teaching, and drawing his inspiration from nature all around him, and wherever he might be, standing on the western edge of Eastern civilization and on the eastern edge of the Western, or at a point where they and their influences reached him and overlapped, found and declared that by obedience to this beneficent world maker and conductor, freedom, the only true freedom, might be obtained. Not an *a priori* freedom, this. Obedience first, freedom afterwards—the means first, the end to follow, not the end first and the means later.

In connection with this branch of the subject, there was one word or expression constantly used by him, especially when he was ministering to the poor, the sick, the crippled and the overthrown. As expressed in the Greek it is *hamartia*, and in the English versions it has been translated to be and mean "sin," as we have heard it called all our lives.

Its meaning seems rather to be such that the "sinner" is one who misses the mark, does not keep step, is out of the march—*ha-martia*—that is to say, out of harmony, out of step with the divine law, with the universe, the kingdom of heaven; in other words, one who is living a non-natural life, conducting himself in a way that is not cosmic, or natural.

This comes quite near to the evolutionary idea expressed by the words, want of adaptation, out of harmony with the environment, not in accord or conformity with the cosmic process, absence of obedience to cosmic law and principle, and is practically the same.

Hence the deep and tender interest, and to us the significance of the interest he showed, in the sick and their healing; and also the meaning of his injunctions to the healed, to "go *and sin no more.*" To him all unsanitary practices appeared to bring misery, disease, sickness, and premature death, and were sins that he warned men to avoid, as violations of the laws of life, and refused to accept as necessary incidents or accompaniments of human life, or as imposed upon men by the Heavenly Father. Hence his like interest in the poor and his denunciation of the rich of his time, whose riches were reduced to possession by far more transparent robbery than are the riches of to-day even in the most extreme cases.

In the mind and declarations of the Teacher, as in those of the prophets who preceded him, the Divine Paternity and Worshipfulness rested upon the solid foundations of the earth, nature, material things like food and raiment, and the laws of their production and distribution, as well as of their use by his children; in fact upon all that is concerned in life connected with and derived from the earth, and with the cosmic title of the meek to the earth; and therefore to all the earth contains and makes possible. But that pathetic scene when he wept over Jerusalem because it knew not the day of its visitation, might represent his feeling and ours toward the entire world of man followed through the succeeding centuries down to this moment;*

*Not essentially different from this are the warning words of Mr. Spencer in our own time in reference to our own civilization. Some will suppose that his words are the products of age or sickness or faintness of heart; but being founded on cosmic principles and laws as permanent as the law of gravity, they will stand, and only those who are ignorant of or willfully ignore those principles and laws will deny or criticise them.

since the children of men and sons of God have not
yet come to their own, nor apparently even in sight
of their own; among which the right to life in a world
administered on sanitary principles is by no means the
least. For it is easy to see not only the fact but the
reason why the system he taught has been set aside
and still waits its realization, while an alien pretense
that ignores nature and the cosmic processes, as well as
their true Author and Organizer, has been so far as
possible put in, or has usurped and still holds, possession. So far as nature and nature's God, such as he
declared to be the only hope of men, are concerned,
they have all these later ages even been classed among
the devils and the outcast. And his system has been
condemned and more effectually crucified by his own
alleged followers than ever was the man himself by
his ignorant enemies. To have expected anything else
would have been to have expected the impossible. He
probably realized it at the last himself. Hence his
Gethsemane. Hence our Gethsemane.

The wealth, the political and social powers, the entire civilization of Europe rested upon and was permeated with an unconquerable spirit of egoistic freedom
and disobedience of cosmic law, a freedom opposed
throughout to an altruistic freedom, such as he taught.
An altruistic freedom that would have permitted all
men to claim and possess their own, was, and there—
in Europe—still seems to be, practically well nigh
impossible, if not unthinkable, since it would not only
break up the foundation of existing society, but would
also overthrow the age-vested titles to the earth itself,
to what it annually produces for the sustenance and
protection of life and to all opportunities whatsoever;
and would also change, to the extent of reversing, the
relations of men to the earth from which they spring
and to which their bodies must return, as well as their
relations to each other.

Notwithstanding the alleged increase of altruistic feeling and action among those in possession of wealth
and power in Europe, due to the influence of religion,
as alleged by a recent writer, strife and threats are
the main reliance of the suffering and deprived classes,
with civil war everywhere in the background and
standing armies everywhere in the foreground.

Of such has been the true, Columbian spirit towards the whole earth until this hour in which its opportunity fails on this continent and in our own country for the present, for want of more wild territory for misappropriation and for unsanitary uses.

Hence the slant taken by Christianity, as organized in Europe and transmitted to America, whereby the minds of men have been and still are diverted by a sacred imposture, that was doubtless at the time a real or seeming necessity, until for the titles to the earth and its means of sustenance, were substituted, in the case of the many, the titles to mansions in the skies and other like at present unavailable assets. The story of how the change in the system became inevitable if not necessary, or was made and has been maintained in spite of everywhere present and active cosmic principle and process dealing every instant with individual life and with the life of all society, states and civilizations, is too long to tell, particularly in view of the fact that the more important question is how mankind may yet and now come by their own through the restoration of the system substantially as originally taught in Judea: at least here in America, this comparatively new country, where, if anywhere, sane living and true sanitary and cosmic conditions are, let us hope, possible and to be first realized.

But even the discovery of America having been made by Columbus under the impulse and control of the European unsanitary spirit of egoistic freedom and plunder, America has, during the whole four hundred years of progressive occupation of the continent down to date, been dealt with in the same old way of irresponsible egoistic freedom to plunder, without regard to the laws of its use as written in every layer of its rocks, mixed into every inch of its soil, permeating not only the earth, but the very air and water everywhere, present in every motion and act involving life whether of plant, animal or man. In other words, America has been developed and is being exploited in violation of the cosmic law and cosmic as well as of Christian ethics. In the meantime the new lease of life and power given to this spirit in Europe by the discovery of, and the continuance of the system of ego-

istic freedom and plunder in, America, results from an
inherited commercial system of the European and
militant type, which the American people have the right
and duty to overthrow, and also the power to repudiate,
as soon as they become intelligent enough to discard and
silence the charlatans who teach them to perpetuate the
system by which they first defraud the earth and soil
by unsanitary practices and are in turn themselves de-
frauded, or by which rather they are induced to directly defraud and destroy themselves and all who
come after them, by throwing away the necessary elements of food supply, and thereby all the due privi-
leges of life and survival. The old commandment
was in effect that if men would have food and raiment they must "seek ye first the Kingdom of
God and his righteousness; and all these things shall
be added" (or given) "unto you." Which was only
another way of saying: Follow strictly the laws
of nature, the cosmic law and process, the biological
and physical laws of the universe and of its maker
or sustainer, which have been so framed that being
followed, food and clothing in ample supply will be
your reward and all forms of human misery and
vice requiring sanitation of the curative type will be
eliminated.

The new, substituted and accepted commandment
is: First, now and forever, abandon the Kingdom of
God and its righteousness and all obedience to cosmic
law and principle, substituting therefor the law of an
all pervading, ignorant and willful self-interest. And
this commandment leads straight to the dominion of
the man of strength, of imperialism and of the sword,
whose rapid approach we see even through the smoke
of strike-battles, social disorders of all kinds and especially through the false teaching, false sympathy
and intellectual torpor of the so-called Christian
priesthood.

Turning now to the message of Mr. Spencer to the
Evolution Congress—Social Evolution and Social Duty
—it will be perceived that it runs parallel to if not
identical with the message of the older Master, the
golden rule, and the gospel of peace and good will
among men. The important point, however, is that,

seemingly unconsciously so, it is derived only from
nature and nature's laws considered from the evolutionary point of view—even if through a psychology cosmic in its origin—thus reinforcing the teaching of the
older gospels, from and by a message derived directly
from science and the most complete modern philosophy.

It is interesting here to note what he says in the
preface of the second volume of Ethics, published in
the epoch-making summer of 1893: "Now that, by
this issue of Parts V. and VI., along with Part VI. previously published, I have succeeded in completing the
second volume of The Principles of Ethics, which some
years since I despaired of doing, my satisfaction is
somewhat dashed by the thought that these new parts
(Negative and Positive Beneficence) fall short of expectation. The Doctrine of Evolution has not furnished
guidance to the extent 1 had hoped. Most of the conclusions, drawn empirically, are such as right feeling,
enlightened by cultivated intelligence, have already
sufficed to etablish. Beyond general sanctions indirectly referred to in verification, there are only here
and there, and more especially in the closing chapters,
conclusions evolutionary in origin that are additional
to, or different from, those which are current."

If he has been thus anticipated, by whom, I would
ask, other than the older Master to whom we have
herein referred? His trouble seems to have been to
find and introduce where needed "the idea of measure"
and "a certain quantitive character" of "the inferences"
which "assimilates them to those of exact science." It
has occurred to me that something of the deficiency referred to might be found in and supplied from the
laws and facts of physical science with which the
acts of men and nations are at any time concerned,
related and correlated, and which would, seemingly,
permit the laying down of more exact sanctions,
conclusions and rules of conduct than Mr. Spencer
ventures to announce.

The real or actual system of the earlier Master, as
given in his own clear and simple words, seemingly
came to hindrance if not defeat through the difficulty
of harmonizing liberty with obedience among both

European and Asiatic peoples, but for different reasons, and of bringing them to a realizing sense of
the universal benefits of compliance with the moral
law of the kingdom of heaven considered as beginning, if not ending, in this physical world, and in
nature as exemplified thereby. And under the
influence of the same European spirit, especially,
the same difficulty remains and dominates the situation and its character in America at this moment,
when the new message to a similar effect as to the relations of the World, Man and Nature is offered us by
the new master in this new pivotal age. But this condition of things is not always to exist; for there seems
to be a peculiar significance and meaning in the coin-
cidence that at the very moment when this message is
offered, the long continued, hungry, egoistic, piratical
grasping for new lands to put to unsanitary uses and
to plunder is necessarily brought by exhaustion to an
end, and that at least the consideration if not the
adoption of a new and better way is practically compelled, that will give the earth to the meek and to
those who will claim the earth, not with the sword of
militancy, but with the meekness of an obedient industrial spirit that will bring in the era of universal
peace and good will.

In that good time the question will not be as to the
right of the private ownership of land, but as to the
right and ethical uses of land, and the possession of its
benefits and bounties by those who have actually, and
not merely theoretically, earned them as earned increments and products of their own labor.

Other coincidences are not wanting, with favoring
associations. Mr. Spencer has just finished with satisfaction the most important part of his system—Ethics
—which is cosmic in its source; it comes at a time
when the principle of conservation of energy has become firmly established and accepted as a law of the
universe and as an increasing practice of men, when
the attention of men in America is especially drawn,
after thirty years of prosperity never before equaled
in the world, and by disaster brought about by alleged
reformers, to the fact that the sources of wealth are not
inexhaustible, as it is now used in modern civilization,

especially if it is deliberately wasted in the use; and also to the fact that the question of the proper production of wealth is not less important than the question of its distribution, if the latter be not in the end controlled by the former, since even if the quarrel over possession is to be the external object and purpose of men, the wealth must be first produced in order to perpetuate the quarrel. Certainly at least the love of money being the root of all evil, the amount of evil should diminish with the increase of money.

Religious implications of these questions are not only being considered by parliaments of religion, but by the people everywhere; and if Jesus founded a new or improved religion and society on the beneficence of the power that rules the world and furnishes food and raiment provisionally for man, what are we to say of a system of science and philosophy fully wrought out, that sustains the proposition as to the same beneficent possibilities after ransacking the universe for their principles.

The power to accomplish, too, is now to be found in the hands of the people, the parties most interested, the only thing lacking being the necessary intelligence and competent subordinate leaders and reformers near to and among the people. True, those who ought to lead—the clergy—manifestly mislead, and are for the most part engaged in promulgating a supernatural kingdom of heaven, wherein food and raiment are unnecessary. But not much longer can such a religious system be palmed off upon mankind.

Sanitation is at bottom a question of ethics, as related to physics. It is also a question of conservation of energy; for wasted energy is wasted wealth and is largely the source or cause of the existence of all that the *post hoc* sanitarian would remove. It is also a question of truth. The motto of this Association is, "The truth shall make you free." The function of the truth is not only to make free, but also to save—to cause or permit to survive.

Neither is it so far as it seems from being a question of religion, as it certainly is a question of sociology.

These things being true, this is no time for this Association to shrink into its shell, or curtail its work.

We are entering upon a new epoch—an epoch which belongs and is to belong peculiarly to evolution, and therefore to this Association as an important factor in the progressive evolution of American civilization. This Association ought to be, and I believe can be made to be, an important instrument of its hope. Its lists of membership should be increased and its meetings ought to be crowded with eager men and women who believe not only in the future of America, but in the future of the world and the race, and who are willing to work and to serve to the ends of their lives in the great cause of human evolution and progress.

But in order to accomplish anything worthy of itself and of its opportunity, it must first believe something, know something and have something to teach, and follow up these with sentiment, feeling, energy and faith in results to come.

The Sanitation of Life, and our work, as well as all other work, to that end, are dominated by two things of only seemingly remote relations, if the views here presented are correct. They are the New Education and the New Religion, both of which must be cosmic and evolutionary, and must supplant the fantastic travesties that now masquerade in their garbs, names and functions.

The phrase "fantastic travesty" will seem, in one case at least, to be too strong if not altogether unwarranted; but only because it is not strong enough, nor descriptive enough.

A system that undertakes to send out missionaries for the purpose of teaching Religion and Life to the heathen and lifts its hands of alleged whiteness in holy horror over and against the throwing of babes to crocodiles, the burning of widows and the bone and body crushing of Juggernaut, must submit sooner or later to inspection of those hands and to tests of their alleged or implied whiteness. Individual motive, however high, cannot satisfy such tests. Only truth and inevitable results can do that.

When under that inspection the civilization to which that system gives its name is seen to permit chariots dedicated to the worship of commerce and convenience

to traverse its streets, and daily crush life and the
semblance of humanity out of men, women and children, those hands begin to take on a perceptibly darker
shade. When it is found to permit a single easily
prevented disease to carry off hundreds of thousands
of babes, every summer, to permit at least ninety per
cent of its people to die from preventable diseases
without the enjoyment of their allotted terms of years;
to permit and promote the pressures and temptations
of life that yearly overcome hundreds of thousands of
mankind and force them through the ranks of misery
and poverty into the ranks of vice and crime; and
when, after considering a long list of other burdens
put upon life that are similarly permitted, it is reluc-
tantly found on careful and candid investigation and
conclusion that such permissions finally rest upon and
receive their ultimate sanctions from a fraudulently
falsified version of the teachings of its master and
founder, then at least will it begin to be seen that
compared with those hands uplifted against the heathen
the hands of the Ethiopian are whiteness itself.

Such fraudulent falsification is everywhere open and
transparent to ordinary schoolboy and sophomore intelligence on almost every page of the record, would be
transparent to all men if the dictionaries had not also
been suborned to utter falsehood before the very altar
of the Most High, and therefore can furnish no excuse
for its existence.

A few samples of the treatment of pivotal words will
show the purpose, scope and general method of the
falsifications made. Æonic life clearly means terrestrial life from age to age. By manipulation it is made
to transfer the center of exploitation from earth to
heaven at one swoop by forcing upon the words "eternal life" the meaning of the future life, or life in
heaven.

In the same way a word meaning the practice of
justice and used in such direct connection with the
words "food and raiment" as to indicate the solution
of the problems of poverty and supply of the means of
life on earth, is made to mean a righteousness that is
a passport to heaven, where neither food nor raiment
are supposed to be required.

Again, it is admitted that there are what may for convenience be considered two fields for human exploitation, viz., the objective, or outward, by way of the five senses, and the subjective, or inward, by way of the inner consciousness; the first belonging to the noetic, and the last belonging to the metanoetic. The metanoetic is to the noetic as the solar to the stellar, the divine to the human. Jesus comes plainly proclaiming the approach of the kingdom of heaven together with a metanoetic era, and their dominion over mankind and the earth. In so doing he proclaims the human intellect as the means whereby man must find his way and do his appointed work in two worlds. By the simple device of a false translation and a perjured lexicon the human intellect is dethroned and an African fetish—Repentance—is established in its place as the central principle of Christianity. Thus a Christian church and society of an acephalic order are made the highest possible products of the ages, and the highest commission for the teaching of Life the world has yet seen, has been turned into a mission for the teaching and practicing of death and decay for Man and Society.

So receptive, however, have been the souls of many that the divine light for the guidance of men transmitted with that message could not be entirely darkened. Consequently we may hope for its complete restoration. When that restoration shall have been made, Religion and Science will be reconciled and the race of mankind will no longer perish from generation to generation, the victims of unsanitary conditions. But meantime the responsibility for all the consequences of permitted and promoted unsanitary conditions must be borne by the church, through whose fidelity to its Master they might be prevented, and through whose recreancy to that Master they are sanctioned and allowed to continue.

The remedy is to be found in a New Reformation to supplement the failures of the old reformation; the Protestant Churches its objectives. For, under the present pope the Romish Church has become the leader of at least social progress, while Protestant Christianity, under the control of an ignorant, arrogant and rich laity, has become the stumbling block of true social and religious progress.

ABSTRACT OF THE DISCUSSION.

Dr. R. G. Eccles:—

The air is filled with myriads of germs, and our bodies are the soil upon which they feed, and, if our bodies are weak, these germs grow and increase in numbers with greater rapidity. These germs may be borne about by the wind, or carried by insects. A single cholera germ will multiply to six millions in twenty-four hours. The infection may be spread by birds, by cats or dogs, or in the milk of cows. A case is recorded of 190 deaths in three weeks caused by diseased milk. Consumption is contagious, and may be communicated through the expectoration of consumptive patients, germs from which, when dried, float through the air. In the matter of contagion much depends upon whether the system has power to resist the attack. These germs when taken into the intestines cause marasmus. Consumption, however, is curable, as has been demonstrated in post mortem examinations. Comparatively few are susceptible to consumption. We are not as careful to protect ourselves against this as against scarlet fever. Sewers would not be so productive of disease if their contents were properly cared for. In Paris it is disposed of outside of the city, and spread over the soil. It was predicted that the result would be fatal, but, upon analyzing the water of the sewers, after it had filtered through the soil, it was found to be purer than the water in ordinary use within the city, and free from germs, though they are there at first. Germs of nitrification are antiseptic, and kill off the disease germs. Wealthy people now reside in the locality where this sewerage is deposited, and land is held at high prices. Such is the case also at Berlin.

The poor of London lived in such utter filth years ago that on the ground or floor were heaped up alternate layers of filth and straw. About one hundred and fifty years ago the houses of these people were cleared by the soldiers of the British army in order to obtain nitrates for the manufacture of powder. These were the people who, when cholera appeared, exclaimed, "God, be merciful to me a sinner."

Dr. Lewis G. Janes:—

In what I conceive to be one of the main contentions in Mr. Skilton's paper, I am in entire agreement with him. In this country, and perhaps in the civilized world at the present day, too much stress is placed on the importance of liberty—mere freedom from restriction—as an end. Liberty is not an end, but a means. Unless we use our liberty in seeking to know the laws by which the cosmos is governed, and in endeavoring to conform to these laws, our liberty is worth nothing to us. Liberty otherwise used may lead to evil instead of good—to devolution instead of evolution. In this country, we incline too much to worship public opinion, to follow the lead of the sensational newspaper, to drift with the current, without knowing whether we are really going right or wrong. The true object should be to ascertain first the truth—to know what conforms to the nature of things, to the laws of the universe; then we should stem the tide of a false public opinion, if need be, in defense of the right.

It seems to me, however, that Mr. Skilton takes too pessimistic a view of our actual situation. From a somewhat careful study of the ancient religions, for example, it seems to me that we have less supernaturalism to contend with to-day than formerly. Eighteen hundred years ago, all religions were supernatural religions. The cosmic elements were confused and distorted by this false bias. Nor does it seem to me true that man has been less successful than the animals in his search for the means of survival. A far larger proportion of animals is cut off prematurely by violence, famine and plague than of human kind. The recent storm, for example, cut short the lives of thousands, perhaps millions, of little birds who were not able to foresee and prepare for the conditions which it invoked. And prior to the last century or two, before science began to dominate the world's thought, how much more frequent and fatal were the famines and plagues which have devastated the human world!

Imperfect as our perception and obedience of the cosmic laws are to-day, we have made a great advance on conditions which were once almost universal. Mr. Skilton would like to see a complete union and co-

operation of Church and State; but it seems to me all
that mankind has gained in these latter days has been
won by the divorce of ecclesiasticism from governments.
The time when such a combination was favorable to social progress has passed by.   It can come again with
advantage only when we get a community of highly
cultured saints—so our first duty seems to be to develop the saints, to act on the individual by all ways that
are educational and morally inspiring.. And when we
get such a perfect community, virtue will be spontaneous; it will not need the forcing of ecclesiastical institutions, backed by the power of the State.   Though
the important thing is to make a good use of our liberty, we should not despise liberty as a means. Though
only a condition, it is an important and necessary condition of progress.

MR. SKILTON IN REPLY:—

The theses I have sought to maintain are: 1.
That Ethics, Sociology and Religion rest upon
and in a Physical Basis;   2. That this physical basis
furnishes the conditions of Life and Survival for
plants and animals, and for Men, Society and States as
well;   3. That the fatal error, particularly in the religious
systems of the world, but also in its ethical, sociological and political systems, is to be found in the universal failure to recognize this physical basis and its
relations in all of these systems; and, 4. That such
recognition, with consequent modifications of current
theory and practice, are necessary to progress and survival, and, in a preliminary way, to the lifting of the
unnecessary limitations, sufferings and burdens now
controlling and resting upon Life everywhere.

The religions of eighteen hundred years ago, certainly
among the Greeks, Romans and other nations living
near the Mediterranean, were more natural than supernatural.   Every department of nature had its own
god, its own worship; and these gods had their own
temples and systems of worship.   In other words, external nature was believed to be governed by divine law;
and hence the strength of their civilizations and their
superiority in many respects over the so-called Christian
civilizations of to-day.

As to famines and plagues, the day is too early for comparisons. We are dealing with a new and unpoisoned, or not entirely poisoned, hemisphere; but we are making rapid, if not satisfactory progress and preparation for famines and plagues in the days to come —one item of which Doctor Janes has heretofore given us when quoting Professor Atwater as authority for the statement that American food products have already deteriorated over twenty-five per cent below those of Europe.

My pessimism is the pessimism that proclaims the duty, the possibility and the glory of prevention. I admit the advance, but I deny its permanence, and I have given a diagnosis of past as well as of present and future advances and of their backslidings, as a warning against impending disaster. My system of saint-culture is of the *Mens Sana in Corpore Sano* order, with the *Sanum Corpus* first. I do not believe in an *insanum corpus* as the possible residence of a *Mens*, or anything else, *Sana*. The true State and the true Church are inseparable; they will come, a unit, together, as body and soul, or not at all. Their separation is the badge of their untruth and want of fidelity to either God or Man; as also was and is and ever will be, the domination of the State by a fraudulently supernatural church. As the true union of State and Church approaches, the day of the translation of the body of the State will also approach; the kingdom of heaven will then be at hand, as eighteen hundred years ago, and the reign of the Higher Law will then have come. Educational and moral inspiration are impossible without an ethics, a sociology and a religion resting on and supported by a true basis of physical law, and an intelligent obedience thereto. Without these all progress can consist only in so many castles in the air resting on nothing, and beguiling men only on the pathways of destruction.

Doctor Eccles has given us a partial list of the proximate causes of disease and of the decay of nations. If he had made the list of the causes of all diseases complete, he could have included none that would not be eliminated and made harmless by sanitary obedience to cosmic law and process.

To be finally compelled, in fidelity to truth and honest conviction, to characterize the Religion that is called Christian as fraudulent, the organized church called Christian as incompetent, and the ministry of both as ignorant and untrue, because not educated in the fundamental elements of Life, and as therefore inevitably unfaithful to both God and Man, is to the last degree painful to one who has, in hope for better things, continued to be a member of an orthodox Christian Church for over fifty years. With increasing clearness during all these years the duty has been seen; but only to be, for the most part, put aside in serenity, patience and faith. The end of the day of probation and the beginning of the day of emancipation have now at last come.

RELIGION AS A FACTOR IN HUMAN EVOLUTION

BY

REV. EDWARD P. POWELL

COLLATERAL READINGS SUGGESTED.

Spencer's *First Principles*, and *Principles of Sociology;* Fiske's *Cosmic Philosophy. Idea of God* and *Destiny of Man;* Powell's *Our Heredity from God;* LeConte's *Evolution as Related to Religious Thought;* Savage's *Religion of Evolution;* Hinton's *Life in Nature;* Picton's *The Essential Nature of Religion;* Max Muller's *Physical Religion;* Gould's *The Meaning and Method of Life, a Search for Religion in Biology;* Chadwick's *Evolution as Related to Religious Thought.*

RELIGION AS A FACTOR IN HUMAN EVOLUTION.

BY EDWARD P. POWELL.

PART I. PRIMITIVE RELIGION.

A. Definitions of Religion.

Schleiermacher defines religion as dependence; Hegel as freedom; which appear to be but opposite, not opposing views. Comte pronounces it to be self-culture; Fichte regards it as knowledge. Kant considers it to be natural morality. Dr. Momerie looks upon it as devotion to goodness. Cicero derives it from *relego* "to be devoted," instead of *religo*, "to bind together." Arnold defines it to be consciousness of a power outside ourselves making for righteousness;and Max Müller believes it to be the perception of the infinite in a way to affect character. Dean Burgon tells us religion can only be "a complete supernatural revelation, not permitting of change or progress;" but Herbert Spencer's religion arises in a Causal Power of which "the nature remains ever inconceivable, and to which no limits in time or space can be imagined." Abbott defines religion as "the life of God in the soul of man."

B. Primitive Religion Traced.

(1) Religion a Family Service.—It was my duty one year ago to trace all secular history back to its origin in the primitive family. It is now my pleasant duty to turn my attention to the evolution of the same family on the religious side. Secular evolution, leading on through towns and commonwealths to States, and to a Federal Union of independent States, has been a noble record; but by all odds the most magnificent half of human life has been the religious. I define religion to be an evolution of family affection; as the state is an evolution of family coöperation.

If you go to the mouth of the Mississippi you find
substantially what you find at the source; only a vastly
increased volume, increased power, increased uses, and
generalizations hardly anticipated where the brooklet
fed violets and filled the pitcher of a rural home; so religion has to-day no new element in it that can not be
found in the earliest cult of the most primitive families. There were from the beginning three conditions
that made religion requisite.

(2) Factors Conditioning Religion.—(a) First to impress the mind were the facts of life and death. Every
myth indicates that no early race thought of beginnings and endings. The babe came to them from elsewhere; the dying only went elsewhere. Religion was
the ligature of these two lives; the science of unity.
What people thought about other lives was of course
diverse; and it grew to be more diverse; but what we
need to see is that they believed in a life beyond, and
that it was associated with this life. They tenderly
cared for the dead as still living. They fed them, consulted them, and had no doubt of their possible help-
fulness or malevolence. Here at the outset lay the
germ of the ideas of revelation, inspiration,and incarnation. It was a matter of course that the dead might
reappear; and that they had their old passions and
desires. So began the utterly natural creed. If you
have wondered why the Hebrew Scriptures never
speak of immortality you may be sure it is because
those ancients never doubted it. It was not open to
discussion, because religion without it would have been
inconceivable.

(b) The second class of facts that bore upon the
mind to initiate religious emotion was that of physical forces. Earthquakes, cyclones, thunder, floods,
serpents, eruptions and disruptions were built into
myths. So also were the benevolences of the sunbeam,
starlight and the seasons. It is easy to accede to Mr.
Spencer that the main cult was family love; but equally
original in all probability was the adoration and the
pacification of the mighty forces that surrounded and
constituted man's home. The commingling of these
two cults was easy. There was an early transference
of heroes to the skies, where they were identified with

stars, winds and storms. The drift was both ways. Some religions became intensely naturalistic; others as intensely spiritualistic. Through all history these two tendencies have clashed, have borrowed, have hated; and out of the two when blended have evolved our richest faiths.

(c) Beyond his relation to other men and to things there was, as there is, in the very selfhood of man, a sense or consciousness of a something or some one above all. Tyler says, "A leading idea in the traditions of the world is really no more than of Somebody." The oldest tradition touched that conception which ever since has been expanding into that still ungrasped idea, the Infinite. In all cases this Infinite was psychical as well as physical. Only late abstractions have led to a notion of a dead universe and a God outside of Nature. So universal was this God-sense that some anthropologists conceive monotheism to have preceded polytheism. The human mind was, as it is to-day, in contact with mind as the body was in contact with matter; and it felt the contact. We must clearly see and stoutly emphasize this religious consciousness as a quality of human nature. Brinton says that the American aborigines everywhere had an abstract word for general spiritual force. Peruvians kissed the air; the Eskimo spoke of the Owner of the Air. The more carefully we study history the more important will appear this native human instinct. Lang insists that the early races felt Power to be universal; and also as consciously intelligent. Earliest men saw that the unity about them was of that kind which is the result of operations similar to their own; it was "the subordination of all things to a harmonious whole," in which unity men had a part.

(3) Religion a Function of the Psychical Universe. —The family relation is distinctively an inheritance of animal origin, and religious culture as well as ethics is integral with the family. Allowing, however, for certain roots of religion in all the diverse branchings and upward yearnings of nature below man, yet when man appears it is with a great leap in the way of religious feeling; having the Lord's prayer not far from his perception and the golden rule in his soul. Re-

ligion thus appears to be more than a phenomenon of
human beings; it is a function of the psychical universe. It is the *religo*, the bond, the tie of life and
of all lives, of gods and men; of God and man. It is
the expression of a moral and purposeful universe. Our
definition thus widens out to include that of Mr. Abbott. Religion is the life of God in the soul of man;
but as a historic factor it is the evolution of the human family in its relation to God.

(4) Earliest Religion a Cult, Not a Creed.—The
earliest religion was almost purely a cult. It consisted
in doing rather than in believing. "It was possible,"
says Schurman, "that there should be heteropraxy in
those days, but not heterodoxy." It is astounding to the
student of ancient religions to find how largely also
our own sacraments, such as eating with the gods and
baptizing the new-born, are a survival of the age of
cult. Yet while not formally expressed, the soul of all
later creeds was implied. All thoughts of the next life
and all obligations in this life found ready place in
this vast science of the right relation of the living
and the dead.

(5) Religion a Social Power. (a) Religion Economic.—On the economic side religion was intensely
fruitful of good. It not only held the family together,
but it was the bond of growing communities. Strong
as might be the hand of the state, as strong was the
heart of the church. The earliest science, the primary
arts, the dawnings of education, the professions of
medicine and theology were due to the religious side
of family life. Face to face with nature, the priest
was also much of a poet, as in simpler races he is to-
day. Yahwehism was one half sanitation. It forbade
suicide; it regulated sexual affairs; it protected woman; it mollified the horrors of wars.

(b) Religion Coöperated with the State.—The capacity of religion to coöperate with the State is seen
in the older civilizations of both continents. Many of
the remains of American plastic art, sculpture and
painting were designed for religious purposes. The
great Pyramid of Cholula, the mounds of the West,
the artificial hills of Yucatan, hallowed great political
events. Their construction took men away from war

and the chase, encouraged agriculture, peace, and settled homes.

The common custom of pilgrimages to the shrines
of heroes, brought peoples into commerce, and widened
both knowledge and sentiment. National unity was
fostered by common cult and common altars. The
Jews never were a nation apart from their relation to
sacred Jerusalem. Brinton tells us the sacred temple
on the island of Cozumel in Yucatan was visited every
year by such multitudes from all parts that roads paved
with cut stones were constructed for their accommoda-
tion. In Peru such vast numbers repaired to the sacred temple for three hundred leagues that houses of
free entertainment were built on all principal roads,
and pilgrims were allowed safe passage through an
enemy's country.

(c) Religious Morals Distinct from Secular.—To
the state at the outset belonged certain duties; to religion also a distinct obligation. Unwritten creeds defined the latter; unwritten constitutions the former.
This involved a distinction in morals; those that were
secular and those that were religious. This distinction
vitally affected all human progress, as it is a vital principle to-day. Beginning with our relations to ancestors, religion peculiarly enforced reverence and piety,
care of the aged and honor for the gods. This widened as the cult widened, into love for the All Father,
and for all men as his children. The tendency was
already toward the principle to be enunciated by Jesus
in the Parable of the Neighbor. Animism required
filialism; this culminated in love. Naturism added the
virtue of rightness as opposed to crooked dealing.
Stealing, murder and other vices concerning family
property and individual safety were secular affairs.
Temperance, honesty, chastity, justice might be fostered by religion, but it was on secular grounds. They
would exist without religion.

PART II. THE AGE OF THEONS AND PANTHEONS.

(a) Absorption and Elimination.—Very early in the
evolution of religion began two remarkable processes,
absorption and elimination. Absorption was a valuable economic principle of antiquity. The dead were

adopted as well as the living; and not seldom a tribe selected its favorite deity from its neighbors. But the overwhelming necessity was to get rid of a superfluity of deities. War, leading to conquest, obliterated not only the living but swept out whole theons. Generous pantheons were established by growing nations; but these were soon overpopulated. Egypt was puzzled more over the relative rank of her gods than over the honor due her princes and priests. Greece made sport of her deities, while India sat down in helpless servitude to three hundred millions. The earliest gleams of history show us that to eliminate gods was already a necessity.

(b) Religious Conflict.—Of nothing are people more sensitive than of their ancestors. You may abuse the living, but speak no ill of the dead. Yet ill was spoken. Gods were defied. Religious wars followed, and history in myth and song shaped itself at the outset into a battle of theologies. Reformers arose who attacked the character of ruling deities and prevalent cults. Old gods and old ideas went out together. About four thousand years ago the first historic reformation took place in Asia. It was a wide-spread effort to cleanse the theons. There was a vast friction of theologies. Thinking grew free; facts accumulated; truths flashed out. Heresy at last triumphed as Brahminism.

(c) Elimination Reaches after a God of Gods.— Original monotheism existed only in the wishes of our more orthodox investigators. Only in all and everywhere there was, penetrating naturism and animism, a God-consciousness, the dim conception of One over all. As elimination went on and even the greater gods were often dethroned, faith reached steadily more and more after the God of Gods, the Father above all, "in whom we live and move and have our being." There were prophetic gleams of monism. Yahweh of the Israelites was the uncaused I Am. Osiris was Cause of the Universe. The Finns to-day represent the least modified form of the original Aryan cult. The spirits whom they worship are a democracy of independent patriarchs, differing in power but not in rank. Over all is the Great Grandfather of the Gods. The Hottentots also speak of the Grandfather in the skies.

(d) Diversions and Perversions of Worship.—As the gods were of both sexes and human desires, religion at once shaped itself to the sexual passion. Theology owes much of its evolution to this sentiment. Self-love, country love, tribal love, also impressed the rituals. Solar worship and rain worship, river worship and mountain worship impinged on animism. It was modified by pestilences, sequences of the seasons, and violent disturbances of nature. Animism, however, furnished in the main the human element in religion; and naturism furnished the poetic as well as the darker shades of brute force. Lightning and other forces frequently destroyed a victim; hence the gods were supposed to desire human sacrifices.

(e) Growth of Creed.—Creeds grew apace. Religion had its birth in poetic sentiment. It begat poetry in turn. The Vedas 2000 B. C., Homer and David 1000 B. C., formulated thought about the gods. The imagination was a growing power. The future world opened a thousand questions demanding answers. Why was suffering? Why death? Great hopes and fears about the next life were the result of the imaginative power of advancing thought. Primitive people had no clear visions of heavens and hells; but as the cults became overloaded with pacificatory sacrifices, the creeds fell into definite opinions of sin, of atonement, of atoners. There was not only feeding of gods, but there was more starving of self. Pacification became the dominant idea. The gods were besought to rescue men from the wrath that is and the wrath anticipated. The way was preparing for our later theologies.

(f) God Comparison.—God comparison began to lead the world into a great idealism. A passion arose for the best. There was a struggle for the true, the beautiful and the good. I think we have never understood the images of the gods. They stood for ideals of the best, as conceived by their worshipers. The Greek gods were smooth limbed, full of grace and ease of action. Oriental gods were huge, powerful and wrapped in meditation. Other gods were meek and fleshless results of self-abnegation. Ideals advanced. Gods, to be entitled to honor, must manifest ideal qualities.

(g) Dualism Developed.—This power of elimination led on to heights impossible for narrow minds. They misinterpreted. They were enthralled by the cult, still more by tradition. The vulgarizing of high ideals followed. All would have been debased but for the few who were hated, stoned or crucified. The spirit died out of reforms, so that about every five centuries a new evolution began to unfold. Richer, broader, deeper was the river that fertilized the world. In Persia was worked out the first great reduction of the gods to dual forces. Henceforth the personality of gods was of importance inferior to character. Two principles absorbed all possible gods and all men. Ormuzd was little more in Persian myth than Goodness personified; and Ahriman was the Evil in nature.

(h) Development of Monism.—Dualism was a magnificent stride away from the chaos of animism. It closed the theons and pantheons forever. But could the two forces of character not be reduced to one? Science rests uneasy till it can find the single element of elements. Philosophy had the same trouble; it could not rest easy short of monism. This was anticipated in the God-instinct of the simplest mind. It was distinctly felt after by the Greeks. It became fundamental in Christianity. Jesus brushed away the dualistic idea as incomplete. He addressed God as the universal Father. Paul fairly turned the young faith over to Him in whom we live and move and have our being. "For there is one God over all, interpenetrating all." Modern science can only supplement with demonstration the faith of the founders of Christianity. "God," says Renan, "it is He that is; and all the rest seems to be."

(i) The Universal and the Infinite.—Here at last the three primeval lines of influence converged: animism, naturism and the God-instinct. The universal took the place of the local, under pressure largely of naturism. But instead of an infinite force man reached the idea of infinite supreme interpenetrating spirit. It is easy to see how dualism might have become a mere clash of impersonal principles, and how monism might have been a universality of physical force. It is not easy to see that animism, the worship of the dead, would have prevented this. But the consciousness of Some One like himself but not himself—the self above himself, came to the rescue, and prevented on the one side animism from resting in an expanded idolatry, and on the other side prevented naturism from ending all in materialism. But the God-instinct did farther service, for animism was ever too familiar with its gods. The Greeks allowed Aristophanes to satirize them on the stage, making Hercules do the work of a scullion, while Bacchus was the recipient of a sound flogging. Prayer and sacrifice were a swapping of favors with the deities. The instinct of the All-Father saved religious evolution from this anarchism. The "One Thinker, thinking non-eternal thoughts," became the Our Father of all men, whose life flows in us all. Religion climbed by simplest concrete to abstract conception, and the cult of the dead rose to self-culture. Max Müller sees man seizing the Infinite Cause "by a spontaneous effort." But it is historically true that what was done was achieved by the trinal influences which I have defined.

(k) These Identified with Jehovah.—That the Universal and Infinite when finally expressed in cult and creed should have been closely identified with some one of the animistic but idealized gods is not surprising. Elimination had gone far to secure the survival of the fittest. Yahweh of the Jews entered the struggle with Osiris, with Apollo, with Chemosh, and he was worthy of the victory he gained over all. He was cold, pure and comparatively just. Libidinous he was not. That his name became transposable with the Universal Spirit we need not regret. The nations turned to him as the holy God. "My house," it was said, "shall be the house of prayer for all nations." The prophets surrounded Yahweh with elements of humanitarian spiritualism. This universalism became the germ of Christianity. It was a culminating protest against priestcraft. It created Jesus and it deified him.

(l) Religion Grows Subjective.—The transfer of religious sentiment from objective duty to subjective feeling was equally remarkable. Primitive religion was family and social. There was little chance for individualism and as little for altruism; for it is true that you can not love your neighbor till you love yourself. The Jewish people were first to pass over from upward looking to inward looking. The Greeks followed. "Know thyself," was the key of the new philosophy. Egyptian faith rested almost wholly in a study of the next world. The Jewish concerned mainly this life. But the nation divided into two schools; the exclusive and the humanitarian. In Greece humanity grew to be the chief object of reverence. The gods were conceived as men. Worship of gods passed over to culture of men. When a Hindoo tried to make a god he carved ideas; when a Greek tried it he carved himself.

(m) The Position of the Jew.—Finally Rome gathered men all together into one empire, and the gods into one pantheon. Universalism was dominant. But while the Jew accepted humanity he rejected the democracy of gods. He held firmly that gods must survive according to moral elimination. That was the true religion in his estimation that could offer the best gods, best morals, best science. Instead of accepting a universal pantheon he begat Christianity.

(n) Economics of This Age.—The economics of the age of theons and pantheons was progressive. There was in the heart of man from the first a feeling of weakness and dependence. Self-consciousness is our distinction above other creatures; but it is our terrible burden. Religion relieved the soul with the conviction that to die was to go to the fathers. At their worst, religions never failed to prophesy a coming redeemer. They were utterances more or less coherent of the yearnings of humanity for betterment; and these yearnings they ever stimulated and fed.

But as thought developed, literature was almost wholly on the church side. Prophets were historians. David and Homer alike sang of the gods. Science was the basis of cult and creed. Philosophy and theology were a long while identical. Architecture, music, painting, sculpture and even dancing were of the gods and for the gods. Prayer, from being simple converse with the dead, became a subjective power. Faith was the corner stone of religion, as physical force was of the state. The twelve commandments, found essentially in all languages, were equally civic and religious. Circumcision and baptism were secular rites as well as sacred.

(o) Conflicts.—The conflict of animism and naturism was constant and valuable. The sensuality of the latter led to a detestation of vice on the part of the former. Even the body became abhorred. The flesh was associated with the devil, and both with worldliness. Other-worldliness, however, arose with a sensuous element quite as obnoxious to pure ethics. But poetry owed gratitude equally to both cults. Naturism made the rainbow a symbol of divine wrath, while animism flung it over the skies as the pathway to the abode of the gods. The virtue of naturism was rectitude, but its worship was unchaste. The free and open sexualism of the universe, from the wedding of sun and earth to that of the flowers, led to a freedom of sex relations that slipped over into Bacchanalian riot. The organs of generation were above all sacred. Unfortunately the cult turned love into a furious passion. Physical ideas of virtue dominated. Next to feeding the dead was the duty of washing before meals, because the living ate with the dead. Sanitation became an exalted rite. Friendship was divine; the family above all was sacred.

(p) Causes of More or Less Arrested Development. —It has been an easy theory that all decadence of mankind is a lapse from the primal consciousness of God; that the soul was originally in clear companionship with Deity, and fell away. But the tendency of early religions to degenerate was precisely that of later faiths. It lay in the conservative nature of religion, tending to inflexibility of ritual and later of creed. Once in the rear of extant knowledge, religion could only yield its authority, or otherwise stand as the champion of ignorance and absolutism. That was to be well on the way to spiritual lifelessness, with moribund manners and dead ideas. Then the very communication of minds with Mind became a lie. "If the light in thee be darkness, how great is that darkness!" The very rise of literature contributed to arrest of religious development. The earliest words were inven-

tions, to the science of those days infinitely more wonderful than our mastery of steam and electricity is to us.
A written manuscript grew easily sacred.   Its words
were law.   To doubt them was heresy.   Homer- sang
religion into fetters; while chronologies became divine
revelations.

(r) On the Whole a Positive Evolution.—Yet on
the whole religious development went forward more
constantly and more firmly than the advance of the
state.   Emerson says:

"One accent of the Holy Ghost
A heedless world has never lost."

The great cycles of reformation were gigantic efforts
to reconstruct creed and cult on the basis of enlarged
knowledge.   Progress fed on decay as our forests feed
on the inferior vegetation of the past.   So out of
Yahwehism was born Christianity.

PART III.   THE AGE OF CHRISTIANITY.

(a) Christianity Born of United Shemism and Aryan-
ism.—In Christianity all religious history culminated.
This was so because Judea was that bowl at the east
end of the Mediterranean into which all nations poured
their ideas as well as commerce.   Here went Grecian
tutors and Hindoo ascetics, encountering Persian spiritualism and Egyptian mysticism.   But the Jewish race
was also, above all, receptive and absorptive, as well
as adaptive.   "Christianity," says Renan, "was at its
origin no other than Judaism."   It was the legitimate
child of the richest religious evolution on earth.   It
could have found no other birth.   Its later foster parents everywhere diverted, where they did not waste its
energy.   Jews were universalists — everywhere — and
everywhere proselyting; therefore excellent disciples
to propagate the higher faith.   Christianity will probably never come to its true and grandest possibilities
until Shemite and Aryan once more unite in defense
of its truths and in antagonism to its perversions.

(b) Christianity both Subjective and Objective.—
Christianity appeared first of all as mediator of the
subjective and objective schools of theology.   It held

tightly to the old cult concerning the next life; but it had also the full Jewish care for the life that is. It looked upward and outward to the Father; but equally it looked inward to self-investigation. It is no wonder that its history has been a continuous battle. Its strongest men have failed to cover the full purport of its founder. The subjective in Christianity produced celibates and ascetics from Simon the Stylite to Cardinal Newman; the objective created Pauls, Luthers and Stanleys. God, not wholly severed from the ghost realm, yet became a life in the soul. Goethe says, "In our innermost life there is also a universe. What each one sees within himself to be best he names God. To this God he makes over heaven and earth." Browning says:

> "All tended to mankind:
> And man produced, all has its end thus far;
> But in completed man begins anew
> A tendency to God."

It was this second chapter of human evolution that Christianity undertook; the evolution not of the highest physical life, but of man as a moral individual.

(c) The Fatherhood of God and Brotherhood of Man.—Jesus joined the kingdom of man to that of God. He was son of God as he was Son of Man. Primitive religion said simply and truthfully, "I am son of a God." Jesus said, "I am child of universal divinity and of all humanity. I am the Father in the flesh. I and my Father are one. So are all men my brothers who do my Father's will." Here was a new social principle, as well as theological. The cult of Christianity created a great human brotherhood. Paul and John placed the work of Jesus fully in the line of evolution.

(d) The Pauline and Petrine Conflict.—It was, however, the inner struggle of Christianity that made it so potent—the eternal combat of narrowness and breadth. Hegel says the greatest moral tragedy is not the conflict of right and wrong, but of right with right. The tragic power of Christianity began to be seen when the Pauline and Petrine schools collided; it is to-day as vigorous as ever.

(e) Christianity Optimistic.—Optimism presided at

the birth of the new religion. Its cradle chant was, "Peace on earth, good will to men." Its founder pronounced a blessing on poverty. The chief apostle rose to his sublimest eloquence in, "Now abide Faith, Hope and Love." The whole history of Christianity has been "I can but trust that good shall fall." The Jewish faith was barely saved by prophets who foresaw better things. Christianity was forward-looking from its origin.

(f) The Economics of Christianity.—Its physical economy was an enormous expansion of love and care for the poor, as the body of God, children of our Father. Incarnation became a universal principle. Jesus did not claim it for himself alone. Animism had made idol-bodies for the ghosts; Christianity gave the body of living man to the infinite Holy Ghost. Tolstoi's race-suicide instead of being original Christianity is, like all asceticism, only undeveloped animism. Jesus stooped to lift the lowest beggar as his brother in God.

(g) Christianity Neglectful of the Dead.—The total completion of the evolution of gods into God, of the local into the universal, tended to the entire abrogation of ancestor-worship, and even of all recognition of the dead as in any way related to the living. Spiritism hitherto had lain in the natural current of human evolution. Religion originated as the tie of the dead and living. Elimination had now gone on until it had left but one God and one Devil; the whole populace of ancestral ghosts was neglected, and then their very existence questioned. Christianity moved off neglectful of the dead. Its cult was for the living. We may reasonably anticipate a degree of reaction that will regard the rights of the dead to our love; and probably our companionship.

(h) Christianity a Protest against Skepticism.—The 500 years that culminated in Jesus are to be considered as a single era; and in most ways the most remarkable chapter of human life. It opened with a crash everywhere of an enormously top-heavy polytheism. India had its 300 millions of gods. Greece had them for every porch and glen. China was exhausted intellectually and morally with God-care. The crash

begat in Greece philosophy as distinct from theology.
India seethed with discussion. China was like a sea
in a storm. This begat great synthetic leaders—Socrates,
Buddha, Confucius—at one world-birth. Confucius
said the less you have to do with the gods the better. Buddha reduced pan-demonium without tolerance.
Socrates did not deny, but he ignored the gods. An
era of criticism, investigation and skepticism set in.
Immortality became a subject of doubt. This world
was of vastly growing valuation. Character-building
was of greater importance than ancestor-feeding. Filialism decayed. Liberty and individualism throve.
The golden rule was formulated everywhere. Only in
such an atmosphere could Athens have been developed
and Rome founded. Plato wrote; Aristotle investigated.
The world worshiped knowledge; it glorified doubt.
It set up altars to the unknowable.

(i) Christianity Constructive.—To all this Christianity came with positiveness. It was not analytic,
but synthetic. It restored faith and love. It gave the
key-note to a new era: "Love God; seek your Father
who fills the heavens; seek first the kingdom of God
and his righteousness." The Gospel rings and sings
with this aggressive idea. To the Greek it was foolishness. With equal beauty beside the doctrine of the
Father was that of human brotherhood: "Love your
neighbor as yourself. If you will be perfect sell all and
give to the poor." This was Christianity—the restoration of God; the equal affirmation of humanity. With
this Jesus brushed away all metaphysics and mysteries,
and taught the simple doctrine that all life is one; that
we live in God. The end of true religion is more life
—not culture, but larger, freer, nobler life. Sin is
self-suicide; righteousness is the enlargement of our
moral, intellectual and physical capacities. Life is
hid in God; death is godlessness.

(k) Christian Heredity.—Christianity was, however,
not only a revolution but an evolution. Its sacraments,
marriage, ascetic orders trickled down from divers he-
redities. Bells, images, holy water, processions, shrines,
pilgrimages, papacies were common heart-beats of
Buddhism and Christianity. Buddha was as genuine
a forerunner of Jesus as was John. He made the great-

est of all joys to be to save the lost, to bring men to the right path. Buddha said knowledge is the aim. Jesus said the truth shall make you free. The vital degeneration of preceding religions had been other-worldliness and much godliness. Buddha began what Jesus closed, the great protest against both these evils. "To save yourself as you are is the worst of disasters," said the former. "Marvel not that I say ye must be born again," said the latter. There was a sweet sympathy between Buddha and Jesus; and a gentle brotherhood. But what Buddha did not do, Jesus did. Christianity not only abolished; it created. It did not cry for unbirth but for rebirth. It was incarnated Hope.

(1) Jesus.—Nothing before on the horizon had appeared so grand as Jesus; nothing so human; nothing so full of the Father. Equally broad in intellect and in sympathies, he stood overtopping intolerance and prejudice. Strong as beautiful, he bore the sins of all men on his heart. Woman as well as man felt salvation from the world's deathfulness. His parables place him uniquely great in literature. His imagination equaled that of Dante; in simplicity he stood beside Homer. His field, however, was his own. He gathered humanity to his bosom, he laid himself in the arms of Eternal Beneficence. Never can we afford to lose Jesus out of our lives or our literature. We may glory in Shakespeare; we may honor Plato; but we must do all this and more with Jesus; we must love him.

PART IV.   THE ERA OF CHRISTIAN CONFLICT.

(a) Conflict with Grecian Philosophy.—Thus, while we see that Jesus restored the natural evolution of religion and built a bulwark against the skepticism of the era, it is not to be supposed that Christianity escaped counter action upon itself of rival ideas and systems. Grecian culture at once entered into mortal combat, and the East was soon strewn with sects that split metaphysical hairs, and lost the spirit of Jesus and the life of his gospel. There was a certain affinity between Christianity and Greek philosophy, for both exalted the human idea. But Jesus also, with humanity, exalted the Father. In Greece the gods were anthropomorphic wholly; with Jesus God was the immanent Love of the Universe.

(b) Conflict of the Councils.—Nor is it to be denied that there were, inherent in Christian simplicity, the germs of many vast problems that sooner or later must become matters of sharp dispute. Was Jesus in any supernatural sense Son of God? This, settled affirmatively in the early Councils, unfortunately led to an infinite train of paradoxes and absurdities as well as a temporary submergence of the whole spirit of religious evolution. Then followed a hierarchy representative of God, a virgin mother, salvation by belief, damnation predominant, a diabolical eschatology, ritualistic death, decreed salvation, thumb screws and brain screws; and ages wasted in inquisitions, monkery, celibacy, and everything but the Father and Humanity and Life. The first evolution out of this myriad-sided development was the new imperialism of Rome. One Church! One Head!

(c) The Papacy.—Entirely natural was the mighty struggle which ended with the establishment of a papacy, because it had for its central thought God on earth. First of all was it necessary to establish with indestructible foundation the doctrine of God in man. "I and the Father are one." Crude or brazen as might be this personal declaration on the part of most of the bishops, yet the idea was ineradicably being worked into human thought. Meanwhile Islam arises with a similar inspiration, recalling the great fact to mind every hour that "God Is."

(d) The Hierarchy.—Another five hundred years were employed apparently in the struggle of this idea to dominate the state and create an overtopping hierarchy. But the times were out of joint. The Empire of the world was rotting like carrion. Rome spiritual rose out of Rome imperial. That it borrowed of the dead and lost much of the divine we need not deny. With Hildebrand came the completion of the hierarchy; and Europe saw the state practically absorbed in the church. Notwithstanding vast corruption, it is nevertheless true that during neither of these two periods of Christian evolution did the church fail to emphasize its struggle with vice, or its determination to confirm the rule of God on earth. It was a superb contest however you view it, and at the end Christianity had not lost the fundamental principle, God Is.

(e) Individualism Arises.—Then began the age of reform, the era that exalted humanity. The Fatherhood had been reaffirmed in history; it remained that man also is God's child. The two sides of Jesus' gospel, as we have seen, were the Universal Fatherhood; the Universal Brotherhood. The historical confirmation of the former had nearly suppressed the latter. That man was more than a moral feoff of the hierarchy was finally nailed to the Cathedral portal by Martin Luther.

(f) Protestant Struggle with Itself.—But so strong had become the sentiment of authority and unity that it was impossible to grasp that of individual liberty. Luther dreamed of a united Protestantism. Calvin built a creed more autocratic than that of Trent, and did not hesitate to use fagots to insure submission. Yet sects multiplied. There was no cement in the walls these men builded—except blood. No one believed in freedom of conscience; but all men began unconsciously to make use of it.

(g) Rome Appeals to Feeling; Geneva to Logic.— Rome remained eminently constructive. Protestantism was substantially what its name implied, a protest. Rome appealed to the emotions; Protestantism, to the reason. The masses feel; they do not argue.

> "We have but faith, we cannot know,
> For knowledge is of things we see,
> And yet we trust it comes from Thee,
> A beam in darkness; let it grow."

Castelar says, "Should I be born again I would not embrace the Protestant religion, whose frigidity shrivels my soul; I would return rather to the beautiful altar which inspired me with the grandest sentiment of my life." These two tendencies have wrought out our modern age by attraction and repulsion. Progress is possible only with both. Catholic emotion would fade out but for the protest of reason. Protestantism would perish but for the emotional life of the older church. The two constantly react on each other. It is a mistake to note only the antagonism. We embrace, we borrow, we love, we wed, as well as quarrel and hate. By and by we shall do better. Catholics are learning to debate freely; Protestants are less afraid of emotion.

(h) Christianity has Controlled Civilization.—I have followed Christianity from its inception as by all odds the most evolutionary religion upon the earth. It has made the end of religion to be the union of God and man. Its ultimate law has been, "Be ye perfect even as your Father is perfect." Our ideal God dies for sinners, our ideal man for the weaker brethren. "You cannot have a perfect life without piety," said primitive religion. Christianity adds, "You cannot have a perfect life without love for God as good." The great gain is in the God-instinct, for now we recognize no piety that is not goodness, nor any God as deserving worship apart from his beneficence. But whatever the cause, Christianity has above all religions adjusted itself to progress, and allied itself to civilization. It has moved on with the conquering and constructive social forces, until the two continents that command commerce, agriculture and industrial enterprise are Christian. This is not a matter of chance, for other religions have had equal opportunities to coöperate with the state for social progress and human betterment. They have signally failed.

(i) Christianity Not a Complete System.—But in selecting Christianity as the representative of all modern religious life I do not assert that Christianity alone is capable of lifting the world to its divinest ends. The life of God which was translated into Shemitic and Aryan sentiment, must be, as it has been, translated into the sentiment and thought of other races. That Christianity introduced any new moral principle is not true. Livingstone says that in nothing did the moral ideas of the tribes he encountered differ from his own, except that a man could have more than one wife. Mencius says all men feel the sentiments of hatred and of vice. The golden rule is common to all religions. Confucianism did not force opium on China; nor did Mohammedanism carry New England rum to Timbuctoo. Lord Bacon in his Novum Organum charges the church with blind zeal for religion at the expense of intellectual life. The church has never quite been

willing to serve God, and leave the state to serve the
world.   One third of Europe at one time was ecclesiastical property.   In America in 1850 such property
was 87 millions; in 1890 it was 679 millions.

Both inherently and organically the era from Luther
to the present has been preparatory.   It is a tempting
field for delay at every point.   It is, however, necessary to hold to the main line.   What are the poten-
cies and tendencies of existing religion, and what are
the promises for the future?

PART V.   THE RELIGION OF THE FUTURE.

Conditioning Forces.—I purpose now briefly to consider the conditions that will determine the religion of
the future.   These are (1) A vast development of
thought expression in the press.   (2) The rise of federalism in government, which enormously increases the
efficiency of the state at the expense of dissociated
churches.   (3) The transference of general education
from the church to the state.   (4) The progress of individualism, involving free thinking.   (5) The consequent equalizing of the sexes in duties and offices.
(6) An immense increase of average wealth and of great
aggregations of capital.   (7) A parallel rise of organized industrialism.   (8) The growth beyond all precedent of a general spirit of investigation.   (9) The
consequent philosophy of evolution, touching theology
at every point.

(1) The Press.—Printing preceded federal democracy by three hundred years; but its potency in
politics began to increase about the days of our own
nation-building. In social affairs it was the middle of the
nineteenth century before the press was supreme.
Then began that enormous multiplicity of papers and
magazines which should carry the widest knowledge
and richest thought into every homestead. Journal-
ism became a new profession, into which now graduates
one seventh of our college classes.   It is in our memory when a new book was a sensation; now the annual
output is four thousand in America, and many more
in England. One hundred new volumes a year will
barely keep the intelligent reader abreast of the age.

This new art of expression has created a revolution.

The age of oratory has lapsed. The pulpit has suffered as well as the platform. Our preachers cannot be expected to give two sermons a week equal to the highest literature. Nor can it be demanded, in justice, of the people to accept the less valuable at a higher price of time and money. The clergy has tried to readjust its work to the new conditions. But the plain fact is undeniable and irrevocable that preaching is no longer a prime social need to the more intelligent classes. The church must give what the press cannot give, or the people will not assemble. The Catholic church understands this and gives art, music and religious drama. The most serious temporary disadvantage is that the people, once accustomed to be educated by the pulpit, are now contented agnostics. Professor Seelye with great force shows the failure of supernaturalism, and urges that the pulpits that have taught miracles should turn to the teaching of natural law. Meanwhile the church falls largely into the hands of peripatetic agitators, whose influence is hypnotic, where it is not closer akin to the incantations of the medicine man of savage races.

(2) Federalism.—The church of the future must exist under the potent influence of federalism. It has felt the power of democracy, and we can fairly say that the church has become as democratic in spirit as the state. But federal union is a later and grander idea; for it makes democracy coherent and coöperative over a whole continent. Protestantism from the start fell into sects. This seemed to men like Calvin most lamentable, and they struggled by all means to establish unity, uniformity and conformity. In reality, however, each church sect corresponds to a civic state, while each church corresponds to a township. Our danger is not from making too much of sects, each one developing a specific idea to its fullness; but our danger is in the lack of federation of sects. Church and state, the two original evolutions of the human family, have always moved on nearly parallel lines. When the state was feudal, the church was feudal. When the state was monarchical, the state was absolute. Now that the state is federal, the church must and will follow.

I am not sure who first flung out the banner inscribed, "A World-wide Democratic Church," but I think it was Taylor Innes in 1891. It was soon after the meeting of Pan-Methodist, Pan-Presbyterian, Pan-Congregationalist and similar conferences. Mr. Innes declared that (1) a union of all the free churches of the world was practicable; that (2) such a union, instead of impairing freedom, might be made a means of advancing it. In fact, as individualism is essential to a perfect society, and as individual states are essential to a perfect nation, so individual churches form compactest sects; and by sects alone can we reach a perfectly free and workable universal church.

But if Christendom can fraternize, why not all upward-lookers and honest strivers the world over? The Parliament at Chicago did not in any sense imply that Buddhism and Jewism and Islamism and Christianism are to move *pari passu* to a common conquest, but it demonstrated that we have begun to see that, as we are all sects of a common Christianity, so all religions are integers of a sole religion of humanity. It was a rediscovery of the unity of the human family on the religious side.

All efforts at religious union by force of authority having failed, Napoleon planned a fusion of this sort. He said, "I would have held my religious as well as my legislative sessions. My councils would have represented Christendom. The popes would have presided." State Churchism and Church Statism, however, are equally untrue to history and evolution. Federalism is the idea of the age, equally adapted to church and to state.

(3) *Education Becomes Secularized.*—It is not long since our whole curriculum of education was tinctured with religious feeling and our higher schools were the property of the churches. Our colleges before 1850 were almost wholly established to educate ministers. A few exist still that must by charter have preachers for presidents. But the Bible is ejected from the common schools, and our universities are almost wholly secularized. The movement was an unconscious drift. The rise of the exact sciences led to a profound conviction that free investigation constituted the essential spirit of education. Meanwhile a vast network of schools

has covered our continent.   The world believes in education as it believes in law.   It is a public instinct.
State universities share with State capitals in being
the center of public life.   We only wait now for a
national university at Washington, toward which all
State universities shall point, as all State legislatures
center in Congress.

Religion is not interested in retaining control of secular education.   It is advantaged by all right secular-
ism.   State and church in their entire course interest
and assist each other.   All knowledge of truth, all real
learning, places the world more directly amenable to
religious influence.   "The foundation of Science," says
Argyle, "is confidence in the intelligibility of nature."
Says Seelye, "Those who study nature study God—a
personal God."   Goethe says, "He who has science
and art has religion."   No mind can secure enlightenment without facing the problems of God, immortality
and brotherhood.

Is the church then forever free from the obligation
to instruct?   Or is the Catholic church right in insisting
that there is a specific religious education apart from
the secular?   Can the common schools teach morals,
and if so can they cover the whole field of ethics?   My
previous sections show that the state does not cover
the whole field of morals; that there are morals which
the church must teach as its own, and is profoundly
sinful if it fails to teach.   These ethical principles may
be summed up as our relations to God, which in character become piety; our relations to the hereafter, and
our human brotherhood as children of God.   The state
school has its own moral obligations; and these are
collateral with those of the church.   It should primarily create good citizenship.   Were I a Catholic, I
would insist on parochial schools for purely religious
culture.   As I am a Protestant, I protest against the
rubbish that with us passes for religious education.
The state and the church must each understand its
field, and unflinchingly resist the encroachments of the
other.

(4) Individualism.—Individualism is comparatively
a modern idea.   It was asserted in the ancient world
only by Jesus and his religious forerunners.   But apart

from the earliest churches, Christendom completely lost the idea of human equality. The Reformation of 1500 began a reaction. Its idea was not so much that current doctrines were false as that intellectual and moral bondage is wrong. This idea was soon passed over to the state as democracy. The church still standing for the mass against the man, the eighteenth century wound up by destroying the church and abolishing God. But the state went down with the church. The two came up together with the nineteenth century, as democracy in state and Protestantism in church; individualism well established.

That the religion of the future will be determined by the individualism of the present is beyond gainsay. Shall we find a platform large enough for free individuals? If so it must omit intellectual conformity and moral conformity and physical conformity. There must be freedom of cult, of character, of creed. Is there a possible union large enough to fellowship those who join no kirk or sect; who keep days, or not, as they choose; who believe in the trinity or reject it?—a church broad enough for Washington, Jefferson, Lincoln, Sumner, as well as Chalmers, Stanley, Leo XIII. and Archbishop Ireland? The future church will not exclude honorable men who are true to humanity.

It is not possible to stay the movement toward unity in diversity, toward fellowship with freedom. Mazzini said of Carlyle, "He stands between the individual and the infinite with a constant disposition to crush the human being by comparing him with God." But our age has turned sharply away to emphasize the moral worth of man. Henry Jones says of Browning, "He believed the Power for Rightness had revealed himself as man." What the people need is not less selfhood, but more; less turning to the state and legislation, and more valuation of each one's "life rent of God's universe," with the tasks it offers and the tools to do them with. It is not enough to cry, "God is on the throne; all's well with the world," unless that throne be our own individual soul. "God works in you; therefore work out your own salvation."

"When the fight begins within himself,
Man's worth something. God stoops o'er his head;
Satan looks up between his feet—Both tug;
He's left himself i' the middle. The soul awakes
And grows."

But individualism invariably refuses to exist for itself alone. There can be no coöperation comparable
to that of strong personalities. Hence it has followed
that never before was there such eager hunting for fel·
lowship and love as now.

(5) Equality of the Sexes.—It was an inevitable consequence of the increasing individualism which I have
noted that woman should be a recipient of its advan·
tages. It was impossible to differentiate the masses
into individuals,and leave women uneducated and dis-
franchised. In fact it was at once discovered that to
breed men we must have mothers. The highest end
of the state is to secure the most excellent conditions
of motherhood. Said a chief of the Cherokees, "We
undertook to civilize by educating our boys; but with
heathenish mothers the children invariably lapsed.There
was no progress. We were compelled to educate our wom·
en." We Aryans have been slower to discover this law
of nature,but we have found it out. Asa Mahan opened
the doors of Oberlin in 1833 amid a storm of shocked
and indignant protests, but the discovery was made,
and the sexes were to be placed henceforth on an
equality. Not only the schools but the trades and professions have opened to women. There are 250,000
women in the ranks of self-supporters in New York City
alone.

Religion has not seldom in the past found it neces·
sary to call woman to its aid as priestess, as vestal, or
as prophetess. Christianity could scarcely have existed but for the baptism of woman's love in the cradle
hours of its weakness. Its least honorable chapters
have been the result of celibacy and monkery. The
liberation of woman from the restraints of prejudice
is steadily calling her to the front as mother of God.
This is no longer profanity; for God in this world is
most manifest as man; and woman bears man in her
womb. The church naturally is her special care. The
love of God is her sublime genius. As preaching

grows less needful and pastoral care more necessary, woman is summoned officially. Men in gowns need not masquerade. If the gowns are needed let us have the women inside of them.

(6) Capitalism.—Organic religion as a social affair touching the people, is conditioned in these days sharply by the vast increase of capital and its large aggregations in the hands of a few. This is not purely a matter of the state—it concerns the character of men as men and as children of God. The capitalist distinctively stands as trustee of the Father, and whether he confesses a creed or not, he is holding office under God. It is necessary for him as controller of a large amount of this world's goods to comprehend not only the laws of trade, of currency, of tariffs; but he must apprehend the inherent laws of nature concerning common rights, the golden rule and the brotherhood of human beings. A breach of trust to God is involved where there may be no breach of trust to the state. So religion, natural religion, finds in this age a new or vastly enlarged sphere. Mr. Carnegie in his Gospel of Wealth has expressed the simple truth that no man owns anything strictly for himself. He is a product of the age; his faculties are results of the social organism. He is created by social heredity to take a certain responsibility, and to bear it nobly and honorably. This certainly does not lead to Tolstoi's doctrine that it is a crime to be wealthy. It is a refutation of the folly that is purling through a good deal of recent legislation. It is a part of the economy of this age to aggregate capital; it is equally a part of its economy to create a race of men capable of managing millions for wise ends. Here the age is magnificently a product of evolution. It has made its men fitted for its purpose; it has created its capital. Is the end of all this purely secular? Clearly you can not rob God of the world. Church and state will move on together. Capital in vastly increased ratio will be used for religious ends. In what manner, I will discuss under the next head.

(7) Industrialism.—Counter to the rise of capitalism is the rise of industrialism. Hundreds of novel forms of individual and social energy

have opened and are opening. Labor has differentiated from capital. It is a force by itself; and it is becoming an organized force. Coincident is the education of all classes; holding common ideals before all and instilling similar desires. When these are not gratified the weaker natures fall off into forms of degeneracy. Trampism develops enormously; dependent classes constitute one-third of our cities and one-seventh of our rural population. When disturbances come either in production or in commerce, society is endangered by the increase of sufferings and crime. Has religion organically anything to do with this? Can religion go over to sociology? Can it legitimately undertake the relief of the poor, the housing of the homeless, the promotion of temperance? Or does this belong to the state, to legislation, and to secular education? Certainly such a demand is made of religion. Canon Freemantle says we must get over the narrow idea that confines the church to public worship and its adjuncts; and take the broad view of religion as embracing the life of mankind and the conditions of life. Jesus made the Parable of the Good Samaritan his typical illustration of social religion. Piety is the practical love of mankind.

Industrialism in reality coöperates with capitalism more than it conflicts. When the adjustment is fully made it will be found to be one of advanced harmony. Together they are improving with decision the economics of religion. The most stupendous business blunder in civilization is the tying up of millions of productive capital in unproductive church buildings, and the withdrawal of the same from taxation. These buildings are almost invariably, if not in debt, at least sustained at a cost far beyond the reasonable contribution of worshipers There is demanded a total readjustment of the whole religious cult to business principles. There is no reason why assemblies should not be held in buildings the rental of which will cover all expenses incident to worship.

Parton, describing an English cathedral, enumerates thirty clergymen associated with the huge building, fourteen of whom drew salaries of over five thousand dollars a year. There were besides in the town sixteen parish churches. In our American towns we often find ten or twelve church buildings, each with its full service and bills of expense; where one-third the number would satisfy every possible requirement. The development of sects I have shown to have been a useful evolution—but such sectarian waste of property is inexcusable. Professor Shaler in his admirable "Interpretations of Nature" calls attention to the shameless waste in services for the dead. The property contained in Mt. Auburn Cemetery, he says, is probably as great as that of Harvard College; it is many times as great as that involved in all the school buildings belonging to the people who bury their dead in that cemetery. Religion must enter fully into the economics of this age. At present it is leading in wastefulness.

But the church as now operative is as careless of moral power as it is of material. Its discussions are in large part practically useless. If orthodoxy could establish every one of its standards, *cui bono?* Can the pulpit afford to ignore the practical topics of present salvation? Will theology give way to sociology? Will the church give up its agnosticism about the present? Is belief in God no longer anything but a belief in a judge of the dead? You have not come thus far with me to lose sight of the fact that religion by natural evolution became not only universal but human, covering the life that is, as well as that to come.

Still it is all important that the passion for heaven that crazed the past shall not drop into an equally absorbing passion for this world. A recent writer says what we need is a development of the amenities of life—the desire for a pleasant life in the place of a passion for accumulation. Did not the Jews develop in Canaan a religion of this life and of home? Did it not constitute the most valuable religion the world had known? Out of whose womb came Jesus? Did not the Greeks develop a religion of beauty and art? And was the result not a boon to humanity, in philosophy, science, hope, beyond all comparison with other races? Little Palestine! Little Greece! Neighbors and dots on the map; but they made the world, and they have ruled its civilization. Why shall we not develop one more religion of pastoral simplicity, yet embracing all that the world has acquired of knowledge and art?

(8) Independent Investigation.—The development of a spirit of independent investigation quite as positively affects religious thought and behavior. The Aristotelian period, beginning four hundred years before Jesus, had much to do with the independence of that teacher's method. It also deeply affected the early churches. That, like ours, was a period of multiplication of sects and free discussion. The era was closed by consolidating power and authority in a papacy. Books grew holy; decrees of councils absolute; popes infallible. Modern orthodoxy is inextricably snarled in an attempt to sustain some portion of this absolutism. The wan hope of authority is shown by the generous effort of Professor Drummond to discover a harmony between modern science and a theology based on science five thousand years old. The wiser plan is to acknowledge that all theologies are stages of progress in man's power to vision the infinite through existing knowledge of the finite.

Creeds will not be less needful than formerly; but they will point the way forward to God rather than require us to camp about them for their defense. Tyndal wisely said that to yield the religious sentiment reasonable satisfaction, is the problem of the hour. Doctor Schurman insists that we should unite with some sect. He omits to add that God and one honest man make a sect. Still Moncure D. Conway is probably right that "historic sentiment united with free thought, the natural fruit of culture, though it now draws scholars out of the church may presently draw them into it over lowered bars." Some of us may for a time be compelled to do as Richter says, "simply sink down into this little earth garden, and nestle so homewise, that in looking out from the warm nest we see no wolf dens, no thunder rods, but only blades and ears of God's love."

The essential spirit of future religion will go to the Father rather than to rewards; not so much in submission to a supreme will as in childlike trust. Faith as it leaves documents will go back to God himself.

(9) The Evolution Hypothesis.   (a) God.—Finally
the religion of the future is conditioned by the evolution
hypothesis.   The idea of an eternal unfolding of ideas
as well as organisms, establishes for us not only a philosophy of history but a philosophy of religion.   We
have forever lost the notion of a supernatural; but we
have caught at last the idea of a nature so complete
that it needs no addendum.   To grapple with monism,
to conceive the universe as an intelligent moral one,
is the great achievement of modern thought.   Hum-
boldt called nature "A Living Whole." The advanced
evolutionist finds no language better than this to express his convictions.

(b) Man.—A new doctrine of man follows.   God,
filling all space and time with continuous self-manifes-
tation, involves the doctrine of continuous inspiration.
Hegel profoundly declares God and man possible only
in each other.   God is; is in man.   Man is; when he
becomes in God.   Mind is in contact with mind, and
everywhere inspirable.   This is our heredity from God.
But mind and matter are no more to be conceived as
separable in the individual than in the universal.   This
universe can be conceived only as an Absolute One,
involving both mind and matter; and man is a child
of the same One.

(c) Immortality.—Immortality was assumed by primitive religion; it was dogmatically asserted by the universal religions; it has been doubted by investigators;
it was made impersonal by a warm altruism; it is now
affirmed as demonstrable by evolution.   Matter is not
destructible; mind is not destructible; only organic relations are temporary.   As the universe reveals the purpose of universal mind, we may justly argue that the
evolution of an intelligent being is for nothing less than
its completest development.

(d) Saviors.—Evolution has by no means displaced
Jesus as a savior.   It leaves him in possession of all
the honor that belongs to the best incarnations of
goodness, beauty and truth.   God as the infinite un-
revealed we can rarely see, even in our most glowing
raptures.   In the sunset's radiance or the morning's
glow of almost personal greeting, we may sometimes
feel Him in whom we live and have our being; but it

is in man that the Father is most sweetly ours. Jesus is forever God in the flesh; our joy and our inspiration.

(e) Morals.—In no direction has evolution worked a greater change than in our estimate of a good man. It requires,in order to morality,the best use of all our faculties in such a way as to best aid our neighbors. Health or *wholth* has become the chief moral end of science. Any one may lose one half his soul; or save but one fourth of it. He is moral who becomes all that,as a human being,he can become in structure and function; for a human being is the crowning work of evolution. Man comes under the inexorable law of the survival of the fittest. The main point is not to be eternally preserved; but to make sure of being worth preservation. Carlyle refers to those "who are worried about the salvation of their dirty little souls."

(f) Piety.—Evolution as either science or philosophy is far from displacing piety. Character is made to depend on obedience and love for personality coincident with nature, not with personality abstracted from nature. Frederick Harrison says, "Morality fused with social devotion and enlightened by sound philosophy is religion." We may amend this formula by adding, religion is sentiment in worship; in action is obedience to law.

(g) Psychics.—The first revelation of evolution concerned physical organism and function. But this led on steadily to an era of psychical investigation. Professor Shaler says, "It seems now as if the end of the long dispute between the materialists and the spiritualists may soon come about through the growing conviction that matter is but a mode of the action of energy." No careful thinker now dares to assert the universe in materialistic terms. We cannot with present knowledge conceive the substratum to be matter and force. On the contrary the underlying fact seems to be infinite purpose and will. Evolution breaks down the division between mind and matter.

(h) The Departed.—Evolution thus steadily brings us back to that primal conception of religion as the bond of union between the living and the dead. Professor Cope believes consciousness is not necessarily confined to protoplasm. On the whole the conviction

grows that we have interpreted the universe too nar-
rowly. Our telescopes have been invented for the
physical eye. But we see God also with the inner eye.
If souls exist out of the flesh they exist as aggressive
facts; as much so as atoms and molecules. They must
in like manner have a relation as positive throughout
the universe as do atoms or stars. The probabilities increase that we shall reach a science of soul collateral
with the science of matter.

Conclusion:—I have not for a moment forgotten that
the Church and the State are collateral developments
of the primitive family; and that it has been by the interaction of these two integral factors of society that
we find brought forth the highest reaches of hope and
life.   But it has been my object, following historic development, to show the greatness of the debt that we
owe to the religious side of evolution.   Normal religion
has ever been the optimistic force of the world.   But
the economics of the Religion of Evolution lies in this
that it teaches us to recognize religion as not a revelation from some supernal sphere, but as a natural unfolding of human nature Godward.   Religion thus binds
two lives together; forbids us to be wholly of the earth
or sensual, and inspires us with the sublime idea that
the family here may at last emerge into the Family
Universal, and our brief lives graduate into immortal
Sonship with the Eternal Father.

ABSTRACT OF THE DISCUSSION.

PROF. E. D. COPE, Ph. D.:—
   The term "religion" requires definition and analysis.
In the popular conception it is a complex idea.   One
conception is that it is a statement of certain facts of
this and the other life, i. e. theology, or the science of
God; another views it in its objective results in society,
i. e. as morals; a third that it is the expression of the
emotional part of the mind, and has its root in our relations to our fellow beings and to a Supreme Being.
The theological view is inclusive of cosmology and philosophy, as evidenced by the religious teachers in all
countries.   But we see on strict investigation that
thought has developed in the direction of rational in-

ference from facts to conclusions, both as regards our ideas of a Supreme Being and our ideas of a future life. All the good there is in theology can now be found in science. Our emotional sentiments do not change or die out, though our intellectual views may change. Our rational faculties serve as our guide, but they do not lie at the root of our being, as does our emotional nature, i. e. our affections. As to the objects for which churches exist, we are puzzled to find a reasonable answer; yet it seems evident that they exist for the purpose of producing good conduct in society. Of course, at the basis of conduct is a certain state of mind which we may term a good will or disposition. This state of mind is increased and strengthened by churches and church relations. In this result faith assists, not intellectual belief merely. Faith is a confidence in the ultimate supremacy of the Lord, and produces a teachable state of mind; a persuasion that the Universe is a good Universe. Were it established on a basis of badness we should *know* it at once.

If we examine the three foundations of religion, we perceive that our emotional nature may be directed to either good or bad ends. Our selfish sentiments are animal in their nature, and demand gratification without regard to the interests of others; they are the inherited selfishness of animal self-gratification. They violate the principle of harmony necessary to the success of coöperative life. Belief in God and a future state serve as motives to action, and have less weight with some than with others. These ideas will probably be found valid. These beliefs are the summation of all life experience. Putting aside all merely vital processes, we infer from the phenomena of mind the existence of minds greater than our own. The mind and conscience differ essentially from all other natures, and from mere energy.

Self-consciousness is sub-knowledge. In its higher forms of thought and in its connection with the lower life, it is radically different. For example, we can bring all our mental energy to bear upon any one particular subject. The qualities of mental processes and physical processes are essentially diverse. That we can cause muscular movement through a mere dictate of the mind is a most extraordinary thing; indeed, it might be called supernatural, as consciousness has no weight; the non-weighable moves the weighable. All other miracles sink into insignificance by the side of this. Do not believe that brain cells are the sole origin of mind; such a view is quite illogical.

There are two views of ethics—the intuitional or sentimental and the rational. Ethics may be conceived either as developed character, or as the greatest good of the greatest number. Human happiness is, after all, the main object in view. We do not know what the laws of God are. Ethics are variable. We must develop both conceptions; the rational by active life, the sentiment of love by and through the domestic relations. Egoism we must have, in order that we may benefit others. The organized ethical sentiment is produced by the conflict of the two ideals.

The church reaches to matters of morals not reached by law, such as falsehood, ingratitude, etc. Theological errors are not of importance in practical life. Rational development prevents distinctions in ethical life where, as among intelligent congregations, the creed is practically given up. As Christ says, "let both grow together."

Rev. John W. Chadwick:—

I think Mr. Powell overestimates the influence of other religions upon Judaism. It did indeed come into contact with the Egyptian doctrine of immortality, but I doubt whether the Hebrews attained any true doctrine of immortality. Sheol was only a formless abode of departed spirits. The first intimation of the doctrine of a future life in the Hebrew writings appeared in Daniel. A little later we have a higher conception in the Wisdom of Solomon.

Jesus was great, but I think the lecturer ascribed to him a larger sense of humanity than he in fact possessed. Jesus believed that his message was only to the lost sheep of the House of Israel. The wider conception came in with Paul. Luke's humanitarian phrases are Pauline in their character, and these reflected back on Jesus' life and work. As we go forward in history from the Christian epoch we find less and less of the human element in Christianity. The slaves, for instance, were manumitted by the Christians on distinctively Christian rather than broad humanitarian grounds; upon the ground that a Christian should not be a slave.

Mr. Benjamin Kidd, in his work on Social Evolution, holds that Natural Selection is the controlling force in that Evolution, in opposition to Professor Huxley, and contends that man would have continued in egoistic courses had not a Supernatural Religion come in, to give to man a sanction for altruistic conduct, which Natural Selection denied to him. I cannot agree with Mr. Kidd. I think Supernatural Religion the parent of all narrowness. The idea of the Jews being a peculiar people led directly to the persecutions of later years, and has been one of the greatest enemies of truth, holding as it did to the basis of an infallible revelation.

The Jewish Yahweh was not a borrowed deity. He survived as the national god, in competition with the admitted existence of many other tribal deities, through a process of "survival of the fittest" as applied to the evolution of theistic conceptions. Notwithstanding the length of time it has taken to civilize the gods, the sweep and impulse of morality has gained. In its earliest phases it produced the "cake of custom," as Mr. Bagehot has termed it; next came the breaking up of this cake. The working of the intellect in history has been quite otherwise than as Mr. Kidd has stated it.

Mr. William O. McDowell:—

Mr. McDowell declined to make any lengthy remarks, owing to the lateness of the hour, but expressed his hearty appreciation of the lecturer's treatment of his subject, and his belief that religion, in its higher ethical development, would prove to be a powerful sociological factor in breaking up national antipathies and promoting "peace on earth, good will to men." He spoke of the enthusiasm with which the new Liberty Bell had everywhere been received by the people, as a harbinger of the day when the sword should be beaten into the ploughshare and nations should make war no more.

Mr. J. W. ALFRED CLUETT:—

I regard Religion as a Factor in Social Evolution as one of the worthiest themes ever discussed in the meetings of our Association. As a question, it fairly assumes the affirmative in the putting of it. A religion not a factor in social evolution, would be such a private concern as to predispose the individual to conceal it from his neighbor. Yet even under such conditions, what might be called a religion would surely have its influence on human progress; but religion is a social thing, and one of its strongest forces is its tendency to attract and keep together bodies or classes of men. In this respect religion is second, if at all, only to government. In fact there are not wanting strong minds who are incessantly declaring that religion *is* government, while just as ardently asserting that government is not even religious. The power of religion to mobilize humanity has been demonstrated by even those beliefs which have contained the smallest kernel of truth. The negative controlling force of such creeds, together with their positive attracting influence over minds seemingly innately disposed to conform to them, has constituted in all ages the dynamics of religion. These claims are not vitiated by the tendencies of the average mind to accept with inadequate examination the varying or contradictory doctrines of its teachers.

While the great governments of the world have by force of arms extended their borders, making mortal enemies where they failed to subject, religious cults have jumped the bounds of government, race, and language, and have been voluntarily accepted by masses of mankind in other respects alien to their originators. These facts stand serenely in their place, despite the teachings of any philosophy that founds itself on mere nature. It is the pride and pleasure of much of our modern philosophy, and its duty, too, to assert that nature is unvarying, implacable, unforgiving, neither relenting nor repenting; that benevolence is the culminating result, and not the incidental intention; but such conceptions of nature are not modern, nor is their acceptance confined to philosophic systems. Certain religions have taught them explicitly, even to the visiting of the sins of the fathers upon the children unto the third and fourth generation, and to demanding an eye for an eye, and a tooth for a tooth; but it may be questioned if such principles have ever been fundamental to any religion, not being of a sort to either attract men or to keep them together. In fact they encroach on the function of government, because pitilessly competitive.

Religion as a factor in social evolution, is such by its recognition of individual frailties and necessities. It does not demand full measure, nor limit survival to the fittest. It does not invite every man to be a judge of his fellow-man, but rather impresses upon its votaries the primal fact of their own ethical and spiritual limitations, teaching them how to forgive and how to be forgiven.

In a society so constituted, the individual man will find the fullest sense of freedom. Without first knowing his fellows, he is assured that the perfection of their knowledge and actions is fundamentally disallowed. He is invited into a society which does not assume that his own conduct is fully exemplifying all the cardinal virtues. In short, if sincere, he joins such an association with the double motive of helping and being helped.

These characteristics of religion, if admitted, throw light on its influence on society. Social evolution I assume to be something far different from the evolution of so-called socialism. That ideal of society is purely governmental and directive. The inducements to adopt it are not those suggested by the impulse to contribute, but rather by the desire to receive, with at least the tacit disposition to avoid responsibility. J. S. Mill finely eulogizes the sense of personal responsibility involved in Protestant church membership.

Religion itself, under the laws of its own development, and as a factor in social evolution, has operated to assuage the severity of law and to modify the rigor of government, to accentuate in the individual conscience its own share in the complexion of society, and above all has developed and maintained the supremacy of the law of forbearance.

INDEX

INDEX.